Crossing the LINE

JANICE WHITEAKER

Crossing the Line, book 1 in the Cross Creek series.
Copyright 2022 by Janice Whiteaker.
www.janicewhiteaker.com

All rights reserved. No part of this publication may be reproduced, stored in a retrieval system, or transmitted in any form or by any means electronic, mechanical, photocopying, recording, or otherwise without the prior written permission of the publisher and copyright owner except for the use of brief quotations in a book review.

First printing, 2022

PROLOGUE
BEN

THE SMALL HOUSE at the center of Cross Creek Ranch sat silent.

Not a single light was on in the place.

Not in the windows.

Not on the porches.

Not in the yard.

If he didn't know better he'd think no one was home.

But he definitely knew better.

Ben slowly made his way to the front door, watching and listening for any sign of where the woman inside might be hiding.

And that was most certainly what was happening.

Liza was hiding.

He stopped at the door and gently rapped his knuckles against it, just like he'd done hundreds of times before.

Always hoping it might be the last.

This time was no different.

The air was still and silent as he waited, hoping to hear her voice.

But there was no answer. Normally he would make himself walk away. Try back later.

This time that wasn't an option.

He cracked the door open, just enough so he could see a sliver of the small living room that took up the front of the house. "Liza?"

Still no answer.

It was the reason he was here instead of sitting at the bar with a few of the other hands, trying to wash away the anger he couldn't seem to shake.

He'd gotten a call from Brooks Pace about an hour into a bottle of whisky. His wife Nora had been trying to reach Liza for an hour. Based on recent events, she was worried Liza might not be making the best decisions and landed herself in a spot she couldn't get out of.

Which was pretty par for the course.

Luckily one of the waitresses was clocking out right when he needed to leave, and she was nice enough to drive him back since he was in no shape to find his own way home.

Ben pushed the door wider, listening for any sound of the woman who never seemed to stop wrecking his world.

"Liza." He said her name louder, the edges sharpened by a frustration he'd planned to bask in tonight, giving it free run until the morning came and he had to put it back in its place.

Right next to everything else Liza forced him to bank.

Ben turned to take one more look across the yard.

He might not be the best one to check on her right now. Not with where his head was.

A soft sound dragged his attention back into the house.

Bringing his boots with it.

His steps barely made any sound against the worn and scarred wood as he moved through the space that smelled like her. Soft and sweet.

Deep and dark.

Just like the woman.

He was almost to the stairs before the sound he'd heard registered.

It was water.

Trickling through pipes.

Ben moved a little faster, taking the stairs two at a time as he raced for the bedroom he'd spent a single night in.

Right before he'd made the biggest mistake of his life.

A mistake he might never stop paying for.

Because while the rest of the world saw Liza as an unbreakable force, he knew the truth.

Liza could be broken.

He knew.

He'd done it.

The door to her bathroom was closed, no sliver of light peeking up at him as he twisted the knob.

Locked.

Ben banged on it with the back of his fist. "Liza."

He tried to take a breath, but there wasn't room inside him for anything else.

Not even air.

He was full up.

Full of anger. Full of hate. Full of frustration.

Full of regret.

And now full of fear.

Something had to come out.

He slammed his fist into the wood again, this time hitting hard enough it rattled on the hinges. "Liza Cross, open this fucking door."

There wasn't anything in him willing to wait for an answer. He took a step back and kicked the center of only one of many things currently lined up between them, fueling the force with everything he'd been bottling up.

Everything he'd been holding back.

The latch failed but the hinges held and the door swung inward, slamming against the wall hard enough to knock the knob into the plaster.

He took two steps into the cool, dark air of the small room, grabbed the shower curtain and whipped it open.

Liza's body was curled inside the basin of the ageing clawfoot, eyes closed, skin pale, lips blue, her right arm draped over the side. Cold water poured from the shower head, pelting her unmoving form.

All the anger. All the hate. All the frustration. All the regret was gone in an instant, leaving a void that fear immediately took over.

He reached for her, scooping her up as the icy water rained down on him, adding to the chill racing across his hide.

Ben pulled her up and out of the tub, holding her limp body close as he angled her through the door and into the bedroom. The covers were already back so he laid her across the mattress, being careful not to bump her injured arm as he rested his hands on her skin.

She was so fucking cold.

He yanked the blankets up and around her, tucking them tight to her body as he scooted closer, pushing at the clumps of wet hair stuck to her face. "Liza."

She was breathing, but not much else, and every second that passed dug dread deeper into his gut.

Deeper into his soul.

He'd spent years thinking she would come around.

Realize the truth of what he said that day.

That she would finally understand he'd done it for her.

But it all suddenly seemed like such a fucking waste.

All the time he could have had.

All he could have given her.

"Liza, please." His hands were on her face, pressing into her skin. "Please open your eyes." He dropped his forehead to hers. "Come on, Sweetheart. Wake up."

Her body had been through so much in the past few days, and she wasn't one to give herself any grace.

Not ever.

She pushed too hard.

Too far.

Always.

Thinking she had to prove something everyone already knew.

He shouldn't have left tonight. Shouldn't have put his needs above hers.

Again.

He reached under the blankets, praying she'd be warmer, but the skin under his palm was just as cool.

She wasn't warming up. Not fast enough.

Ben kicked off his boots and knocked the hat from his head before stripping off his shirt and jeans and sliding under the covers with her, pulling her close, one hand pressed to the side of her face as the minutes ticked by.

Suddenly she started to shake, body quaking, teeth chattering. Her lids lifted, but her eyes didn't seem to find focus.

"Liza." Ben turned her face toward his, thumb stroking her cheek as she seemed to finally see who was there with her.

Just like always.

In spite of what she thought.

What he'd made her believe.

Her blink was slow and heavy.

He pulled her closer, bringing more covers in around them as she continued to shiver.

Liza stared at him, the pink slowly coming back to her cheeks as her skin warmed against his.

The panic pushing him along slipped, making space for old anger to flare. "What in the hell were you doing?"

She never thought before she acted.

Never considered danger.

Never worried about getting hurt.

Or worse.

And a few days ago it could have been worse.

Much worse.

She came inches from that fucking car crushing more than her arm.

He could have lost her forever. Lost the chance to figure out how to make it all right.

And it pushed him over an edge he didn't know existed.

Sending him into a freefall he didn't know how to stop.

Liza's expression was blank as her eyes held his. "Leave me alone."

The request was raspy and rough.

And denied.

"No."

He'd left her alone once. Walked away when she needed him most.

Left her to the wolves thinking they were sheep.

Her chin trembled, but her expression remained flat. "Go."

He'd given her time.

He'd given her space.

Now he was clean out of both.

The fall he was caught in stopped, slamming him into the one place he should have claimed as his own long ago.

Ben shook his head, holding Liza's gaze as tight as he held her as he offered up the first of many promises he intended to make and keep.

"I'm not goin' anywhere."

ONE

LIZA

"MORNING." TROY, ONE of the newer ranch hands wandered into the building that served as a community mess hall at Cross Creek Ranch, his eyes wary as they fixed on where Liza was putting together the morning's coffee.

One-handed.

"You need help with that?" He didn't come any closer, but his desire to take over the task was clear. His clear blue gaze followed her every move as she portioned out the grounds and dumped them into the line of filters set down the counter. "Cause I'm happy to help."

Normally she would say no. Just to prove she was as capable now as she was before some prick ran her over with an aging sedan, shattering her right forearm and causing a ridiculous amount of soft tissue damage to everything above it.

While also pissing her off to epic proportions.

But this morning she was tired. Tired in a way that sleep hadn't fixed.

"That would be great." Liza dropped the scooper into the economy-sized bucket of coffee they went through each week. "Thanks."

"No thanks needed." Troy stepped in and went to work filling the last filter before sliding each one into place on the four pots they brewed at least twice each morning. "No reason for you to go around killin' yourself when there's plenty of us here to help."

"Pretty sure I'm not killable." Liza went to the fridge and wrestled out a flat of eggs, balancing it carefully with her one good hand as she carried it to the counter. "And I'm not so sure there's as many people willing to help out as you think."

She'd always struggled to find enough hands to keep the ranch up and running, which forced her to rely on people she'd prefer to keep her distance from.

One in particular.

"Yeah." Troy shot her a look over one shoulder as he filled the first maker with water from the decanter. "I noticed you've got some dead weight hanging around."

"If you know of any live weight looking for a job let me know." It was one of the many never-ending tasks she faced at Cross Creek. Finding quality people who wanted to work and didn't mind having a woman for a boss.

Lots of men claimed they didn't mind, but when it came right down to it, more than a few ended up having big problems with the fact that Liza was in charge and calling the shots.

Add on the fact that for many years she could barely afford to offer the low end of the going pay scale, and that left her with a pretty steady turnover rate.

But now the ranch was finally turning a decent profit and she had a little more financial leverage to work with, which was good, considering most of her *actual* leverage was shot now that she was the one-armed queen of Cross Creek.

"I might know of a few." Troy finished filling the coffee makers with water and turned to her. "What now?"

"Now we start breakfast." She turned back to the fridge. "There's a few packs of bacon in there, wrapped in butcher paper."

Since she was down an appendage for the foreseeable future, Liza tried to keep the first meal of the day as simple as possible. Eggs, a meat of some sort, toast, and grits.

Her grip was almost as shot as her flexibility, so potatoes of any kind were out until she could peel and chop again, which, according to her physical therapist, could be as far away as six-months from now.

One more piece of crap in the bullshit pie her life was baking into.

"Got 'em." Troy stacked the packs along the counter next to the eggs. "You just want it all fried up?"

"You know of a better way to make bacon?" She hated jabbing at the guy, especially since he was being helpful, but it was a necessary thing.

Which was starting to get depressing as hell.

"Actually," Troy's blue eyes came her way again, looking completely unfazed by her abrasiveness, "I do."

Liza lifted her brows in question as she went to work cracking the eggs into a giant bowl.

Troy settled one of the large skillets onto the cooktop and switched on the flame before going to work adding the strips of bacon across the non-stick surface without explaining this magical bacon-cooking method he claimed to know about.

Liza tried to wait him out, but honestly her patience was pretty much non-existent at this point. "And it is?"

Troy shot her a grin that probably had panties dropping all the way in the next county over. "In the oven."

"Seriously?" She was expecting, or maybe hoping, that Troy had some genius way to whip out four pounds of cooked bacon. "That sounds like a huge pain in the ass."

To be fair, everything was a huge pain in her ass now.

Including wiping her own.

"It's not that bad." Troy went to work slapping a second package of bacon across another giant pan. "You don't really have to flip it or anything. You just line it up on a baking sheet, put it in the oven, and pull it out when it's done."

Liza studied the ranch hand beside her. He was tall and lean. Muscular without being overly bulky. He had sky blue eyes, shaggy blonde hair, and a set of dimples that could tie a woman's tongue.

He didn't, however, look like a man with a lot of experience in a kitchen.

"You cooked a lot of bacon in your life?"

Troy dished out another grin. "I've made breakfast more than a few times in my day."

The suggestion in his tone was clear.

Troy wasn't exactly a baby, but he certainly wasn't what she would consider a full-grown man yet either. He was probably in his mid-twenties, about the same age as Brett Pace, the baby brother of the family that owned Red Cedar Ranch.

Maybe in another life, she might have considered exploring the opportunity anyway.

But in this life, she was his boss.

A boss who also tended to lean towards men with a little more experience under their belt.

Not that that had ever worked out well for her.

"That doesn't surprise me." Liza turned to one of the ovens under the counter behind her. She snagged a baking sheet, pulling it out before slapping it against Troy's broad chest. "Show me what you've got."

Troy's blue eyes held hers. "I'd be happy to, Ms. Cross."

The complete confidence in his response managed to rattle her enough that the next egg she cracked dropped a bit of shell into the bowl.

"Dammit." Liza used the remaining shell like a spoon as she scooped at the offending shard, but without the use of her other hand it was impossible to catch the elusive bit.

"Let me help." Troy was suddenly very close, the heat of his tall frame impossible to ignore as both his arms came around her. "Those shells can be persnickety."

She hadn't been this close to a man in so long she almost forgot how good they could smell.

Because while Troy might be a little below the age requirement to ride her Ferris wheel, he certainly seemed to possess just about every other quality she would look for.

If she was looking for that sort of thing.

Troy's long fingers slid over hers as he took the shell from her hand. "You only lose this one little bit here?" He expertly scooped the piece out before dropping it into the scrap bowl.

Liza nodded, being careful not to move any other part of her body since the tiniest flinch would result in the feel of some part of Troy against some part of her. "Thank you." She shot him what she hoped was a threatening look from the corner of her eyes. "Now get back to your spot at the counter."

Troy wasn't the first ranch hand to attempt to sneak their way into her bed.

It usually happened at least once a year, sometimes twice.

And while she would love to think it was because of her statuesque frame and wicked sense of humor, the more likely reason was a thirst for power.

In her experience, most men liked to get drunk on the shit.

Most. Not all.

But Troy looked undeterred. He tipped his head her way, adding on another drawer-dropping smile for good measure. "Yes, ma'am."

She almost rolled her eyes at him, but at this point he might think she was flirting back with him. Because while Troy was cute and possibly slightly sexy, he also seemed to not be very good at picking up on context clues.

Liza went back to cracking eggs, doing her damnedest to avoid noticing the masculine presence at her side.

She wasn't interested in Troy, not even a little bit.

But having him standing beside her did threaten to remind her of another man.

A man she should not have any interest in. A fact she had to remind herself of regularly.

"You ready for a cup of coffee?" Troy slid the baking sheet of bacon into the oven before grabbing two mugs from the collection on the counter.

She was ready for a cup of coffee, but normally did everything in her power to avoid help from anyone, especially the ranch hands.

The clearer she made the lines, the easier her life was. It kept any confusion about her position on the ranch to a minimum.

These men weren't her friends, and they definitely weren't her suitors. They were her employees.

And she was their boss.

But after too many weeks struggling as a one-armed bandit,

she was beginning to peter out. "Sure." Liza turned as Troy started to fill the cups. "Cream and sugar."

He went straight to the fridge. "Yes, ma'am."

This time Liza did roll her eyes, but waited until she was turned away from the baby cowboy jumping at the opportunity to help her out.

If she wasn't careful, she was going to end up accidentally genuinely liking Troy. Not as a man she'd be interested in, just as a human.

And men had a habit of disappointing her.

Liking one was generally the kiss of death.

And right now she couldn't afford to lose any of the men working at Cross Creek. They needed everyone they had.

And probably a few more.

"How's this?" Troy was back and just as close as ever, holding her cup of coffee between them as he waited for her approval.

But he didn't look like the eager little puppy dog she was starting to peg him as.

He looked more like a wolf, dressed up in a cowboy hat and boots, trying to lure Little Red Riding Hood into his bed.

Maybe little boy Troy wasn't as harmless as she thought he was.

"What in the hell is going on in here?"

Troy slowly leaned away from her, the devilish smile he wore easing into a more good-natured line. "I was helping captain one-arm here get breakfast started." He held the cup in his other hand out at the older, more problematic cowboy coming their way. "You ready for some coffee too, boss?"

Ben's eyes didn't even come close to going Troy's way.

They were firmly fixed on her.

And while she might only be suspecting Troy wasn't the sweet young man she initially thought, Liza was fully aware of how dangerous Ben Chamberlain could be.

Knew it for a fact. Found out firsthand.

And there was only one way to handle him.

Liza gave Ben the sweetest smile she could manage. She cracked another egg into the bowl, keeping her gaze on Cross

Creek's head ranch hand. "Troy's been helping me get breakfast ready."

For the first time Ben's eyes moved to the man beside her. "He's helping you?"

His skepticism was well-founded. She didn't have a history of allowing men to help her.

Because the last time a man helped her, she almost died.

"That's right." Liza grabbed a fork and went to work mixing the eggs together. "He's helping me."

And while it was annoying at first, Troy's help was turning out to be a bright spot in the clouds that filled the past month.

Not because she really needed his help. She'd successfully made breakfast almost every morning since she came home from surgery all by herself.

And not because she almost accidentally enjoyed the company of a man. Technically she could get the company of a man anytime she wanted, all it would take was a look and a smile down at Paige's bar in town, and she could have her pick of any unattached man in Moss Creek.

Her appreciation for Troy's assistance rested solely on the fact that it would help put Ben back where he belonged.

Which was as far away from her as possible.

Unfortunately, that distance was limited, but any little bit helped.

Sadly, Troy seemed to pick up on the tension that suddenly filled the air in the mess hall, and he was inching farther from her with each passing second.

Hopefully, the damage was already done.

Liza finished mixing up all the eggs and turned to the fridge, pulling out a gallon of milk and setting it on the counter.

As luck would have it, this particular gallon of milk was unopened, and while she did possess the strength to unscrew the lid, she did not have the second hand required to hold the jug steady, so the whole damn thing spun in place as she twisted.

And, confirming her earlier suspicions, Troy made no move to come to her aid.

"You need some help with that?" Ben stepped in close at her side, his low voice laced with something she chose not to identify.

"Nope." Liza changed tactics, using the heel of her hand to brace the jug while she attempted to work the lid loose with her fingers. But after weeks of abuse, her single hand just didn't have what it took to get the job done.

She was going to have to stab it.

Liza grabbed a knife.

"Is this how it is?" Ben closed in on her, coming even closer than Troy had.

Or maybe it just seemed that way.

He leaned in, bringing the weight of his presence. "You'd rather waste a whole fucking gallon of milk than let me help you?"

Where Troy's nearness had been mildly pleasing, and a gentle reminder of how it felt to be around a man, Ben's body being mere inches from hers brought a completely different reaction.

One she couldn't control, even after all this time.

And that was frustrating as hell. Possibly even more frustrating than trying to maintain the status quo one-handed.

"I don't need your help." It was a lie. They both knew it.

She absolutely did need Ben's help. Without him Cross Creek Ranch would fall apart.

"But you do need *his*?" The last word was practically a hiss.

"He's just frying bacon." She shouldn't have to justify any of this to him.

Especially considering it was Ben's choice that put him where he was.

"And this is just opening a goddamn gallon of milk." Ben's eyes stayed on her as he reached out and twisted the lid free one-handed before slamming the blue cap down onto the counter. "The task isn't the issue, is it?"

He stayed close a few seconds longer, jaw set tight as he stared her down, the devastatingly familiar scent of his skin burning through her brain like wildfire.

Then he turned and walked out, slamming the door behind him as he left.

Liza closed her eyes, taking a deep breath as she tried to reset her mind and her mood.

She'd been hoping things would get back to normal, but it

didn't appear that was going to be as expeditious of an event as she was anticipating.

"Everyone else is going to start heading this way soon." Troy's reminder was soft and carried less than none of the flirtation from earlier.

"Then you better get on that bacon." Liza dumped some milk into the eggs, gave them another stir, and poured them into a pan.

She couldn't keep letting Ben affect her this way. Not if she wanted Cross Creek to be truly successful.

And she did. She lost everything because of it. If it failed...

Then it was all for nothing.

TWO

BEN

"EVERYTHING OKAY?" DARRYL, one of the newest ranch hands, stood just outside the barn, finishing off the last of his morning cigarette.

"Fine." Ben went straight past him, going inside to where the giant bin of chicken feed sat.

Darryl poked his head through the open door. "You sure?"

"Yup." His current disposition was not up for discussion.

Definitely not with one of the ranch hands.

If he was going to talk about it, which he wasn't, there was only one person who would be hearing what he had to say.

And right now if he talked to her there was a damn good chance the conversation would take a turn. One he wasn't in any place to handle.

Ben grabbed one of the five-gallon buckets stacked beside the bin and went to work filling it to the brim with crumble. Once it was full he locked the bin's lid back into place and hauled the bucket outside, past where Darryl was now lighting up a second cigarette.

"Need any help?"

Ben didn't bother slowing down. "Nope."

Darryl might be new, but he'd been at Cross Creek long enough for it to be clear he didn't plan to do anything that wasn't explicitly required of him. That meant his offer of help had more to do with nosiness than with an actual willingness to help carry some of the weight around Cross Creek.

Ben stopped outside the overcrowded chicken coop, wrestling the rusty hinges of the door open before carrying the crumble in and dispensing it between the rubber tubs spread throughout the run. This time of year they had triple the number of chickens they kept on hand through the winter, so feed went fast and the chickens were already jumping into the tubs and kicking crumble across the dirt.

Once the bucket was empty of feed he went to work refilling it with all the eggs the hens laid overnight, stacking them up as he went from one nesting box to the next.

This was normally a chore Liza handled. One she continued to tackle even now, with her dominant arm still almost completely useless, swearing she didn't need any help.

And while he didn't actually believe that was true, he'd had no choice but to go along with it.

Until now.

Ben hauled the eggs across the yard and right into the mess hall where Liza was still standing a little too close to Troy, smiling wide at the young, good-looking ranch hand.

By now most of the other men who worked at the ranch were scattered around the tables filling the space, nursing cups of coffee while they waited for breakfast to be finished so they could eat and go out to tackle the tasks of their day.

Ben gritted his teeth as the woman who'd been refusing any help he offered stood by and watched Troy flip the last of the bacon onto a serving platter.

Liza leaned to look around him, surveying a separate platter of bacon. Troy picked a piece up and held it out.

Liza took it, sampling one end, her eyes widening as she nodded in approval of Troy's bacon cooking skills.

Ben dropped the bucket onto the cement floor beside Liza, letting it hit hard, not caring if they lost a few eggs because of it.

Her attention snapped his way, like she didn't notice he was there until just that second.

Probably because she was too busy being distracted by bacon boy.

Her eyes dropped to the bucket of eggs. "What are those?"

He could barely unclench his teeth as she continued to eat the strip of bacon. "Those are your chickens' eggs."

Liza's gaze lifted to his, narrowing when their eyes met. "*I* collect my chickens' eggs."

Ben took a step closer, driven by an urge he didn't care to name. "I thought you needed help."

Liza's nostrils barely flared, her attention moving to where the rest of the room had suddenly gone silent, before finding its way back to him. "I don't."

Ben edged in a little more, unable to make himself care about all the eyes they had on them. "Funny. That's not what you said earlier." He slid his focus to where Troy stood, much farther away now than he was a few seconds ago.

"What are you getting at?" Liza's tone was steely and strong, the way it usually was while other people were watching. Normally it wouldn't bother him.

But right now it grated on his hide, sending his aggravation at the situation soaring. "I think you know what I'm getting at, Elizabeth."

Her eyes barely widened at his use of her given name.

For a second Ben thought she would fight back with him, give him the outlet he desperately needed.

Instead she cut him off, turning her back his direction before continuing her discussion with bacon boy. "Would we be able to cook all the bacon this way?"

To his credit, Troy looked appropriately concerned about his safety. The younger ranch hand took a slight step away from Liza, disguising it as he reached for a cup of coffee. "Sure. Yeah." He met Ben's stare for half a second before taking another tiny shift away from the woman dragging him into the middle of something he couldn't begin to understand.

Ben struggled with it himself, and he was living it.

"I think your helper is having second thoughts, Elizabeth." He couldn't resist the urge to say her name again. He loved the way it felt coming out of his mouth. He loved the sound of it as it hung in the air between them, a reminder of what should have been.

Liza spun back toward him, narrowly missing catching her

elbow against the counter. Her voice was low as she glared up at him. "What in the hell are you doing?"

It was a good question. One Ben didn't currently have an answer to.

He knew what he was supposed to be doing.

He was supposed to be making sure Cross Creek stayed afloat. That the one thing Ed Cross managed to not completely ruin didn't sink the woman he tried to take down with him.

It was a task that was far-reaching and life-changing. One he'd managed to handle just fine for almost five years.

But now it was getting harder. The tightrope wasn't so easy to walk anymore. Every day he got closer and closer to falling.

And there was no net to catch him.

"I'm collecting your eggs, Ms. Cross."

The instant flash of anger in her eyes settled him as the playing field between them leveled.

"I don't need you to collect my eggs, Mr. Chamberlain." Her chin lifted. "You have your chores and I have mine. Stick with what's yours."

It was the delicate balance they'd existed within for the past five years.

He needed her. She needed him.

They were forced to face each other down every single day. Forced to pretend there was nothing between them.

Forced to accept nothing ever could be.

Ben stepped in a little more, coming toe to toe with her. "Then it looks like tomorrow I'll be frying the bacon since you do need help with that, Ms. Cross." It was the one thing he had. The only bit of her that was still his to cling to.

Knowing he was the man she relied on, even if neither of them would admit it.

Liza held his glare a few seconds longer before turning away once again.

It's what she always did. Stared the truth in the face until she couldn't stand it.

And then she ran away.

"Food's done, boys." She tipped her head at Troy. "I appreciate your assistance this morning."

Then she spun on her heel and marched away, heading straight out into the yard.

Normally he would let her go.

Normally he would bide his time, knowing there would come a point where she couldn't avoid him any longer.

But nothing had been normal since Liza's accident, especially him.

Ben used one boot to shove the bucket of eggs out of the way, making sure no one would trip on it and ruin the ones he hadn't already managed to destroy.

Then he went after her, because they had some things to talk about.

He caught sight of Liza just as she ducked into the back door of her house, thinking she would be safe from him there.

It was the one place on the ranch he didn't go, not if he could help it.

It made the regret harder to bear.

But right now frustration and anger were doing a hell of a job beating regret into oblivion.

When he reached the back door he didn't even bother knocking, just went right into the small kitchen of the tiny farmhouse.

The smell of her hit him like a wall, threatening to stop him in his tracks. The sweetly soft scent almost turned him around, sending his boots back out into the yard.

But then he heard a sound.

A soft, shaky breath that had his feet moving fast, across the kitchen and up the stairs.

He stopped in his tracks at the open door to her room.

A room he had been in not so long ago.

And also very long ago.

Liza's watery eyes came his way and her head dropped back, tipping toward the ceiling. "Oh, for the love of God." She sucked in a loud breath, sniffing in the air through her nose. "Why can't you just leave me alone?"

It was something he'd asked himself a million times.

And never managed to come up with an answer.

"What's wrong?" Ben went straight into her room, not caring

about the unspoken rules that stood between them. Rules that once kept Liza safe from an uncertain future.

She was clearly in pain. He could see it in her eyes. Hear it in her voice.

"You're here. That's what's wrong." She cradled her injured arm a little more carefully than normal. "You're not supposed to be in here."

He ignored her. Ignored the truth in her words.

Because right now the reasons for that truth didn't matter at all.

All that mattered was that Liza was hurting.

"What happened?" Ben knew the basics about the injury to her arm, thanks to her friends' willingness to include him the day she had the surgery intended to repair the extensive damage caused by too many bad decisions to list. But that's all he knew. Anything beyond that he was completely in the dark on.

"Nothing happened." Liza's smile carried no humor or happiness. "I'm fine."

The way her fingers wrapped around her elbow offered a hint he didn't miss. "You hit your arm on the counter."

He thought she'd narrowly escaped the impact, but apparently he'd thought wrong.

"It's fine."

"If it was fine you wouldn't be up here." He might have had to keep his distance from her, but Ben still knew this woman better than anyone.

And Liza would never let anyone see her suffering.

Because Liza would never allow anyone to think she wasn't perfectly capable.

Perfectly fine.

It was ingrained in her. Deep enough it would probably never escape.

Which meant the only way she allowed someone to help her was out of complete necessity.

And occasionally because there was no way of getting out of it.

"Come on." Ben straightened, turning toward her door. "Let's get some ice on that elbow."

"I told you, I'm fine." The fire was back in Liza's words, making him feel a little bit better about her condition.

But not much.

Liza was notoriously skilled at hiding her pain. She was good enough that no one else would notice the tightness of her jaw. The pinch of her eyes.

But he did, and it would eat him alive if he didn't do something about it.

Not that there was much left of him to go around.

Ben turned back toward the woman capable of making his life both heaven and hell. "Elizabeth Cross." He pointed toward the stairs. "If you don't get your ass down to the kitchen I will haul it there myself."

He'd stood by for years while she worked herself to death, managing to go far beyond proving she was capable of running Cross Creek Ranch.

He'd seen her exhausted. Worn down. Stressed over debts and labor shortages.

And never once had he stepped in.

But apparently there was a line.

And they had reached it.

Liza's glare was strong and steady. "I don't know what makes you think you have the right to talk to me like that."

"Someone has to." He walked back her way, boots moving over the scarred wood floor. "And it seems like I'm the only one with enough balls to take you on."

It was what saved him all these years.

He wasn't stupid enough to think no one around here desired Elizabeth Cross. She was beautiful. Tall, strong, smart as a whip, and funny as hell.

But she was also a notorious pain in the ass.

By design.

A design he was grateful as hell for, because he wouldn't have been able to stand the sight of her with someone else.

Clearly, considering his reaction to Troy.

Ben stopped right in front of her.

Dangerously close to the only woman he'd ever loved.

"Now," he inched in a little more, craving a closeness he'd

been without for so long, "are you going on your own, or am I draggin' you?"

Her cheeks barely pinked up, but it was impossible to tell if it was from anger or the same thing making his own blood heat. "You wouldn't dare."

Maybe not yesterday, or the day before, but this morning something flipped a switch.

"Have it your way." He immediately reached out, being careful as hell not to hurt the arm she'd already aggravated as he scooped her up off the floor and headed to the door.

"I swear to God, if you don't put me down right now—"

"You'll what?" Ben angled her body to the side, making sure not to knock any bit of her on the doorway. "Fight me one-armed?"

She would.

And he honestly didn't hate the thought of it. Maybe it would make her feel better, take out some of the anger she carried for him.

Because Elizabeth Cross was most definitely pissed as hell at him.

She was in good company.

Ben took the stairs as quickly as he dared, knowing each second she was in his arms would bring on a special kind of pain he'd be stuck dealing with for days.

Because while he may have been the one that made the decision that changed everything between them, she was the one who made sure it stuck.

The second they were in the kitchen he set her down, depositing her into one of the kitchen chairs before going to the freezer and pulling out the tray of ice. "Where are your pain pills?" He started opening drawers looking for a baggie. "Because I know you haven't been taking them."

The night he found her in the shower, passed out and so cold her lips were blue, scared the shit out of them both. He would put money down that she hadn't taken a single pill from that point on.

"I got rid of them."

Of course she did. "It's not an all or nothing thing, you know that right?"

"They weren't good for me. I didn't like how they made me feel." Liza refused to look his way.

But he couldn't keep his eyes off her. The memory of the night he held her close, while her body shook from the cold water that had been pelting it for God knows how long, refused to be ignored. "That's because you weren't taking them right."

She'd been exhausted and unwilling to let anyone help her, which led to Liza accidentally taking more than she was supposed to.

If he hadn't come home early—

Hadn't known something was wrong—

Hadn't found his way into her house and up to her room—

"I don't need them." She said it like she believed it. Like she was somehow above the effects of physical pain.

"Of course not." Ben zipped the top of the baggie closed. "You don't need anything." He leaned on the table, waiting until her eyes finally met his. "Except for help from Troy."

THREE

LIZA

THIS WAS WHAT she got for letting someone help her.

She should have sent Troy the baby cowboy back on his way and finished the day, and breakfast, all on her own.

"Is that what this is about? Your ass is chapped because I let someone else fry a pack of fucking bacon?"

It was ridiculous.

"My ass is chapped because you will ask anyone else for help but me." Ben picked up the ice pack and came closer, his eyes hard as he leaned down to rest the ice against her elbow. "You paraded everyone you knew through this house when you came home from the hospital."

Liza couldn't help the laugh that jumped out. "You think I had a choice?" She snorted. "Have you met Maryann Pace?"

She couldn't have kept that woman out of her house with a moat and a drawbridge.

Ben's eyes barely narrowed.

Probably because that wasn't the answer he wanted to hear. He wanted to be angry that she didn't come running to him in her moment of need.

Well that ship had sailed.

Then it hit an iceberg and sank epically, taking down more than she realized in the process.

"Hold this." Ben's hand shifted off the ice pack, lingering just until she took over. Then he walked away, disappearing into the small half-bath on the main floor.

She listened as the medicine cabinet opened and he started to dig through the bottles. "So now you think that since everyone else was here you can come into my house and do whatever you want to do too?"

"I think I *have* to come into your house to make sure I do what *needs* to be done." He slapped a bottle of anti-inflammatories down on the top of the table before going to the cabinet beside the sink. "Because you sure as hell aren't doing it."

"If you think I'm not doing everything that needs to be done then you clearly haven't been paying attention." She wasn't going to let Ben pretend like she wasn't completely capable. Especially when she'd busted her ass proving she was. "Because I have managed to do everything I did before," Liza lifted up her one remaining useful arm, "and I've done it with one damn arm tied behind my back."

"I'm not talking about the ranch, Elizabeth."

There he went. Acting like he got to use her name again. "Don't call me that."

It wasn't right, and it sure as hell wasn't fair.

"I think I'm done letting you tell me what to do," Ben set a glass of water in front of her, his dark eyes steady on hers, "Elizabeth."

Oh, that was rich. "I'm not the one who decided what you were going to do, *Benjamin*."

Maybe if she were a better woman this would all be water under the bridge by now.

Maybe she would have moved on, like any normal person would have.

Found a different man. One who was willing to take a risk to have her.

Ben picked up the bottle of pills, cranking the lid off as he held her glare, taking them right back to where they started.

An impasse.

He tipped out three pills and held them in her direction. "Take these."

"You're still acting like you get to tell me what to do."

"I let you tell me what to do."

"You're full of shit." If Ben really did what she wanted him to do then her life would be completely different right now. "And you know it."

Ben leaned down, lining his eyes up with hers. "Elizabeth, you are the only reason I do anything."

It was a ridiculous statement for him to make. Ridiculous, and unfair as hell.

"I—"

"*Hello.*" Maryann Pace's voice carried in through the house. "Knock, knock."

If it was possible for Ben to frown any harder, the lower half of his face would probably fall off. He was obviously not thrilled at the interruption.

He was the only one.

"I'm in here." Liza gave him a sweet smile as Maryann came into the kitchen. "Was there anything else you needed, Mr. Chamberlain?"

"*Ben.*" Maryann set down the bags in her hands, dropping them right beside the bottle of pills Ben probably thought she was going to continue taking. "I am so glad you are here." Maryann immediately dug into one of the bags, coming out with an unmarked cardboard box. "I found the most beautiful set of wind chimes today at the garden store and I thought to myself," she shoved the box into Ben's hands, "wouldn't these look beautiful hanging on the back porch at Liza Cross's house?" She gave him a smile. "Would you do Liza a favor and go ahead and hang those up for her?"

Liza accidentally scoffed, dragging Maryann's attention her way.

"Do you not like wind chimes?"

Oh hell. Now she seemed ungrateful for all the wonderful things Maryann had done over the past month. "I love them, but I can handle hanging them myself."

Maryann waved one hand at her. "Oh honey, don't be ridiculous." She patted Ben on the shoulder. "Why would you do it when you have such a strong, capable man here who's ready and willing to help you in any way he can?"

Up until this very moment she'd been thrilled every time Maryann Pace pulled into her driveway. She always brought food and conversation, serving as a welcome distraction for the current state of Liza's existence.

But now, it suddenly felt like she might end up making her current state of existence even more problematic.

"I'm happy to help Elizabeth in any way I can." Ben shot her a smirk as he tucked the box under one arm and backed toward the door. "You ladies enjoy your visit."

Maryann watched Ben go, her eyes hanging on him until he was completely out the door. "Did he just call you Elizabeth?"

"Nope." Liza would rather convince her friend she needed a hearing aid than admit the truth of what Ben called her. But she shouldn't have to. The easiest way to distract Maryann Pace was by picking a fight. And the easiest way to pick a fight with the Pace family matriarch was to tell her she didn't have to do something. "You didn't have to bring me wind chimes."

Maryann's fists immediately dropped to her hips. "I don't do anything because I have to." The scolding tone to her voice gave Liza hope that Ben's use of her given name was all but forgotten. "I do it because I want to." Maryann went back to digging through the bags on the table. "I was here the other day and noticed you didn't have a single wind chime, which is a complete shame considering the breeze you get across this place."

"I haven't really had time to think about wind chimes." She hadn't really had time to think about anything that didn't involve running the ranch. The one luxury she gave herself was the weekly lunch she shared with Mae, and now the rest of their friends, at The Wooden Spoon in town. It was the one afternoon each week she could dress up in something other than jeans and boots.

"Well of course you haven't." Maryann pulled out a few containers, stacking them at the center of the table. "You've been working your fingers to the bone trying to bring this ranch back after Ed did his damnedest to run it into the ground."

Her assessment of Liza's life was spot on.

Ruining Cross Creek was the one thing Ed turned out to be good at. When he died, she was left with a mountain of debt and a ranch that was worth practically nothing. "Well, a few of my bones are bionic now, so hopefully that will help."

"And how is that bionic arm of yours feeling?" Maryann picked up the stack of food from the table and carried it to the fridge.

"Fine." Granted, it felt much less fine than it did before she banged her elbow against the counter in the mess hall, but the throbbing should start to subside soon.

Hopefully.

"Well I noticed you had ice on it, and I've never seen you ice it before." Maryann finished packing up the fridge before turning her way. "Don't you have ice packs?" She frowned at the makeshift medical device Ben threw together. "Because I can get you some next time I'm out."

"I do have some ice packs." They'd sent them home with her from the hospital, but she wasn't pointing out where they were to Ben. That would just make him think she was giving him permission to be a pain in her ass. "I just forgot they were there."

"Well let's get rid of that then." Maryann snagged away the ice pack Ben crafted. "That looks like something one of my sons would use, and it's going to end up leaking all over you." She took it to the sink, unzipped the top, and dumped out the contents. "Have you had breakfast yet?"

"I made breakfast earlier." Lying to Maryann wasn't high on the list of things she enjoyed doing, so over the years Liza learned to craft her sentences carefully, stating the truth while still managing not to disclose everything.

"Good." Maryann grabbed one of the ice packs from the freezer and came back to her side, gently laying it in place. "Because you can't be taking those anti-inflammatories on an empty stomach. They'll eat your guts up."

Good to know. She definitely didn't want her guts eaten up, so it looked like now she had the reason she needed not to take the pills Ben so aggressively laid out for her.

"I won't." Liza carefully slid the pills under one hand, managing to scoop them up and out of Maryann's sight. "What are you doing out and about so early today?"

Normally, Maryann Pace showed up closer to lunch time,

frequently bringing along one of her daughter-in-laws to help browbeat Liza into behaving better.

Up until today it had been slightly irritating, but now that she'd seen Ben's version of help, Liza was grateful as hell for Maryann.

"I needed to go to the post office, and a few other little errands." Maryann went back to the bags, pulling out the final few items she brought. "You like chocolate, right?" She didn't wait for an answer, which was pretty normal for her. "I brought you some of that chocolate cake from the new bakery."

Moss Creek finally had its first independent bakery, and holy cow was it amazing. "The one with the mousse filling?"

The tiny little storefront opened up just after her run-in with a car, and while Liza hadn't been able to see it in person, she had been lucky enough to try cake, doughnuts, and strudels from the place. Each one had been amazing.

"You know they sell that mousse in little cups?" Maryann made a scooping motion. "So you can just eat it with a spoon."

"Sounds like I know the first stop I'm making as soon as I can drive again." Hopefully that wouldn't be too terribly far away, but given the fact that her pickup truck was a stick shift, she might be stuck for a while.

Maryann pulled out one of the chairs and dropped down into it. "Do they have any idea when that will be?" She reached across to cover Liza's hand with hers. "I know you don't like having to rely on other people."

It made her sound kind of like...

An ungrateful bitch.

"It's not that I don't like to rely on other people." Her reasons for the way she was weren't usually something she shared. They made her feel guilty and like maybe the decisions she'd made in her life were not as right as she wanted to think they were. "I just don't like to inconvenience other people."

Plus, relying on other people put you at their mercy. Made you vulnerable. And no matter how much you loved or trusted someone, there was always the risk that they would take you down.

Sometimes even claiming it was for your own good.

"Honey, no one would ever call you an inconvenience." Maryann patted her hand. "Do you need anything else before I go? I've got to get home and get my pot roast started for dinner."

"I'm okay." Liza tapped the clear clamshell container of cake with one finger. "And thanks for the chocolate fix."

"It is no problem, honey." Maryann stood up, hooking her purse over one shoulder. "It gives me an excuse to sneak a piece for myself too." She gave her a wink. "Enjoy those wind chimes."

Those damn wind chimes. "I will."

She would not, especially since there was a very good chance Ben would use them against her. Was probably already planning his attack.

Liza gave Maryann a wave as the older woman left the house to go about her day.

Her perfectly happy day, in her perfectly happy life.

Maryanne had moved to Moss Creek in much the same way Liza had. Lured away from an acceptable life in the city by the promise of security and adoration.

Only Maryann's husband kept his promise, giving her a beautiful home, attractive children, and all the love and affection she could stand.

All Liza got was stabbed and ownership of a worthless business and all the debts that came with it.

Which was definitely not what she signed up for.

A soft knock rattled the back door and sent her heart racing.

Which royally pissed her off.

Liza eased up from the chair, making sure she was steady on her feet before making her way across the kitchen.

It was a cowboy on the other side of the paned glass, but not the one responsible for the unfortunate incline in the rate of her pulse.

She opened the door, lifting her brows at his handsome face. "Do you need something?"

Troy held his cowboy hat in his hands, blue eyes filled with concern as they moved over her face. "I just wanted to make sure you were okay."

"I'm fine." She managed a little bit of a smile. "I'll be out to clean up breakfast in just a few minutes."

"Oh you don't need to worry about that, Ms. Cross." He thumbed over one shoulder in the general direction of the mess hall. "I already took care of it."

"You did?" It was unusual to have one of the ranch hands step up and take on additional work, especially given the demographic of the men she could afford to hire. "Thank you. I appreciate that."

Troy tipped his shaggy blonde head. "No thanks necessary. I'm happy to help."

"*Troy.*"

The ranch hand filling up her doorway barely jumped at the sound of Ben's voice behind him. He slowly set his hat back on his head, offering her a wink before turning toward his other boss. "I was just letting Ms. Cross know that I handled KP duty." He grinned at Ben as he passed by, tipping the front of his hat back with a flick of his finger.

The baby cowboy had swagger, that was for sure. And balls, considering the fact that he didn't flinch at the glare Ben was shooting his way.

Her head ranch hand currently looked ready to spit nails.

Good. At least she wasn't the only one pissed off.

"Hey, Troy." Liza waited until the younger man turned to face her. "I could use some help with lunch too."

Troy tucked a toothpick between his teeth, his grin from earlier holding strong. "I am at your service, Ms. Cross."

FOUR

BEN

HE WAS GOING to string Troy up by his belt buckle. Bacon boy didn't even have the sense to look scared about it either.

Ben glared at the kid as he walked away, keeping his eyes on Troy until he was out of sight.

Out of sight, but not out of mind.

He was going to have to keep an eye on that one. If for no other reason than for his own sanity.

If there was any of it left.

If he hadn't needed a damn eye hook to hang the wind chimes then he would've been able to fend off Troy's arrival and the subsequent invitation to lunch it earned him.

An invitation that didn't matter at all considering he was the one responsible for the midday meal.

Not Liza.

Which meant she was planning to dig her heels in and keep bein' a pain in his ass.

The sound of Liza's door slamming shut dragged him back to his purpose for being there.

Purposes.

Ben went to work screwing the eye hook into the fascia of the farmhouse. Thirty seconds later he was looping the chimes into place. They were close to the kitchen window and tucked under the slight overhang shading a tiny strip of the back deck.

He took a step back and looked around the space as the wind chimes started to dance, their sound soothing and soft.

Unfortunately, there wasn't a good place on the small deck to sit and enjoy them.

He and a couple of the other hands put the deck on the back of the house when the original cement steps crumbled away enough he was worried Liza would take a tumble one morning on her way out the door. It wasn't a big space, but it was sturdy and well-built enough that Liza should be able to enjoy it for years to come.

Not that it appeared she was enjoying it now.

There wasn't a scrap of furniture in the space. Not a bird feeder. Not even a grill.

Just the wind chimes Maryann Pace brought.

He was going to have to come up with something, otherwise the chimes were pointless.

Ben collected the cardboard and plastic sleeves the metal tubes were packed in, stacking all the trash together before heading back toward the barn where the rest of the ranch hands were going about the day's chores.

In the years since Ed Cross's death, they'd managed to come up with a system that kept their costs to a minimum while still helping the ranch run as smoothly and efficiently as possible. One of the most important things they'd done was confined their calving season to a short window in the spring. It was a rough couple of months while it was happening, but once it was over and all the babies were born, it was smooth sailing from there on out.

As smooth as sailing ever got on an understaffed cattle ranch.

Right now they were in a holding pattern, taking care of the cattle and horses while they waited for the next big task, which was cutting and bailing the Labor Day hay.

That meant he had plenty of time on his hands. Time that, up until now, was driving him slightly crazy.

Too many unfilled hours gave him too much time to think.

Too much time to regret.

Too much time to worry about a woman who didn't even worry about herself.

"Everything okay?" Darryl was back outside the barn, puffing on one of the cigarettes that always seemed to be dangling from the corner of his thin lips.

But this time he had a couple of other hands loitering with him. The three men were the oldest of the crew.

And the least likely to be found doing any actual work.

"Everything's fine." Ben almost went past them, his focus zeroed in on the new plan he had.

But then he realized Darryl and his cohorts looked awfully clean.

He gave the ranch hands a once over. "You been out in the fields?"

Right now the ranch hands did the same exact thing every day. They made sure all the calves and their mamas were healthy and accounted for, mucked horse stalls, and made sure everyone was fed and watered, hogs and chickens included. And while none of that was the dirtiest work on a ranch, it also wasn't clean.

"We hung back. Figured we'd stay around the house in case anyone needed anything." Darryl said it like he had the authority to make that decision. Like he wasn't less than a month into an entry-level position.

"That's not your job." Ben was used to dealing with men who didn't fully comprehend what the life of a ranch hand was actually like. In the last five years they'd gone through more men than most ranches employ in a lifetime. "Your job is to go out with the rest of the hands to check on the cattle." He pointed one finger at the horse barn. "Then you muck stalls."

Darryl took a slow drag on his cigarette, blowing out the smoke like he wasn't remotely concerned he'd been caught not doing his job. "I'm not really cut out for mucking stalls." He arched his spine. "Got a bad back." He tipped his head toward the yard of Liza's farmhouse. "I figured I was more useful around here."

It was sounding like Darryl might not be useful anywhere. "You were hired as a ranch hand, not the yard sitter." Ben wadded the trash in his hands tighter as he scanned the faces of the three men. "You can either work here as ranch hands, or you can go find yourselves another place of employment."

He walked away before he risked saying anything more.

Nothing aggravated him worse than when someone tried to take advantage of Liza.

And that was most definitely what this was.

Darryl got here and discovered that the man in charge was actually a woman, so he decided to make things more flexible for him and his friends.

It had happened countless times before, and almost every one of them ended in a fist fight.

And right now Ben didn't have time to kick Darryl's ass.

He had a woodpile to pick through.

Ben chucked the garbage from the wind chimes into one of the cans on his way to the back of the biggest structure at Cross Creek. The metal-sided pole barn was where they stored anything that needed to stay dry. Feed, straw, tools, gear.

And the pile of old barn wood he salvaged from anything he could. So far the continuously growing stash contained hundred-year-old boards from the original Cross Creek barn, the bits and pieces left from Liza's new deck, and the remnants of the old smokehouse they tore down to make way for the mess hall.

Surely, between all that, there had to be plenty for him to work with.

Ben started digging through, pulling out anything that looked like it might be useful for the project he had in mind.

Thirty minutes later he had a stack of wood that was more than enough to make a couple of chairs and a small table. Liza's little deck wasn't big enough to house much more, but that was all she really needed.

Ben collected the wood, stacking it into small, carryable piles that he then hauled to the bed of his truck, lining them into place one by one.

He was just finishing up when Darryl and his buddies wandered back over, testing the limits of his patience. "You need any help with that?"

This dude really wasn't getting the message. "What I need help with is mucking the stalls." Ben closed the tailgate and turned the ranch hands' way. "Are you capable of mucking stalls, or not? Because if you're not then like I said, you need to go find a new place of employment."

"It seems like not everyone around here has to muck out stalls." Darryl squinted in the direction of the mess hall just as Troy came out with Liza at his side. "Seems like some people get to do other things."

Ben forced his eyes from where Troy followed Liza into her house. "Some people do get to do other things." He leaned back against the tailgate of his truck, trying to look more relaxed than he felt. "But you are not some people. You are ranch hands who were hired to muck out stalls."

Normally, he waited for any problematic additions to figure out they were not Cross Creek material on their own. It made things simpler and resulted in fewer bruised knuckles.

But right now the idea of bruised knuckles, along with the outlet of the fight that went with them, was getting more appealing with every second Troy spent in Liza's house.

"You don't have to muck out stalls," Ben straightened, gearing up for what he hoped was coming, "just like you don't have to work at Cross Creek Ranch."

Darryl's slick-smile barely slipped. "I belong at Cross Creek Ranch."

"Then you belong mucking stalls." Ben's fingers were practically itching at the opportunity to let off some steam. Work out some frustration.

Frustration that had been building for five fucking years.

Darryl ran his tongue across his teeth. "I guess we'll go muck stalls then."

Ben watched his much-needed stress relief turn and walk away, heading for the horse barn.

"This is an awful big tray of coleslaw, Ms. Cross." Troy was putting on his best smile as he followed Liza across the yard, carrying an aluminum serving tray wrapped in foil.

"You boys eat a lot of food." Liza pulled open the door to the mess hall with her good arm, holding it wide as Troy passed.

"That's because we appreciate good cooking." Troy's smile barely dimmed as he caught sight of Ben.

He should probably feel lucky that it had taken this long for someone to attempt to crawl under Liza's skin. Even with her reputation as a handful, it was a miracle no one had tried their hand at getting into the jeans she wore like a second skin.

But in this moment he was not feeling grateful. Not at all.

Ben took off across the lawn, going straight for the mess hall. He unlatched each of the sliding doors before pulling them open wide. It was something they did when the weather was tolerable. It kept them from having to cool the space in the summer and reduced the number of days they had to heat it in the winter.

But his reasons for opening the doors today had nothing to do with the weather.

"You starting lunch already?" He crossed his arms, watching as Troy's skin paled.

"Did you not want to eat lunch today, Mr. Chamberlain?" Liza knew exactly how to piss him off, and she did it with a smile on her face.

That was fine. If she wanted to play, then he was happy to join the game.

"Lunch is normally my duty, Elizabeth." They split the chores around Cross Creek between them. They'd done it from the beginning and stuck with it over the years.

"I assumed that since you decided to collect the eggs this morning I should pick up lunch." Her expression was sweet enough that no one else would realize the true intention behind her words.

Which was to prove she didn't need any more of his help than she was already forced to accept.

"I chose to collect the eggs this morning because I wanted to." Ben slowly crossed the mess hall, closing in on where Liza stood next to bacon boy.

"Well I am choosing to make lunch today." Liza's tone carried the slightest edge.

Maybe he would get the fight he was looking for after all.

And this one would be infinitely more satisfying.

"Then I'll go ahead and let you know that I'm going to choose to make breakfast tomorrow." He would get up in the middle of the night if that's what it took to ensure bacon boy was not spending the predawn hours cuddled up next to Liza. Following her around like a puppy dog as he did her bidding.

Liza's eyes narrowed. "Breakfast is not your job."

Ben smiled at the aggravation in her voice. "Maybe it is now."

They had followed the same rules for too long.

Rules that were outdated at best.

Rules that maybe should have never been.

"Fine." Liza's lips curved in a way that no one would call a smile. "Then lunch will be my job."

"I just remembered," Troy backed away, "I was supposed to call and check in with my mom."

Liza didn't even glance his direction as bacon boy fled the scene without looking back.

At least someone could read the room, but it definitely wasn't the woman staring him down like he was a chunk of manure stuck to her boot.

It wasn't how she used to look at him.

At one point Elizabeth Cross looked at him like he was everything that mattered.

Everything she needed.

Everything she wanted.

But then it ended. Like all good things do.

"Why are you being so stubborn?"

Her humorless smile didn't fade. "I have always been stubborn, Mr. Chamberlain."

The name chapped, sending his teeth tight together. "Stop calling me that."

"Then stop calling me Elizabeth."

"It's your name." One no one else used. Not ever.

No one but him.

It was a reminder of the time they shared so long ago. A time he usually tried to pretend hadn't happened, thinking it might help keep him from losing his mind.

But it was looking like he'd been unsuccessful.

Because right now he was feeling it start to slip.

"My name is Liza."

Ben shook his head. "No. It's not." She might be Liza to everyone else, but to him she would always be Elizabeth. The woman who was breakable and soft. The woman who needed to be protected from the evils in this world.

It's what he'd done. What he tried to do.

Even at a cost that was almost too much to bear.

"Yes. It is." Her voice barely wavered, the only sign that the woman he knew was still there, hidden beneath the layers of armor he'd forced her to wear.

Ben moved in closer, giving in to a need he'd been denying for years. "Don't pretend like I don't know the truth about you, Elizabeth." He inhaled slowly, savoring the sweet scent of the air around her. It was like a spring day, fresh and warm and new.

But nothing between them would ever be new.

"I know who you are." He inched in a little more, daring to brush his body against hers. "I've seen what you hide from everyone else."

It was the only thing that got him through these years, being so close to her but still so far away.

Knowing that he was the carrier of all her secrets.

Knowing that he was the one keeping her safe.

"I don't want to talk about that." Liza tried to back away, but he followed her, bracing both hands against the counter and boxing her in.

"I don't care what you want."

"I know." Her cool blue eyes held his, steady and unwavering. "You never did."

FIVE

LIZA

BEN'S EYES NARROWED, dark and stormy as they moved over her face. "Fine."

She thought he would move away and finally give her room to breathe.

But Ben's large body didn't budge. If anything he came closer. "What do you want, Elizabeth?"

Her name rolled off his tongue, slow and seductive in a way her treacherous body refused to ignore.

Because even after everything that happened, Ben Chamberlain still affected her.

Which is why she had to lie.

"I want you to leave me alone."

It shouldn't be hard. He'd done it before.

"Are you sure that's what you really want," he was so close his nose almost touched hers and she could feel the warmth of his breath skate over her skin as he spoke, "Elizabeth?"

She wasn't sure of anything at this point, outside of the fact that she was positive she needed to figure out how to breathe again.

Because for some reason, her lungs decided to stop working.

"Is lunch almost ready?" One of the hands peeked in through the open doors, eyes going wide the second they landed on her and Ben. "I'll come back."

Liza tried to move away, put some distance between her and the man who could be her undoing, but Ben's arms kept her caged in.

He tipped his head at the fleeing ranch hand. "Good idea."

"What are you doing?" She shoved at his chest with her hand, but being down an arm's worth of strength meant Ben didn't budge at all. "People are going to get the wrong idea."

Ben's dark eyes slowly came her way, lingering on her lips before lifting. "I'm not so sure I care about that either."

If it was possible for her to become any angrier at Ben Chamberlain then that comment would have done it.

"Convenient that you stop caring when it suits you."

She wanted to scream. Wanted to kick and hit and fight.

But all that would do was make everything hurt worse, injured arm included.

"That's where you're wrong, Elizabeth." Ben tilted his head to one side, each word coming out of his mouth slow and smooth, like he had all the time in the world. "Caring what other people thought never suited me." His nostrils barely flared. "But I didn't have much of a choice before."

"Stop." Now he was just being mean. "Just shut up and leave me alone."

"Not happening." Ben continued dominating her personal space, taking it over with his heat and his presence. "Not ever."

"Then we're definitely remembering things real different." She snorted out a bitter laugh. "Because you sure as hell left me alone."

Ben walked away from her easily. Like nothing ever happened.

Like nothing ever mattered.

"Did I?" He leaned down a little more, dark eyes staring directly into hers. "Because it sure looks a lot like I'm still right here."

She laughed again. It was hard not to. "Where else were you going to go?"

Neither of them could leave Cross Creek Ranch. It was what tied them together.

Even now.

It was Ed Cross's final stab, and the one that brought her the most pain.

Having to look at Ben every day for the past five years, rain or shine, might have been a fate worse than the death Ed tried to bestow upon her the night he lured her back to Cross Creek.

"Is that what you think?" Ben's eyes barely narrowed. "That I'm only here because I have to be?"

Of course that's what she thought. It was the truth.

"Are y'all going to serve lunch or are you just going to stand there?" Darryl's cigarette-roughened voice scratched through the mess hall. "Because if you're having a hard time getting lunch ready then I'm happy to provide my services."

Ben's eyes left her face for the first time in what felt like forever, squinting into slits as he glared at one of Cross Creek's newest additions. "We discussed which of your services are needed here." Ben barely straightened, his arms dropping from where they pinned her into place. "If you have a problem waiting five minutes for your lunch, then you're welcome to go find your own food."

Darryl's eyes moved from Ben to her and then back to Ben again. "I can wait." He went to the table closest to where they stood and dropped down onto the edge of the bench, leaning an elbow against the table. His eyes stayed on Ben and Liza as two other hands sat down on either side of him, all three staring in unison.

Normally, she would light a man like Darryl up, give him complete hell for being a pompous pain in the ass.

But right now he and his sidekicks were saving her from digging any deeper into a wound that might never heal.

So she would wait until tomorrow to put him in his place.

"If you'll excuse me." Liza edged her way past Ben. "I have work to do." She glanced across the space and caught sight of Troy. "Are you helping or not?"

Troy hesitated, his gaze moving to where Ben stood looking ominous and a little threatening.

But instead of tucking tail and running like she expected, the baby cowboy came her way.

"I'm happy to help with anything I can, Ms. Cross."

"I appreciate that." Liza opened the fridge and pulled out the pack of pulled pork sitting on the top shelf. "But right now all I need help with is lunch."

As convenient as Troy's sudden interest was, it was still something she had to keep a tight leash on.

Giving him, or anyone else, the wrong idea could cause problems she might never recover from.

As someone once not-so-kindly pointed out to her, women didn't play by the same rules as men.

"You want me to heat this up?" Troy sliced across the top of the sealed bag with a pair of scissors.

"I can't imagine everyone wants to eat it cold." Liza reached into the fridge again, this time going for the large tray of coleslaw she spent two hours assembling last night.

It was one of many downsides to getting your arm run over by a car. Everything took twice as long to do as it normally did.

But she would do it again in a heartbeat. Knowing she helped keep a child safe was worth every bit of pain and suffering.

The large aluminum tray was a little more unwieldy than she expected and required a tiny bit more balance than her single arm provided. She barely got it off the shelf before it started to tip, threatening to go down in an explosion of cabbage and carrot.

The only thing that saved her was the open refrigerator door. Liza managed to catch the lip of the tray against one of the shelves, keeping the side dish intact.

Unfortunately, with only one arm in action, she couldn't negotiate the adjustment required to get it out of the position it was in.

"You need some help?" Ben leaned one arm across the top edge of the refrigerator door, lips almost threatening to become a smirk as he watched her struggle.

"No." The response was second nature at this point. "I'm fine."

"Are you?" Ben leaned in a little more, looking down at the precariously perched tray. "Because it looks like you're about to wear whatever's in that pan."

"I'm fine."

Ben came around the edge of the door, moving in close.

Close enough she should be trying to get away.

But she couldn't, not without sacrificing two hours of hard work and a much needed lunch addition.

Ben's hand held the door firmly in place, keeping it from swinging wider and stealing the only thing standing between the pan and the floor. He leaned in, lips almost touching her ear. "If you're not going to start asking for my help when you need it," his other hand braced against the inside edge of the refrigerator, successfully boxing her into his space once again, "then I guess I'll just have to start following you around." He let the refrigerator door go and it immediately swung wide, sending the tray of coleslaw into the freefall she was trying to avoid.

Ben caught it, easily steadying it as the smirk from earlier showed its face. "To make sure you get the help you refuse to admit you need."

"I have help." She tipped her head toward Troy. "So you are more than welcome to go back to your regularly scheduled programming."

There had to be five hundred other things Ben could be doing besides annoying the shit out of her and the sooner he got back to doing that, the sooner her life would go back to normal.

Ben slid the tray onto the counter before tipping back the front of his cowboy hat. "I've got a secret for you." He leaned in again. "You are my regularly scheduled programming."

"Are you drunk?" It was the only explanation for the sudden shift in his behavior. For five years they'd managed to work on this ranch together without getting in each other's way. Now suddenly he was everywhere she went, being a complete pain in her ass.

"Ms. Cross?" Troy edged in, eyes wary as they moved to Ben. "You got anything else you need me to heat up?"

Liza turned to Troy, offering him a sweet smile as she ignored Ben. "Nothing to heat up, but we need to put out the pickles and the chips." She started to walk away, needing space from all of this. "Oh, and the buns."

Troy tipped his head. "Got it."

She sure hoped he did because she was done with this day.

And it was barely noon.

Liza walked straight out of the mess hall, heading to the back door of her house.

This time when she went inside she locked the door behind her, ensuring no one would take the liberty of letting themselves in.

She'd just finished digging out one of the containers Maryann Pace brought over and shoving it into the microwave when her phone started to ring.

She picked it up and swiped across the screen. "Please tell me you're not canceling our date tonight."

"What?" Mae scoffed. "Of course I'm not canceling our date tonight." The clanging of plates and silverware carried through the line. "I was calling to see what you wanted to eat."

Liza glanced down at the gapping waistband of her pants. Her stomach had been pretty touchy since the surgery, and since she hadn't been able to do as much activity wise, she wasn't as hungry as normal. "Something with lots of carbs."

"Dianna's got that chocolate cake in her bakery today. I could stop and get us some of that."

"Maryann brought me some this morning." Liza popped open the microwave and stirred around the mashed potatoes before doing her best to flip the generous slice of meatloaf Maryann packed.

"How many pieces?"

Liza leaned back to glance at the table. "Looks like two."

"Perfect."

"I didn't say you could have one of them." Liza smiled as her best friend scoffed again.

"Fine. I'll bring a pie and you don't get any of it."

"Liar. You can't eat a whole pie by yourself." Liza reset the timer and turned to lean back against the counter. "What time are you coming over?"

She and Mae hadn't been able to partake in their regular weekly lunch dates, so they'd had to move them back to dinner dates, at least until Liza could drive again.

"Five?"

"I'll make sure I look pretty for you." Liza grabbed a bottle of water from the fridge, getting it all the way out before remembering she couldn't open them easily.

"You're always pretty." Mae paused. "Except for right after surgery. You looked rough then."

"I'd just been hit by a car. What do you want from me?" Liza grabbed a glass and filled it with water from the tap. It wasn't as good as the stuff from the bottle, but it was independently accessible.

"I expected you to look just as ravishing as you always do." Mae's grin was obvious, even through the phone line. "It did make me feel a little better to know that even you aren't always drop-dead gorgeous."

Liza rolled her eyes. "Happy to help."

Something crashed in the background. "Gotta go. The new server just lost her tray."

Liza slid the phone back onto the counter and went to work pulling out her lunch.

It was yet another thing that was much trickier to do one-handed. Between the steam, and the heat coming through the sides of the container, there wasn't really any way to manage it unscathed.

The best plan of attack was to do it fast, so her suffering was as short as possible.

Liza pinched the edge between her fingers, holding tight as she raced from the counter to the table.

But, like the coleslaw before it, this food refused to be agreeable. It started to shift around inside the plastic tray, redistributing the weight just enough to make the side she wasn't holding droop. And since that drooping wasn't part of her initial calculation, the edge caught on the back of the kitchen chair she planned to sit in, directing all the momentum right back at her and sending the lid to the floor as the scalding hot meatloaf and mashed potatoes splashed all across her shirt.

The potatoes and sauce from the meatloaf immediately sank through the thin cotton fabric, sucking it directly against her skin. The burn was sharp and immediate, and shocking enough to make her scream out a list of obscenities any cowboy would be proud of.

Maybe not *any* cowboy.

Probably not the one kicking her door in.

Ben rushed into the kitchen, chest heaving, eyes wild.

When his focus landed on her sauce-streaked chest all the blood drained from his face the same way it did on the night that stole him from her.

He raced toward her, boots loud against the worn linoleum.

Then he was holding her, pulling her close before she could offer any sort of explanation.

"Everything is okay." He tried to scoop her up, almost managing to get her feet off the floor.

"Stop it." She shoved at his chest, doing her best to stay upright as Ben pulled her back into a moment she tried hard to forget. "It's just sauce."

His hand went to her shirt, pulling it up to reveal her sticky, barbecue sauce tinted skin.

Along with something else.

Something that explained both the past panic making it hard for her to breathe.

And the haunted look in Ben's eyes.

SIX

BEN

HE THOUGHT SEEING the red splashed across Liza's shirt would be the worst part of this moment.

It wasn't.

The worst part was seeing the scar she still carried from the night he caused.

The shining line of white skin ran from just under her left breast, over the smooth skin of her stomach, angling down until it almost touched her right hip.

He couldn't stop himself from reaching out to trace it, following the same path Ed Cross's blade did that night.

When he tried to turn the threat he used to terrify and control Liza into reality.

"I'm fine." Liza grabbed at her shirt, yanking it down to cover the evidence of the night that was supposed to be a beginning, but turned out to be an end. "It's just barbecue sauce."

She said she was fine, but the shake in her voice made it clear Liza was struggling with the same thing he was.

A past neither of them could escape.

"What happened?" It was a pointless question, considering the container at her feet and the meatloaf and potatoes splattered across the linoleum.

"I dropped my lunch." Liza held the fabric of her shirt away from her skin. "It's not a big deal."

Technically she was right. Meatloaf and mashed potatoes weren't a big deal.

But they didn't come alone. They dragged up memories he worked hard to bury away.

And the guilt that came along with them.

Ben jerked his chin toward the stairs. "Go put a new shirt on. I'll take care of this."

Liza didn't argue with him, which was a testament to just how much this moment affected her, and it made Ben want to bring Ed Cross back from the grave so he could be the one to put him there.

Maybe he should have been in the first place.

Then it would have been his life on the line that night.

And in the years that followed.

Ben waited until she reached the top of the stairs safely before dropping to his knees to clean up the mess.

A mess that was significantly easier to handle than the one that came before it.

He scooped as much of the meatloaf and potatoes back into the container as he could before wiping up the remaining sauce with a handful of paper towels. All of that went into the trash, not including the container, which he dropped into the sink.

He was just finishing up wiping down the floor with a clean rag when Liza came back downstairs.

"You didn't have to clean that up." The anger she'd been throwing his way seemed to have dissipated, but it was replaced by something that might be harder for him to handle.

Fear.

That night changed her. Dug its way into her soul, burrowing deep enough it would never be gone, no matter how much she tried to hide it.

"I know." Ben finished removing any trace of stickiness before standing back up and rinsing the rag off in the sink.

Liza watched him silently, rubbing her lips together as her eyes followed his every move.

There was so much he wanted to say to her, but right now he didn't know where to start.

Right now he was almost as lost as he was that night. Unsure what to do next.

So he did the only thing he could.

What was best for Liza, and maybe it was the same thing now that it was then.

Ben went to the back door, glancing at the ruined lock. "I'll come fix that later on."

Then he walked out of the little house without looking back.

It's what he did five years ago, and what he should have stayed doing.

Being close to her was too hard.

Pretending they could ever be what he wanted was a waste of energy.

So it was time to go back to the way things had to be.

"Ben." Troy hustled across the yard, coming his way. "You got a minute?"

Troy was the last person he wanted to talk to right now.

Ben's eyes flicked to the little farmhouse as a movement in the kitchen window caught his eye.

Troy was the *second* to last person he wanted to talk to right now.

He barely slowed down as the younger man raced to catch up with him.

"I wanted to talk to you about Ms. Cross." Troy was a little out of breath, but he managed to keep pace as Ben continued toward his truck. "I'm not trying anything funny with her."

"It's really none of my business what you're trying with her." It was true, and something he should have remembered from the very beginning.

Troy's brows came together under the brim of his cowboy hat. "Oh." He slowed down, falling behind for just a second.

Ben continued on, intent on getting the fuck away from this house and the woman inside of it.

But Troy must not have realized their conversation was over. He walked faster, managing to catch up to him again in a few long strides. "At any rate, I just wanted to let you know." He barely paused. "I really like working here, and I was more so looking for a way to maybe make myself a little more essential."

That stopped Ben's retreat. "Essential?"

"Right." Troy shifted on his feet. "I heard from some of the other hands that no one stays here for very long, on account of the low wages."

"I think you've got it backwards. Wages stay low because no one stays here very long." It was a blessing and a curse. They'd dished out very few pay increases over the years, which meant they never had to struggle for the extra money.

But it also meant they never maintained quality help.

"See?" Troy held out one hand. "That's what I tried to tell them. You've got to stick it out long enough to earn a raise." He glanced from side to side before stepping closer and lowering his voice. "And then you've got pricks like Darryl who could stay here for a hundred years and never earn a raise."

Ben gave the ranch hand a once over. He'd assumed Troy was too young to be much more than manual labor, but maybe he'd been wrong. "What exactly are you looking for here at Cross Creek?"

Troy stood a little taller. "I'd like to work my way up to a position like yours." He looked out toward one of the pastures, where a handful of this year's calves were in view. "There's no way you can take on any more growth without a second, and I'd like to prove that can be me."

Ben reached up to rub across the rasp of hair peeking out of his skin, scratching at one more thing that was irritating him. "That's not a quick position to earn." He'd been the head ranch hand at Cross Creek for almost eight years now. Three of them passing before Ed Cross met his untimely end.

Untimely only because it didn't come soon enough.

In those eight years, he'd done everything in his power to make the place run as smoothly as possible. Sometimes that was easier than others.

"I don't expect it to be quick." Troy tucked a toothpick between his teeth. "But I also don't want to stay at a place that has no intention of letting me move through the ranks."

In all Ben's years at Cross Creek he'd never had a ranch hand approach him like this, certainly not one willing to work for what he wanted. "Is that what you thought helping Ms. Cross would do? Help you move through the ranks?"

"She's the boss, isn't she?" Troy flipped the toothpick with his tongue before clasping it back between his teeth. "I figured the first step to getting where I wanted to go was to make sure the boss knew who I was."

Ben really didn't want to like Troy after having to watch him be so close to Liza all day, but the ranch hand's recognition of Liza as the main boss made it real hard not to at least respect him. "I'd say she knows who you are now."

Unfortunately.

"You got any other skills? Anything else that might come in handy around here?" The day-to-day running of the ranch was only a portion of what Ben needed help with. There were a hell of a lot of other tasks that went into keeping a property like Cross Creek moving, and right now most of them fell on his shoulders.

Troy propped against the side of Ben's truck, giving the wood in the back a once over. "I know my way around a saw, if that's what you're asking."

It wasn't, but maybe it should have been. "Anything else?"

Troy shrugged. "I've done this and that. I'll try just about anything."

That bit of information could be good or bad depending on how things shook out.

Because as much as Ben wanted to pretend it wasn't a possibility, there was no denying the fact that Troy was a decent-looking guy who possessed an inordinate amount of charm.

And the more time he spent around Liza, the more likely she was to notice.

"I was just about to go start making Ms. Cross a couple of chairs for her back deck." Ben resisted the urge to look toward Liza's house, knowing full well she was still watching through the window because he could feel the weight of her stare. "That something you'd be capable of helping me with?"

"Course." Troy turned his head, shooting the toothpick from his mouth across the grass with a sharp puff of air. "She know what she wants?"

Ben laughed. He couldn't help it. "No."

"Fair enough." Troy went to the passenger's side of Ben's deep green dually, pulling the door open with a loud creak. He pointed to the obnoxious joint. "I know how to fix that."

Ben climbed behind the wheel. "Good to know."

He fired up the engine and pulled away from the main yard, heading down the gravel drive that led to the bunkhouse where a handful of the ranch hands chose to stay, Troy being one of them.

Troy hung his arm out the window as they passed the bunkhouse, continuing down the lane as it narrowed, cutting a thin line into a copse of trees.

The small frame structure tucked right into the center was practically invisible from outside looking in. Even in the winter months, when the cold temperatures stripped the leaves of their trees, there were enough evergreens to camouflage Ben's tiny home.

Troy leaned forward as they came to a stop in front of the two-room building. "I didn't even know this place was back here."

"There's a reason for that." He liked his privacy. Even more so now than before. The less people knew about you, the less they had to use against you.

Troy climbed out of the truck, looking the house over as he closed the door. "Wouldn't mind having a little place like this myself." He shot Ben a grin. "Definitely be better than listening to Darryl snore after he finishes jacking off."

"What in the hell is wrong with him?" Even knowing as much as he did about Darryl, the revelation that he'd jerk off in a room full of coworkers trying to sleep was still shocking.

"I'd say more than you've got time to hear about." Troy tipped his head toward the roof of Ben's house. "You're going to need to replace that soon."

"Soon has already come and gone." Ben dropped the tailgate, and started unloading the wood, carrying it to the small shed where he stored his tools. "It needed replaced a couple years ago."

About the time Liza's back steps crumbled into nothing. The ranch had the spare money to replace one, but not both, and doing it himself would raise suspicions he wasn't prepared to deal with.

"You know how to replace a roof?" Troy grabbed a pile of wood, hauling it over and adding it to the stack Ben started. "I bet between the two of us, we could get it done in a weekend."

"I might take you up on that." Ben grabbed the last of the wood and added it to their growing pile.

Maybe Troy was going to turn out to be more useful than he realized.

And maybe it was going to be easier to find ways to keep him as far away from Liza as possible.

Troy stared down at the wood. "So what are we thinking?"

AN HOUR LATER they had all the pieces cut for the first chair. Between the two of them, they came up with a design that made the best use of the wood they had available. It was a simple style with no frills and clean lines, but the wide seat and angled back should make for a pretty comfortable chair.

"You going to put cushions on these?" Troy plugged an extension cord into the single outlet inside the shed before dragging it out to where Ben stood with a hand sander.

"Don't have any." He hadn't really made it that far ahead in this process, which wasn't surprising, considering pretty much everything he'd done so far today was based on a knee-jerk reaction.

"You know how to sew?" Troy plugged the sander into the extension cord then stood back as Ben fired it up.

"Nope." He ran the medium-grit paper along the first piece of wood. "You?"

Troy shook his head. "Nope."

Finally. At least there was something bacon boy couldn't do.

"But I'm willing to try to figure it out." He sorted through the rest of the pile, pulling out pieces, and lining them up according to length and width. "I bet they'd be more comfortable to sit in with somethin' under your ass."

Ben kept his eyes on the wood, methodically working his way across the surface to buff away any sharp or rough edges.

Troy was right, as much as he hated to admit it. The chairs

would be significantly more pleasant to sit in with some cushions.

And there was one person he knew who might be capable of helping him out with that.

Ben shut off the sander. He stood up and fished his keys out of his pocket. "You feel like going for a ride?"

Troy propped his hands on his hips, looking Ben up and down. "You gonna kill me and dump me in the woods for getting close to Ms. Cross?"

The implications of Troy's understanding of the situation were problematic.

Too problematic to address right now.

Ben turned to the truck, spinning his keys on one finger until they dropped into the palm of his hand. "Not today."

SEVEN

LIZA

"WHAT DID YOU bring?" Liza held the door open for Mae as her best friend angled through the opening carrying two large paper bags.

She wasn't even all the way inside and the house was already filling with the amazing scent of whatever was inside the giant shopping bags.

"You said carbs, so I brought all the carbs." Mae went straight through the small living room and into the kitchen, setting both bags onto the table. "I made fettuccine Alfredo with crispy breaded chicken, and I brought an entire loaf of Carmen's farmhouse white." She pulled out a clear plastic bag and dangled it between them, the circular loaf spinning as she held it. "I didn't even bother slicing it. I figured we could just tear off chunks like the savages we are."

"I'll do my best." Liza lifted her healing arm, stretching it the way her physical therapist showed her. "I'm not quite my normal savage self right now."

"I would say that you're still twice as savage as most of the men we know," Mae pulled out a container and stacked it next to the bread, "even one-armed."

A week ago Liza might have agreed with that assessment, but today she was feeling the strain of everything.

And there was a lot of it.

"I packed the pasta and the chicken separately." Mae pulled out another foam container and popped the lid. "I was hoping it would keep the chicken crispier on the drive over." She poked at one nicely browned chicken chunk, lifting her brows in approval. "Not too bad."

"Pretty sure I would eat it if it was complete mush." Liza already had plates and silverware stacked on the table. "I'm starving."

Between her sudden exit at breakfast, and her mishap with lunch, she'd managed to make it through the entire day without eating.

A problem that was becoming a little too regular of an occurrence.

"Good, because I brought enough to feed an army." Mae scooped out a heaping portion of noodles, before sliding on a healthy topping of chicken. She carried the first prepared plate out and set it on the coffee table in the living room. "You go get started since it takes you twice as long to eat now. I'll be in in a minute."

Normally Liza would argue with her and insist on waiting until everything was ready so they could eat together.

But the smell of garlic and cheese had her empty stomach growling so hard it hurt. "I'll take the bread with me." Liza grabbed the plastic bag on her way into the living room, carefully cradling it in her injured arm.

This was how their dates went now. Instead of enjoying tea and talk at The Wooden Spoon, Mae's restaurant in downtown Moss Creek, they piled up on Liza's couch while they stuffed themselves silly and watched the latest episode of 90 Day Fiancé.

"Do you want some wine?" Mae hollered in from the kitchen like the house wasn't small enough she would have been able to hear it in her regular voice.

"Yes." She'd skipped out on the anti-inflammatories Ben tried to make her take this morning, thinking that sooner or later her arm would stop throbbing.

Apparently it was going to be on the later end of the spectrum, but hopefully a glass of wine would move the process along.

"Good. Me too." Mae came in a minute later, carrying her plate, two glasses, and a bottle of wine like the skilled professional server she was. "How is it?"

Liza didn't even bother covering her full mouth. That wasn't the kind of relationship they had. "Amazing." The word came out a jumbled mess, but she'd been friends with Mae long enough to know that was how her best friend preferred to get praise where her food was concerned.

"Good." Mae settled her plate onto her lap and leaned back, kicking her socked feet up onto the coffee table. "Eat a lot, you've got a bunch of weight to put back on."

"How can you tell?" Liza made sure she always wore a baggy shirt when Mae came over, knowing her friend would be concerned if she saw how much weight she'd lost.

"What do you mean, how can I tell?" Mae shot her a glare. "I'm your best friend. I know how stress affects you." She looked Liza up and down. "How much have you lost?"

"I don't know. Don't have a scale. Threw mine away when I moved here." It was the first thing she got rid of when she came to Moss Creek, thinking she was finally leaving her days of obsessive calorie counting behind and moving on to a better, brighter, healthier future. One where she didn't feel like she was in constant competition with the women around her.

She was right about the calorie counting and female competition part, but the better, brighter, healthier future was still in question.

"Good." Mae shoved in a bite and continued talking around it. "Those things are the devil." She glanced Liza's way. "Do you ever miss New York?"

"Sometimes." She twisted the fettuccine on her fork, continuing to spin even after the bite was ready for eating. "It was fun in a lot of ways."

Her days working as a model, and then scout, in New York were some of the most exciting she'd ever experienced.

Exciting and short-lived.

Stopped before it really started, because she was naïve enough to believe hard work would make her irreplaceable.

"Maybe I should have—"

"Nope." Mae held up one hand. "We're not talking about our bad decisions right now." She snagged the remote. "We are relaxing, and not worrying about anything, while we watch people who make worse life choices than we do."

Liza smiled as Mae went to work pulling up their entertainment for the evening.

This was why they were friends. Mae understood her in a way few people did. Maybe that was because Mae knew what it was like to live with regret.

And what it was like to have to kill or be killed.

Unfortunately Mae wasn't as successful at that as Liza was. She managed to knock Junior Shepard out a window before he could shoot her, but the cast iron pan he took to the face, and the two-story fall that followed it, didn't turn out to be as lethal as they sounded.

Which was probably for the best. Killing a man, even in self-defense, wasn't as easy to live with as she expected.

"Stop." Mae dropped the remote between them. "You're thinking about it again."

She'd been thinking about it a lot actually.

Ed was a loose cannon. She knew that. Found out the hard way more times than she could count.

It was how she and Ben started talking in the first place.

He'd found her alone in the barn one night, waiting out another of Ed's whiskey-fueled rages, icing one of the many black eyes the asshole gifted her over the course of their two-year marriage.

It was the beginning of a connection that started out innocently enough, but grew into something more.

Something neither of them could pretend wasn't there.

"So do we think that the woman this guy has been talking to is really a woman?" Mae's eyes were fixed to the television screen as she leaned forward to tear two big chunks off the bread, passing one to Liza before taking a bite out of the other. "Or do we think it's some dude in a headset who tries to get people to pay their tax debts with Target gift cards?"

Liza forced her focus to the television and took a big bite of the bread. It was chewy, and yeasty, and still a little bit warm. A surprisingly effective distraction from things she shouldn't be dwelling on. "My vote is dude in a headset."

Mae nodded as they watched the man profess his love for a woman he'd been text messaging for less than two months and had never actually talked to or seen. "Same."

They were halfway through the episode, and halfway through the bread, when something moved around outside the front window.

Mae leaned to one side, squinting through the sheer curtains. "Are you expecting company?"

"Just you." Liza slid her plate onto the coffee table as she stood up. The improved angle gave her a better view of the car pulling up in front of her house. "It's Nora."

Nora was one of the newer transplants to Moss Creek. Like Liza, she'd enjoyed a glamorous, but soul sucking, life in the city before being lured into cattle country by the promises of a man.

Lucky for Nora, the man making her promises was raised by Maryann Pace, so her happy ending was as real as the one his parents shared.

Liza opened the front door, stepping out onto the porch with Mae close behind her.

Mae waved at her sister-in-law. "What are you doing here?"

"You didn't know she was coming?" Mae and Nora were each married to one of the Pace brothers, Brooks and Boone respectively. They both lived at Red Cedar Ranch in beautiful new homes built within a stone's throw of each other.

Mae shook her head. "I came straight from work." Her brows pushed together as Nora unloaded something from the back seat of her car. "What in the hell does she have?"

"A sewing machine." It was something Liza had seen numerous times in her life, but never managed to learn her way around. "Why in the hell does she have a sewing machine?"

The sound of crunching gravel sent Liza's attention to the drive leading back across the ranch. A second later a familiar truck pulled into sight.

"You've got to be kidding me."

Ben parked right next to Nora, immediately getting out and taking the sewing machine from her hands.

Another man climbed out of the passenger's seat, going to retrieve a giant stack of fabric from Nora.

Mae let out a low whistle. "Who is that?"

Her friend's attention was completely focused on Troy, like he was the best thing out there worth looking at.

And while Liza could admit that Troy was attractive, he was definitely not the most attention-grabbing man currently occupying her driveway.

One more issue she'd had to deal with every day for the past five years.

Being around attractive men usually wasn't an issue for her. Moss Creek was stacked full of them. Hell, all her best friends were attached to men that made good women stupid and bad women dangerous.

With all her best friends falling into the latter category.

But Ben Chamberlain was on a whole different level, and had a history of making her both stupid and dangerous.

It really wasn't fair.

She struggled not to watch the flex of his forearms as he shifted the sewing machine in his grip, long fingers easily managing the odd shape.

It was almost impossible not to let her eyes drag down the well-muscled line of his tall frame as Ben sauntered across the gravel of her driveway, proof positive that there was nothing sexier than a man in a pair of Wranglers and cowboy boots.

Except maybe a man in Wranglers, cowboy boots, and a cowboy hat.

"Liza?" Mae elbowed her without looking away from Troy. "Are you going to tell me who that is?"

"That's Troy. One of the ranch hands." Luckily her friend was too busy ogling the blonde flirting with Nora to notice Liza hadn't even glanced Troy's way.

How it was possible for her to hate a man as much as she did Ben Chamberlain, while still being able to appreciate the fine form that the good Lord gave him was one of life's great injustices.

But while Mae might not have noticed her perusal of the finer parts of Cross Creek's head ranch hand, someone else definitely did.

Liza nearly jumped when she finally made her way up to Ben's face and found his gaze leveled squarely on her. When he shot her a knowing smirk she couldn't decide between throwing something at him or turning tail and running away.

Since there wasn't anything heavy enough to do damage within grabbing distance, the universe made that decision for her.

She turned, abandoning Mae on the porch as she ducked into her house, fleeing the scene of the crime.

And noticing Ben Chamberlain as anything other than a thorn in her side definitely qualified as a crime.

Mae could handle whatever was going on out there. She was going to hide out in the kitchen, polishing off the last of the wine they shared over dinner.

Straight from the bottle.

Liza had it tipped back, opening against her lips as Nora's voice carried into the house.

"Let's put that in the kitchen on the table."

Damn it.

She barely had time to swallow what was in her mouth before Ben strode into the room, carrying the sewing machine like a tall dark and handsome Suzy Homemaker.

He set the appliance down on the table as his eyes scanned the bottle in her hand. He continued around the circular pedestal of oak that she ate breakfast at every morning, deftly snagging away the remnants of the Chardonnay before immediately tipping it out into the sink.

"*Hey.*" Liza followed behind him, her voice a low hiss. "I wasn't finished with that."

"Yes, you were." Ben turned to face her, looking much more dangerous up close. "Remember what happened the last time you drank with one of your friends?"

Vaguely, and she preferred not to dwell on the tidbits she did recall from the night she and Nora split a bottle of Sloe Gin and a tray of banana pudding.

Tidbits that involved the man currently glowering at her. "I am a grown woman. If I want to drink, then I will drink."

Ben shifted on his feet, a move that brought his body closer to hers. "When you start eating three meals a day, then we'll talk about it."

"We won't talk about anything." She fixed her eyes on his face, hoping for a fight that would take this odd warm feeling in her chest and smother it into dust. "You don't have a say in anything I do."

He gave that privilege up.

But Ben didn't look deterred. "I might not," his eyes slid toward the front of the house as the door opened, "but I know a few people who do."

"You can put the fabric right here on the table, Troy." Nora swept into the room, all her attention focused on the lanky ranch hand currently doing her bidding.

Poor Troy was going to have to be careful, otherwise he was going to end up with Brooks Pace's boot wedged between his butt cheeks.

"Yes, ma'am."

Nora continued on, like Troy wasn't laying out the cowboy charm in a layer so thick it could smother out midday sunlight. "What kind of fabric are you thinking of, Ben?" She started pulling out individual bolts. "I brought a couple stripe patterns." She stacked a cheery yellow and white mix on top of a deeper green and black. "I brought a couple solids." Those went into a pile of their own. "And a couple florals." Liza picked up the last two fabrics together. "One of them is daisies and the other is—"

Ben pointed at the final fabric. "The sunflowers."

Nora shot him a smile. "That was easy." She reached down to unzip the rolling bag she brought in. "We need some thread that matches the fabric," a pale turquoise that perfectly matched the background of the sunflower print hit the table, "and how do you feel about trim?"

"I want whatever you say is going to look the best." Ben picked up the thread, pinching the spool between his finger and his thumb as he compared it to the fabric.

"I mean, adding some cording around the seams will look

really nice," Nora gave him an apologetic-looking cringe, "but it's more work."

"Not scared of work." Ben set the thread down on top of the sunflower fabric Liza was itching to get her hands on.

Hand on.

It was beautiful, and she was a sucker for sunflowers of any kind.

It was one of her favorite things about Cross Creek Ranch. There was a huge patch of sunflowers that grew every year in a spot she could see from every window across the back of the house. Each year the section got bigger, probably from the flowers re-seeding themselves in the fall.

"Good, because I brought cording hoping you would say that." A bundle of twisted white cotton rope came out of Nora's magic interior designer bag.

"I'm sorry, I think I missed something here." Liza focused on Nora since she was the one most likely to explain the situation. "What is happening?"

Nora's dark brows came together as she looked from Ben to Liza. "Oh, I assumed since the chairs were for you—"

"Chairs?" She wasn't following along. "What chairs?"

Nora looked just as confused as she was. "The chairs for your deck." She focused on Ben. "Did I misunderstand you?"

"Nope." Ben jerked his chin toward the front door, eyes on Troy. "Go unload Ms. Cross's chairs from the back of my truck."

Liza slowly turned toward the man still hovering at her side. Ben shot her another little smirk that heated her belly with an emotion she was going to choose to believe was anger.

He had her between a rock and a hard place. Also known as Mae and Nora.

Arguing with him now would only lead to questions later. Questions she definitely didn't want to have to answer.

So she forced on a smile, doing her best to make it seem like everything was fine. Like Ben Chamberlain wasn't suddenly becoming a huge pain in her ass.

"Oh." Liza tried to look as sweet as possible, but her left eye started to twitch as she stared Ben down. "*Those* chairs."

EIGHT

BEN

MAYBE THIS WAS the best idea he'd had all day.

Having Liza's friends around seemed to make her a little less hostile than when he had her completely alone.

Not that he minded the thought of having her completely alone.

"You are really good at this." Nora leaned over his shoulder, watching as he fed the fabric through the foot of the machine. "I was a little worried you would end up with one of your fingers stuck under the needle."

Ben lifted his eyes over the machine, catching Liza staring at him once again. "I'm pretty good at keeping my hands where they belong."

Liza snorted loud enough to make the whole room turn her way. She immediately started to cough, trying to cover up the unintentional sound. "Sorry. Swallowed wrong."

She waited until everyone went back to what they were doing before narrowing the glare she'd had focused on him since he walked in.

It's like the woman didn't appreciate all he was doing for her.

"I thought we were both going to learn how to do this." Troy sat in the chair beside him, arms crossed over his chest as he waited his turn at the sewing machine.

It had to be one hell of a sight, two cowboys fighting over which one got to make a pillow first.

"Calm your tits. You'll get your turn." Ben slowed down, lifting his foot off the pedal as he came up on a turn.

"Good job." Nora could have been one hell of a kindergarten teacher the way she dished out praise for completing the simplest of tasks. "Make sure you get all the way into that corner before you stop."

Sewing a chair cushion was turning out to be surprisingly complicated. He'd been expecting a couple pieces of fabric with a line of stitches around the outside, but Nora Pace clearly had a different vision for the project.

And in all fairness, her vision was a huge improvement.

Ben reached the corner, stopped the machine, and lifted the foot, carefully working the bulk of outdoor fabric as he pivoted.

Nora nodded in approval as he lowered the foot and took off again. "You know," she rested one hand on his shoulder, "if you're ever looking for a new line of work I could definitely find you something to do."

"I'll keep that in mind if I'm ever in the market for a career change." His eyes lifted of their own accord, just like they had countless times before, going to the spot Liza stood.

Only this time the spot was empty.

He didn't expect her to be interested enough to stand and watch him all night, but he did expect her to be pissed off enough to stand there and glare at him until he left.

And as much as he hated to admit it, he didn't mind the idea of spending the night in Elizabeth Cross's sights.

At least then she was acknowledging he existed instead of walking past him like he was a ghost, which was exactly what she'd been doing since Ed Cross died.

"Are you about done?" Troy leaned forward. "I'm tired of hearin' Miss Nora talk about how excellent you are." He shot Nora the kind of smile men gave to women across dimly lit bar rooms and crowded dance floors. "I want to hear her talk about how fantastic *I* am."

"She talks too much about you and you're going to end up

getting a visit from Brooks Pace." Ben reached another corner and slowed his speed. "And I don't want to clean up the mess that comes from that."

Troy scoffed. "How come she can talk about you?"

It was a valid point, one Ben never really thought about.

Maybe it was because the Pace brothers knew he'd never even think about trying to touch something that was theirs.

Or maybe the Pace brothers knew something else. Something he worked hard to conceal.

"Finish up this last bit and then we'll let Troy try his hand at the other seat cushion." Nora moved the conversation along, keeping it from sticking at a point he wasn't entirely interested in lingering on.

Ben hurried up and finished the last seam of the seat cushion, backstitching to make sure none of the stitches would pop, exactly the way Nora showed him earlier, before lifting the foot and pulling the completed cover free.

"Now all you have to do is wrestle this chunk of foam in there." She held up the all-weather insert they'd trimmed down to size before starting.

"That should be the easy part, right?" Ben took the foam and tucked it under one arm, stepping away from the machine, using his new position to scan the house in search of the woman hell-bent on being a pain in his ass.

Nora laughed, reaching out to poke the foam under his arm. "You ever tried to get a big guy into a little jacket?"

Ben looked down at the cover in his hand, guesstimating at the opening left along the seam. It was probably only three inches wide, significantly smaller than the width of the foam he was about to shove through it.

"I think I'm gonna make my hole bigger." Troy was already working his way down the first side of his cushion.

Nora passed Ben a needle and thread. "Then you'll just have to hand stitch more of it when you're done."

Troy wiggled his brows at her. "It's okay. I'm good with my hands."

"And that's the story of how you're gonna die." Ben pinched

the needle between his teeth. "Trying to flirt with one of the Pace brothers' wives."

Troy might not be a bad guy, but he definitely needed to get a clue about what was in his best interest, and what would lead him to a short hospital stay.

"I'm takin' this outside." Ben started for the front door. "I need some fresh air."

He'd skipped dinner, and the smell of garlic and chicken inside Liza's little farmhouse had his stomach growling.

But that was only one of the things pulling him out of the house.

Ben headed out onto the narrow front porch, taking a deep breath of the heavily humid evening air, giving the yard a quick scan.

He shouldn't be surprised that Liza found a way to escape his presence. It was an art form she'd perfected in the past five years. One minute she'd be there, and the next she'd be gone. Disappeared without a trace, like she never existed at all.

And maybe his life would have been easier if that was the truth.

Maybe he wouldn't be busting his ass to revive the ranch, pretending like he didn't have any other choice.

Ben dropped his ass onto the edge of the porch, letting his legs swing over the edge. Liza wasn't the only woman who'd gone MIA, which led him to believe she was safely in Mae's care, and if there was any other person in this world he trusted to take care of Liza, it was Mae.

He stabbed the needle into the cushion for safekeeping and went to work turning the cover right side out, stuffing the bulk of fabric through the narrow hole he left himself. It was surprisingly challenging, which didn't give him much hope that he'd be able to squish the cushion inside.

Once the cover was right side out, Ben went to work compressing the foam and inching it through the opening. It was a slow and tedious process, but one he didn't hate.

Recently, every task he took on felt infinitely more tedious than it used to. It was frustrating as hell.

But this didn't feel that way, even though it actually *was* tedious as hell.

Maybe it was because it was something different. Outside of the way he normally spent his time.

Or maybe it was because he was doing it for someone who shouldn't matter to him as much as they did.

"How's it going out here?" Nora came out the front door and sat down on the porch next to him. "Wow, you're plugging along."

"I was hoping to get this done tonight. I don't have time to mess with it tomorrow." It wasn't true. Tomorrow was just as much of an uneventful day as today was.

"Now I definitely want to hire you." Nora leaned back, propping herself in place with her hands. "It's not easy to find someone willing to put in a good day's work."

"Tell me something I don't know." It was one of the never-ending tasks in maintaining Cross Creek Ranch. "Our turnover is unbelievable."

"I feel your pain." Nora shook her head. "Sometimes it seems like we go through contractors like water."

Nora and her husband Brooks started up a house flipping business that she was in charge of. They'd been in the process of buying, renovating, and selling every run-down, dilapidated house in Moss Creek.

And they were making a pretty big dent in the inventory.

"It doesn't seem like it's slowing you down much."

Nora rolled her eyes Ben's way. "I could say the same thing to you." She smiled. "From what I hear, you and Liza have managed to bring Cross Creek back in a big way."

"Didn't make sense to let it go into bankruptcy."

Even though it would've been the easiest option.

In some respects.

"That would have been a shame." Nora swung her feet a little where they dangled over the edge of the wooden plank porch. "It's such pretty land."

She was right. It was pretty.

But much of what made Cross Creek pretty, also made it less conducive to raising cattle.

It was something Ed Cross hadn't considered when he decided to try his hand at being a cattle rancher. All he saw was an opportunity to pretend to be something he wasn't, at a price he could afford.

Partly.

"Pretty isn't always best." While the Pace family's land was primarily flat and even, Cross Creek Ranch was situated on the complete opposite end of Moss Creek, bringing it much closer to the mountains edging the little town.

That meant their terrain was rougher, and the weather routinely had a hitch in its giddy-up. More than a few rain clouds stalled out on their way across the mountains, dropping down unmanageable amounts of water across the area that flooded the intersecting wet weather creek beds cutting through the fields.

It washed away everything from fence lines to alfalfa to baby cattle.

"Pretty can be helpful though." Nora nudged the almost complete cushion on his lap. "Ugly pillows would sit just the same, but pretty ones will put a smile on your face."

Ben grinned at Nora. "You're starting to sound like a country girl."

Like Liza, Nora came from the city. Maybe not the same city, but close enough to make it count.

"Am I?" Nora's smile was wide and bright. "Good."

Ben finished tucking the foam into the pillow. "Now we've just gotta get you picking up snakes."

It was one of his favorite stories. The day Mae told him about Liza picking up a dead snake and scaring the shit out of Nora with it he laughed for almost three hours straight.

Partially because he could imagine the look on Nora's face, and partially because at one point in time Liza had the same exact look on her own face.

"I'm going to take a hard pass on that one." Nora shook her head. "I'll leave the snakes to Liza."

Ben picked up the needle, mulling over his next words. "I can tell you a secret that might make you feel a little better."

He never talked about Liza, not to anyone. Hell, he did his best not to think about the damn woman.

But Nora Pace wasn't just anyone.

She watched him, her eyes moving over his face with suspicion. "Ben Chamberlain has a secret?"

Her surprise made him feel better and worse at the same time.

Better because he'd clearly been successful at keeping the biggest secret of his life.

Worse because he'd been successful at keeping the biggest secret of his life.

"I've got one or two." He carefully pushed the needle through the fabric, poking it right behind the seam of the cord. "The first time I met Liza she was standing on top of a fancy black car in a pair of high heels, screaming at the top of her lungs."

He thought for sure she was lost. No way would a woman like her be caught dead out in the middle of nowhere Montana, especially looking the way she did.

"What?" Nora's eyes widened. "Why?"

It was one of the many moments he'd done his damnedest to push into the darkest parts of his mind, hoping to smother them out.

"She saw a snake."

Nora covered her mouth. "So she climbed onto the car?"

"Absolutely she did. Wearing a little bitty black dress and a pair of shoes that made her taller than me." He laughed, almost not recognizing the sound when he made it. "I have never heard anyone scream as loud as she did that day."

And he hadn't been the only man in town rushing to her rescue that afternoon, just the fastest.

At least he thought he was.

"It was just a little bitty garden snake. I picked it up and she started to scream louder." Never in his wildest dreams would he have thought that woman would be the same woman making breakfast for a bunch of cowboys every morning at four-thirty. "I got rid of it and helped her down off the car without losing either of my eardrums."

It was in that first moment with her, holding her hands to keep her steady, catching her as she slid to the ground that he knew Liza Cross was something special.

"Then what happened?"

That was where the story took a turn, one he never would've seen coming. "Then her new husband came walking out of the bank."

NINE

LIZA

"WHERE ARE YOU going?" Mae chased Liza across the grass, working hard to keep pace with Liza's longer strides.

"I needed some fresh air." Fresh was exactly how you would describe the air out here. It smelled like dirt, and grass, and animal.

And shit. Lots and lots of shit.

This was not where her life was supposed to end up.

But she had no one to blame but herself.

"Your sudden need for fresh air doesn't have anything to do with a certain cowboy, does it?" Mae wiggled her brows in a move that sent Liza's stomach dropping to her shoes.

"No. Of course not."

"I wouldn't blame you if it did." Mae shook her head. "Troy is pretty easy on the eyes."

Liza almost laughed, barely catching the burst before it broke free.

Her best friend thought she had the hots for the baby cowboy.

"I am not sure that Troy has quite enough years under his belt buckle for me." She was probably more than a decade older than the young buck serving as Ben's partner in crime.

Mae rolled her eyes. "Oh come on. He's not an 18-year-old kid." She pursed her lips, clicking her tongue when they separated. "That one is definitely a grown man." Mae gave her a little nudge with one elbow, being careful not to bump Liza's injured arm. "And I'm pretty sure you're overdue for a visit with a grown man."

"I don't have time for whatever it is you're suggesting."

Mae's eyes went wide. "Oh my God." She put one hand in the center of her chest. "It's worse than I thought if you don't even know what I'm suggesting."

Liza stopped, dropping her head back to look up at the heavy clouds moving across the evening sky. "And how do you think I'm going to secure a visit like you're suggesting?" She straightened, huffing out a breath that was definitely not built of sexual frustration. "Can you imagine what the ranch hands who work here would think if I had some man stay the night with me?"

As much as Liza wanted to think she was on the same playing field as a man when it came to running a ranch, it wasn't the truth.

Because even if they were both on the same field, they definitely didn't have to play by the same rules.

"They would probably think you would be in a way better mood when they woke up the next day." Mae's brows came together. "And last time I checked, most men had their own place."

"And I get there how?" Liza lifted her arm. "I can't drive. I can't ride a damn horse." She managed to work the thumb of her damaged arm into the air. "I can barely hitchhike."

"You are absolutely not hitchhiking to a booty call." Mae shook her head. "That seems like all sorts of a bad idea."

Everything about this conversation seemed like all sorts of a bad idea. "I am not booty call material."

She might have been at one point in her life, but the last casual encounter she partook in didn't shake out so well in the long run.

Not well at all considering he tried to kill her for having the audacity to think she could leave him.

"So what? You're just going to be a nun for the rest of your life?"

"Do I look like I'm a saint?" Liza snorted. "I would get kicked out of the convent before my second foot crossed the threshold. Maybe even the first."

Mae pressed her lips together, pinching them tight. Then she started to laugh. "Can you imagine us in a convent? Just for a second. Just think about it."

She and Mae had been best friends almost since the second she arrived in Moss Creek, looking and acting like a completely different person than she was now.

But even then their friendship was easy and strong.

And primarily built on sarcasm, inappropriate comments, and a mutual appreciation for violence.

But only when it was warranted.

Like the time Mae smashed Junior Shepherd in the face with a cast-iron pan, knocking him out of a second story window.

Or the time Liza nearly snatched a woman bald to keep her from kidnapping their friend Camille's little boy.

Or the time Liza had to shoot Ed Cross before he made good on his promise to cut her up into little pieces and feed her to the hogs.

And then turn his rage on someone else.

Mae continued on with the conversation. "I think we would definitely liven the place up a little."

It wasn't an unappealing thought. Getting to hang out with her friends all day. Plant a garden. Drink some wine.

No tall, dark-haired cowboys making her flee her own house so she could take a deep breath.

She would have issues with not being allowed to cuss though. "Only a little?"

"I was being conservative." Mae glanced up at the clouds rolling in. "Is it supposed to rain?"

"There was a small chance according to the weatherman." Liza scanned the sky, looking over the thick band of gray moving their way. "Those look low."

Low clouds tended to be a problem.

"They do, don't they?" Mae was familiar with the issues Cross Creek had regarding rain and flooding.

"We should get back to the house." Normally going to find

Ben in a situation like this would only cause the slightest uptick of her heart rate.

But that was before he started acting the way he was acting now.

Which meant that tonight, her pulse started to race the second her little house came into view.

"I should have known not to believe that damn Jamie Foxworth." The weather was something she kept a close eye on, especially this time of the year when storms were frequent and fierce. "He's always wrong." Liza forced in a slow breath, hoping to stabilize the heart threatening to beat its way out of her chest. "And why do all weathermen have ridiculous names?"

"It'll be okay." Mae stuck right by her side as they ran up the stairs and across the porch. "I'm sure Ben will get everything secure."

Liza rushed into the house, seeking out the same man she normally avoided, using the rain as an excuse to do what she was too afraid to admit she might be wanting anyway.

But Ben was nowhere to be seen.

Neither was his new best friend Troy.

She hurried into the kitchen and found Nora sitting at the table stuffing one of the cushions. "Where's Ben?"

Nora huffed out a breath, blowing back a chunk of hair dangling across her face. "He and Troy rushed out of here. Something about moving cows?"

"I should go help them." If history taught her anything, it was that storms could be unpredictable as hell. One minute they were fine.

The next they were wailing on you.

Sort of like men.

"I'm pretty sure they can handle it." Mae frowned in disapproval. "You have a fucked-up arm. You need to stay inside and let them deal with it."

Yeah. That wasn't really how she lived her life.

"It will be fine." Liza grabbed her raincoat from the closet just inside the back door. She shoved her good arm in and wrapped it over the sling she'd hooked onto the other one to keep it more stable after her mishap with the counter.

Then she went straight out the back door, leaving Mae hollering behind her.

"Dammit, Liza."

Her feet barely stalled out at the sight of two chairs angled on her back deck. A small circular table sat between them.

They were nothing like anything she'd ever seen in a store. They were sturdy and strong and solid.

Someone definitely made them by hand.

Probably the same someone who insisted on taking over her kitchen table and sitting at a sewing machine, reminding her just how skilled he was with his hands.

The same someone who was hell-bent on making everything harder than it already was.

And unfortunately, the same someone she was about to chase across the ranch.

But the ranch came first. Always.

Liza moved as fast as she could, cutting across the front pasture on her way toward the area they were currently using to contain this year's calves.

They were the most likely to have issues if a large storm came. Over the years they'd lost more than a few when the creek beds flooded and dragged them downstream.

It was just starting to sprinkle when she reached the gate, huffing and puffing and wishing like hell she could drive a truck or ride a horse.

A low rumble of thunder moved across the fields as the first strike of lightning lit up the sky.

There wasn't much she could do to help at this point, but she could sure as hell still work a gate.

Liza yanked on the strings of her hood, cinching it down tight as the soft spatters turned to bigger drops.

The sky went impossibly dark as the thick clouds drowned out what little was left of the day's sun, forcing her to squint through the downpour, looking for any sign of Ben and the rest of the ranch hands as they collected the heifers and calves, but it was next to impossible to see anything.

The only warning she got was the steady fall of hooves against earth.

Unfortunately, that warning blended in with the nonstop drum of thunder from the storm that was now directly over her head.

She didn't realize they were coming until they were almost on top of her. A few slashes of lightning lit up the scene bearing down on her.

Usually one ranch hand stayed in front of the rest, making sure the gates were open and the first cattle through went where they needed to go. But between the chaos of the storm and the dark, a handful of heifers and their calves managed to get ahead of the group, the glossy wet slick of their hides blending almost perfectly into the night.

Liza didn't have a prayer of getting the gate open in time. The best she could do was unhook it and hold on tight as the first heifer hit.

The impact was shockingly hard and made it perfectly clear she wasn't the only one who couldn't see well.

The gate swung fast and sharp, sending her sailing through the night and the rain.

Liza managed to maintain her hold on the gate through most of the opening arc, but her skin was soaked, compromising the grip of her already exhausted hand.

She slipped free but kept moving, even without the gate to propel her along, continuing through the air a few more feet before dropping to the sloppy, mucky dirt.

There was nothing she could do to brace for impact, the best she could hope for was that all her weight would fall to her left side and reduce the impact and jostling of her injured arm.

Liza hit the ground with a grunt that stole every bit of air remaining in her lungs, leaving her fighting for breath as thousands of pounds of beef came dangerously close to her body.

A sharp whistle was barely audible over the herd and the storm.

The rush of cattle came closer as more and more of them fought their way through the opening and toward the higher ground of the pasture the hands were driving them toward.

Liza tried to fight her way toward the fence at her back, but the mud was already slick as hell, and no matter how much she struggled, it was impossible to get any sort of leverage.

It also didn't help that one arm was currently pinned to her chest.

"*Ben.*" One of the hands hollered from the other side of the fence. "Liza's down beside the gate."

She gave up fighting the mud and switched tactics, swinging her arm back in an attempt to grab a hold of the fence.

She was so focused on reaching the worn wood, that she didn't see the hoof coming straight for her thigh.

Which also meant she couldn't try to dodge it.

And when it came down hard, rolling her leg and pinching a good bit of her flesh under a calf that outweighed her by hundreds of pounds, Liza couldn't contain the scream of shock and pain.

The clouds and rain were gone, replaced by more stars than a person could count in a lifetime, each one narrowing to a fine point before exploding, chasing a pain so intense she could barely breathe.

"Goddammit, Liza." Ben dropped to the ground next to her, his large form barely discernible as he crouched close. His knees hit the mud beside her a second before his arms were around her, strong but careful as they worked her up from the muck. He started to scoop her up and the pressure of his hold sent a stab of heat through her leg.

She didn't mean to scream, or whatever that sound was that broke free. It was feral and a little unhinged.

And completely indicative of how she was feeling in this specific moment.

"Hell." He carefully moved her, one hand running over her shin and knee. The second he hit the spot the calf kicked like a doorstop she sucked in a sharp breath.

Ben hovered over her, blocking most of the rain wailing down on her from the unforgiving sky. His face turned away as he whistled between his teeth.

Then he was close, shielding her body with his, protecting her from the rain and the last of the cows and calves as they escaped to safer pastures.

Just as the last one cleared a second man dropped to her side. Troy's eyes were full of concern as he looked her over. "She okay?"

"She's never okay." Ben pushed to his feet. "Help me get her up on the horse." He pointed to the thigh that was throbbing like it had its own heartbeat. "Watch her leg."

"Damn." Troy carefully lifted her up. "You wantin' a matching set, Ms. Cross?" He managed to get her up and against his chest without jostling her leg or the arm she did manage to mostly protect. "Cause I'm sure there's easier ways to accomplish that." He eased her higher. "Maybe a fall off the porch or a trip over a shoe."

"She doesn't do anything halfway." Ben grabbed on as Troy started to let go, lifting her up and onto the back of his horse, carefully situating her across his lap so neither her leg or arm had any pressure on it. He jerked his chin toward the ranch hands closing the gate behind the last few stragglers. "You got this?"

"Sure do." Troy tipped his hat at her. "Try to stay out of trouble."

"I don't see that happening." Ben gave the horse the tiniest of nudges and they started to move, his arms bearing most of the impact each step created.

Liza forced herself to keep breathing, even as the throb of her leg edged deeper, turning into an almost unbearable ache. She couldn't move without making it worse, and unfortunately the angle of her body only gave her one other thing to focus on.

Ben Chamberlain's angry face.

He was silent, his jaw tight as they slowly moved through the rain, dark eyes staring straight ahead.

He didn't say a word to her the whole way back to the house. Kept his mouth shut as he slowly worked her battered body to the ground and carried her inside to where her friends were waiting, looking just as pissed off as the man who finally decided to do exactly as she'd been asking.

He set her on the couch and turned and walked right out of her house, leaving without so much as a 'fuck you for being a pain in the ass'.

TEN

BEN

BEN ROLLED OVER, peeling his eyes open as the knocking on his front door picked up in volume and speed.

He slowly sat up, rubbing one hand over his face as he tried to get his bearings.

No one knew where his little cabin was outside of a few of the longer lasting ranch hands, and not a single one of them would be wailing on his door at four in the morning.

He grabbed a blanket off the couch as he made his way through the small space, past the open-concept kitchen that took up one wall of the front portion of the house. He haphazardly wrapped the blanket around his waist, shoving one corner into his makeshift sarong as he yanked open the door.

Nora Pace's hand hung midair, primed and ready for another series of brain rattling knocks. Her eyes went wide. "Oh." Her gaze slowly dragged down his bare chest. "I thought you would be awake."

He should have been, but last night was a rough one. One he wasn't interested in being reminded of. "Do you need something?"

"Um." Her lids lifted even higher as her focus zeroed in on the low-slung blanket barely covering everything the good Lord gave him. "Yeah."

If she looked any harder her eyes were going to pop out of her head, and he was going to be the one on the wrong end of Brooks Pace's boot.

Ben turned, leaving the door open as he walked toward his room. "Come on in."

"Am I imposing?"

He turned to find that Nora hadn't budged from her spot on the tiny porch. "Are you asking if I have company?"

She chewed her lower lip for a second. "Kinda?"

"No." He grabbed the blanket as it started to work loose, barely managing to save the muscles of her eyeballs and his own decency. "I don't have company."

"I wasn't trying to be nosy." Nora inched her way over the threshold, eyes sweeping the front of the house. "I just didn't want to interrupt."

"Are you saying that if I did have company you would've gone away?" Ben ducked into his room and snagged a pair of jeans, pulling them on as he peeked out to find Nora looking exactly as nosy as she claimed she wasn't trying to be.

"No." She leaned in close to the line of pictures taking up the wall above the couch. "But I would've felt bad about it."

Ben buttoned the fly of his jeans before returning to the living room area. "At least there's that."

"You've got a big family, huh?" Nora was about halfway down the line of photos, which meant she was at the one he took with all his siblings, lined up across the yard in front of the house where they all grew up.

"Most people would call it that." He didn't particularly enjoy talking about his family. Mostly because there wasn't much to discuss.

They weren't close.

Actually that wasn't true.

He wasn't close. Everyone else decided to keep on living the same life as their parents did, having kids and working the ranch that had been in their family for generations.

Hopefully they were all happy with that choice.

He sure as hell wouldn't have been.

"I'm an only child, so most families are big to me." Nora turned to face him.

That was when he noticed that Liza's good friend looked a little worse for the wear.

Maybe not quite as rough as she looked the night he had to call Brooks to come pick her up off the kitchen floor, after she and Liza imbibed in too much sloe gin and banana pudding, but it was definitely a close second.

Her hair was flat and messy on one side. Her eyes were droopy and edged in pink, with shadows tinting the skin beneath them.

She yawned loud and long, confirming his suspicions.

"You going to tell me what brought you to my doorstep, or are you going to make me guess?"

"I'm pretty sure you could guess." Nora dropped down onto the couch, her head going into her hands. "She's being difficult."

"Not sure why that would surprise you." Ben went to the kitchen to start his first coffee of the day. "She's always difficult."

"Yeah, but normally it's funny." Nora straightened, only to yawn again as she fell back against the cushions. "Right now it's not amusing at all."

Ben dumped the grounds into a filter before switching the maker to run.

He'd left Liza with her friends last night, knowing they would take better care of her then he could.

Considering he was ready to throttle her.

Or kiss her.

Or both.

But, based on the exhaustion paling Nora's skin and making her yawn every minute and a half, it looked like he might not be the only one ready to throttle Moss Creek's most stubborn inhabitant. "She givin' you a hard time?"

Nora dropped her head to one side, brows lifting as she stared his way across the room. "You're kidding, right?" She sucked in a long breath that ended on another yawn. "Of course she's giving us a hard time."

Ben leaned back against the counter, crossing his arms over his chest. "That sounds like her."

Last night his heart almost stopped in his chest, might have for a second, when he saw her laying on the ground, forced to watch as the cattle he was moving came closer and closer to

Liza's crumpled body. It was a terror he'd felt twice before in his life.

The only difference was this time Liza wasn't broken or cut. She was just a little bruised up and sore.

It should have made it easier for him to handle.

It didn't.

And that meant he had to get the hell away from her before he did something they would both regret.

"Mae and I talked about it," Nora hesitated, looking like she didn't really want to have to continue, "and you're the only one she listens to."

Ben couldn't stop the bark of laughter that jumped free. "If you think that woman listens to me then you clearly haven't been paying attention."

If she listened to him, she would have taken the time to let her damn arm heal before jumping back in the way she did.

She would've stayed in the house last night instead of chasing him across the ranch, insisting on putting herself right in the middle of a dangerous situation to prove she was capable.

And she would've never come back to Cross Creek that night five years ago. She would have stayed as far from Ed Cross as she could get and done all her talking through a lawyer.

They would be together and Cross Creek Ranch, and everything that came with it, would be nothing more than a speck in the rearview mirror of their life.

"But you work together." Nora waved her arms around. "You run this whole ranch together. She must listen to you at least a little bit."

"Just because we work together doesn't mean we interact." It was something that used to make it all easier.

Used to.

Not so much anymore.

"Well someone has to do something." Nora flopped back against the couch, arms dropping to her sides. "And we already tried."

Ben rubbed his face, wishing like hell he already had some caffeine in his system. "What is it that needs to be done?"

He'd checked Liza over on the ride back to the house, making sure nothing was broken or required a trip to the hospital.

"Well she needs to put ice on her leg for starters."

Ben stared across the room at Nora. "She didn't put ice on it?"

Nora shook her head slowly.

"Are you kidding me?" He left her there thinking she would be better off with her friends, assuming that she'd be more likely to take care of herself when she didn't have to prove to him that she was fine.

Nora shook her head again, wincing a little. "She said she didn't need it."

"Of course she did." Ben abandoned his plan for a caffeinated morning, going back into his bedroom to yank on a T-shirt before stepping his feet into some boots. "How could you not have gotten her to put ice on that thing?" Just because it wasn't broken didn't mean it wasn't still in need of some basic first aid.

Nora scowled at him. "I think you know exactly why we couldn't get her to put ice on her leg." She crossed her arms over her chest. "You work with her all the time. You know exactly how stubborn she is."

Ben grabbed his keys on his way to the door, tucking the closest hat he could find onto his head. "I've also met you and your friend Mae, and you two are just as stubborn as she is. I figured between the both of you you'd be able to get her to do what she needed to do."

He shouldn't be as pissed as he was. He knew exactly how strong-willed Liza could be.

And he knew exactly how hell-bent she was on proving herself capable of handling anything.

"Don't worry about locking the door behind you." He went out onto the porch and straight to his truck, leaving Nora sitting on his couch.

At some point, he'd have to figure out how in the hell she knew where to find him, but that point wasn't now.

Ben kicked up gravel as he drove to Liza's little house, headlights cutting through the last darkness before morning. The storm had passed in the middle of the night, but the ground was still soggy and wet, and the air was heavy with humidity and the smell of wet cattle.

He pulled in front of the small farmhouse, expecting to see Mae's car, but the only vehicle parked in front of Liza's place was her old blue pickup truck.

Ben skipped the steps, taking the height of the porch in one leap, driven by a level of frustration he'd never experienced. Not even in all his years working at Cross Creek Ranch.

The front door was unlocked and he went straight inside. "Elizabeth Cross, where in the hell are you?"

A slight scuff of movement led him into the kitchen to find Liza sitting in a chair next to the back door, a screwdriver in hand.

"What in the hell are you doing?" If it was anyone else he'd be shocked to see her sitting there like nothing was wrong.

But nothing shocked him with this woman. Liza was predictably problematic.

"What does it look like I'm doing?" She turned back to where she was working on loosening the doorknob. "Someone kicked in my door yesterday and didn't come back to fix it like they said they would."

"So you thought you would fix it at four in the morning?" His aggravation at the situation amped up even more.

Maybe he was tired.

Maybe he was hungry.

Maybe he just needed a pot of coffee.

Or maybe he was at his limit with this woman.

"Why does it matter to you?" She shifted on the chair, her flat expression almost concealing a slight wince. "Why are you even here?"

Any other time he would work hard not to throw Nora under the bus. She and Liza were close, and Liza needed friends who looked out for her. Risking putting one of them in a bad position wasn't something he would normally do.

But he'd lost his hold on normal the day he watched her fall in front of that damn car.

"I'm here because you won't listen to anybody who's trying to help you." Ben went to the freezer, whipping it open with a plan to make another ice pack. This time he noticed a whole stack of medical-grade cooling packs lined down one side of the freezer.

They were right there. Easy to see. Easy to reach. Easy to use. All she had to do was grab one.

Something inside him snapped.

"Elizabeth," he could barely grate out her name between the clench of his teeth, "are you telling me that there's an entire pile of ice packs in this goddamned freezer and not a single one of them is on your leg?"

She didn't answer him, just kept jabbing at the damn doorknob like she had any clue how to fix it.

Not that he doubted she would do whatever it took to figure it out if it kept her from having to ask him for help.

At this point, he would believe she'd gnaw her own leg off to avoid admitting she needed him for anything.

Ben grabbed the biggest ice pack from the stack before slamming the door shut hard enough to rattle the whole appliance.

Liza's eyes finally snapped his direction. "What is wrong with you?"

Ben crossed the kitchen and grabbed the back of her chair. "The same thing that's been wrong with me for years." He dragged the chair across the floor, hauling woman and all toward the living room. "You."

She'd been a problem for him from the beginning. One he couldn't seem to make himself escape.

"Stop it." Liza gripped the seat, hanging on for dear life.

"Get up and make me." The chair jostled a little over the transition connecting the kitchen linoleum and the wood floor of the living room. He did his best to keep the ride as smooth as possible, knowing she was in pain.

Pain that was her own fault, but that didn't mean he wanted her to suffer any more for it.

Because he understood what it was like to be in pain that you brought on yourself.

Ben stopped just beside the couch. "You're getting on this couch one way or another." He dropped the ice pack onto the coffee table. "You can get your own ass there, or I'll put it there."

Liza glared at him, working her jaw from one side to the other as she weighed her options.

There weren't many. Probably even fewer than she realized.

But telling her that would only result in him having to drag her onto the sofa, which would make her leg hurt more. The best option was to let her think she was going to spend this day alone as long as she did what he said.

"I can move just fine." Her unquenchable desire to prove independence propelled her from the chair to the couch.

But Ben didn't miss the careful way she pivoted, keeping all her weight on one foot as she slowly lowered into place, working hard not to bump the thigh that had to be sporting a softball-sized bruise.

Once she was in place, Liza smirked up at him. "See?"

He was seeing a lot of things. Things he'd been ignoring for way too long.

Ben grabbed the ice pack and carefully set it into place over the soft fabric of her flannel pajama pants.

Liza barely jumped at the added weight, sucking in a breath as the cold from the pack sank into her skin.

She had to be in a ridiculous amount of pain.

Additional pain.

Between her arm and her leg, she was dealing with something most grown men couldn't handle.

Then again, most grown men were pussies.

"You've gotta ice stuff like that." He should have sucked it up and stayed last night. Should've found a way to power through the feelings he'd been fighting for over half a decade.

"It's just a little bruise." Liza tried to brush it off, the same way she tried to brush off getting hit by a damn car.

The same way she brushed off every struggle she faced, trying to prove to him and the rest of the world that she was fine.

Always fine.

"I've been stepped on by a cow, Sweetheart." He grabbed a couple of the decorative pillows from the other end of the sofa. "There's nothing fine about it." Ben eased down to one knee, carefully working his hand under the back of her leg.

"It's really not a big deal. It will be fine." Liza winced as he lifted, raising it up until there was enough room to prop the pillows beneath it, offering as much elevation as he could manage given the location.

"It will definitely be fine." There was no doubt about that.

Ben stood, giving Liza's leg and ice pack one more look before going into the kitchen. He grabbed the coffee pot off the maker and went to work filling it in the sink.

"What are you doing?"

"I'm making some coffee since someone had to drag my ass out of bed to come take care of you." He poured water into the reservoir before adding grounds and switching it to start.

"You took care of me. Your job's done. You can go drink coffee at your own house."

"Not happening, Sweetheart." Ben paused the machine, pouring the first of the pot into his cup before setting it to go again. He took his mug out into the living room and dropped down into the chair across from Liza, then took a long sip, staring over the rim at her. "Because I'm pretty sure the only way that leg is going to get taken care of is if I sit here and make sure it happens."

ELEVEN

LIZA

HE HAD TO be kidding.

"You can't sit here all day." He couldn't. It was impossible.

Even though that was exactly what it appeared Ben planned to do, based on the relaxed way his long body was draped across one of the cream-colored armchairs in her living room.

Ben took another leisurely sip of coffee. "Actually," he offered her a smirk, "I can."

A beeping from the kitchen pulled his attention to the doorway. "Do you want to take your pain pills with water or coffee?"

She thought getting Nora and Mae to go home would mean she would get to sit in pain by herself.

Her friends meant well, but the last thing either of them needed was to worry about her. They both had businesses to run and husbands who were lost without them.

Plus, it was really hard to carry on a conversation when your leg and arm were both throbbing.

But she was starting to get the idea that her friends being here would have been the lesser of two evils.

"I already took pain pills." She was tired. She was sore. All she wanted was to go to sleep.

Not that it would be an easy thing to do, considering every inch of her ached, and a few parts did way more than ache.

"You are a liar, Elizabeth Cross." Ben went down the short

hallway leading to the half bath and laundry room that completed the main floor of the house. "And while your friends might be afraid to call you out on it," he turned and looked her way as he flipped on the light, "I am not." He disappeared into the small room, coming back out a few seconds later with the same bottle of pills he tried to feed her yesterday.

He was unsuccessful then, and he would be unsuccessful now.

"I don't need pain pills."

Ben's dark eyes lifted from where he was tipping a few gel tabs free. His gaze moved over her face at a leisurely pace.

She always hated when he looked at her like that. Like he was trying to see what else was there.

It worried her, because at this point she wasn't sure what he might find.

"I know you don't need them." He capped the bottle before setting it on the coffee table. "You'll survive without them." Ben closed his hand around the pills, shaking them in his loose fist as he went back into the kitchen. "Coffee, or water?"

Liza rubbed across her temples, squeezing her head like it might ease the stabbing pain working its way behind her eyeballs. "Neither."

"Both it is." Ben came out a minute later with a coffee cup and a glass. He set both on the table before holding out the pills. "Just because you can handle the pain doesn't mean you have to."

Liza eyeballed the turquoise tablets cupped in his hand.

They were tempting.

She'd managed to wean herself off the stronger stuff they sent home after her surgery pretty quickly. She didn't like feeling groggy, and she sure as heck didn't like collapsing in the shower.

Especially considering that collapse resulted in Ben being in her bed, his scent permeating her sheets and pillows, reminding her of everything she almost had.

And reminding her that she couldn't be close to him. Not without losing the tentative grip she currently had on her life and the tiny bit of happiness it offered.

"Fine." Liza grabbed the pills and popped them between her

lips, swallowing them down with only the spit in her mouth to help ease their path. "Now will you go away?"

Ben shook his head at her. "No."

"Are you serious?" She'd only taken the medication thinking it would get him to go.

Leave her some time to figure out how in the hell to stop thinking about him.

Ben tipped his head to one side, the baseball cap he was wearing making him look deceivingly innocent. "You, Ms. Cross, have proved yourself to be non-compliant," he backed toward the kitchen, "and in need of a babysitter."

"Then I guess I should be lucky that you're in charge of running this ranch and not a babysitter." She adjusted the ice pack as it dropped down between her thighs. "I'll call one of the high school girls that works at the Dairy Dream and they can come babysit me."

She didn't need a babysitter, but it was seeming like Ben was no longer the only one conspiring against her. That meant she wasn't going to get away with being left alone. And if she wasn't going to be alone, then she sure as hell wanted to pick who she was stuck with.

And it couldn't be Ben. It just couldn't.

"Not happening, Sweetheart." Ben's deep voice carried in from the kitchen, along with the sound of pots and pans banging together. "You would steamroll those poor girls."

That is exactly why she wanted one of them here. They would sit on their phone and let her do whatever in the hell she wanted to do.

And their presence wouldn't drag up things that were better left alone.

Things that *had* to be left alone, because anything else would be too painful.

"You fucked around too long and found out your friends aren't willing to let you cut off your nose to spite your own face."

"My friends apparently don't understand that I am a grown woman capable of taking care of herself."

"Your friends realize that you are a grown woman refusing to take care of herself." A sharp sizzle came from the kitchen. "And they're tired of your bullshit."

Liza's next breath smelled like bacon and it had her stomach growling immediately. "Then they should be the ones here annoying the shit out of me instead of you."

"Seems to me like they came up with something worse than sitting here annoying the shit out of you." Ben came out of the kitchen with a glass of orange juice that he set down on the coffee table in the line of beverages collecting there.

"And what's that?"

He gave her another smirk that threatened to tingle its way down her insides. "They sent me to annoy the shit out of you."

"You don't annoy me." She returned a smirk of her own. "You piss me off."

"Good to know we're on the same page." Ben sauntered back into the kitchen, leaving her with an unfortunate view of his backside that her eyes wouldn't give up until it was fully out of sight.

Liza dropped her head to one side, letting it fall against the back of the sofa.

She'd made a lot of bad decisions in recent years. Some proved to be life-altering.

Some just chapped her ass.

And some had the potential to do both.

Ben was falling into the latter category.

She glanced around, leaning forward until she could see the back half of the kitchen.

She'd tried running him off and been highly unsuccessful.

Maybe her only option was to run off herself.

She carefully pulled the pillows under her leg loose, silently stacking them onto the cushions as she gently worked her feet over the edge of the couch. They hadn't even hit the floor when Ben's sharp voice made her jump.

"I know you're not out there trying to come up with a way to get out of this house."

The man was nowhere in sight. There was absolutely no way he could have known—

Ben's head popped around the edge of the doorway. He

pointed at where her feet were almost on the ground. "Get those back up on the damn couch right now."

"Or what?" She slowly let the soles of her feet rest against the area rug spread across the wood floors. "You're going to make me?"

She was an adult, and while she might require Ben's assistance to keep the ranch up and running, she did not need him outside of that very narrow scope.

And it was his own fault. He's the one who made her learn how to live without him.

Ben slowly came into the living room, wiping his hands on a dish towel before swinging it over one broad shoulder. "Sweetheart, I have half a mind to make you do a lot of things."

She accidentally gulped.

He didn't mean it in any sort of a suggestive way, she knew that.

And thank God he didn't, or she would have to figure out how to run from a man when she was one leg down.

And it was hard enough to accomplish when she had use of all her appendages.

But...

The thought of Ben Chamberlain trying to make her do things still wiggled its way into her brain.

And not things like take a pill or eat a balanced breakfast.

Debaucherous things.

She accidentally let her eyes fall down his body, dragging over the spot of skin just over his ribs where she knew he had a scar from his days in the rodeo.

Down to where there was a bit of dark hair hiding just below his belly button that ran lower, disappearing down into his jeans.

"Sweetheart."

Her eyes jumped to his face. "Don't call me Sweetheart."

Ben eased her way, looking like he wasn't in any hurry at all in spite of the aggressive sizzling continuing in the kitchen. "Fine." He bent down, forcing her to lean back as his body crowded closer to hers. "Elizabeth," his hands came to rest at each side of her thighs, pressing into the cushions as her back shoved deeper into the couch, "if there's something you want to see, you just have to say it."

Liza held her breath, primarily so she didn't notice the way he smelled and risk letting it drag her back in time. "I would love to see your backside as you find your way out of my house."

She'd been caught ogling him, there was no point in denying it.

She could plead exhaustion. She'd been up all night convincing her friends she did not need to go to the ER.

Or she could plead insanity, because this man was running off the final bit of right mind she'd managed to cling to.

But in reality, it was neither of those things that led to her wandering eyes, which was a very big problem.

Ben clicked his tongue, hovering in her space a second longer before straightening. "You're just going to have to settle for watching it while I walk back in your kitchen to finish our breakfast."

"Our breakfast?"

"You definitely owe me breakfast, Elizabeth." Plates clattered against the counter. "Considering I had to haul your ass back to this house in the rain, and then had to drag mine out of bed to come here and take care of you."

"You didn't have to do either of those things." Sure, she'd been slightly stuck in the mud last night.

But she absolutely would have gotten up eventually.

And at some point would have made it back to the house.

She would have been fine.

Ben came out of the kitchen carrying two plates. He set them both down on the coffee table before grabbing the pillows she'd moved out of the way. "I'll keep that in mind next time."

There wouldn't be a next time. "I don't plan to get kicked by a cow again."

She'd managed to spend over seven years at Cross Creek Ranch without ever coming close to being assaulted by a cow. The chances of it happening again were slim to none.

"That's good to hear." Once again Ben gently lifted her leg, sliding the pillows underneath it as he worked her back onto the couch, taking full advantage of the fact that she couldn't do much to fight him off.

Each press of his hands against her body was like a brand, hot and unforgettable.

But she had to forget.

Had to pretend none of this mattered. Including him.

Ben added an additional pillow on her lap before balancing a plate full of food on top of it. "Now eat so those pills don't upset your stomach."

"You upset my stomach." The fact that she was resorting to juvenile comebacks wasn't a good sign.

She was coming to the end of her rope, and once she reached it there'd be nothing left to hang onto. She'd fall into the pit she'd been working to stay out of for five years.

And if she fell in that would be the end of it. The end of everything.

Her happiness, what little she managed to possess.

Her peace.

Her hope.

Her life here in Moss Creek. She would have to leave. Walk away and never come back.

And that wasn't a viable option.

Which meant she had to find a way to climb back up that damn rope, away from the pit and the man who dug it.

"Then you'll definitely want to eat up, because I plan on being here for the foreseeable future." Ben lowered into the chair he'd occupied earlier, balancing his own plate of food as he set his coffee onto the small table beside him.

The thought of being forced to sit in the same house as Ben Chamberlain for an extended period of time twisted panic into her gut, right next to the other unfortunate emotion it caused. "I'll call Nora. She can come back and sit with me."

"You can call her, but I've got a feeling that ship has sailed, Sweetheart." Ben shoved an entire piece of bacon into his mouth, watching as she picked up her cell phone.

"Stop calling me Sweetheart." Liza tapped out Nora's number and pressed the phone to her ear, waiting as it rang.

Then went to voicemail.

Ben's grin was as irritating as everything else about him was becoming.

What happened to the man who understood their unspoken rules?

The one who did his best to stay as far away from her as possible, giving her the room to pretend she didn't wish with every fiber of her soul that he could be close?

"I believe Nora's probably gone to bed." He tipped his head toward the stairs. "Which is exactly what you're going to do as soon as you're finished with breakfast."

She let out a little breath, relieved at the bossiness allowing the tiniest bit of outrage to creep in, crowding out the warmth resting soft and comfortable in her chest. "I'm not a child."

"Good." Ben leaned forward, eyes narrowed. "Then stop acting like one."

"How is taking care of myself acting like a child?" She hadn't asked for help from anyone. She'd pushed through and figured out how to do for herself as soon as she possibly could, powering past pain and frustration to avoid burdening anyone else.

"It's not." Ben's eyes held hers. "But you're not taking care of yourself."

Well that was offensive.

"I'm clothed." She used her good arm to motion at the pajama bottoms she managed to put on all by herself last night after struggling through a shower to rinse away the muddy mess caked into her skin and hair. "I'm bathed. And I'm fed."

Ben's eyes dropped to the plate he provided her.

"I was fed even before you got here." Technically Mae is the one who fed her yesterday, but she wasn't bringing that fact into this conversation.

"If I remember correctly," Ben's dark eyes took on an edge, "your track record with bathing isn't so good either."

"I don't want to talk about that." She snapped it out as fast as she could, hoping everyone in the room would listen.

Herself included.

Nothing good would come from remembering the night Ben held her so gently, the heat of his body sinking into hers as she shook so hard she was sure she'd lose half her teeth.

"Imagine that." Ben picked up a fried egg, cramming it between his lips as his eyes stayed on her. "Elizabeth Cross doesn't want to talk about something."

It was a new dig into an old wound. One she didn't intend to reopen.

Liza turned away, angling her body straight ahead so she was staring at the blank screen of the television instead of Ben.

"That's right. Switch it all off." The bitterness in his tone was familiar.

She'd heard it before, back when she thought she had options.

Back before she realized she didn't actually control anything that happened in her life.

Liza bit off a chunk of toast, needing some sort of a distraction from the weight of the air compressing the atmosphere between them.

There was so much there. More than she could ever consider trying to wade through.

And when through wasn't an option, you had to go around.

That's what she'd done for the past five years. Gone around. Giving Ben Chamberlain, and all the problems that came with him, a wide berth.

Liza swallowed the toast, but the crusty bit of bread scratched a little on its way down, forcing her to pick up the glass of orange juice to wash it away.

She didn't need Ben to take care of her.

She didn't need anyone to take care of her.

But unfortunately, she did end up needing that orange juice.

And maybe the bacon.

And one piece of the toast.

All of which she was almost completely through when her cell phone started to ring. She snatched it up, thinking it was Nora calling to save her from this mess.

But it wasn't Nora.

And her claim of independence was about to have to get a lot more convincing.

TWELVE

BEN

HE CAUGHT THE look of panic that crossed Liza's face before she expertly hid it behind a mask he knew well.

She snagged her phone from where it was ringing on the coffee table and held it out in front of her, angling the screen so only her face was visible. She plastered on a bright smile and connected the call. "Hey. How are you guys?"

"Good. How are you, Honey?" The older female voice on the other end of the line could belong to only one person.

The person that Liza lied to just as much as she lied to him.

"I'm good." Her voice was light and cheery.

And fake as hell.

"Oh, that's so good to hear." Liza's mother was one of the kindest women he'd ever met.

Not that he'd met her many times. Carol Galloway lived on the opposite end of the country in New York and had only been to Cross Creek Ranch a handful of times since Liza moved to Moss Creek.

And he might be overestimating.

It wasn't an easy trip, and Liza's parents had responsibilities that made it even more difficult to accomplish.

Ben slowly stood from his chair, taking the rest of his coffee and food with him as he silently stepped across the room. Liza's eyes connected with his for just a second, unspoken words passing between them the way they used to.

Back when he did his best to keep his interactions with the primary owner of Cross Creek to a minimum.

Ben quietly opened the door Liza attempted to repair and stepped out onto the deck. The chairs he and Troy made the day before sat in the small space, each one topped with a sunflower cushion.

He considered sitting in one of the new chairs, testing it out, but then he noticed the lights were on in the mess hall and the scent of frying sausage filled the cool morning air, so he headed that direction.

Troy was inside the building, working at the main island with one of the other hands at his side.

The younger ranch hand looked up when Ben stepped into the building. "Morning."

Ben tipped his head at Troy and Dustin. "Morning."

He went to the island and set his plate down, leaning one elbow against the counter as he went to work polishing off his first meal of the day. "You boys are up early."

"Figured we might have some cleanup to do after all the rain last night." Troy slid a flat of eggs onto the counter. "Thought I'd drag Dustin in with me to make breakfast so we could get a move on." He glanced Ben's way as he went to work cracking eggs into a hot pan. "How's Ms. Cross doing?"

"Like you'd expect." He had the unusual urge to say a little more. "Some ice and ibuprofen and she'll get back to bein' just as rowdy as ever."

Troy went back to cracking eggs. "Good to hear."

Dustin nodded along as he flipped the sausage patties sizzling in a pan. "Real good."

The two men appeared to have breakfast under control. Hopefully they could juggle a little more.

"I'm going to have you handle whatever has to be done today." Ben swallowed down the last of his coffee. "Is that something you think you can do?"

Troy's brows barely lifted, the only sign that he was surprised at the delegation. "Sure thing."

"Appreciate it." Ben used the last of his toast to sop up what remained of his eggs. "I've got a repair to make here at the main house. Just holler at me if you need anything."

It was a weak excuse, but hopefully one that would fly enough not to raise any suspicions.

Not that he thought suspicions would matter anymore.

They certainly wouldn't put Liza at risk like they might have at one time.

Ben grabbed his empty plate and cup, stacked on his silverware, and headed out of the mess hall before anyone else could witness him making his way in through Liza's back door.

He was as quiet coming in as he had been going out, just in case Liza's call with her mother wasn't over yet.

Carol called at least once a week to check in on her younger daughter. Their calls were usually short but sweet, with Liza painting her mother the rosiest picture possible of Cross Creek in the life she lived there.

To this day he didn't think Carol knew about ninety percent of what her daughter had gone through since moving to Montana.

Ben carefully stacked his plate beside the sink before creeping back into the living room.

Liza sat silently on the couch, eyes unfocused as she stared straight ahead.

A trickle of dread slid down his spine. "Everything okay?"

There was so much that could go wrong in New York, and right now it wouldn't take much to push Liza over the edge.

Hell, she might be over the edge as it was.

Her focus sharpened, eyes darting to his face, fake smile immediately lifting her lips. "Everything's fine."

It was too fast to be the truth.

Ben leaned over, peering down into her empty coffee cup. The glass of orange juice was empty too, and the water was half gone. Unfortunately, a good bit of her breakfast still covered the plate.

Exactly what was there when her mother called.

He reached down to snag the empty mug. "How about some more coffee?"

She didn't put up any fight, one more sign that something was wrong.

Ben poured himself a fresh cup of coffee before making Liza's, adding in the caramel flavored creamer she loved, before carrying both cups back out to the living room.

He held out the coffee. "Here."

Her gaze went to the cup, lingering for a second before she finally took it, her hand a little shaky as she brought it to her lips.

Ben went and sat down in the chair, waiting her out.

He'd known her long enough to know there wasn't any way to force Liza to talk to him.

Elizabeth Cross was a woman who required an immeasurable amount of patience, primarily because she possessed very little herself.

The best thing he could do was just be quiet. Luckily he was normally pretty good at that, the last couple of days being an exception.

Liza balanced the cup in the center of the pillow on her lap and stared down into it. She rubbed her lips together, working them from one side to the other as the quiet settled between them.

"That was my mom." She said it matter-of-factly, without emotion. "She said Dawn has been having some issues."

Ben took a drink of coffee, forcing himself not to immediately respond. He slowly set the cup down on the table before leaning back in his seat. "What kind of problems?"

Liza lifted her left shoulder in a one-sided shrug. "Some things are going on with her heart." Her next breath was shaky. "Again."

He watched her closely, witnessing the only moment Liza would give herself to process this new information.

Because she would never ever wallow in it. She would immediately suck it up and go on like nothing was wrong.

Like she was fine.

Because that's the way she'd always done it. From the second she came into the world Elizabeth Cross was destined to always be perfectly fine.

"Anything specific?" He met her sister Dawn the one and only time Liza's parents brought her to the ranch. The woman was full of joy in a way he'd never seen. Never once did he see Dawn without a smile on her face. She was all laughter and happiness and sunshine.

"I mean she's always had heart issues, ever since she was born." Liza sniffed. "They're pretty common in people with Down Syndrome."

There wasn't much in this world that could rattle Liza. She'd been through more things in the past five years than most people saw in a lifetime.

But right now Liza looked scared.

"Maybe it's something simple." He wanted to believe it was possible himself. Dawn was a beautiful soul who didn't deserve suffering of any kind. "They'll just fix it like they did everything else and move on."

He only knew a little of what Liza's childhood was like, but it was more than enough to explain what her adulthood turned out to be.

"Yeah." Liza nodded. "Maybe." She took a deep breath, pulling it in through her nose before shifting around on the sofa like she was getting up.

"Whoa." Ben was up and out of the chair before her feet hit the floor. "I'll get you whatever you need. You just stay there."

Liza huffed out a breath, shooting him a glare that made him feel a little better.

If she was mad at him then she wouldn't be upset about Dawn.

"I have to pee." She frowned at the empty cup in her hand. "Someone keeps bringing me coffee."

"Someone knows you haven't been eating or drinking right for the past month." Aggravation slid in easily, probably because Liza wasn't the only one that would rather be aggravated than concerned about the situation with her sister. "If you lose any more weight you're gonna blow away in the wind."

"Wouldn't that make life easier for you?" Somehow Liza managed to get herself up off the couch. "Then the ranch would be all yours." She started to tip to one side.

Ben reached out, grabbing her in the only way he knew he wouldn't hurt her.

But having his arms around her again was a mistake.

One of many he'd made recently.

"I don't want the ranch, Elizabeth." He never did.

Liza snorted. "Right." She tried to break free of his hold, but only managed to start to tip over again. "That's why you're still here."

That's the reason he wanted to believe he was still here. To make sure his partial ownership in Cross Creek didn't end up being a worthless investment.

If you could call it that. He'd always thought of it as a gamble where the chips weren't what he initially thought they were.

Liza tried to get away again, but he just held her tighter, pretending it was only to keep her from falling. "You know that's not why I'm here."

Liza went still, blue eyes on his, her expression unreadable as the seconds slowly ticked by.

He hadn't held her in what felt like forever, not counting the night he found her in the shower, unconscious and cold. Lips so blue he thought he'd lost her forever.

It was one more night he tried not to think of.

Unsuccessfully.

"Ben?" Troy rapped against the open back door. "You in here?"

"He's in here." Liza's chin lifted, a conquering smile on her lips.

She believed she would win this battle.

She thought he would do anything to keep Troy from seeing them like this.

Normally she would be right.

"Come on in." Ben pulled Liza closer, the arm around her back supporting more of her weight as he turned them toward the kitchen doorway.

Liza's eyes widened, realization dawning just as Troy stepped into the room.

"Looks like a couple of our ATV roads got washed out. I'm gonna take a few guys out and see what we can do to clean those up." Troy tipped his head at Liza. "Ms. Cross."

"Sounds good." Ben turned, lining Liza's side up against his. "Let us know if you need anything."

Troy gave him a nod. "Will do." He shot Liza a grin. "Don't let him work you too hard."

Her wide eyes moved from Troy to Ben and then back to Troy again, but she didn't say a word as the younger cowboy turned and left the house.

Ben started to move, walking toward the bathroom.

"I don't know what you think you're doing, but it's not funny at all." Her voice was a sharp whisper, like she thought Troy might be waiting just outside the door, eavesdropping on everything they said.

"I agree." Ben continued moving her toward the bathroom, more carrying, then helping.

Nothing about their situation was amusing. Never had been.

"And *us*? Why did you say Troy should let *us* know?"

"Like it or not, we run this ranch together, Elizabeth." He flipped on the bathroom light, his eyes meeting hers in the small mirror over the sink. "Just like we own it together."

Her lips pressed to a flat mine, nostrils flaring as she glared his way. "Trust me. I remember."

It was what tied them together and forced them apart. The ranch neither of them could leave for completely different reasons.

Liza reached out to brace one hand on the sink, using it for leverage as she stepped away from him.

The second she was clear the door slammed closed in his face.

He could take it personally.

Technically, there was a lot he could take personally.

Since her surgery, Liza had told him to leave her alone more times than he could count.

She'd yelled at him, glared at him, fought with him, and threatened him.

But at least she was talking to him, and that was more than he'd gotten from her in the past five years put together.

He would take angry Liza over the woman who was careful never to look his way or be alone with him.

At least now she acted like he existed.

Ben crossed his arms and leaned back against the wall behind him, waiting for her to finish up so he could help her back to the couch.

He straightened at the sound of the toilet flushing, preparing to fight her all the way back to the living room.

But instead of the sound of the faucet kicking on, he heard a bump and a gasp.

Ben hit the door with his knuckles. "Elizabeth?"

"I'm fine." Her voice was tight, but not from anger.

From pain.

"You've got three seconds and then I'm comin' in."

"I'm fine." She said it again but the whimper that came after her words made it clear they weren't true.

Ben twisted the knob, opening the door slowly in case she was just on the other side.

Liza's lower lip was pinned between her teeth. Her face was pale and pinched. Her eyes were squeezed shut tight and her breath was coming in short bursts.

"What happened, Sweetheart?" He edged his body into the tiny room, being careful not to bump her.

As soon as he cleared the door he realized she hadn't been able to work her pajama pants all the way up. They were tangled around her knees, giving him a perfect view of the purple and black knot taking up a huge part of her right thigh.

"Christ." It was worse than he expected it to be. Swollen, and angry, and raised.

He grabbed the elastic of her pants and worked them up, making sure not to bump her injured leg in the process.

Maybe he should have taken her to the hospital. Maybe he was just as guilty of giving in to Liza's lies as Nora and Mae.

"I'm taking you into town."

"I'm fine." She sounded a little bit more convincing this time, but he knew Liza well enough to know she was a good liar.

"You are not fine." Ben worked the door all the way into the room so he could get her out. "You probably broke the damn thing if it hurts this bad."

"That's not why it hurts." The volume in her argument made him feel a little better.

"That's exactly why it hurts. It hurts because you're too stubborn to tell someone when you're miserable." He hooked one arm around her, almost managing to get her out of the room before she shoved at him with her left hand.

"That's not why it hurts." She huffed out a loud breath, head dropping back until she stared at the ceiling. "It hurts because my grip slipped when I was pulling up my pants and I accidentally punched myself right in the bruise."

THIRTEEN

LIZA

SHE COULD BARELY stand, let alone form words, and it would figure the man wanted a detailed explanation of why she couldn't even breathe right.

Liza blinked a few times, trying to clear the tears edging her eyes. She wasn't actually crying, it was just a reflex to the surge of pain that happened when her knuckles connected with the spot the damn calf stepped on.

"Okay." Ben adjusted her shirt, making sure everything was in its right place before he carefully scooped her up, lifting her off the ground in one smooth movement.

And there wasn't shit she could do about it. Everything hurt. She'd managed to piss off both the injured parts of her body at once. When she hit her leg, everything else tensed up in response, including the mangled muscles of her right arm, which were now cramping hard enough that there was a good chance they might twist themselves right off her body.

"Let's get you back on the couch," Ben carried her down the short hall and into the living room, gently setting her back into the same spot he clearly believed she needed to be occupying, "and ice the shit out of this thing." He stacked the ice pack back on her leg, holding it over the spot that was accumulating more heat with each passing second. "Deep breaths."

"I'm breathing." She forced the words out before squeezing her eyes shut as cold and hot warred it out above her knee.

"You're hyperventilating." Ben's hand came to her face, fingers resting just under her chin. "Look at me."

Looking at him was normally the last thing she wanted to do.

Looking at him reminded her of everything she could've had. Everything she didn't want to admit she still wanted.

But right now keeping her eyes closed only amplified her awareness of the pain.

Ben smiled when she opened her eyes. "Good girl." His gaze was soft but focused as it held hers. "Now breathe."

She sucked in air through her nose, fighting the urge to immediately blow it back out again, dragging out the inhale as long as she could.

"That's it." His fingers barely moved over her skin, sliding along the side of her jaw. "Now let it back out."

She slowly released the breath from her lungs, holding his gaze as the air slid free.

"One more time." The heat of his palm sank into her clenched jaw, relaxing it a little more as she slowly took another breath and let it back out.

Ben barely tipped his head. "There you go."

She expected him to move away, but Ben didn't budge. He stayed right beside her, one knee pressed into the shag carpet and both hands resting on her body.

She hadn't been touched like this by a man since...

The last time this man touched her like this.

And it made her aware of just how much she missed this kind of contact.

How much she might miss—

"I'm okay now." Liza managed a little smile as she clamped off the wayward and useless thought. "I promise."

Technically it was the truth. She was okay. The throbbing in her thigh was already starting to ease, along with the ache in her arm.

And no matter which way she tried to spin it, that had everything to do with the man she was supposed to be pretending not to see.

Not to hear.

Not to want.

Ben's thumb slowly dragged across her cheek in a touch that lit every nerve ending in her body on fire.

But that was only because she'd been starved of contact for so long. That was all.

That had to be all.

"When will they know more about what's going on with Dawn?" His question was soft, like he knew what was actually causing her the most pain.

Being so far from her parents had always been hard, even when she first came here.

But back then she thought she was making the best decision, one that would take away any concern her parents had for her future.

And they deserved to have at least one child whose future they didn't have to worry about.

"My mom said they're taking her back for more tests in a few days."

Ben's hand stayed on her face, providing an anchor that kept her from spiraling down a path of fear and uncertainty.

Dawn was her parents' whole world. Everything they did centered around her older sister. It had to.

Dawn was unable to care for herself. She couldn't live alone. Couldn't manage her own medical issues. Couldn't ensure her own safety.

But the list of things Dawn couldn't do paled in comparison to everything she could. Dawn was the kindest, most compassionate, most beautiful soul that existed. She faced an unkind world with bravery and strength.

And she inspired everyone around her to do the same.

"They know about your arm?" Ben was one of the few people who knew anything about the life she lived before coming to Cross Creek. Mae was the only other one who knew anything about her family.

But even Mae didn't know everything Ben did.

Liza chewed her bottom lip, knowing Ben wasn't going to like her answer. "No."

He stared at her, long and hard, the outside corner of one of his eyes twitching the tiniest bit.

"I didn't want to worry—"

"They're your parents. It's their job to worry about you."

"They have enough going on. They don't need to worry about me." Her parents were amazing people and she didn't doubt for a single second how much they loved her.

Which is why she loved them enough to keep her own issues to herself.

"So you don't even let them know what's happening in your life?" Ben shook his head. "You've gotta see how fucked up that is, Elizabeth."

She scoffed. "You're right. I'll just dump my load of bullshit onto them and steal the time and energy my sister needs."

No way. That wasn't the way things worked.

She wanted to be sure her sister always got what she needed, and there wasn't a doubt in her mind that Dawn would do the same for her if the tables had been turned.

Dawn had always been there to hug her when she was down and celebrate when she was up. She was Liza's number one fan, and Liza was hers.

Being away from her was the hardest part of living in Montana.

And almost everything about living in Montana was hard.

"You act like they don't have enough for both of you." Ben shook his head. "I don't think that's how parenting works."

In theory, he was right. But her parents were human, and humans had limits.

The day she realized she was pushing those limits was the day she decided to accept the proposal from a man she thought would take care of her.

"They're still people, Ben." She swallowed hard. "They can only handle so much."

"I don't think you give them enough credit, Sweetheart." His thumb continued to smooth over her skin. "And I'm not sure this is about them as much as you want to think it is."

It was about them. It would always be about them. They were what mattered most.

Liza's phone started to ring again, making her jump and sending Ben's hands off her body. He grabbed her cell from the coffee table and passed it over.

She answered the call from her physical therapist's office. "Hello?"

"Hello, Ms. Cross. We need to reschedule your appointment for tomorrow."

"Okay." She didn't like the thought of missing an appointment. Physical therapy was the only thing standing between her and the possibility of a lifetime without full use of her arm.

And that was not an option.

"We do have an opening this morning at eleven. Would you be able to make that?"

"Eleven today?" That didn't give her much time to arrange a ride and take a shower. "Um."

"If that doesn't work we will have to put you down somewhere next week."

Ben watched her closely, still kneeled beside her.

The chances that one of her friends would be awake and able to haul her ass around were slim to none, especially considering she'd kept the only two without children up the whole night.

"I really don't want to wait until next week. I was supposed to get new exercises tomorrow." She'd been working hard, doing exactly what the physical therapist wanted her to do, and finally getting some new exercises made it seem like she was getting somewhere.

Even when it didn't feel like she was.

Ben leaned close, keeping his voice low enough the woman on the other end of the line wouldn't be able to hear. "I will get you wherever you need to go."

Liza rubbed her lips together, debating her options.

Neither of them were great.

But one was definitely less appealing than the other.

"I'll be there at eleven."

"THIS IS A pretty fancy place." Ben was close at her side, one hand resting on her lower back as they slowly worked their way across the lot toward the building that housed her physical therapist's office.

"Wait till you see the inside." She was trying hard not to limp, and actually doing pretty well based on her reflection in the glass vestibule flanking the entire front of the structure. "I can't imagine how much money is wrapped up in all the equipment they have."

Physical therapy days were one of the bright spots in her currently crummy life.

The appointments weren't fun. They were painful and challenging.

But every one she ticked off meant she was one step closer to being her normal self again.

And living her normal life.

Liza started to reach for the door.

"Don't even think about it." Ben beat her to the handle, pulling it open wide with one hand and keeping her steady with the other as she wobbled her way into the building.

He stayed close by her side, keeping a hand on her at all times as they made their way through the lobby and into the physical therapy office.

The place was huge. As far as she knew it was the only office like it around, so they probably saw every patient within fifty miles.

"Sit." Ben stopped her right in front of one of the waiting room chairs. "I'll go check you in."

Liza opened her mouth to argue, then realized they were being watched by an older woman a couple chairs down. So instead she worked on a smile that was anything but amused as she slowly lowered into the seat, smoothing out the flowing skirt of the dress she wore to avoid another pants-punch mishap. "Fine."

Ben's eyes slid to the grey-haired woman before coming back to her. He gave her a grin and a wink. "Don't get in any trouble while I'm gone."

She glared at his back as he walked away, trying to find a comfortable position in the barely-padded chair.

The older woman waited until she stopped wiggling around before leaning across the table separating them. "What are you in for?"

Liza twisted to give her a better view of the brace covering most of her right arm. "Got in a fight with a sedan."

The woman's eyes went wide. "You got hit by a car?"

"It didn't really hit me so much as rolled across me." She got lucky. As lucky as being run over could ever be.

The injury could have been much worse if her arm had been at a slightly different angle. Possibly to the point that her arm would have been too mangled to regain any sort of functionality.

As it was, she had a new set of scars that she would carry forever, but hope that this would be one more incident she would come out of relatively unscathed.

Relatively.

The little woman let out a low whistle. "That's impressive."

Liza's smile turned a little more genuine. "Thanks."

The lady held out one hand. "Muriel." She looked at Liza's right hand. "Oops." She switched hands, giving Liza's left a tight squeeze with her left. She had a surprisingly good grip and her hold was warm and solid.

"Liza."

Muriel's eyes lifted. "And who is this handsome man taking such good care of you?"

"Um." She cleared her throat at the thought of trying to explain Ben's connection to her.

"Ben." He easily relieved her of the burden of condensing a history that was long and complicated. "We run Cross Creek Ranch out in Moss Creek."

"That explains the boots." Muriel blushed a little when Ben took her hand with both of his.

Liza watched as Ben eased down into the chair next to Muriel instead of the one next to her. "Where abouts are you from, Miss Muriel?"

"Not too far from here." She folded her hands over the purse in her lap. "My husband and I moved closer to town once our boys grew up and moved away."

"Boys?" Ben's entire focus was on Muriel.

Making it a little easier to let her eyes wander.

The man was aging like fine wine. Well enough it almost pissed her off.

While she had to start adding highlights to blend away her greys starting at thirty-five, the sprinkle of silver dotting Ben's dark hair at the temples made his own forty-two years look anything but old.

More like experienced.

Even the tiny crinkle of lines at the corners of his eyes added to his already good looks, leveling them up in a way that really didn't seem fair.

"Muriel?" One of the assistants stood at the door leading back into the treatment area.

"That's me." Muriel hooked her purse over one hand before gripping the arms of her chair tight as she slowly tried to get to her feet.

Ben was up in an instant, watching closely as his new friend finally managed to straighten.

Muriel's eyes softened when they landed on Ben. "Things don't work as well as they used to."

Ben held out one arm, offering it to Muriel. "Looks like you're in the right place then."

Muriel slid her hand into the crook of Ben's arm. "It looks like I am." She beamed at him as he helped her across the room and through the open door, disappearing with the new woman in his life.

It was exactly what she would have expected of him. The man had a soft spot for old ladies and animals.

Hopefully they didn't come across a stray dog in the parking lot.

"Liza?" Another assistant stood in the doorway with a clipboard, waiting as Liza got on her feet, managing to do it without causing too much additional aggravation to her bruised thigh.

Damn calf.

Liza fought to keep the smile still lingering from watching

Ben and Muriel as she walked across the floor, unsuccessfully disguising the slight limp that kept her thigh from aching.

The assistant's brows came together. "What happened?"

"Oh it's nothing." She waved the woman's concern off. "Just a little mishap with a cow."

"She got stepped on." Ben's deep voice carried around the corner, ratting her out.

"It was more of a bump." Liza tried to minimize the situation as the assistant's eyes got wider.

"With a hoof." Ben eased into view. "That the cow then stepped on her with."

Liza turned her attention his way. "Weren't you helping Muriel?"

"Miss Muriel is in capable hands, doing exactly what she's supposed to be doing." His lips twitched at the edges. "Unlike some other women I know."

FOURTEEN

BEN

SHE WAS GOING to kill him.

But not right now, because he was smart enough to make sure they brought a witness with them when they left the physical therapist's office.

"You really didn't have to drive me home. I could have called for a taxi." Muriel sat in the passenger's seat of his truck, hands stacked on top of her purse.

"Now why would I make you take a taxi when we are heading right past your house?" When he found out that Muriel's husband passed away six months ago and that she couldn't drive, Ben knew they would be making a pit stop on their way back to Moss Creek.

Muriel's brows lifted. "I'm just saying. I'm sure you two have better things to do than chauffeuring an old woman around town."

"You obviously think we live a much more exciting life than we do, Miss Muriel." Ben glanced up in the rearview mirror at where Liza was sitting in the backseat. "The only thing I have planned for today is arguing about whether or not the physical therapist really meant it when she told someone they needed to take it a little easier."

Muriel glanced toward Liza before looking back his way. "Don't give her too hard of a time." She pulled a crumpled tissue from the front pocket of her purse and wiped at her nose. "It's not easy to be patient when you just want to feel better."

"But if you don't give your body time to rest, then you won't ever feel better." It turned out he wasn't the primary reason the physical therapist knew Liza was overdoing.

Apparently, it was pretty evident and had been from the beginning, which led to her receiving a lecture at every appointment.

One she promptly decided to ignore each and every time.

"Well, I suppose that's true." Muriel twisted in her seat, giving Liza her full attention. "You can always come spend the day with me. I'm very good at taking it easy."

"Which one of these houses is yours, Miss Muriel?" Ben slowed down as they got closer to the address Muriel had given him. It was a cute little neighborhood, with small story-and-a-half houses similar to the one Liza lived in. Most had been updated with vinyl siding and new dimensional roofing. All the lawns were neatly trimmed with flower beds full of petunias.

All of them except for one.

"That one there." Muriel pointed at the house that stuck out like a sore thumb.

The wood siding was peeling and chipped, with long strips of paint dangling down into the overgrown flower beds.

Could you call them flower beds if they didn't contain any flowers?

The lawn was way too tall, with more than a few patches almost going to seed.

The sidewalk leading to the porch was cracked and crooked, with uneven ledges that made wicked tripping hazards.

One of the gutters running across the front was sagging, weighted down by grass almost as tall as the weeds filling the flower beds.

He put the truck in park, his stomach sinking at the thought of Muriel sitting alone all day as her house crumbled around her. "I'll walk you in."

"You don't have to do that." There was something off in Muriel's tone. "I'll be just fine." She pushed open her door, looking like she was in a hurry.

Ben jumped out, rushing to beat her as she managed to slide free of the seat, landing on both feet only by the grace of God. "I know you'll be fine." He offered her his arm. "But I'll feel better knowing you made it inside safe."

Muriel hesitated. For some reason she did not want him getting close to her house.

And that made him even more sure he did want to get close to her house. "I won't take no for an answer." He offered a smile, hoping a little cowboy charm would smooth the situation over. "I'd have more than a few cowboys ready to kick my ass if they found out I left you here to fend for yourself."

"Pshh. I'm sure all the cowboys you know have more to worry about than an old woman." She continued to argue, but finally tucked her hand into his arm. "And you have your wife to worry about." Muriel shuffled along beside him. "You already made her sit in the backseat." Her eyes rolled his way. "I'm sure you're going to hear about that too."

Of all the things Liza would give him hell about, putting Muriel in the front seat would not be one of them.

Now, if he hadn't walked her to her door?

Liza would've gotten her ass out of that backseat and done it herself then ripped him a new one over it the whole drive home.

Because while Liza didn't think anyone should worry about her, she was more than ready to worry about everyone else.

"Of course," Muriel gave him a sly smile, "you can always make it up to her later." She wiggled her brows like he wasn't already following.

"I guess we'll see about that." He was working hard to keep up with the conversation, but the closer they got to Muriel's little house, the clearer it was that the place needed some significant work. "Have you lived here long?"

"Oh," Muriel slowed down as they came to a large gap in the cement, "I guess about thirty years." Her eyes lifted to the structure in front of them, turning wistful. "It was such a pretty place." Her expression dropped, taking on an edge of sadness. "Oscar just had a hard time keeping up with everything the last few years."

"Taking care of a house is a lot of work." Ben frowned as they reached the stoop. The steps leading to the porch were loose and rotting. "They always seem to need something."

"They do, don't they?" Muriel gave him a little wink. "Sort of like us women." She glanced back at where Liza sat in the truck. "You should take her for ice cream. She worked really hard today."

"So did you."

"Well it's too late to get me ice cream. I'm already home." Muriel dug out the keys to her house. "Are you sure I can't pay you?"

"If you keep offering me money I'm gonna get insulted eventually." Ben lingered, waiting as Muriel worked her way to the door. She was moving a little slower than before her time with the physical therapist. "You need help getting in?"

"Nope." Her answer was short, sharp, and firm.

"Why don't you write my number down? Just in case you ever need a ride."

"I'm not going to bother you when I need a ride." Muriel unlocked her door, opening it just enough for her to squeeze through. "Now go take your wife for some ice cream." She shot him a wink as she shut the door in his face, the deadbolt immediately sliding into place.

At least that made him feel better, knowing she was locked in.

He still wasn't happy. Not knowing Muriel was sitting alone, and definitely not knowing whether or not she'd make it down those damn steps safely the next time she left home.

Ben turned to find Liza worming her way up into the passenger's seat.

These damn women were going to make him lose his mind.

He jumped straight off the porch, skipping the steps just in case they only had one or two more good uses in them. "What are you doing?"

Liza winced a little as she worked her butt up and in, using her left leg to shove herself onto the seat. "Did you want to pretend you were my chauffeur for the rest of the trip?"

"What I wanted was for you to be better off than you were, and I'm pretty sure the last thing the physical therapist said to you was to take it easy." He reached her just as she got herself fully into the truck.

Liza shot him a smile, clearly proud that she'd accomplished yet another thing entirely on her own. "I am taking it easy. I didn't climb between the seats."

Ben shook his head. "This is why your friends don't want you to be alone." He grabbed the belt and pulled out some slack, stretching it across Liza's lap. "Because you don't know how to act right."

Apparently she was in good company, because he was starting to think maybe his new friend Muriel wasn't so good at acting right either.

And Liza looked like she was thinking the same thing. Her gaze drifted over his shoulder toward Muriel's dilapidated home. "Did her house look better on the inside than it looks on the outside?"

"Don't know. She made sure I didn't see it." Ben lingered, staying close to Liza.

She hadn't been putting up as much of a fight, which worried him a little.

Made him think she might be in more pain than he realized. "How are you feeling? Are you sore?"

"I'm okay." She continued to study Muriel's house. "Those steps don't look very safe."

"They look better from far away than they do up close."

Liza's lower lip barely pushed out. "I wonder where her sons are."

"Don't know. Probably far enough away that they don't realize what the place looks like." *Hopefully* they didn't realize what the place looked like.

Liza's eyes jumped to his. "Maybe they *had* to move far away."

"Maybe they did." Ben still held the upper portion of the seatbelt, his hand close enough it barely brushed Liza's hair. "Life's different now than it used to be. Lots of people move away from home for lots of different reasons."

Like Liza did.

Not that he necessarily agreed with her reasons.

"I'm sure they still check on her though." Liza was back to looking at the little house. "Right?"

"I would hope so." The only thought that was worse than imagining Muriel sitting alone all day, was Muriel being alone completely.

"But if they checked on her wouldn't she tell them that she needed new steps?"

"Maybe she doesn't want to bother them." He wasn't trying to be an asshole, but it might do Liza some good to see what happened when you didn't let people help you.

"Maybe." Her eyes finally came back his way, holding a second before dropping to her lap. "We should get back."

"Miss Muriel said I should take you for ice cream." He left off the part about Muriel thinking Liza was his wife. Not because it bothered him.

More because it didn't.

Liza's brows lifted as her expression turned skeptical. "Sure she did."

"She really did." Ben leaned away, forcing himself out of Liza's space. "She said you did such a good job at the doctor today that I should get you a treat."

Liza dropped her head to one side, but a smile played at the corners of her mouth. "I told you. I'm not a child."

"That is a fact I have not missed, Sweetheart." Ben closed the door as her eyes went wide.

It was getting harder and harder to pretend like they didn't have a past.

That he didn't still wish they could have a future.

Ben opened his door and climbed into his seat, feeling a little lighter for the first time since he found Liza on the ground, broken and bleeding after being hit by that fucking car.

In that second it was like his whole world stopped, every hope and dream he had crashing down around him.

Because even though she wasn't his, she was still there. Still alive and breathing. Still close.

Until she almost wasn't.

"I think Miss Muriel might be right." Ben shifted the truck into drive and slowly pulled away, casting one last glance at the rundown little house. "I think you do deserve some ice cream." He shifted his eyes to where Liza sat beside him. "And I know I sure as hell do."

Liza snorted what almost sounded like a laugh.

"You think it's funny that you give me such a hard time?" He struggled not to smile about it himself.

Liza tipped her head away, hiding the curve of her lips. "It might be a little funny."

"It's only funny until you get stepped on by a cow." He shook his head. "How in the hell did you end up on the ground anyway?"

Liza groaned. "A couple of the cows got ahead of the group and ran into the gate."

"What?" He'd been at the back, pushing the herd forward while everyone else kept them in line. He'd assumed Liza was pulling the gate open when she slid and fell.

"It was so dark I only saw them right before they hit." She turned his way. "And I still almost managed to hang onto the gate the whole time."

"Almost only counts in horseshoes and hand grenades, Sweetheart." It was a miracle she didn't end up right in the middle of everything, trampled by every mama and baby rushing through the night.

Ben took a deep breath, slowly letting it back out. "You are going to get yourself killed, Elizabeth."

"You would think so." Her eyes went out the windshield, lips flattening into a thin line. "But no one's succeeded at it yet."

And it wasn't for lack of trying.

"And that's why you get ice cream."

Liza peeked his way, looking across the truck from the corner of her eyes. "Then why do you get ice cream?"

"For not locking you in a room to make sure it doesn't happen again."

Liza's head fully turned his direction. "I'm not sure that's ice cream worthy."

Ben turned into the Dairy Dream, pulling straight into the drive through. "Oh it definitely is."

Liza scoffed, rolling her eyes as she turned to look out the side window.

He pulled up to the speaker and ordered two chocolate-dipped ice cream cones. At the window he passed the first one to Liza, making sure she had a good grip on it before snagging the other one and pulling away.

They ate in silence, with Liza finishing hers first. Maybe that was the key to getting her to eat. Buy her something that would melt all over her if she didn't.

Once they were home Ben parked in front of her little house, backing in so her door was as close to the porch as he could get it. As soon as he got her inside, he went straight to the freezer to pull out an ice pack.

The physical therapist had been nice enough to offer some care tips for the bruise on Liza's leg. Her primary suggestion was to start rotating cold and heat therapy after the twenty-four hour mark, along with maintaining a steady dose of anti-inflammatories to reduce swelling.

Liza carefully worked her way down the hall and into the bathroom.

He watched her over one shoulder. "You need any help in there?"

She shot him a glare, but it didn't carry the same venom it usually did. "I think I can handle it."

"Says the woman who accidentally punched herself a few hours ago." He offered her a little grin. "Hurry up so you can get some ice on that thing."

"I don't remember you being so bossy."

Her comment threatened to stop him in his tracks, but calling attention to the fact that Liza mentioned their time together probably wasn't a good idea.

"Then I'd say you're not remembering correctly." He held up the ice pack, tilting it from side to side. "Get moving. I've got things to do."

"Fantastic." Liza flipped on the light to the bathroom. "That's the best news I've heard all day."

She definitely thought she was getting rid of him.

She was wrong.

Ben grabbed a glass and filled it with some water. Then he snagged a banana from the bunch on the counter and set both on the coffee table.

He'd learned a lot today. Apparently nutrition and proper rest affected healing just as much as the exercises printed on the stack of paper Liza left the physical therapist's office with.

And the fact that the physical therapist pointed that out made him pretty sure Liza was only doing one of those things correctly.

And was probably even doing that to a fault.

She wanted to get better, he understood that completely.

Unfortunately, her desire to get better directly conflicted with her desire to be entirely self-sufficient.

"I thought you had things to do." Liza stood in the doorway, eyeing the set-up he was working on.

"I do." Ben finished getting the pillows adjusted. "But so do you."

FIFTEEN

LIZA

SHE DIDN'T LIKE where this was going. "I do have things to do."

She had a whole list of things to do. Always.

She was busy from sunup to sundown. All day. Every day

"Very important things." Ben made it seem like he was agreeing with her, but she'd known him long enough to recognize that wasn't the case.

There was a glint in his eyes that said he was about to be a pain in her ass.

"The most important thing, I might argue." He grabbed the blanket she had folded across the back of the couch, pulling it free and shaking it out. "You, Ms. Cross, need to come sit your sweet little ass on this couch and rest." He stretched the blanket between his hands, long fingers gripping the fabric tight. "Doctor's orders." His lips lifted in a smile that would make almost any woman do whatever he said.

Almost any woman.

"I knew I shouldn't let you drive me to that appointment." Liza fished through her brain, trying to come up with a way to get out of this.

"I hope you're not trying to think of a way you won't have to do this." Ben's tone softened. "If you want to get better then you need to rest."

He wasn't telling her anything she hadn't heard before. Her

physical therapist droned on about the importance of rest every time she went to see her.

"Elizabeth." He slowly came her way, the soft pile of the plush blanket just as tempting as the man behind it. "I know you don't like listening to what I say."

"You don't have a history of saying things I enjoy hearing." She pressed her lips together, but not soon enough to halt the second mention of the past she should be over.

Ben stopped, the tips of his boots so close they almost touched her bare toes. His eyes moved over her face, dark and focused in a way that made her stomach clench and her heart race. "I just want you to get better." He came a little closer, his voice soft and low. "I want you to be happy, Elizabeth, and I know you're not happy right now."

"I'm fine." It was an automatic answer. One she'd been giving everyone since she learned to talk.

Since she understood what it was like to not be fine. Since she watched her sister struggle with medical issues and hospital stays and mean kids and asshole adults.

And none of it was fair. Dawn deserved so much better than the world offered her, and yet she smiled. Loved everyone she met with her whole heart.

If she could be fine, then so could Liza.

"You're allowed to be fine and still need rest." Ben's arms shifted, carefully wrapping her favorite blanket around her shoulders. "You can be fine and still in pain." His hands came to rest against her shoulders, the one on her right side moving with a gentle touch. "How does your arm feel?"

She started to say it was fine, which it was. It was put back together like Humpty Dumpty, but it got better every single day. Stronger. More flexible.

But that's not what Ben was asking, and for the first time in a long time she accidentally told him the truth.

"It's a little sore."

"I can imagine. You did some pretty impressive stuff today." He'd taken full advantage of her unwillingness to kick him out when Muriel was having such a good time flirting with him to distract herself from the stretches helping her get mobility back after her knee replacement. Ben stayed back for her whole treatment, and she caught him watching her more than a few times.

"They told me if I do everything they say I should be able to get back to normal." She followed every instruction they sent home down to the letter, doing every exercise as perfectly as possible.

"They told you to rest."

So maybe she didn't follow *every* instruction they sent home.

Ben's hands slid higher, easing up the column of her neck. "I know it's not in your nature, but sometimes we all have to do things we don't want to do."

"Don't act like you do things you don't want to do."

Ben's expression suddenly turned very serious. "Elizabeth, I have done what I didn't want to do every single day for the past five years." The heat of his palms sank into her skin as his thumbs traced each side of her jawline. "Except for this one."

The air sucked into her lungs all by itself. She didn't mean to breathe.

Couldn't have done it if she wanted to.

It would be easy to convince herself that Ben didn't mean it the way she was taking it.

Definitely easier than seeing it for what it was.

"Don't." It was the only word she could manage, both a plea and a threat.

Because considering what Ben was suggesting might be the one thing that could break her. Split her open along a scar cobbled together with nothing more than denial and willful ignorance.

"I should have never left you, Elizabeth." The width of his body brushed hers as he eased in a little more. "I should have stayed right where I wanted to be."

Liza closed her eyes, trying like hell not to let his words sink in. "Stop it."

"No. I won't." Ben's touch slid higher, fingers dragging up the side of her face. "I'm done pretending things went the way they were supposed to go."

"Things went the way they had to go." She opened her eyes, meeting his gaze easily now that the old anger was working to the surface. "You were the one that said it had to be that way, remember?"

The reminder should be enough to send him running.

But Ben's boots didn't budge.

His head tipped in what was almost a nod, bringing their lips closer together. "I remember." His nose almost brushed hers. "I was wrong, and I've suffered for it every goddamned day."

"Good." She wanted him to suffer. Wanted him to feel the same pain she did.

"And that suffering isn't going to ever end." His head barely tipped. "It'll go on forever." The drag of his thumbs moved higher, making a slow slide across her lower lip. "But I'm not going to do it from the outside looking in anymore."

He was so close his breath skated across her skin, teasing her with a sensation she'd almost forgotten.

"Knock, knock." Troy's actual knock came two seconds later, right as he stepped into the back door.

Normally Ben would step as far from her as possible, but for the second time today he didn't budge, his hands staying on her even as his eyes moved over her shoulder toward the back door. "Come on in. I was just about to come look for you." Ben's hands slowly slid from her face, moving down to gently turn her toward the couch, one of them pressing against her back. "Let me get her all set up."

Liza shot him a look over one shoulder. "I'm fine."

"I know." Ben didn't argue about her fineness, just kept pushing her toward the couch he'd set up with pillows, remotes, beverages, an ice pack, and even a snack. "And you want to be better than fine, which is why you're going to rest." He unwrapped the blanket as he backed her toward the cushions.

"I definitely shouldn't have let you take me to that appointment." She scowled as he urged her down onto the sofa.

"Looks like we both have some regrets to deal with then." Ben lifted both legs over the pillows before settling the ice pack onto her thigh and covering her with the blanket. "Now watch some television and eat your damn banana." He picked up the fruit, peeling it for her. "The doctor said it would help keep you from getting muscle cramps."

Liza grabbed it and shoved it into her mouth, biting off a quarter of it at once. "There." She could barely talk around the mouthful. "Happy?"

His eyes held hers. "I'm getting there."

———

LIZA SUCKED IN a deep breath, sitting up fast enough to make both her arm and her leg offer sharp reminders of their current states.

Which weren't as bad as they were before.

The living room was darker than it should be. Shadowy in the way it was late in the afternoon.

The screen saver floated across the television screen, slowly bouncing from one corner to the other, replacing the episode of Schitt's Creek she was watching.

Her eyes were gritty and her mouth tasted like old banana.

Not a great flavor, but better than sloe gin *and* old banana which was another flavor she was unfortunately familiar with.

She reached for the glass of ice water Ben left on the coffee table, taking a few big gulps before holding what was left of it up in front of her face.

There wasn't a trace of ice in it. Even the outside of the glass was dry, not a hint of condensation anywhere.

"Goddammit." She freaking fell asleep.

Liza started to put the glass down, but decided to knock the rest back first. A few swallows later she was on her feet, the no-longer-ice pack hitting the floor with a thud as she gimped toward the bathroom.

The whole house was quiet as she did her business. Not even a hint of the man proving himself to be significantly more overbearing than she realized.

Liza was extra careful as she worked her skirt back into place and washed her hands, managing to get the whole bathroom process done in under a minute.

She might finally be getting the hang of this.

And only because of practice. Definitely not because of the nap.

That probably set her progress back at least an hour.

Liza opened the bathroom door, expecting to find that Ben sensed her uprightness and came to pee all over her parade.

But the hall was empty.

Which was not disappointing at all.

She leaned to peek out the door. He was probably in the kitchen, excited about the prospect of sending her back to the sofa.

But the kitchen was as empty as the hall.

Also fine. Better than fine. Fantastic actually.

She needed some time to herself. A break from whatever wild hair brought Ben back into her personal space.

A few items were lined down the table, none of which she'd set there.

A single-serving size bag of pistachios. A pack of beef jerky. A cardboard carton of protein shake.

That one she didn't remember buying.

Liza picked it up, looking the label over before setting it back in place and snagging the pistachios.

Normally she would leave everything as it was out of spite, but the damn nuts sounded good. She snipped them open with a pair of scissors, only fumbling them with her left hand once, before heading outside through the back door.

The knob was surprisingly smooth in her hand, dragging her attention down to the shiny, new hardware replacing the one Ben broke the day before.

She could have fixed that herself. Eventually.

The backyard was just as empty as her house, no sign of Ben or anyone else. Which wasn't technically unusual this time of the day. The men were responsible for their own dinner most nights, and tended not to stick around unless they were being paid for it.

And she didn't blame them. Cross Creek didn't have the same atmosphere as Red Cedar Ranch. Never had and after all these years she was pretty sure it never would.

Liza popped a few nuts into her mouth, managing to hold the bag in her right hand as she crossed the small deck Ben and a few of the hands built a couple of years ago even though she made it clear her old steps were more than fine.

A gentle breeze caught her hair and the wind chimes Maryann Pace brought her, sending the hair up her nose and the chimes bouncing off each other, in what was definitely the more appealing of the movements.

She eyed the chairs sitting in the small space, their sunflower cushions luring her across the smooth boards to test one out.

It was surprisingly comfortable. The back was angled in a way that offered support but also allowed a slight recline. The arms were wide and sanded to the point there wasn't a single sharp edge or rough spot to be found.

She relaxed back, breathing in the warm air and closing her eyes.

A banging noise mingled with the chimes, sending her eyes back open and her spine straight. She listened, trying to determine what it was as it happened again.

The sharper sound seemed to be coming from the large building they used to store feed and gear.

Liza ate a few more nuts as she stood and headed toward the open door, slowing a little as she closed in.

A couple of male voices carried out of the building, luring her closer.

She crept along, hoping to keep her arrival a secret as long as possible. If Ben could infiltrate her life, then she could sure as hell infiltrate his.

"What about this one?" Now it was easy to tell that the second voice belonged to Troy, who was all the way in the back of the barn, holding a board that had to be at least eight feet long.

"Is it pressure treated?" Ben leaned into view, giving the board in Troy's hands a once-over.

"Looks like." Troy dropped one end to the ground before lining his eye up with the edge. "Pretty straight too."

"Toss it in the take pile." Ben waited while Troy deposited the board before adding one of his own. "I'd rather have more than we need. I don't want to get her steps all torn out and then not be able to get them all put back."

"When you thinkin' about doin' this?" Troy added another board to the pile, the wood hitting with a loud bang.

"As soon as we can. She just had her knee replaced and it

won't be long before those steps give out." Ben picked up the baseball cap on his head, raking one hand through his dark hair as he looked over their collection. "I think this should be plenty." He shifted a few boards. "Probably got enough to make her a rail too."

Goddammit.

He was going back to fix Muriel's steps.

The urge to throttle him was strong.

Maybe not throttle him.

Maybe just throw something at him. It wouldn't even be with her good arm so she probably couldn't hit him anyway.

Ben's eyes snapped toward the open door, fixing on where she stood just inside, eavesdropping with a mouth full of nuts.

He stood silently while she decided what to do next.

She couldn't run, not with her leg still upset over last night.

And she'd decided throwing something at him probably wasn't a viable option. She was already carrying pistachios so her hands were pretty full.

Troy cleared his throat. "I'm gonna go check on my truck. Make sure it's still where I left it."

It was the lamest excuse she'd ever heard.

Second lamest.

Once upon a time a man told her he couldn't be with her for her own good.

The same man who was now watching her every move, like he wasn't sure what she was going to do next either.

But not knowing what to do next stressed her out, which resulted in decisions that usually weren't the best.

Unfortunately, her options were limited.

Since she couldn't run Liza marched into the barn, managing a pretty impressive stomp for a woman who got stepped on by a cow less than twenty-four hours ago.

She didn't stop until she was right in front of him.

Still without a plan of attack.

And that's what this should be. An attack.

He was attacking her.

Her privacy.

Her independence.

Her peace.

She glared up at him, poking one finger into the center of his chest. "I hate you."

Ben's dark brows lifted like he was surprised, but a hint of a smile teased at the corners of his mouth.

"Are you smiling?" She jabbed him again. "I mean it. I hate you."

"Good." Ben moved in closer, her finger moving right along with him. "I've been waiting a long time for you to hate me."

"Why?" Her lack of plan and forethought was showing, but there was no going back now.

She'd clearly crossed a line somewhere and her only choice was to power through.

Ben snagged the finger poking his breastbone. "Because I can work with hate." He lifted her hand, dragging his lips over the inside of her wrist.

She gasped at the contact.

The closeness.

The intimacy.

It was all bad.

Bad because it proved something she'd been trying hard not to admit.

She didn't hate Ben Chamberlain.

Not even a little.

SIXTEEN

BEN

HE KNEW TOUCHING her earlier was a mistake.

It was one he'd made before, back when he was naïve enough to think things could be simple when they were right.

"How much do you hate me?" He wanted to hear it. Wanted to know Liza still had feelings for him.

Because that's what the hate stemmed from.

"A lot." Her claim was unconvincing.

"Good. You should hate me."

Liza's eyes followed the path his lips were making up the inside of her arm, her brows pulling together. "Why?"

"The same reason I hate me." He still remembered how she tasted. The way she smelled. The way she moved. It was burned into his brain. A brand he would carry for the rest of his days. "Why are you out here, Elizabeth?" He wrapped her arm around his neck, stepping in close as he dragged his nose up the line of her throat, breathing the scent of her skin deep into his lungs.

"Because of all the noise." She sucked in a breath as he reached the spot just beneath her ear. "I thought you were out here tearing the barn apart."

"You're a liar." He knew exactly what brought her into his path, and it was leading him to make some very bad decisions.

Decisions he would probably not be able to make himself regret. "You came looking for me."

Liza made a sound, but it was impossible to tell if it was a scoff or a gasp as he nipped her skin, taking another taste of the woman he'd denied himself for so long.

"You always come looking for me." He worked hard to put as much distance between them as he could, since being around Liza was the worst kind of pain.

Pain he brought on himself.

He should have been more patient. Should have held back when he saw the signs that Ed and Liza's marriage wasn't all it was cracked up to be.

But he didn't. He couldn't.

And his impatience cost him everything.

He didn't intend to make the same mistake twice.

That's why he'd waited for almost five years. Biding his time, hoping for something that might never happen.

A moment that might never come.

But now it was here.

And he still had to be patient.

Still had to bide his time.

"You run the ranch. Of course I have to come look for you."

It was the same excuse he'd fallen back on time and time again when Liza would find her way wherever he happened to be.

But that's exactly what it was. An excuse.

"Say it again. Maybe this time it will be true." Ben slid his fingers into her hair, the soft sound that slipped through her lips sending all his blood rushing south.

"It is true." Her eyes dropped closed as his fingers worked over her scalp.

"Anyone else would believe it was." Liza lied to people every single day, and each one of them believed her. "But not me."

He'd always known when she was lying. Saw it on her face when she said her first black eye was nothing more than an accident.

He knew the truth. Knew Ed Cross put his hands on her.

The memory of that day was just as fresh now as it was five years ago. Back when he thought there was only one person he had to protect Liza from.

"Tell the truth, Elizabeth." He needed to hear it. Needed to know she understood what she was doing.

"Why are you still calling me that?" Her eyes stayed closed and her voice was barely a whisper.

"Because it's your name."

Her lids slowly lifted, gaze meeting his. "Now who's lying?"

This was what drew him to her from the very beginning. She knew him as well as he knew her. Knew when he was being honest.

And when he was stretching the truth.

Ben took a long, deep breath, setting it free along with the answer she wanted. "No one else calls you Elizabeth. Only me." He ran his nose along the side of hers. "It's the only piece of you that was ever just mine."

He'd had very little in his life that belonged to only him. Growing up as one of ten kids meant he shared everything. Rooms. Clothes. Toys. Attention and affection, both of which were in short supply to start with. His family owned and ran one of the largest cattle ranches in Texas, and kids were expected to do as their parents had done before them.

Work hard.

Be quiet.

Sacrifice any semblance of a normal childhood for the greater good.

Liza's eyes softened. "Ben—"

His phone started to buzz in his front pocket, stealing the moment in an instant. He pulled it free, swiping off the alarm he'd set not realizing what it would ultimately interrupt. "We need to go."

Liza blinked a few times, looking a little disoriented. "Go?"

"Go." Ben slid his hands free from her hair, savoring the last few seconds of her in his arms.

They couldn't be late. There'd be hell to pay if he didn't produce a perfectly healthy and hale Liza Cross at six sharp.

"Where?" Liza didn't seem to notice as he took her hand in his, holding tight while he led her through the barn and out into the sun streaking across the ranch.

"We've got a dinner date." He opened the back door,

managing to get her into the house as she continued to fire off questions.

"Where?" Liza let him move her through the house. "With who?" She leaned closer, catching his eyes just as he picked up her purse and slung it over his shoulder. "What for?"

"Are you gonna let me answer one or are you just gonna keep thinking up new ones?" Ben opened the front door, working her out onto the porch before closing and locking it behind them. When he turned around she was glaring at him, head tipped to one side.

Looking so much like the woman he used to know.

Which is why he couldn't keep himself from aggravating her a little more. "It's a surprise."

Liza scoffed.

"Come on. We can't be late." He tried to drag her along, but Liza's feet stayed firmly planted. He lifted his brows. "I will carry your ass to the truck, Elizabeth."

Actually, he liked the thought of that.

Ben didn't give her the chance to change her mind. He scooped her up, smiling as she yelped. "Shoulda come the first time." He managed to get her door open with the hand tucked under her thighs, pulling it wide before depositing her into the seat.

"You can't just—"

He shut the door and walked around the back of the truck, whistling as he dug out his keys. She was glaring when he climbed in beside her. "This might be considered kidnapping, you know."

He passed over his phone as he started the truck. "Call, Grady. I'm sure he and the rest of the station would love to hear how I'm forcing you to go eat dinner."

"Fine." Liza shot him a smirk. "Maybe I wi—" Her eyes landed on his phone, fixing on the screen a second before lifting to his, wide with shock.

Hell.

He didn't think that one all the way through.

"YOU MADE IT." Maryann Pace came rushing down from the porch of Mae and Boone's house, her arms stretched wide as she went straight for Liza. She grabbed her in a hug that wasn't quite as tight as the ones she normally dished out, before leaning back. "How are you feeling, honey?"

Liza managed a weak smile that was completely unconvincing. "I'm good."

Maryann's smile froze on her face, making it clear she picked up on the fact that something wasn't right.

"She had physical therapy today." Ben offered up the excuse, knowing full well it wasn't even close to the truth of what had Liza looking the way she did.

He was completely to blame for this one.

Maryann's expression was filled with sympathy as she wrapped one arm around Liza and led her toward the house. "You've had one hell of a day then." She shook her head. "Between the cow and all those damn exercises they make you do it's a wonder you aren't passed out on the couch right now."

Liza peeked his way. "I did take a little nap."

Maryann's smile was instant and wide. "Wonderful." She stayed at Liza's side as they went up the stairs leading to the house. "There's nothing quite like a good nap, is there?"

Liza gave her a little smile. "I guess not."

"Well hopefully you woke up hungry, because I think Mae made your favorite." Maryann opened the door and the sounds of the Pace family all talking at once spilled out into the quiet evening. "I know she's been worried about you."

"There's nothing to worry about." Liza stood a little taller. "I'm fine."

Maryann's eyes slid Ben's way before going back to Liza. "I'm sure you are."

Ben held the door as Liza and Maryann passed through, going straight into the madness that was dinner at Red Cedar Ranch. Now that all three boys had their own places, family dinner rotated around the property, and tonight was apparently Mae and Boone's night to host.

In some ways it reminded him of his childhood.

In other ways it was the exact opposite.

Brody's twin daughters ran around the space, laughing and giggling, their piercing voices bouncing off the walls and high ceilings. His other set of twins were currently being passed around, entertained by whoever was closest and available.

Wyatt and Calvin, the two older boys who came to the family when their mommas accidentally stepped into the Pace's gravitational pull, sat side-by-side on the couch, playing a video game, their eyes locked onto the television as they jumped around with excitement.

"Ben Chamberlain." Brooks slapped him on the back with the hand not currently holding one of his matching nieces. "How's it going?"

"Fair." Ben worked his eyes away from where Liza stood in the kitchen, being fawned over by her friends. "You?"

"Hangin' in there." Brooks bounced a little as the girl in his arms started to fuss. "Heard you got a fair bit of rain last night." He started patting the baby's back. "You end up getting washed out?"

"One spot, but it wasn't bad." He risked another look in Liza's direction, the sight of her drinking a large glass of water while Maryann stacked food on her plate making this whole trip well worth it.

"Brooks." Maryann waved her son over. "Can you come carve this roast?"

Brooks sighed. "This is what I get for being an ass and betting Brody I could slice roast beef thinner than he could five years ago." He turned toward Ben, passing off the girl in his arms. "Hold this."

"I don't—" He couldn't get any more out before Brooks was already walking away, off to fill his role as family beef carver.

That was the way things happened in big families. One misstep and you were stuck carving every roast until the day you died.

Or repairing every fence and barn and stable from sunup to sundown. No matter how much you hated it.

No matter how much you wanted to do something else. Anything else.

Anything except whatever Brooks just stuck him with.

Ben tipped his head, looking at the baby dangling from his hands. "You just got screwed little girl."

"Not into babies?" Nora swept in, snagging the twin and balancing her on one hip.

"No." He crossed his arms, hoping it would deter anyone else from trying to pass him another one. "I've had my fill."

He came pretty much right in the middle of his brothers and sisters, number five out of ten, giving him plenty of exposure to kids and babies and everything that went with them.

Especially since his parents subscribed to the belief that kids were more than capable of helping to raise each other. Taking care of his younger siblings was one more thing he ended up being tasked with.

Nora gave him a smile. "Be careful. They kind of grow on you."

"It's not that I don't like kids." They were cute. Wyatt and Cal were old enough to be fun and interesting.

Kids just...

Reminded him of times he wasn't so interested in revisiting.

Nora carefully worked a chunk of her dark hair away from Brody's daughter. "Just got it all out of your system taking care of your siblings when you were younger?"

He shouldn't be surprised at how astute Nora was. The woman had proven herself to be smart as a whip and one hell of a good business owner. "I guess I did."

She nodded. "Makes sense. There were a bunch of you in that picture I saw at your house." She leaned back as the girl made another grab for her long hair. "How's our patient doing?"

"Not too bad." He reached out to offer a finger to the baby hellbent on yanking out a clump of Nora's hair. "The physical therapist lectured her."

"She does that every time." Nora huffed out a breath. "Liza never listens."

"That's because she's too busy being fine." He smiled as the little girl grabbed onto him, her grip as strong as he would expect considering who her parents were.

"She doesn't look too fine tonight." Nora's lips twitched. "She actually looks like she's ready to pass out."

Ben immediately turned, expecting Liza to be propped somewhere, ready to fall asleep.

Instead she stood across the room, watching him with wide eyes, her skin a little pale.

A sharp pain cut through the tip of his finger as Brody's daughter sank her brand new teeth into his flesh.

But it didn't matter nearly as much as the look on Liza's face.

Nora was right. She looked about thirty seconds from hitting the floor.

But he wasn't so sure it was from exhaustion.

"If you'll excuse me." He gently pulled his assaulted finger from the future hellion giving him a drooly grin, before making his way across the room.

Liza's eyes followed him the whole way, her gaze as uncertain now as it was when she saw the picture serving as the wallpaper on his phone.

Ben stopped at her side and dug into his pocket, pulling out the baggie of anti-inflammatories he'd tucked away just in case. He fished out two. "Arm hurtin'?"

"Arm's fine." Liza had the pills before he had the chance to offer, knocking them back without the aid of the water sitting on the table beside her. "But you're giving me a migraine."

SEVENTEEN

LIZA

BEN'S PICKUP TRUCK smelled like mashed potato bake and roast beef.

Definitely not the worst scent in the world, but it wasn't doing much for her headache.

If that's what you could call the feeling throbbing through her brain right now.

It didn't technically hurt, just felt like it was packed so tight it might explode.

Which made it sound more painful than it was.

"Mae makes a pretty wicked roast beef." It was the first thing he'd said to her the entire trip. A generic observation that would lead to a safe conversation. The sort they'd been having for five years.

But the thought of one more meaningless conversation with this man about food or the weather or the market outlook for beef prices, made her want to scream.

And would probably also lead to the head explosion she predicted.

"Why is my sister on your cell phone?" That wasn't the entire question she wanted to ask. The entire question she wanted to ask was...

"Why is a picture of me and my sister on your cell phone?" If it was anyone else she might have thought it was weird. Possibly even creepy.

But considering it was Ben, the candid photo of her and her sister serving as the background on his phone was borderline enraging.

Except it didn't really make her angry. One more problem to add to the pile stacking up around her.

Ben sat silently, looking straight out the windshield as he pulled down the short lane leading to her house.

"Are you going to answer me?" Normally his silence would've afforded her the opportunity to escape the situation.

Which is exactly what she should be doing now. It's what she'd been trying to do since the night Ben told her he had to walk away from the future they planned.

A future that looked incredibly different from the reality she now faced.

Ben parked the truck in front of the house and got out, the slam of his door a little harder than normal.

He didn't get to be mad. She was the one who should be mad.

And yet she wasn't.

Ben opened her door, reaching in to unlock her seatbelt.

"Answer me." Liza stared at his face, but his eyes refused to meet hers. "Ben."

He stood in the opening of the door, head down, arms braced against the door and the truck.

"Answer me –"

His head snapped up, dark eyes meeting hers for the first time since they left Mae's house. "I don't know how."

"You know how." She shook her head. "You just don't want to." Liza tried to scoot out beside him.

This conversation was over, and not because she was running away from it.

This time she was walking away. By choice. Because it was going nowhere.

She stomped across the lawn and up the steps, unlocking her door and going straight inside. She chucked her purse, missing the seat of the chair she tried to throw it into, sending it spilling to the ground.

Which is where it could stay. She didn't give a shit right now.

"Liza." The name was enough to send her spinning to face him. "So I'm Liza again?" She forced a smile. "Great. I'm glad things are finally getting back to normal."

Ben stood just inside her house, his shadowy presence sucking every bit of air out of the room.

Which meant she was back to suffocating, fighting for every breath in a life she didn't choose.

Didn't particularly want.

Liza waited for him to leave, walk away so she could go back to pretending everything was fine.

It was the way things had to be. It was the way they'd always been.

Even when the world fell down around her, which happened more times than she could count.

But instead of leaving, Ben took a step, kicking the door closed behind him. "Are you?"

Her brain fumbled the question. "Am I what?"

"Are you glad things are getting back to normal?"

She lifted her chin, trying her best to look unaffected. "Of course."

Ben slowly continued coming her way. "Liar."

The anger she couldn't find earlier flared to life. "You son of a—"

"You can call me anything you want when we're done here." Ben closed in, his wide body blocking out the bit of light filtering in through the window. "But not until then."

"I think we are done." It was a reality she'd been struggling to accept, and right now she felt like a fool. "We've been done."

"Liar."

The name-calling pissed her off just as much this time as it had the time before. "I'm not."

"You are." Ben stopped, his expression unreadable in the darkness. "And so am I."

Liza stood straighter, refusing to back down. "I can agree with the second part."

"Then you agree with the first part too." Ben's voice was low. "Because we're both lyin' about the same thing."

She snorted. "Right. And what would that be?"

"The fact that this," his finger barely touched her breastbone before turning back towards himself, "this thing between you and me is over." He shook his head. "Because it's not."

"That's funny, because it sure looked a hell of a lot like it was over considering the way things have been for the past five years." She leaned in, getting in his face a little bit. "And considering the fact that you yourself said it was over."

"I know what I said." Ben sounded just as angry as she was, words short and sharp as he closed more of the almost nonexistent distance between them.

"Good. It's settled then." She turned.

"You're not walking away from this, Elizabeth." A hint of a threat edged his words.

"You're right." She glanced his way over one shoulder. "Because there is no *this* for me to walk away from." She stood a little taller. "I'm not sure there ever even was." Liza spun away again, intending to go upstairs and lock herself in her room.

She made it one step.

Ben snagged her hand, spinning her to face him, his chest hitting hers with enough force to send her stumbling back.

And Ben kept right up with her, following her across the room until her back met the kitchen wall. "Don't you dare try to take that from me."

She sucked in a breath as he pressed against her, pinning her into place.

"I lost everything else, Elizabeth. I won't fucking lose that too."

"Don't act like you lost everything." Bitterness was sour in her mouth. "You still have your portion of the ranch."

Thinking it was anything else that kept him here all this time would be foolish.

Unfortunately she was a fool.

Over and over and over again.

"I don't give a shit about this ranch." Ben shook his head. "Never did."

"Right." She would roll her eyes if she wasn't fighting for air from the solid press of his frame. The fact that he could still affect her like that, even now, only pissed her off more. "That's why you're still here."

The tip of Ben's nose barely touched hers. "You know why I'm still here." His body was warm and hard where it pressed against hers, making it a struggle to focus on what he was saying. "And it's got nothing to do with the money I gave Ed Cross."

"I don't believe you." She couldn't, because believing him meant—

Something she couldn't handle.

"I don't give a shit what you believe." Ben's voice was barely a whisper. "It doesn't make it any less true." His head tipped to one side. "And that picture? The one of you and your sister?" He put one hand against the drywall just beside her head, leaning down until his eyes lined up with hers. "That picture's there because that's the only happy day I've had since Ed Cross died."

All she could do was stare at him.

In shock.

In disbelief.

In confusion.

"No." Liza shook her head. "That's not true."

It couldn't be true.

"It is." Ben's mouth barely lifted in a shadowy smile. "Well it was." His lips hovered over hers. "Until today."

She swallowed hard as he moved in closer, the heat of his body stealing any thought her overwhelmed brain might have tried to work up.

"And tomorrow." Ben's lips barely ghosted across hers. "And the next day." Another pass of his mouth that almost didn't count as a touch. "And the day after that." His hands slid into her hair, fingers spreading wide, thumbs resting just under her chin, lifting it up. "Because I'm done stayin' away from you, Elizabeth."

His mouth hit hers, as hot and hard as the body keeping her upright. It was old and new at the same time.

Familiar and unknown.

Real and imagined.

And it forced her to face down a truth of her own.

Liza pressed one hand to the center of his chest. Ben immediately pulled back, breathing heavy as his eyes held hers.

Then she pulled him close again, one arm wrapped tight around his neck as she leaned into his weight.

Into his strength.

Knowing he wouldn't let her fall.

He never had.

Not one single time.

Ben caught her easily, keeping her close as they spun away from the wall, knocking over one of the kitchen chairs as they went.

He was like a drug, one she tried to quit.

Apparently unsuccessfully.

It had always been like that. From the first time she saw him.

The air around him always seemed charged, filled with an energy she craved.

And it was almost her undoing.

"I still hate you." She couldn't make herself pull her lips from his. Not to breathe and sure as hell not to speak.

"Good." Ben sucked her lower lip before setting it free. "You'll have to show me how much sometime."

Heat immediately flamed through her body, setting her skin on fire. "I can show you now."

It was easy to admit how much she needed a man to touch her now that it was happening.

But not just any man. That she could have arranged. Easily.

It wasn't what she wanted though. Liza couldn't actually stomach the thought of another man's hands on her body.

"Not happening." Ben spun her again, pressing her back against the wall just beside the stairs.

"What?" There wasn't an ounce of her capable of controlling her outrage right now. "Are you fucking kidding me?"

Ben's chuckle was more of a low rumble, one she could feel everywhere.

Everywhere.

"I have waited years to have you here again," his mouth dragged along the side of her neck, "with me," he paused at the spot where her shoulder curved, raking his teeth across her skin and sending goosebumps racing free, "like this." His hand slid up her side, coming dangerously close to her breast and the nipple already pulled tight in anticipation. "And I can promise you I'm going to savor every last fucking second of it."

Someone scoffed.

It was her. Most likely.

And it made Ben chuckle again, sending that delicious rumble back between them.

Which only aggravated her more. "Fine." Liza bumped his body with hers, shoving him out of her way.

She was going to bed. Alone apparently.

But Ben snagged her hand, reeling her back in. "Simmer down, Sweetheart." He looped her arm around his neck, pulling her close again. "I don't remember you being this impatient."

She lifted a brow as his lips curved in a smile. "You can't even say that with a straight face."

"Fair enough." His hand slid down her spine, pressing her to him. "Maybe I was hopin' you might have come across some recently."

"I haven't." She gasped when he pinned her to him, the tips of her toes dragging across the floor as he hauled her into the living room, the long length of her dress tangling with his legs as they moved, each step winding her closer to him. Wrapping them together.

Until the back of her legs bumped something and she started to go down.

Her fall stopped suddenly when her ass hit the soft cushion of the chair Ben sat in this morning, eating breakfast with her like it was the most normal thing in the world.

It was way more normal than this. Not that she was complaining.

He went to his knees in front of her.

Liza sat straighter. "What are you doing?"

He grabbed the fabric of her skirt. "You know exactly what I'm doing." He flipped it back, sending a rush of cool air over her bare skin.

"But why?" The last bit came out a little strangled as he leaned down to run his lips over the purple bruise just above her knee.

"Lots of reasons." Ben grabbed her around the calves and

pulled, tugging her ass right to the edge of the seat and hiking her dress up far enough to reveal the decision she thought was smart earlier in the day.

Back when the thought of anyone seeing what might or might not be under her dress was laughable.

"Christ." His gaze was dark as he shoved her dress higher.

"I didn't want to risk punching myself again." She'd practically patted herself on the back at her forethought.

And maybe she still should, because right now Ben was looking at her like he might swallow her whole.

His touch slowly slid up, inching higher at a painfully slow pace. "I think it was a good call." His eyes fixed on her pussy. "You should make it again tomorrow." His head dipped, giving her zero time to brace for the feel of his mouth on her skin.

Her reaction was immediate and uncontrollable.

"Oh my—" Air no longer filled her lungs as her back arched and her fingers dug into the upholstery.

There was no pretense. No way she could ignore or deny her body's response to him.

It was as unexpected as everything else in this day was.

Unexpected and over as fast as it started.

She couldn't help it.

Couldn't do anything but grab his head and hold it in place as she came, the steady flick of his tongue stealing her sight and her sanity.

Because she'd definitely lost it.

Ben lifted his brows at her as he slowly dragged her skirt back into place.

"Don't look at me like that." She lifted her eyes to the ceiling. "I've been busy."

Ben eased up her body, dragging his nose between her breasts. "Is that your way of telling me it's been a while?"

"Obviously." She yelped a little as he wrapped one arm around her back, bringing her front to his, his body pressed between her thighs.

"How long?" His voice was rough.

"That's irrelev—"

"It's not." Ben's lips worked along her neck, managing to

stoke a flame she thought he'd extinguished. "Not even a little bit."

Liza tipped her head, offering him more space as she hooked one leg around his waist, looking for a little more pressure in a spot that didn't seem as satiated as it should be.

"Elizabeth." Her name was sharp and ragged as he leaned to meet his eyes to hers. "How long?"

He looked a little wild. A little like he might be feeling the same way she felt most of the day.

She lifted one shoulder. "You can do the math." His skin paled and it made her smile. "You were there."

EIGHTEEN

BEN

"GOOD MORNING." LIZA stood at the base of the stairs, watching him with a wary gaze.

"Morning." Ben grabbed one of the mugs he set out and filled it with coffee, making a stop at the fridge to doctor it up, before setting it at the table next to one of the two plates out and ready to go. He went back to the stove to give the gravy simmering there a final stir. "How's your leg?"

"Fine."

He turned, looking her way over one shoulder.

"It really is." Liza walked to the table without a hint of the limp she'd been sporting the day before. "It doesn't even really hurt when I walk on it."

He pointed to the pills he'd set beside her place. "Take those anyway."

She rolled her eyes but did as he said, popping them both in her mouth before washing them down with the coffee he poured her. "There? Happy?"

He let his eyes drag down her frame and the slip of the nightgown that covered it. "I am."

A week ago this moment was impossible to imagine, but nothing about it felt strange.

It never did with her.

"Breakfast will be done in just a minute." He'd already been out to check on Troy, ending up pleasantly surprised when the younger hand was already in the mess hall working on the morning meal.

"What about everyone else?" Liza took another sip of her coffee. "They need breakfast too."

"They're getting breakfast." Ben grabbed the scrambled eggs and went to work dishing them out. "You've been usurped. There's a new chef in town."

"Troy?"

"Troy." He scooped out a healthy portion for Liza before dropping the rest on his own plate. "He's got Dustin helping him. Between the two of them they should be fine."

Up until now, he'd managed nearly every task that required any sort of responsibility, partly because he didn't have anyone he trusted to delegate to, and partly because he needed it.

Needed the distraction.

But now he had a different distraction. One he was much more interested in pursuing.

"I hope so, otherwise we'll probably lose a few men, and I'm not sure we have very many to spare." Liza watched as he grabbed the biscuits from the oven and set the cast-iron pan down in the center of the table. "I almost forgot what a good cook you are."

"That's not something you can forget, Sweetheart." He brought over the gravy, setting it down between them before taking his place across the table. "Especially since I've been making lunch every day." He gave her a little smile. "And sometimes dinner."

"Not breakfast though." Liza drank down a little more of her coffee as he worked the first biscuit free, splitting it in half before setting it onto her plate.

"That's because you took over breakfast." Lots of things changed when Ed died, some good, some bad. One of them was that they started offering breakfast and lunch for anyone willing to come work for them. It was an easy way to sweeten the deal, without having to fork over money they didn't have. A byproduct was that it offered a taste of the family life many of the ranch hands wanted.

Even if they wouldn't admit it.

Ben poured a spoonful of gravy over the top of the biscuit on Liza's plate before going to work on his own. He had his first bite in his mouth before he noticed Liza hadn't touched her breakfast. He set his fork down and waited until her eyes met his. "Talk to me."

What happened between them last night was one thing. They'd never been short on attraction and all that went with it.

But that wasn't what he really missed about her.

What he missed was where they started. The long nights spent talking about their lives.

Their hopes.

Their dreams.

He wanted that back more than anything.

Liza took a shaky breath. "About what?"

"About whatever's got you pretending you don't like my biscuits and gravy."

She lifted one shoulder. "I just don't want you upset that I took over breakfast."

"Do I look upset?"

Her eyes moved over his face before dropping to her plate. She picked up her fork and cut off a chunk of gravy covered biscuit before shoving it into her mouth.

"Elizabeth." He wanted her to open up to him. Wanted to think things could be as simple as they were before.

But maybe they weren't simple then. Maybe he just thought they were.

"Why did you take over breakfast?"

He'd been focusing on the whats. What was wrong. What he could do to fix it.

But maybe he needed to think about the why.

Because that was what usually mattered the most.

"I don't know." Liza stacked another bite onto her fork, adding a chunk of scrambled egg on top of her biscuit and gravy.

"I think you do. I think you just don't want to tell me."

"Or maybe it just really doesn't matter." She shoved the giant bite in her mouth, barely managing to keep her lips closed as she chewed.

"If it didn't matter you would've told me." He waited until she swallowed what was in her mouth. "Tell me." It shouldn't be important, but something about the way she was acting told him it was. "Please."

Liza rubbed her lips together, eyes holding his as the seconds ticked by.

He could wait her out. He'd waited five years, he could wait a few minutes longer.

"I didn't want you to make breakfast for me ever again."

It was hard to hear. Hard to stomach

Their time together had been short, a few days that changed everything in ways he never would have imagined.

But for those few days he went to sleep next to her every night. Woke up to her every morning.

And made her breakfast.

Until the day he didn't.

The day he almost lost her. Did in some respects.

The day she had to take a life to protect her own.

Realizing Liza didn't carry those days close, thinking of them the same way he did, was like a punch to the gut.

"That's fair." Ben focused on his plate, shoveling in the food without really tasting any of it.

Maybe he didn't really want to know the why. Maybe some things were just better left alone.

"I don't know that I'd call it fair." Liza poked at her eggs. "It's actually really unfair when you think about it."

He'd thought about it. Plenty.

Agonized over it. Second-guessed and reconsidered every decision he made.

And it didn't change any of it.

"But I guess that's just how life is sometimes." Liza set down her fork, abandoning what remained of her breakfast. "I should get ready." She stood up, moving faster than he expected.

Fast enough he had to hustle to catch her before she reached the stairs. She stopped when he blocked her path but didn't look at him.

"You can't keep running from everything that's hard, Elizabeth."

This time her laugh had a bitter edge. "You think I run when things get hard?" She lifted her arm. "I've got proof you're wrong."

"I'm not." He reached out to run the tip of his finger over the scars etched into her skin. "Because that wasn't hard for you."

Liza would put herself on the line to save someone else in a heartbeat, without thinking twice.

And she would never regret it. Never think she did anything special.

Sacrifice came easily to her. Always had.

Physical suffering she could deal with.

That's not what this was.

And as much as he wanted to fix everything right now, find their way back to what could have been, it wasn't going to be possible.

He was going to have to be patient with her.

With himself.

Ben took a deep breath, reaching up to rest his hands on each side of her face. "What are your plans for the day?"

"MY STAIRS ARE fine." Muriel frowned down at the missing deathtrap that used to sit in front of her porch. "Were fine."

"Don't argue with him." Liza passed over the milkshake they brought for the older woman. "There's no point."

Muriel looked Troy up and down as he set up the saw they brought from Ben's shed. "Who's he?"

"He works on our ranch." Liza took a long pull from the cherry chocolate milkshake she chose. "His name's Troy." She leaned Muriel's way. "He's a good cook too."

Muriel harrumphed her way into the other chair sitting on her porch. "Good cook, knows how to build things, and fills out a pair of jeans." She took her milkshake, giving Liza a sly smile. "Seems like he's a triple threat."

"He's somethin'." Ben wasn't still sour about Troy flirting with Liza.

He just didn't necessarily appreciate Muriel pointing out the way Troy looked in his jeans.

"Don't get all butthurt." Muriel gave him a wink. "I think you're somethin' too."

"He's definitely somethin'." Liza took another drink from her milkshake, trying to hide a little smirk behind the straw.

Ben stopped what he was doing and took a nice, long look at the flowery dress draped over her long body. "Did I tell you how much I like that dress?"

Her cheeks instantly flushed, accompanied by a scowl that threatened to heat his blood and distract him from the task at hand.

And he was already struggling. Had been since she came downstairs wearing that damn thing.

"I used to wear dresses a lot." Muriel reached over to pinch the flowing fabric of Liza's dress. "They're cooler in the summer." She leaned closer to where Liza sat at her side, but didn't lower the volume of her voice. "On account of you don't have to wear anything under them."

Hell. He'd found a partner in crime for a woman who could already torture him with nothing but a glance.

"I'm thinkin' we might want to make them a little wider than they were." Troy came to stand at his side, brows together as he surveyed the task at hand. "Nothing too big." He held out his hands, spacing them apart. "Just a little more room for her to get her footing."

"Agreed." Ben pulled out the tape measure from his back pocket and went to work marking cut lines on their first board. "And we'll need to come back before it gets cold and add some grip strips."

Troy squinted up at where Muriel and Liza were chatting. "She got anyone to come shovel her out when it snows?"

Ben shook his head. "Doesn't seem like it."

Troy took off his hat and ran a hand through his mashed hair. "Hell."

Ben lined up his Speed Square and marked another line. "Yup."

CROSSING THE LINE

"THANK YOU FOR helping with Muriel's stairs." Liza glanced up at Troy in the mirror on her visor.

"I can't believe her kids haven't taken care of all that shit." Troy was frowning in the backseat. "How can you let your mother live like that?"

"Maybe they don't know." Liza snapped her visor back into place. "They don't live around here."

"And they don't ever come to visit her?" Troy shook his head, not realizing he was treading into some very dangerous waters. "If that's the case then they're even worse than I thought."

"I'm sure they check in on her." Liza snapped it out. "Maybe they can't leave where they are."

Troy tipped his head to one side, bobbing it in a small sign of agreement. "I guess they might be in prison. I didn't think of that."

Liza stared out the front, nostrils flared. "Life is complicated, Troy. People can't always do what they want."

"We're not talking about doing what they want." Troy held his ground. "We're talking about making sure their aging mom has what she needs."

If it was any other conversation Ben would appreciate Troy's commitment to his opinion.

But not on this one.

"I've been thinkin' maybe we could bring her to the ranch one day. Get her out of that house and into some fresh air." He still hadn't gotten a good look inside Muriel's house, but the way she worked hard to keep everyone out didn't bode well for the condition of the interior.

"I can go pick her up." Troy leaned back in his seat, finally looking a little more relaxed.

Ben could imagine the two of them together for an extended period of time. A set of flirts each trying to outdo the other. "You'll probably have her talked into marryin' you before you even get here."

"Hey, hey, hey. That's uncalled for. And I'm sure she's looking for someone her own age." Troy leaned between the seats, shooting Ben a grin. "Someone like you."

"Real fuckin' funny." Of all the men on the ranch to finally decide to step up and take on some responsibility, it would figure he'd get stuck with a damn comedian.

"You're probably right." Liza nodded her head like she agreed with Troy. "She seems like the kind of woman who would want a man with stamina."

Troy put one hand over the center of his chest. "You just hurt my heart." He shook his head in mock despair. "No one told me you were so vicious." He fell back, dropping dramatically against the back of his seat.

"I know that's not true." Liza folded her hands on her lap. "I'm sure there's a whole PowerPoint presentation on the topic."

"I think you're seriously overestimating the digital skill set of most of the men." Troy crossed his arms over his chest. "It's a flip book."

Liza snorted out a little laugh at a conversation that normally bothered the hell out of her.

She could put on one hell of an act, but deep down what people said bothered her.

One part in particular.

"Is it true?" Troy had the decency to sound hesitant to ask the question everyone who worked on the ranch eventually wanted to know.

"Yes." Liza answered immediately, the way she always did.

Only this time she didn't stop there.

"I left him and moved on with someone else." She sucked in a breath. "He found out and wasn't appreciative of the new situation." Each word was clipped and concise. "He tricked me into coming back to talk to him and then ambushed me." Her hand went to the spot Ed Cross's blade managed to slice open. "So I shot him."

Troy let out a low whistle. "Damn."

Liza nodded. "Pretty much."

NINETEEN

LIZA

SHE KNEW WHAT everyone said about her.

About what happened the night Ed Cross died.

It was like a legend, passed down over the generations of ranch hands they'd gone through since it happened.

"I didn't poison him."

"That's good to know." Troy tipped his head. "Honestly that was the real reason I wanted to help you make breakfast." He almost managed to keep a straight face.

Almost.

Once he started laughing it was impossible not to laugh with him.

And it felt good to laugh about it, which probably said more about her than she really wanted to consider at this moment.

"I never figured you were the black widow kind of woman." Troy stretched his arms across the back of the seat, looking relaxed. "Definitely not after you jumped in front of the car to save that kid."

Yet another legend she would never live down. "I didn't jump in front of a car to save a kid." Although that scenario was significantly closer to the truth than the one she knew ran rampant through the bunkhouse. "But I may have had a physical altercation with the woman trying to take him, which led to both of us ending up on the ground in front of a car."

Troy bobbed his head in a nod. "Fuck yeah."

"And it was a terrible fucking idea." Ben finally contributed something to the conversation, although he looked significantly less impressed than Troy was at the discussion.

"You would've done the same thing."

Ben's grip tightened on the wheel, squeezing hard before releasing. "That would have been different."

"Of course it would." Liza let out a long, strangled-sounding sigh.

She busted her ass to prove that she worked just as hard as any man in Moss Creek. To prove herself just as capable as any man around.

Because like it or not, she was stuck living in a man's world, one filled with old-school cowboys who thought she'd be better off baking bread and raising babies.

Neither of which were on her agenda.

Ben parked in front of her house and she immediately got out, managing to negotiate un-belting herself, opening the door, and climbing free with little problem or pain.

Maybe Ben was on to something with the ice packs and anti-inflammatories.

Not that she had any intention of telling him that, especially not now that she realized he still looked at her much the way he always had.

Which was exactly the same way everyone else did.

Liza went into the house, kicking off her shoes just inside the door and dropping her purse into the chair. She hadn't done much today, but she was almost more tired than she'd ever been.

Tired of the bullshit. Tired of the expectations.

Tired of the games.

"What's wrong?" Ben closed the front door behind him as he came in, looking comfortable as hell walking into her house.

"Currently?" Liza went to the fridge and pulled out a bottle of wine. "I still can't use my right hand, my thigh is the color of wilting spinach, and you think I'm incapable because of my vagina." She set the bottle onto the counter and dug out her corkscrew, realizing too late there was one more task she still couldn't accomplish on her own. "Goddammit." Liza slammed the corkscrew down on the counter.

Then she reconsidered, picking it up and chucking it down the hall.

She tried not to get angry. It wasn't a useful emotion, not unless you had to kill someone before they killed a person you loved, and hopefully that situation never arose again.

But right now she was angry. For a lot of reasons, most of which had nothing to do with the list she'd offered Ben.

"I don't think you're incapable because you're a woman." Ben's eyes moved over her. "And honestly, I'm not sure how in the hell you came up with that."

She laughed and it sounded a little unhinged. "You're not sure how I came up with that?" Liza marched up to him, going toe to toe. "How about the fact that I shouldn't ever try to protect a child again and that it would have been a different thing if you were the one who had done it?"

One of Ben's dark brows slowly lifted. "You assumed all of that had to do with the fact that you're a woman?"

"Of course it had to do with the fact that I'm a woman." She glanced down the hall where her corkscrew laid on the floor. "Hell." Liza marched after it, snagging it from the ground before going back to the bottle of wine.

"Maybe you don't know me as well as I thought you did." Ben came up behind her, stealing the corkscrew before pressing the point into the mouth of the bottle, his arms around her as he cranked it down into the soft cork. "Or maybe, you're looking for reasons to be pissed at me."

"I'm not sure I would have to look far." She tried to ignore the feel of him behind her, around her.

But it was almost impossible.

And that pissed her off a little too.

"You can't just come back into my life like this," she turned, planning to face him down, but only succeeded in coming nose to nose and belly to belly with the man who always managed to turn her whole world upside down, "and expect everything to be fine."

"Who said I expected everything to be fine?" The cork popped free behind her.

"That's how you're acting." Liza waved one hand toward the table. "You're making me breakfast, and opening my wine, and," her waving hand started to motion toward the living room and the couch he'd parked her on, but instead her brain tripped over the chair, getting caught on what happened last night, "and... And..."

"Meeting your needs?"

Liza snorted, caught in the snowball of emotions that had been bottled up so long they started to turn. "I'm not sure that's what I would call that."

"Interesting." Ben rested one hand against the counter at each side of her hips, leaning down to bring their eyes level. "What would you call it then?"

"Just..." Unfortunately her brain was still in the chair. "Like a..." Liza squeezed her eyes shut, trying to stop the spinning. "It doesn't matter. What matters is that you still think I shouldn't do certain things because I'm a woman."

"I've never thought that." He said it completely calmly, like she should just believe him because the words came out of his mouth.

"You just said—"

"I just said that you won't be jumping in front of anymore cars, or inserting yourself into anymore kidnappings." Ben barely shook his head. "And that has nothing to do with the fact that you're a woman." He leaned in a little closer. "But it has everything to do with the fact that I won't survive you almost dying again."

She wanted to punch him. Right in the face.

Maybe scream a little.

But she couldn't do either, so she had to settle on the next best option.

"Dammit." Liza lunged at him, wrapping one arm around his neck as her lips hit his.

The man was frustrating as hell. Always had been.

He laid out the truth in a way that made her crazy.

He also had a habit of making her wild. Two things that tended to go hand in hand.

Along with the bad decisions they brought along to spice things up.

But Ben never felt like a bad decision. Not ever.

Definitely not right now.

"Why are you such a pain in the ass?" She grabbed at his shirt, yanking it free from his jeans. "You should have just left well enough alone."

"Not a chance." Ben's back slammed into the wall beside the stairs, knocking his cowboy hat loose and his breath free in a rush. "I never could leave you alone."

"Now you're the one who's lying." Liza gathered the front of his shirt in one upward motion, gripping it tight, using it as leverage to pull his mouth back to hers. She could barely breathe when she pulled back. "Because you left me alone for five fucking years."

"Like hell I did." Ben fisted one hand in her hair, holding on as his lips crushed against hers, sealing them together once again.

Liza leaned back, tugging on his shirt as she stumbled toward the center of the room. "What would you call telling me that we couldn't be together because the whole town would know?"

"It's called looking out for your best interest." Ben wrapped one arm around her waist, lifting her up and backing her across the kitchen until her butt landed on the counter, knocking over the bottle of wine he'd opened seconds before. "And it was a bad fucking call." He shoved up the fabric of her skirt, the width of his body pressing her thighs apart. "I should've never made it." Ben grabbed the bandeau style top that was held in place by nothing more than gathered elastic and yanked it down, baring her upper half. His eyes moved over her naked flesh, the heat of his gaze making her nipples pull tight in anticipation.

She could barely breathe. Barely think.

This was never supposed to happen again.

They were never supposed to happen again.

Ben's eyes slowly lifted to meet hers.

She leaned for him the same time he grabbed for her, each of them latching on tight, fed and fueled by years of unspent anger and lust.

And probably something else, but thinking about that would only piss on her parade.

Liza yanked at his shirt, unable to do much more than drag it over his face without the use of her right hand. It hadn't even occurred to her that undressing another person would be as much of a struggle as it was to dress herself, but that wasn't really on her radar until recently.

Very recently.

"Get this freaking shirt off." Any patience she might have possessed had abandoned her, and it showed.

Ben easily shucked his shirt, tossing it to the side before leaning in, the heat of his mouth closing around her nipple before pulling it deep. Her head dropped back, hitting the cabinet behind her surprisingly hard.

Ben lifted his head.

Liza grabbed him by the hair, putting his mouth back in place. "If you stop I will kill you."

She tried not to threaten people, mostly because everyone in town knew what she'd done, and most of them questioned just how capable she was of doing it again.

She never had to worry about that with Ben. He knew the truth. About everything.

And there was a certain amount of freedom in that. Someone who knew all her sins. All her flaws.

Ben's mouth latched back onto her breast, the slow suck shooting straight between her thighs, dragging out a groan she couldn't control.

"Christ." Ben growled the word out against her skin.

Then he grabbed her tight, hauling both her legs around his waist before pulling her flush against him, the worn fabric of his jeans rubbing right against her throbbing pussy. "Hold on."

He dragged her off the counter, lips on her neck as they crossed the kitchen.

Liza gasped as he bounced her body, adjusting his grip. The move rubbed her clit right against him, clenching her thighs tighter. "Where are we going?"

They shouldn't be going anywhere. He should've left her ass on that counter, pulled out his cock, and given her what they both wanted right then and there.

"Upstairs." Ben's boot hit the bottom step.

Unfortunately, it also hit the hem of her skirt, so when he tried to take a step there was nowhere to go.

Her ass immediately dropped to one of the stairs as momentum tipped Ben forward. He caught their descent, bracing one arm against a tread, softening the landing for both of them.

Liza hooked her hand in the front of his jeans, dragging him close. "What happened to the man who couldn't wait to have me?"

"He got older." Ben grabbed her again, hefting her up, only this time he managed to keep the bulk of her skirt pinned under his arm. "He realized the benefits of a soft mattress." His lips quirked in a little smile. "And a tough woman."

"I'm going to choose not to be offended by that." Liza gave up on being sweet and soft a long time ago.

That wasn't the hand life dealt her.

"If that offends you then you might not be as tough as I thought." Ben stomped his way up the steps, going straight into her room. "Because I'm pretty sure you know exactly how tough you are." He crawled onto her bed, dragging her up the mattress. "Pride yourself on it, actually."

"I'm tough because I have to be." She didn't mean to let anything besides lust find its way into the moment.

She wanted this.

Needed it, really.

Ruining it with feelings and emotions was not an option.

Ben didn't seem to get the memo though. His eyes moved over her face as his thumb stroked her skin, sliding across her cheek in slow passes. "I know." He leaned down, his lips as soft as his touch. He rested his forehead against hers.

He wanted to say something else. She felt it. Braced for whatever it might be.

Because Ben wasn't one to shy away from hard conversations. He asked tough questions and gave difficult answers.

It was once a blessing. It made it possible for them to get incredibly close incredibly fast.

Now... It was definitely feeling more like a curse.

One she wasn't quite ready to deal with.

So she pulled him in again.

But the lust and desire from earlier were gone.

Replaced by something dangerous.

Something she should run as far from as possible.

Need.

But her leg was still a little sore, so running was out of the question.

That left her with one option.

To ignore it. Pretend this could be easy and mess free.

So that's what she was going to do.

Ben tugged her dress, working it free from her body as his mouth followed the same path, leaving a trail of heat in its wake.

"Ben, I can't—" She grabbed at him, not really sure how to explain what she needed.

No. Wanted.

This was want.

Not need.

His mouth came back to hers as his boots hit the floor, dropping one after the other onto the scarred wood. Then his weight was on her, warm and solid. Familiar and settling in a way she didn't expect.

Grounding at a time when so much seemed to be spinning away.

Just like it was before.

She held him tight, unable to do much else as his hands slid over her skin, leaving fire in their wake until she was burning. Ready and willing to incinerate if that's what needed to happen.

Liza fought his jeans, needing him as naked as she was. Stripped bare until there was nothing else between them.

Physically.

Ben pushed up on his knees, gaze dark as his eyes met hers. He flipped the button of his jeans free, shoving them down his hips before kicking them away. His eyes dragged down her as his fist gripped his straining cock, pumping it slowly as his fingers traced the seam of her pussy.

She sucked in a breath as he teased across her clit, sliding in slow circles that threatened to make this night just as speedy of a performance as the one before.

Liza shoved his hand away, hooking her leg around his back to pull him closer. "Come here."

Ben eased back over her, the rigid line of his cock pressing against her belly. "We need to talk about some things, Sweetheart." Ben dragged his dick down her slit.

"I don't want to talk anymore." Liza angled her hips, trying to work her way closer.

"Has to be done." He flexed his hips, thrusting against her in a move that made them both groan. "I need to tell you something important."

There was something ominous in his tone.

Something that said she wasn't going to like whatever it was he had to say.

Ben leaned down, dragging the tip of his nose up the side of her neck until his lips brushed her ear. "I haven't been with anyone since you."

TWENTY

BEN

IT WAS A confession he never planned to make.

Not because he wanted Liza to think he'd been fine.

Mostly because he didn't want her to know he wasn't. Not yet.

But now it was out there, one more thing stacked between them.

Liza's eyes held his as all the air rushed from her lungs. "You're serious."

He tipped his head, managing a nod. "I'm serious."

"Hell." She pressed both hands to her head. "It's been five years."

"I feel like now's a good time to point out that you haven't been with anyone either." It was the only thing he could fall back on. Hopefully it was enough.

Liza huffed out a breath. "That's different."

"Why?" He traced down the side of her face, running his finger over the smooth skin of her cheek. "Because I'm a man?"

"Yes." She nodded. "That's exactly why."

"I think you have some archaic opinions on men." He smiled, feeling light in spite of the weight of the admission he'd been forced into offering. "Especially for someone so progressive."

She scoffed, her mouth hanging open like she wanted to argue but nothing was there to come out.

She scoffed again, this time following it up. "But it's been *five years*."

"I realize that." He'd been there for every damn day of it.

"But why?" She seemed shocked. Maybe a little confused.

Like she fully believed he'd been out living life as normal since walking away from the first person who ever treated him like he was special.

The first person who ever really listened when he talked.

The first person to care enough about what he thought to talk back.

"Why haven't you been with anyone since me?" He turned the question back on her, fighting the distraction of her body under his.

She'd always been all but impossible for him to ignore, and right now he was suffering for it.

All he wanted was to prove she was still his.

That deep down she always had been.

But he wanted her to know the full truth of the situation.

That he'd always been hers too.

Liza lifted her chin the tiniest bit. "I told you. I've been busy."

His smile was easy, holding as he brushed his lips over hers. "Then I guess I've been busy too."

She wasn't ready for the truth. That was fine.

Didn't change it.

"One more thing." They were almost there. Almost back to the beginning. One that was new and unhindered.

Ben couldn't resist the need to thrust against her one more time, teasing them both with the slide of his body over hers.

"You better start talking." Liza hooked her legs at his waist, wincing a little when the inside of her bruised thigh pressed tight to his side. "And you better talk fast."

Knowing she wanted him too might have made him put this conversation off in his younger days, skipping it in favor of instant gratification.

But after five years there would never be anything instant about this.

And this conversation was important. Difficult, but important.

He struggled to come up with the right words. "I don't think either of us want anything extra to come of this."

"It's handled." She picked up on his meaning instantly, ending a discussion neither of them wanted to have.

Not right now.

Liza ran her hand down the center of his chest. "Anything else?" The tips of her fingers dragged over his sternum.

She no longer sounded impatient. Her mood had shifted in the way he expected.

But it had to be done. Liza never wanted kids and neither did he. Pretending it wasn't a concern would be stupid and careless.

And he would never avoid hard conversations with her. Never had.

Even when they almost killed him.

"Elizabeth."

She didn't look up at him. Her gaze stayed fixed on where her fingers traced little circles in the hair of his chest.

"Look at me, Sweetheart." He waited until her eyes slowly lifted to meet his.

There was so much he wanted to say to her.

So much he needed her to know.

Liza's fingers trailed across his face, slowly tracing the line of his lips. "What?"

He couldn't look away from her. "I just need to know you're here." He leaned into her hand as the soft brush of her touch slid along his cheek. "With me."

Liza was quiet for a minute, her touch slow and unhurried as it moved over his face.

Then she leaned up, catching his lips with hers, pulling him down with her as she fell back to the pillows.

There was something different in the way she kissed him. The roughness from before was gone, replaced by something he couldn't blame her for.

Hesitancy.

Caution.

They could never pick back up right where they left off. He knew that.

But knowing she didn't fully trust him was a knife to the gut. One more wound he would happily carry for her.

She carried so many because of him.

The reminder burned inside him, driving him forward with purpose and need.

A need to prove she hadn't suffered for nothing.

He'd intended to take his time with her. With this.

Thought it would be a simple task, given how long he'd been waiting.

What was a little more?

But a little more turned out to be too fucking long.

One second turned out to be too fucking long. He'd gone too many as it was.

He needed her.

Always had.

Always would.

That's why he didn't leave Cross Creek. Not because of money or ownership.

Because of her.

Ben angled his hips, lining himself up before pressing in as slow as he could stand, gritting his teeth as her wet heat engulfed him.

Liza's eyes held his as he started to move, each liquid glide of his body into hers threatening to be his undoing.

Threatening to push him over the edge.

He dropped his forehead to hers, fighting for some semblance of control.

But his balls were already pulling up tight, already aching.

Which left him no choice but to hit the brakes.

Ben pulled free of the perfect squeeze of her pussy, drinking in air like it might be the key to survival. "I need a minute." He rested one hand on her middle, fingers splayed across the scar that would forever remind her of that night.

Liza's lips pulled into a slow smile. "That's what you get for going five years without sex."

"I'm not sure that has anything to do with it, Sweetheart." He ran his fingers over the fading white line. "I think my primary issue is you." Ben traced over the reminder of what his presence in her life caused. "Always has been."

Liza caught his hand, lacing her fingers with his, using the hold to pull him back to her.

It was easy to go. Easy to let his body fall onto hers.

Into hers.

Wanting her was always easy.

Having her was the hard part.

She held him tight, moving with him, her hips meeting every thrust, her sharp, short breaths mingling with his.

"I'm—" It was the only warning he got. A second later she clenched around him, her whole body going tight as her fingers dug into his skin and her sweet moans filled the air.

He powered through, fighting for those last few strokes that would carry her over and along, until she dragged him down with her.

Pulling him under the same waves they almost drowned in.

"YOU'RE UP EARLY." Liza yawned as she came into the kitchen, looking like she was still half-asleep.

"I've got some things I need to get done." He'd been in the process of making a batch of French toast she could warm up when she came downstairs, hair mussed with a sleep line indented across the pink skin of her left cheek. "You hungry now?"

"Definitely." She picked up the full coffee pot, holding it up and squinting at the level of the brown liquid. "Did you already drink a whole pot?"

"I haven't been up long." He thought he'd be able to sneak out and let her sleep in, hopefully spending most of the time he was gone in bed.

Liza filled a coffee cup almost to the top, setting the carafe back in place before passing him the mug. "You could have woken me up."

"You need sleep." He slid the first slices of egg-dipped bread onto a plate. "Remember?"

"What about you?" Liza filled a second cup. "You were up just as late as I was."

"I'm not still healing." Ben set the plate on the table next to the syrup and sliced strawberries. "You are." He snagged the pills he set out. "Speaking of." Ben held out the ibuprofen. "The physical therapist said you need to keep up with these until tomorrow."

Liza snagged them from his palm and popped them into her mouth, immediately washing them down with the coffee in her cup. "Oh, God." She cringed, sticking her tongue out. "That's terrible." A second later she was in the fridge, digging out the creamer to add to her coffee. "I don't know how you guys all drink that shit."

"It's hot and easy."

Liza spun toward him, hiding a little smile behind her cup. "Sorta like you."

"If I was easy then I would have had half of Mae's waitstaff by now." Ben dropped two more slices of soaked bread into the buttered pan. "And a few of the girls at The Creekery."

"Maybe easy is the wrong word." Liza picked up a slice of bread from her plate and took a bite. "Maybe picky is a better term."

Picky didn't quite explain the reason he'd struggled to convince himself to move on. "Picky wasn't the problem either."

He flipped the toast before turning to face Liza, leaning back against the counter and crossing his arms. "I had to be around you every damn day, Elizabeth, and it was a mind fuck I couldn't find my way out of."

She stopped chewing, swallowing the bite in her mouth as her hand dropped, setting what remained of the slice back on her plate. "I'm sorry I couldn't buy you out."

"I didn't want you to buy me out." He tried not to sound angry, but he was.

Angry that Ed Cross wouldn't take no for an answer.

Angry that the only way to keep Liza safe was to give her up.

"I wanted you."

And he couldn't have her. Not when the whole town and the

state police were watching her every move, looking for some sign she'd killed Ed Cross in cold blood.

And finding out she'd already moved on would make it look like exactly that.

A light rap on the back door cut the conversation short. Troy peeked into the room. "You ready, boss?"

"Almost." Ben forced his eyes from Liza. "I'll be out in a second." He waited until Troy was off the deck and halfway to the mess hall. "I've got some repairs to do on the bunkhouse. Storm blew a few shingles loose."

Liza nodded, the shift in her mood evident. "Okay."

"I'll be back before lunch." He crossed the room and took her face in his hands. "We have to talk about this, Sweetheart. There's no way around it."

If there was, they would have both recovered long ago.

She gave him a little nod, but that was the only hint of agreement she offered.

Ben leaned down, resting his lips against her forehead. "Please rest. I'll be back as soon as I can."

He didn't want to leave her. Not now.

Not like this.

Not again.

But it was set to rain this afternoon, and unless he did something about the roof there'd be one hell of a mess to clean up.

Ben forced his feet out the door and across the deck. Troy had already collected a crew to help make the process as speedy as possible, and they were out and getting started just as the sun came up, barely peeking through the heavy clouds already threatening rain.

The pitch on the bunkhouse roof was just a little steeper than he was comfortable being on untethered, so each man was tied down with a rope hooked over the peak and tied to a tree on the other side. It was how he'd reroofed the building four years ago, bringing it back from the brink of complete ruin just in time.

"I've never seen them come loose like that." Troy stood at his side, looking over the bare patch. "They usually end up twisted at least a little."

"The wind out here gets pretty unruly." Ben didn't have time to really consider the means.

Just the repair of the result.

He went down to one knee, grabbing a shingle from the stack Dustin brought up before sliding it into place.

Troy worked right beside him, helping line things up and hold shingles out of the way as Ben nailed the replacements down. Once they were done you'd never know anything ever happened.

"Looks good." Troy scrubbed one hand against his jaw. "I still don't see how they came loose like they did."

"Not sure how great the job was done in the first place." He'd had help from men who'd moved on long ago, so there was a good chance they'd be losing more shingles in the future. "I didn't do it alone."

"Guess we'll just hope for the best then." Troy grabbed the hammer and tucked it into his waistband before heading for the ladder.

"Guess so." Ben straightened, glancing up at the sky as the first spit of rain hit his skin. "Looks like we got done just in time."

He took one step back and immediately started to slide as another shingle came loose, stealing his balance. He grabbed the rope hooking him in place, gripping tight as he skidded toward the edge.

For a second he slowed, but instead of the hard catch he'd been expecting, the rope provided a slowly releasing tension.

Until it completely broke free, going slack in his hand.

There was nothing he could do. No way to regain his footing.

No way to stop the slide as the grit of the shingles ate into his skin, peeling away at his palms as he tried to hold onto something.

Anything.

TWENTY-ONE

LIZA

"HOW IS EVERYTHING going?" Her mother smiled out from the screen of her phone.

"Fine." Liza managed a genuine smile back. "How about you? Is everything okay? Is the house okay?"

Her mother laughed a little. "Of course the house is okay. Why wouldn't it be okay?"

"No reason. I just wanted to make sure there wasn't anything that needed to be done." Liza adjusted her positioning, making sure her arm was completely out of view. "If you ever need help with anything you should let me know. I'll figure out a way to get it done."

"Oh, honey." Her mother waved one hand at the camera. "You are so busy. Besides, your father and I are completely capable of handling any little projects that need done."

"So there are projects that need done?" The longer she sat and stared at Muriel's house yesterday, the more concerned Liza became that maybe Muriel's kids weren't the only ones dropping the ball.

"There's always projects that need done." Her mother leaned in close, her face taking up the entire screen. "Your father just had to rebuild all the toilets because they stopped working."

"All your toilets just stopped working?" How in the hell did something like that happen? "Is there something wrong with your plumbing?"

Liza had a vision of her mother washing dishes in the bathtub, unwilling to tell her because she was sure she was too busy to be bothered.

"There's nothing wrong with our plumbing." Her mother leaned to look over one shoulder, before facing the camera again. "There was just a little mishap." Her voice was quiet enough to make it clear she didn't want her husband hearing about this mishap.

"What sort of a *mishap*?" Liza's mind was already running through all the possible avenues she could use to help her parents.

There weren't many, considering they lived on opposite ends of the country.

"I found these neat little bleach tabs at the store." Her mother's expression was serious. "They sounded amazing. You just drop them in the back of the tank and they keep your toilet clean all the time."

"Are you having a hard time cleaning your house?" Maybe she could hire them a housekeeper.

One that didn't cost an insane amount of money.

A very not insane amount of money.

"I'm going to choose not to be offended by that." Her mother continued on. "Anyway, they worked like a charm. No more of those ugly little hard water rings in the toilet." Her mother tipped her head to one side, squinting one eye. "Unfortunately, they also destroyed the inner workings of the flushing mechanism."

"How can they sell something like that? What's the point of it?"

Her mother's eyes widened, brows lifting as she pointed at the camera. "Exactly. It never occurred to me that they'd sell something that would eat up your toilet's insides, causing it to run around-the-clock, doubling your water bill and generally driving everyone inside the house insane with the constant noise."

"Does dad know why the toilets all needed to be rebuilt?"

"Of course he doesn't know why all the toilets needed to be rebuilt."

Liza pressed her lips together to smother out a smile.

Her parents had been married for almost fifty years, and the majority of those involved her poor father cleaning up random household messes her mother inadvertently created.

Like the time she was sure that dumping a combination of baking soda and lemon juice down the drain would unclog it.

Spoiler alert: It didn't. It just made the clog fizzier and lemony fresh.

Or the time she laid blankets over the driveway before a snowstorm, thinking it would be easier to just lift them up, knocking any accumulation off and out of the way.

Which technically might have worked if the snowstorm hadn't been immediately preceded by freezing rain, which pelted the blankets, sinking into them and fusing them to the concrete. It took days of work and ultimately a saltwater slurry, to get the blankets free.

"I was just trying to make life easier." Her mother retired from teaching when Dawn was born. And while no one would question her mother's commitment to raising children, she was definitely always looking for something to stimulate her mind. "I have all these ideas. I have to try at least some of them out."

"I understand." Liza balanced her cell phone against the syrup bottle still sitting on the kitchen table. "How's Dawn?"

Her mother's eyes shifted away. "She's fine."

"Did she have her follow-up appointment?" Liza picked at a tiny crumb she'd missed when wiping up after breakfast.

"That's next week, but I'm sure everything will be okay." Her mother was creative and kind and loving, and an eternal optimist who sought out the best in every situation and every person.

It was one of the many reasons Liza held so much about her life close. Outside of the fact that her parents already had enough to worry about, she didn't want to risk crushing her mother's sweet spirit.

And that's what would happen if her parents ever found out what her life in Cross Creek was really like.

They would be crushed. No way would she ever do that to them.

"You'll call me as soon as it's over though, right?" She'd been lucky in the years since she left New York. Her parents and Dawn had all been relatively healthy and happy.

It was still hard to be away from them, but at least she didn't worry.

"Of course, dear." Her mother's smile was off, and it stoked the worry she'd been fighting since they last spoke.

"Is Dawn there? Can I talk to her?"

"Oh honey, she's at one of her classes." Her mother lifted one hand, showing off an elastic bracelet made of brightly colored beads. "Look what she made me last week. Isn't it cute?"

Liza's throat suddenly went tight. "It is."

She and Dawn used to sit together for hours, making bracelets, painting figurines, and weaving potholders.

Dawn definitely inherited their mother's creativity, and spent most of her time making gifts for the people she loved.

And Dawn loved pretty much everyone.

"Maybe I can come see you soon." She'd taken very few trips to New York, always using the ranch as an excuse.

But that's what it was.

A way to avoid going home and risking spilling her guts to the people she wanted to protect most in the world.

Her mother's brows lifted in surprise. "Well that would be lovely, if you had the time."

An alert flashed across her screen, dropping down from the top. It was a local number, but one she didn't recognize.

Liza swiped it away, intending to continue talking to her mother. "I can make the time."

"Are you sure? Your father and I understand how much pressure you're under. We don't want you coming here if it will only make that worse for you."

It almost seemed like her mother was trying to put her off. "Are you sure everything's okay?" The alert dropped down again, displaying the same phone number from before. Liza swiped it away again.

"Of course everything's okay." I just don't want you flying all the way here when you should really be doing something else."

The alert immediately dropped down again. "Is it okay if I call you back? The same number keeps calling me."

It was probably the surgeon's office trying to reschedule one of the many follow-up appointments marked across her calendar.

"Of course, honey." Her mother looked relieved.

A little too relieved.

Liza ended their chat and answered the call, ready to quickly deal with whatever appointment needed moved so she could call her mother back and continue their conversation. "Hello?"

"Liza, it's Troy."

There was something in his tone that made her sit straight in her seat. "What's wrong?"

"Ben told me not to call you."

It was an odd way to start a conversation. "Why would he tell you that?"

"I think he didn't want you to be worried."

Her stomach dropped. "Worried about what?"

"I want to start by saying he's gonna be okay." Troy barely paused. "Probably."

Liza was up and out of her chair before the next words came out of her mouth. "Listen to me carefully, Troy." She slung her purse over one shoulder and grabbed her keys from the counter. She had no clue how she was going to drive her stick shift, but she'd figure it out. "You've seen my nice side, and if you don't want to see what else I have to offer then you need to start talking."

"I'm starting to figure out why he didn't want me to call you."

"Too late for that now, cowboy. You've got three seconds to start talking before I run you over with my truck on my way to wherever he is." Patience was never her strong suit, and she had the bad decisions to show for it.

But what was one more?

"Are you allowed to drive?"

"Pretty sure you can't arrest me." Liza was out the front door and halfway to her truck when an ambulance came flying down her driveway. "Troy. Why is there an ambulance here?" She ran at it, ignoring the cramp of pain in the muscle under the bruise on her thigh. The squad slowed, the passenger side window rolling down as they started to come to a stop. Travis Moore leaned out the window. "Where we headed?"

"We're back by the bunkhouse." Troy must've been able to hear Travis's question on his end of the line.

Travis relayed the information to whoever was driving and the ambulance started to move again.

"Travis Moore, if you don't stop that fucking ambulance and let me in I will make sure Cecily never waits on you again at The Wooden Spoon." Liza grabbed a hold of the handle and yanked, wrenching the door open just as the vehicle finally stopped. "Scoot over."

Travis lifted his hands. "There's no place to scoot to, Liza. It's one fucking seat."

"Fine." She grabbed the handle just above the door and swung herself in, landing her ass on Travis's lap hard enough to make him grunt. She turned to find Dane Carter in the driver's seat. "Go."

"Jesus Christ." Travis grabbed the door and yanked it closed. "I knew this was going to be a pain in the ass call."

"You don't know what you know Travis. You're too busy chasing Cecily to know your ass from a hole in the ground."

"How do you know that?" He leaned around her shoulder to peek at her. "She say something about me?"

"Shut up." Liza pressed the phone tighter to her ear. "Troy, what the fuck happened?"

"Ben slid off the roof."

Everything fell silent around her, drowned out by the ringing in her ears. She turned to Dane. "Faster."

She couldn't tell if they sped up or not. Either way they still weren't moving fast enough. She smacked her hand against the dash. "I said faster."

"I'm going as fast as this thing can handle gravel, Liza." The lane split in two and Dane started to slow down. "Which way?"

All she could do was jab her finger to the right as Troy's words flashed through her mind on repeat.

Ben slid off the roof.

"How did he fall off the roof?"

"I don't know for sure. All I know is he lost his footing and the rope didn't hold like it was supposed to." Troy sounded upset, which didn't make her feel any better at all.

If anything, it worried her more.

"Is he okay?"

"Define okay."

The first thing she was going to do when she got there would be firing Troy. "You know exactly what okay means."

"I see you guys." Troy stepped right in their line of sight, waving one arm.

Dane pulled to a stop, but Liza was already out, shoving her way free of the ambulance before it was even in park. She ran, dropping her purse and her phone into the grass as she raced toward where a group of cowboys was kneeled on the ground.

She grabbed the closest one by the back of the shirt, yanking him out of the way before falling into his place, going straight to her knees. "Oh my God."

Ben was lying very still, his hat over his face.

"No. No, no, no, no." This couldn't be happening. Not to him. Not now.

Sweetheart, I really need you to calm down right now." His voice was muffled and strained.

Liza snatched away the hat. Ben immediately winced as a streak of sunlight snuck through the clouds, hitting him right in the face, along with a few of the random raindrops that had been falling for the past thirty minutes.

"We had that there to keep the sun out of his eyes." Dustin took his own hat off his head, moving it around until the shadow it cast covered Ben's face.

"Are you okay?" Liza struggled to breathe. He was talking and awake, but that didn't necessarily mean anything. "Does anything hurt?" She carefully laid her hand at the center of his chest.

"Everything hurts." Ben's eyes moved beside her. "Have them check Troy out too. He tried to catch me."

Dane crouched down beside her. "How long ago did this happen?"

"About thirty minutes." Dustin answered. "He accidentally slipped and came right over the edge."

"Did you hit your head?" Travis dropped down at Ben's other side, a neck brace in his hands.

"Hit pretty much everything." Ben winced as Travis worked the brace around his neck.

"Did you lose consciousness?" Dane leaned over him, flashing a light into Ben's eyes.

"No." He looked Troy's way again. "And I'm not the only one that hit the ground."

"I'm fine." Troy was holding his right arm close, keeping it remarkably still.

Something Liza had been doing for almost a month now.

"What's wrong with your arm?" She wasn't willing to leave Ben's side, but she was more than happy to call Troy out.

Especially since he'd waited twenty minutes to call her.

"It's fine." Troy took a step back. "Just strained it a little. He tipped his head at Ben. "Get him all taken care of."

"Let's get Ben loaded up and then we'll see if anyone else needs to go in." Dane tucked his tiny flashlight into the front pocket of his shirt. "You comin' with him, Liza?"

"Yes." She was fighting the urge to panic. "Will they keep him?"

"Don't know. Depends on if they find anything wrong." Dane stood as Travis brought the stretcher their way, the wheels moving surprisingly well over the grass and gravel.

Liza stood back as they dropped it down and carefully transferred Ben, earning another wince of pain from the man she'd never seen so much as bat an eye in discomfort.

A fact that tightened her throat and twisted her stomach.

As soon as he was up she moved back in at his side, staying close while they loaded him into the back of the ambulance. Dane got in, reaching out to help her inside before sitting down to take Ben's vitals using the equipment lining the interior.

Travis went back to check on Troy, looking over the arm he was favoring before making his way their direction.

"Looks like your buddy is okay." Travis tipped his head to one side. "Okay enough that he doesn't have to take a ride with us."

"Good." Ben stared up at the ceiling, his face lined with what she could only imagine was pain.

"I'm going to get us moving." Dane passed on all the information he'd collected as Travis took his spot.

Travis motioned to a seat just at Ben's other side. "Get buckled up so we can go."

She immediately sat down, but struggled to negotiate the lap belt.

"Here." Travis leaned over her. "I'll get it."

"Don't get any ideas, Miller." Ben's voice was surprisingly strong. "I can still kick your ass." He closed his eyes, looking remarkably relaxed, all things considered. "Even in a neck brace."

TWENTY-TWO

BEN

"I'M FINE."

Liza glared at him. "You are not fine. You have two broken ribs and every bit of you is covered in bruises."

"You haven't seen every bit of me." Ben smirked a little as she helped him up the steps and into the house. "But I'd be happy to show you."

Liza eased him down into the chair just inside the door. "The doctor said no strenuous activities."

"Sounds an awful lot like a challenge to me." He laughed and immediately regretted it, banding his arm across his middle at the stab of pain that stole his breath. "Hell."

"That's what you get." Liza went into the kitchen and flipped on the light. "Are you hungry?"

"No." Ben leaned his head back against the chair and closed his eyes. Whatever they gave him for the pain was making most of him feel like it might melt into a puddle.

"Ben." Liza's voice jolted him awake, making him jump and offering an immediate reminder that his ribs were no longer entirely intact. She was crouched down in front of him, her eyes filled with concern.

"I like that you're worried about me." It wasn't easy to get all the words out. They felt thick and heavy on his tongue. "Even more than I liked you hatin' me."

Liza's head tipped to one side. "Did you really like that?"

"Mm-hmm." Ben nodded his head, rocking it against the back of the seat.

"Why?"

He smiled. "Cause it meant you still loved me."

"I think your reasoning might be a little flawed." She pressed a glass of water into his hand. "Drink this."

Ben did as she said, chugging the water as fast as he could, so it was over with and he could close his eyes again. He burped, passing the glass back. "My reasoning's not flawed."

"Agree to disagree." Liza took the empty glass and stood.

"It's a thin line between love and hate, Sweetheart." He fought his eyes open so he could look at her. "I knew you'd cross it eventually."

He held her gaze as long as he could manage keeping his eyes open.

"What about you? Do you hate me?"

Ben shook his head, fighting the sleep trying to drag him under. "No. Didn't have time." He started to doze, jerking a little as he came back out of it. "Cause I never stopped loving you."

"HEY. I'M SO happy to see you."

Liza's voice roused him from the deepest sleep he'd had in a long time, her words carrying up the stairs and into the bedroom he didn't remember finding his way into

"How are you doing?"

Ben started to sit up, but a sharp stab of pain across his middle stopped him in his tracks, forcing him to move slower as he pushed his way upright.

"I miss you too."

He worked his feet over the edge of the mattress, letting gravity do most of the work in pulling them to the floor. Getting upright was actually easier than sitting up had been, so the walk to the stairs was relatively pain free, outside of the general ache radiating through every part of his body.

An ache that would've been considerably worse if Troy hadn't managed to hang onto him for a couple of seconds, slowing the speed of his fall to one that didn't manage to break every bone in his body.

"Your hair looks so pretty today." Liza's tone was light and easy, filled with a joy he didn't see in her often.

A joy she generally reserved for one person.

He hit the bottom of the steps and immediately found himself in the frame of Liza's phone.

Her eyes widened just a bit in the reflection of her face on the tiny screen.

"Ben!" Dawn's delight in seeing him made the pain it took to get down here infinitely more bearable.

He moved in behind Liza, peeking over her shoulder. "Hey there, pretty lady."

Dawn waved vigorously into her camera. "I made you something." She disappeared, leaving them both staring after her.

Liza's smile held, like it was frozen in place. She leaned his way, voice low. "You don't have a shirt on."

Ben angled his upper body so most of it was blocked by Liza, getting in place just as Dawn came back into view.

"It's a dream catcher." Dawn held the combination of yarn and sticks up. "It will catch your dreams."

"I could sure use that, because my dreams run faster than I expected them to." Ben leaned in, looking over the carefully wrapped web of multicolored yarn. "That's about the most perfect dream catcher I have ever seen."

Dawn set it down, the smile she wore nearly every second of the day making his own smile a little easier to come by. "Yeah. I practiced." She turned to one side. "Do you like my hair?"

"That's real pretty. What do you call that?"

"A braid. My mom did it." Dawn patted the plait twisted together down the back of her head. "I like it when she takes it out."

Liza's eyes got a faraway look to them. "Mermaid hair."

"Yeah." Dawn smiled wide at Liza. "You remember mermaid hair?"

Liza nodded, blinking a few times as she pressed her lips together.

Ben rested his hand against the center of Liza's back, rubbing in slow circles. "I've got a friend here that I think could use a dream catcher too. Do you think you could make him one?"

Dawn's head bobbed in an eager nod. "Yeah."

"How about you go do that and we will call you later?" Ben rested one hand against the table, using it for support as he leaned in a little more. "Maybe you can show us how you make those next time we talk."

"Yeah." Dawn gave him another wave. "Bye." Then she reached out and abruptly ended the call.

Liza sniffed. "She likes pressing the button."

"I wasn't offended." Ben lowered to his knees, taking it slow so he didn't have to deal with one of the shooting pains that stole his breath. He waited until Liza tipped her head to look his way. "She knows you love her."

Liza's chin barely quivered, the movement smothered out almost instantly. "I know." Her eyes lifted to the ceiling, lids blinking furiously as she tried to control the tears threatening to break free. "Did I do the wrong thing?"

"Wrong is relative." He reached up to swipe at the first tear as it snuck loose. "And completely depends on how you look at things."

Her eyes slowly dropped, fixing on his. "Did *you* do the wrong thing?"

"Lots of times." Ben smoothed a bit of loose hair back, tucking it behind her ear. "Probably more than I can count." He managed a little smile. "But you're not asking about all those times, are you?"

Liza shook her head.

"I don't know." At the time it seemed like the only option he had. The only way he could make sure Liza was safe. That everyone saw what happened for what it was.

A man who tried to hurt his wife one too many times.

But maybe they would've seen that anyway.

"But if I think about it too hard I'll drive myself crazy." Almost had.

"Why didn't you try to be with me sooner?" There was so much lingering in Liza's question. Hurt. Confusion. Longing.

But it was missing one important thing.

Anger.

"Because you didn't believe I did the right thing." He struggled to swallow. "And it broke you."

Ben knew what he caused her. Forced himself to look at it every single day.

But then he realized the way she looked at him changed. The pain was gone. Replaced by a much more manageable emotion.

"I wasn't broken." Liza sounded offended he would even consider it. "I was angry."

"No you weren't. Not at the beginning." Watching her at the beginning nearly broke him too. Looking at her every day, knowing he was the reason that the light went out in her eyes, was a special kind of torture he wouldn't wish on his worst enemy.

"I don't even remember the beginning."

That wasn't surprising. She'd been almost like a zombie, going through the motions. Living on autopilot.

That was the first of the reasons why he told himself he couldn't leave Cross Creek. Because she needed him. "I know."

Liza's eyes moved over his face. "And you're still not sure if you made the right choice?" There was no accusation in her tone. Not even any anger.

Ben shook his head. "No. I'm still not sure."

He would never be sure. There was no way to know if he did make the decision that kept Liza safe. "All I know is that I would make the same choice if it meant keeping you out of jail."

He would go through it all over again, the days of her staring at nothing. The nights alone, knowing she was so close and could never be his.

Watching her find happiness everywhere but with him.

He would do it all again to keep her safe.

"I don't think I would have gone to jail."

"I wasn't willing to take that risk."

"But you were willing to risk that I would hate you forever?"

Ben nodded. "Yes."

"Even though you—" she took a little breath, short and sharp. "Even though you loved me?"

"Yes." He didn't hesitate at all. "Even though I love you."

Liza didn't miss the twist of the word. "Loved."

He shook his head. "Love."

He always thought he loved her, even at the beginning, but the way he felt for her five years ago was nothing compared to the way he felt about her now. It was one of the worst parts about everything, he was forced to fall a little more in love with Liza every day.

He had to watch as she rebuilt Cross Creek, bringing it back from the brink of ruin. Proving she was so much more than the pretty face Ed Cross believed he was getting.

He had to see her with her friends, defending them. Standing up for them. Supporting them.

And then he almost had to watch her die, putting herself on the line to protect a little boy.

"I—" Liza's eyes went to her hands, focusing on where they rested in her lap.

"I'm not worried about what you feel for me, Elizabeth. Not even a little bit." He wasn't interested in putting pressure on her.

They had time. It's all they'd ever really had.

"What I am worried about," he slowly stood, holding his breath as he got to his feet, "is what's for breakfast."

"Oh." Liza jumped up from her chair. "I forgot about it." She yanked open the oven as she shoved her left hand into a mitt, fumbling a little as she tried to work it into place.

"I can get that." Ben plucked the oven mitt off her hand before reaching in to slide the slightly overcooked quiche from the oven.

"You are supposed to be resting." Liza glared at him as he set the savory pie onto the cooktop. "I'm supposed to be taking care of you."

"How's that working out for you?" He leaned over, taking a deep breath of the eggy warm air lifting out of the pie. "That smells amazing."

"Probably because you're starving." Liza grabbed a plate, setting it on the counter before having at the quiche with a knife. "You wouldn't eat anything last night before you fell asleep."

"Maybe you just didn't offer me the right thing." His eyes dragged down the length of the dress she was wearing.

Liza's eyes went wide.

"Don't act innocent." He ran one hand down the lean line of her body. "Especially since you're not wearing any panties."

"I'm not acting innocent." Liza scooped out a healthy chunk of quiche and stacked it on a plate. "I'm acting like you just fell off the roof yesterday and you're supposed to be resting." She held out the dish. "Not trying to get in my pants.

"First of all," he took the plate to the table and set it down, "you're not wearing pants." He went back to her side, stealing the second plate just as Liza finished dropping the quiche onto it. "Second of all, there's no tryin' about it."

The glare she shot him was enough to make him laugh.

Which was enough to make him groan as his ribs protested.

"That's what you get." Liza pulled out the chair in front of the larger portion of quiche. "Now sit down and eat your breakfast."

"You're awfully good at dishing out demands for a woman who doesn't like being told what to do." Ben eased down into the chair, finally managing a deep breath once he got seated.

"And you're awfully good at ignoring your own double standard." Liza set a glass in front of him before filling it to the top with orange juice. "It's like you've never had anyone try to take care of you before."

Her observation carried more of a sting than he expected.

Liza's eyes slid his way as the orange juice stopped flowing. "I didn't mean it like—"

Ben shoved in a quick bite of quiche. "This is really good." He focused on the plate in front of him. "Is that asparagus?"

Liza's gaze lingered on him a second longer. "And mushrooms."

"It's good." He risked a peek her way as she sat down across from him. "Mae teach you how to make this?"

Liza came to Cross Creek from a very different sort of world. One that was significantly more glamorous.

And significantly more cutthroat.

"She did." Liza took a little bite of her food. "She's taught me to make a lot of things."

"I noticed your skill set started to broaden once you two got close." He always assumed Liza and Mae bonded over their mutual hatred of the men who'd done them wrong. It made sense.

But then Boone Pace came back into town and figured out a way to smooth things over with Mae, eventually managing to work his way into her bed.

And a ring on her finger.

Mae and Liza no longer had scorn in common, but they remained as close as ever.

It gave him hope. Hope that maybe things weren't as lost as he thought.

Hope that seeing what happened to her best friend would make Liza wonder if it could happen to her too.

TWENTY-THREE

LIZA

"HEY." TROY LOOKED up from where he and Dustin were wiping down the counter after lunch. "How's he doing?"

"He's okay." Liza watched Troy for any sign he'd been injured worse than he let on. "What about you? How are you doing?"

Troy stretched out his left arm, flexing his fingers. "Sore." He shot her a wink. "But worth it."

Liza glanced toward Dustin, making sure he was out of earshot. She leaned closer to Troy. "Thank you."

Troy tipped his head. "No thanks necessary."

"They are though." She'd been through plenty of ranch hands in the time she ran Cross Creek, and there weren't many she could think of who would have done what Troy did. "He could have just as easily taken you down with him."

"But he didn't." Troy brushed it off. "That's all that matters."

Maybe Troy was more annoying than she realized. Annoying in the same way Ben was annoying. "That's not all that matters, but I feel like we're going to have to agree to disagree."

"Sounds like a fancy way of saying you're not gonna admit I'm right." Troy shot her a grin as he turned to wipe down the counter behind him.

Liza rounded the island between them, moving in close at Troy side. "Are you sure you're okay?"

"He turned to face her. "I am okay. I promise."

She tipped her head. "Good. Because I need someone to take over while Ben's recovering."

A week ago she would have been completely screwed. But Troy had proven himself to be more than a decent ranch hand.

And after watching him with Muriel she knew he was also a decent human.

"I'm happy to help in any way I can." Troy leaned one hip against the counter, crossing his arms over his chest. "But I'm still only one man. Ben does the work of at least three men."

"I know." She'd watched Ben practically work himself to death, always assuming it was to protect the investment her piece of shit dead husband swindled him into making.

But maybe that wasn't the only thing motivating him.

Either way, there was no reason for him to continue on the way he'd been going.

"That's why even once he's recovered, I want you to start carrying more of the weight."

Ben could give her shit all he wanted, but the man was just as guilty of not accepting help as she was.

But at least she had a reason.

"You talked to him about this?"

Liza stood a little taller, lifting her chin. "I don't have to talk to him about this. I'm in charge."

Ben always deferred to her. She was the primary owner of the ranch. She was also the owner of a vagina which meant, given the opportunity, the ranch hands would walk right over her and only listen to Ben.

So, from the beginning, Ben always made it clear who ran Cross Creek.

And today, for the first time, she was going to use it against him. But only because it was for his own good.

"I didn't mean it that way." Troy reached into his pocket, digging out a slim case. He knocked a toothpick free and pinched it between his teeth. "He's already talked to me about takin' over some responsibilities. I thought maybe he'd told you about it."

Liza stared at him for a minute. "Interesting."

She wasn't mad, not in a way that made any sense.

"At any rate." Troy tucked the toothpick case back into his pocket. "I'm happy to help out in any way I can. Like I told Ben, I'm looking to move up in this world, not stay at an entry-level position shoveling shit."

Liza nodded. "Good for you." She ran her tongue across her teeth, thinking her way through the situation. "You know anyone else looking to move up?" She lifted one finger, adding on an addendum. "Someone who's willing to work for it?"

There was always someone who wanted to move up, usually lots of somebodies. But most of them didn't want to work for it. Most of them thought if they managed to hang around a year, doing the bare minimum, they would get where they wanted to go by default.

And that's not how things worked. Definitely not at Cross Creek.

Troy tipped his head toward the man she'd seen hanging around him lately. He was a little shorter than Troy and a decent amount thicker, with a face that reminded her of someone, but she couldn't quite put her finger on who.

Probably one of the many other ranch hands that passed through Cross Creek.

"Dustin's a hard worker. Seems to know his way around things."

"Good. Let him help you." Liza turned, looking through the open sliding doors of the mess hall as Ben stepped out onto the back deck, a towel slung across his shoulders and a pair of jeans draped low on his hips. "Call me or Ben if you need anything." She started to walk away, then turned back. "And thank you for handling breakfast and lunch."

Troy bent at the waist, offering her half a bow. "I'm at your service."

Liza rolled her eyes, but couldn't stop her grin, as she turned to make her way back through the mess hall, following the sidewalk that connected it up to her house. The wind chimes Maryann brought her caught in the breeze, sending a light and airy tinkle of music through the air.

They were happy and bright and relaxing, and maybe eventually she would sit down and enjoy them.

But right now she was aggravated.

"I heard you asked Troy to start taking on more around the ranch."

Ben lifted the edges of the towel, moving slow as he raised them up and rubbed them against his wet hair. "I did." His eyes skimmed down her body as she climbed the handful of steps up onto the deck. "I made an executive decision. I didn't think you'd mind."

She didn't. Ben had made countless executive decisions about the ranch hands in the day-to-day tasks he took care of. That wasn't the issue.

"Were you ever going to tell me that you needed a break?"

He lowered his arms, hands still gripping each side of the towel where it hung over his shoulders. "I just thought it would be good for us to have someone else capable of running a few things."

Liza considered continuing the discussion, but technically right now Ben was being forced into a break, so was it worth arguing about something that was essentially a moot point?

Especially when she could be focused on his mostly nakedness. "Do you feel better after your shower?"

"I do." He paused, waiting until her eyes jumped to his. "Do I look better?"

"You smell better, I know that." She forced her eyes to stay on his instead of accidentally dropping back down to the low line of his waistband. "Do you need to go get anything from your place?"

"YOUR PLACE IS the other direction."

"Is it?" Ben glanced her way as he turned out onto the road, offering a smirk.

"Smartass." Liza watched as he drove, looking for any sign that he was uncomfortable. "Are you sure you should be driving?"

"Pretty sure being a smartass doesn't make me dangerous behind the wheel." Ben looked pretty damn relaxed for a man who just fell off a roof.

"You know that's not what I meant." Liza was a little jealous of how well he was doing.

But to be fair, all of him was relatively intact. Nothing that was supposed to be inside was on the outside.

That was the worst part of what happened to her arm. She'd never get over seeing the jut of bone poking through her skin.

It still turned her stomach.

"You okay?" Ben reached out to adjust the settings on the thermostat, lowering the temperature before angling one of the middle vents right at her face. "You look like you're about to pass out."

"I'm fine." She closed her eyes and rested her head back against the seat. "It's probably just your driving."

She missed sparring with him.

She missed a lot of things.

"I'll make sure I start keepin' a bucket in the back." His tone carried a hint of amusement as the warmth of his fingers laced with hers. "Until you can start driving us around."

Liza huffed out a breath. "Who knows when the hell that will be."

"I know you love that truck of yours, but maybe you could drive around an automatic until your other arm can handle shifting."

"That would be great if I had an automatic to drive." Liza opened her eyes and rolled her head Ben's direction. "But buying another car really isn't in the budget right now."

They were finally getting ahead and the best place they could spend their money now was on quality help.

Like Troy.

Ben hit the brakes, bringing his dually to a complete stop in the middle of the country road.

"What are you doing?" Liza watched as he climbed out, wincing a bit and proving that he wasn't nearly as fine as he was trying to make it seem like he was.

Ben rounded the front of the truck, coming to her side and pulling the door open. "Come on. Let's see what you can do."

Liza stayed put. "I'm not ready."

"That sounds like we're about to have an eventful drive then." Ben reached up, holding his hands out. "Come on."

She shook her head. "It's not time yet."

Ben lifted a brow. "That what your physical therapist said?"

"We've never discussed whether or not I can drive." She leaned back as Ben reached in and snapped her belt loose.

"Probably because she figured you were already driving." Ben stepped back. "Come on out."

"I can't." Liza's voice broke, betraying her in the worst possible way.

And Ben didn't miss it.

His gaze stilled, resting on her face. "What are you afraid of?"

She swallowed down the panic tightening her throat. "Nothing."

He tipped his head. "Someone's gonna come down this road eventually and it's gonna be real frustrating to them when you won't move your truck."

"It's your truck." She looked both ways just in case Ben spoke the threat into existence. "And we're the only people who drive down this road."

"That's why it's the best place to test out ol' lefty there." He tipped his head to her arm. "If you can't do it then no one knows but me."

"I would know." She pressed her lips together, unsuccessfully catching the tiny admission.

"So what?" Ben came close, leaning into the open door. "Then we wait a little while and try again." One finger came out to tip her chin. "Just because something doesn't work the first time doesn't mean it won't the second."

Liza couldn't even focus on the double meaning she was sure his words had.

Her palms were sweating and her mouth was dry. Her skin was clammy and her stomach was rolling.

Ben's head tipped as his hand slid up the side of her face. "Talk to me. What's wrong?"

It was one of the many things that drew her to him in the first place. Ben was shockingly open to discussing her feelings back when no one else really was.

But confessing about an abusive alcoholic husband and digging into personal demons were two totally different things.

One was something she could escape.

One was not.

"You know I'll stand on the side of this road forever." Ben's eyes slowly drifted down her body. "Might even come up with a hell of a good way to pass the time."

"We can't do something like that out here."

"All I'm hearin' you talk about is how much you can't do." He leaned against the side of the opening. "That doesn't sound like the Liza Cross I know."

"You didn't call me Elizabeth." It was a strange thing to hurt her feelings, especially considering how much it pissed her off not long ago.

"I know." Ben's tone was surprisingly soft. "We're not talking about Elizabeth right now. We're talking about Liza." His smile was genuine and easy. "And there's nothing Liza Cross can't do."

She glanced down the street before resting her eyes on Ben's face. "What about Elizabeth?"

Ben held out one hand. "Elizabeth is worried she might not be able to make Liza proud."

Liza's gaze went to his hand.

Once again Ben was leading her through fear and uncertainty, just like he did the day he found her in the barn with a black eye and a busted lip, lost and alone.

She slowly put her palm against his, carefully sliding out of the truck without putting any pressure on him. She rounded the front of the cab, her heart racing as she took a careful step up onto the running board, gripping the handle just inside the door with her left hand as she managed to adjust the skirt of her dress with her right. She dropped into the seat and all the air rushed from her lungs.

Ben slowly eased into the seat beside her, the careful way he moved planting the seed of resolve in her belly.

If she could drive then he wouldn't have to. He could keep his movements to a minimum and hopefully wouldn't end up in as much pain as he appeared to be in now.

Liza grabbed her dress, making sure it was clear of the door before pulling it closed.

Which was much easier to do now that her left hand was on the correct side of the car.

Buckling up was easier too. A simple grab and stretch instead of the twist and wrestle movement she'd been trying to negotiate in the passenger's seat.

Shifting into gear was another issue though.

Using her left hand was awkward, but not impossible, and once the truck was in drive everything else she needed was well-within reach.

She eased onto the gas, managing to steer the big truck with no problem.

"I figured you could do it." Ben relaxed back in his seat, tipping the front of his cowboy hat down over his face.

"You've got an awful lot of faith in the fact that I'm not going to kill us once I have curbs and other vehicles to worry about."

"I have a lot of faith in *you*." He lifted his hat to look her way. "Both of you." He set the hat down on the console between them. "Always have."

"I'm not sure it was always warranted." She and Ben started out as friends.

An innocent connection between two people with a mutual enemy.

One who wanted nothing more than to control as much as he possibly could.

And while he tried to control Ben with money, Ed Cross's control of her was of the more physical variety.

"And why's that?" Ben was watching her closely now, but his attention had nothing to do with her driving.

"I should have left Ed a lot sooner than I did." She'd been planning it for a year. Maybe longer if she was honest.

But leaving would mean telling her parents more truth than she wanted to burden them with.

It would mean admitting failure.

That she wasn't fine.

That she wasn't even okay.

"You can't change it, Elizabeth."

"I know." She forced in a slow breath as the past she tried to pretend didn't exist made her chest squeeze tight. She turned onto the main road that led into downtown Moss Creek and came to a stop at the light.

"Look at me, Sweetheart." Ben waited until she fought her eyes his way. "Ed Cross has already controlled you for too long." He shook his head. "Don't let him do it anymore."

TWENTY-FOUR

LIZA

HE WAS RIGHT.

She hated when Ben was right.

Especially considering what happened the last time he was right.

But this time Ben was even righter than he realized.

"I don't think I'm the only one letting him control my life." Liza held Ben's gaze for just a second before the light changed and forced her eyes back to the road.

She pulled onto Main Street, easing past The Wooden Spoon as Ben sat silently beside her. Every table in the place was packed and a few groups stood outside waiting for space to open up. She couldn't be more proud of Mae and the success her friend found in her business life.

And her personal one.

"Turn in here." Ben pointed to the small public lot situated at the center of the street that provided parking for all the businesses lining downtown.

Liza did as he said, picking a spot with open spaces on each side so she didn't have to worry about hitting anyone if her parking skills were rusty.

Ben stayed quiet as they unloaded, the process proving a little easier on the driver's side than it was on the passenger's, since she could use her left arm to open the door. She was all the way out, purse draped across her shoulders when a few of the ranch hands from Red Cedar pulled in, no doubt on their way to fill up another table at The Wooden Spoon.

They climbed out of the extended cab pickup, each tipping their head her way in greeting. "Ms. Cross."

She offered a smile just as their eyes moved to her side.

"Afternoon, boys." Ben greeted the men as his hand slid into hers, holding tight as she instinctively tried to pull it free. "You on your way to go see Mae?"

The group of men looked down at their joined hands, almost in unison.

An old panic crept into her belly, clawing at the first bit of peace she'd found in years, threatening to scratch it away.

The first of the ranch hands to meet her gaze offered an easy smile. "Sure are." He leaned in. "I heard she's got that cheesecake cherry pie she makes on the menu today."

"That one's good." Liza could barely squeak it out, fighting around the squeeze that had worked its way up her throat.

"They're all good." Another of the ranch hands stepped forward, nudging his buddy. "Which is why we should get going before it's all gone."

"Good point." The ranch hand closest to her tipped his hat. "You two enjoy your afternoon."

Liza was still frozen in place as they walked away, leisurely sauntering toward the front of the buildings lining Main Street.

"Breathe." Ben's thumb dragged across her hand.

Liza nodded, but struggled to follow his direction.

Ben came closer, his other arm wrapping around her back as he rested his lips against her forehead. "It's okay."

She sucked in a breath through her nose, pulling it in as hard as she could, hoping to control the sudden onslaught of emotions threatening to make it run. "I just got scared."

Ben pulled her closer. "I know."

It shouldn't have scared her. It had been five years for God's sake. They investigated the shit out of the situation and proved beyond a reasonable doubt that she acted in self-defense. But in that moment, all she could think of was that someone was going to tell on them.

That she would be dragged in and tried. Convicted of something she didn't do.

No matter how it might look on paper.

"For a second I felt exactly the same way as I did back then." The night Ed Cross tricked her back into the farmhouse she'd still been new to town, at least by Moss Creek standards. She'd lived there for two years, but two years was nothing when everyone else had been there their whole life.

Liza wasn't yet one of them, and suspicions were strong.

The only thing that saved her was her close friendship with Mae, and the weight her friend pulled in the court of public opinion.

"So did I." Ben took a slow breath against her skin.

Liza leaned into him, closing her eyes as her heart rate finally started to slow. "I shouldn't have to feel like this. I didn't do anything wrong."

She thought eventually she would be over it. That the nightmares would subside.

But then Ed Cross would creep back in, the ghost of all he did coming along when she least expected it to smother out any happiness she'd found.

"I know that, Sweetheart." Ben leaned back, his hands coming to cradle her face. "And so does everyone else." His lips slowly brushed across hers, a move she would have never ever considered allowing in broad daylight.

Definitely not in broad daylight in downtown Moss Creek.

But in this moment she needed him. Needed Ben to help carry her through this moment of darkness, brought on by the man who'd made every decision in her life for almost a decade, half of it done from the grave.

Well fuck Ed Cross and fuck the hold he still had on her.

Liza wrapped one arm around Ben's neck, pulling his lips back to hers, keeping him close as vehicles and people passed.

No cars slowed down to gawk. No one called her a murderer from the sidewalk. No one raced to report her to Grady at the police station.

No one really seemed to care at all.

Maybe one person seemed to care.

Ben's lips curved against hers.

"Why are you smiling?"

"Because I've waited a long damn time for this town to know you're mine."

Liza scoffed, leaning back. "That's awfully presumptuous of you."

"Fine." Ben reclaimed the bit of space she put between them. "I've waited a long damn time for this town to know I'm yours."

She pressed her lips together, unsuccessfully smothering out a smile. "Is that why we're here?"

"No." Ben backed away, but immediately caught her hand with his and started walking toward the sidewalk.

Without offering any further explanation.

"Are you going to tell me why we're here?" Liza's eyes scanned the street. She was still expecting someone to be shocked by the sight of them together, but not a single person who crossed their path batted an eye.

"I could, but what would be the fun in that?" Ben stopped in front of a small storefront and pulled open the door. The air was immediately saturated with the scent of sugar and spice.

Liza glanced up at the awning over their head. The Baking Rack was printed across it in scrolling gold letters. A matching design was displayed across the front window, the logo there completed with a set of swirl-topped cupcakes.

"I might have heard something about you being interested in Dianna's mousse."

"I wonder where you would've heard something like that?" There was only one person that could have come from, and it only raised more questions. "I didn't realize you were close with Maryann Pace."

"Sweetheart, everyone is close with Maryann Pace. Whether they like it or not." Ben rested one hand on her lower back, urging her into the small space. "And we have a common interest."

"You do?" Liza leaned to peek into the first glass-front case. "And what is that?"

"You."

A woman wearing a white apron dusted with cocoa powder came out from the back room. A name tag fixed to the apron identified her as Dianna, the owner of The Baking Rack. Her shiny dark hair was pulled up at the top of her head, twisted into an elaborately effortless messy bun, the kind only women with insanely thick hair could accomplish. Her eyes and the long lashes surrounding them were just as dark, and framed by perfectly arched brows. She wasn't tall or short, but that was the only unremarkable thing about her.

Dianna was unquestionably stunning.

"Ben." Her whole face lit up. "I haven't seen you all week. How are you?"

"I'm good." Ben leaned against the counter between him and Dianna. "Looks like business is booming."

Dianna continued to beam at him. "I can hardly keep up." She pointed toward one of the trays of cookies in the case. "I have to shove the baking sheets in the deep freezer to cool them off so I can get them out here."

Liza peeked through the cases. There were tons of labels marking empty cake stands and crumb filled trays, but as far as actual inventory went, things were looking pretty low.

"I guess it's a good thing I put my order in early then." Ben looked completely at ease conversing with the bakery owner.

"It pays to be smart." Dianna continued to smile, her face glowing as all her focus remained on the cowboy across from her.

But Ben just looked like his normal self, carrying on a conversation with a person who crossed his path on a regular basis.

Which sort of made Liza wonder if he was oblivious to the fact that Dianna was clearly into him.

And if he was oblivious to the fact that Dianna was into him, how many other women in Moss Creek were lusting after him while Ben was completely unaware?

Probably a lot.

"I guess it does." Ben's eyes slowly came Liza's way. "Dianna, have you met Liza Cross?"

Dianna's eyes slowly came her way, widening just a little bit and proving Liza's suspicion that the other woman hadn't really noticed she was there. "Oh my gosh," her smile only faltered for a second then came right back, "I've heard so much about you."

Well that could go either way.

Liza managed to smile. "And I have enjoyed quite a bit of your chocolate cake."

"Maryann said that you loved it." Her eyes went back to Ben, but this time they only stayed a second before coming right back to Liza. "That explains the mousse order." She backed away from the case. "I'll run and get it real quick so you guys can go do," she took a little breath, "whatever you're doing."

"It's a nice place, isn't it?" Ben watched Liza as she continued to peruse the bare cases, trying to look as interested as possible in anything besides the beautiful woman who had probably been flirting with him on a regular basis.

She couldn't blame her, not even a little bit.

Ben was handsome. And charming. And kind.

And a whole list of other things that Liza worked hard not to think about.

Until recently. Very recently.

But Dianna probably thought about those things a lot, and it made her feel.... Guilty.

"Here it is." Dianna came out of the back room carrying a brown paper bag emblazoned with the same logo from the front window. She set it on the counter before dropping in two plastic spoons and a little stack of paper napkins. "I threw in a couple of cookies that accidentally broke in half." She kept her smile and her focus on Liza. "I'm so glad I finally got to meet you."

"I feel the same way." Liza leaned closer. "What would I have to do to order one of those cakes?"

Dianna's brows jumped up. "Do you know when you want it?"

"Maryann has done a lot for me while I have been recovering from an accident, and I would love to show her my appreciation." Not only that, but she knew what it was like to be a newcomer in a town where everyone knows everyone else by name, and while it was clear Dianna probably didn't need it, Liza wanted to offer support to her business.

Dianna rubbed her lips together. "If it's for Maryann Pace then could I make a suggestion?"

"Of course."

"Maryann mostly bought the chocolate cake because she

knows you love chocolate." Dianna pointed to an empty cake stand with a label that said *lemon supreme layer*. "But the lemon is her favorite."

Liza's smile came easily. "Thank you." She tapped the window in front of the cake stand. "Let's order her one of those then."

Ten minutes later she had an order placed for Maryann's favorite cake, a few more mangled cookies added to her bag, and a cowboy who definitely had plenty of options on her arm.

"She's beautiful." There was really no other way to describe Dianna, and it wasn't just referencing her looks.

"She is." Ben's hand was warm in hers. "She's also one hell of a businesswoman."

"And an amazing baker." There was probably a list a mile long of the positive attributes Dianna possessed.

Which led to Liza's next question. "Why didn't you ask her out?"

"Are we back to pretending we don't understand certain truths about each other?" His answer was not really an answer.

"I guess maybe I don't completely know what the truth is."

Ben stopped, turning to face her right in front of the only jewelry store downtown. "Then you haven't been paying attention, because I've made my truth pretty clear." He pressed one finger under her chin. "There will never be anyone else for me, Elizabeth. Not ever." His fingers slid down the front of her neck to tap against her breastbone. "Just like there will never be anyone else for you."

"How do you know that?" He seemed so certain, completely confident in spite of the fact that they effectively spent five years apart.

"Well, the fact that you have *fuck off* written across your forehead is a pretty good indicator."

For some reason she slapped her hand against her forehead, like the words were literally there and not just figuratively. "I do not."

"You absolutely do, and I appreciate the hell out of it." Ben's lips teased a smile. "I really didn't want to have to go around beating the shit out of all the men in town."

"I have to act a certain way so the men who work for us will listen to me."

Ben laughed, long and loud, and right in her face. "If that's what you tell yourself."

"Stop laughing. It's true."

"You're absolutely right. It's completely true." Ben moved one arm across her shoulders and started walking again. "You should keep doing it."

Liza rolled her eyes up toward the sky. "Are you actually trying to argue that a bunch of cowboys would have listened to me if I'd been sweet to them?"

"I'm not sure I should tell you this, considering the fact that I still have a hell of a lot of pain in my ribs, and that might make it a little bit less comfortable for me to go around kicking ass, but I can guarantee you that if you had been sweet you probably could've gotten a hell of a lot more work out of them." Ben fished the keys to his truck out of his pocket and passed them over to her. "Of course, you might've also had to carry a stick to smack them up the side of their heads when they tried to put the moves on you, but that would've been fun to watch too."

"See?" She pointed at him. "That's what I was trying to avoid."

"My point exactly."

"I don't think that was your point."

"It was. If your reasons for being," Ben hesitated.

"Bitchy."

"Your words, not mine." He opened the driver's door. "If you were acting that way thinking it would make them more likely to listen to you, then my point was that you were going about it the wrong way." He held out one hand, letting her use it for added support as she climbed up into the seat. "But you weren't acting that way to make them more likely to listen to you. You were acting that way to make them less likely to hit on you."

"So you're saying I should have been nice, let them hit on me, and then smacked them with a stick."

Ben grinned at her. "Exactly."

TWENTY-FIVE

BEN

HE SHOULDN'T BE so amused at the thought of Liza with a stick and a sweet smile, but it might have made the years pass a little quicker.

"I feel like we would have gone through at least twice as many ranch hands that way."

"I bet you would have been surprised." Ben shut the door, closing Liza into his truck before heading around to the opposite side. He slid their bag of goodies from The Baking Rack into the back seat before climbing into the passenger side, being careful not to jostle his ribs any more than absolutely necessary.

Unfortunately, even only doing what was absolutely necessary still caused a decent amount of pain. Pain he must not have concealed as well as he thought.

"How are you feeling?" Liza already looked skeptical, like she was pretty sure he was going to lie.

But what kind of an example would that be? "I feel like someone beat the shit out of me with a baseball bat."

"We should have stayed home." Liza started the truck, almost managing it with just her right hand before having to add a little extra torque with her left. "I should have made you stay in bed."

"While I don't actually hate the thought of that, I didn't want to stand Dianna up." He'd had a whole plan for this damn chocolate mousse, and at this point most of it was shot to hell.

And maybe that wasn't the worst thing that could have happened. He didn't get to surprise Liza with the treat Maryann assured him was one of Liza's favorite things, but he did get to do something he never thought he would.

Publicly make it clear that they were together.

"Something tells me she would have easily been able to sell your abandoned chocolate mousse." Liza shook her head as they waited on a gap in traffic. "There was nothing left in those cases."

"I think maybe Miss Dianna understands the art of flirting with cowboys."

"I didn't see a stick." Liza eased out onto the road looking a little more confident than she did when he first convinced her to get into the driver's seat.

"She doesn't need a stick. The fear of not being allowed in her bakery again is probably enough to keep them all in line." He'd seen everyone in Moss Creek in Dianna's bakery, and just about all of them were sweet on Miss Dianna. Old, young, men, women. They all loved her.

"I could see that." Liza slowed as she went past The Wooden Spoon, her brows coming together. "That probably worked for Mae too."

"I think anyone with two brain cells is smart enough to have a healthy dose of fear when it comes to Mae." Liza's best friend was hell on wheels.

They were two peas in a pod. Thick as thieves.

"She's really not that scary once you get to know her." Liza turned at the light and headed out of town.

"I would argue she's scarier once you get to know her." Ben reached across the console to slide his hand into Liza's. "Then the filter's gone and she tells you what she really thinks."

He'd been schooled by Mae more than a few times over the years.

Usually in regards to Liza.

"It sounds like there's a story there." Liza relaxed a little as the congestion of town got farther behind them.

"Let's just say she never held back when she thought I needed to do something to make your life easier."

Liza's expression went soft. "I think she just worries about me."

"I know she worries about you. Like a damn mother hen." If Liza seemed upset one day at lunch then Mae was calling him asking why. If she didn't laugh right at a joke, Mae was calling asking him what happened to put her friend in a bad mood.

"I used to worry about her too." Liza was quiet for a minute. "For a while we were sort of in the same boat." She took a little breath. "Then her boat came back."

He hadn't really thought through the way Boone Pace's reappearance in Mae's life would affect Liza.

Mostly because he saw it as another bit of hope to cling to. When Mae forgave Boone, it meant that maybe Liza could forgive him.

"Were you surprised when they got back together?"

Liza shook her head. "No."

"Really?" *Everyone* had been surprised when Boone and Mae got back together, including Boone, and probably Mae.

Liza lifted her shoulder in a shrug. "She still loved him, even after everything."

"I'm not sure she knew that." He'd seen Mae point a knife at Boone, definitely not something you would expect from a woman in love.

"I think she did. I think that's part of the reason why she was so mad at him." Liza chewed her lip for a second. "Because life would have been easier if she didn't love him."

Ben sat with that for a minute, letting it settle. "You said you and Mae were in the same boat."

Liza stared straight ahead, eyes completely focused on the road in front of them. "We were."

Ben did his best not to react to the revelation.

He took a slow breath, putting his eyes in the same spot Liza's were, watching as the dually ate up the road between them and Cross Creek.

Liza stayed silent the rest of the trip and he let her. Pushing her for more information, more explanation, didn't seem right.

Especially when she'd already offered so much.

Instead of going to the farmhouse she drove right past,

heading down the narrow lane that led to the small house he'd called home since moving to Montana looking for a life he chose.

One that ended up having a hold on him he could never seem to shake.

Liza parked in front of his place, sitting for a minute and staring at his little cabin in the woods. "It feels like forever since I've been back here."

"It does." She'd been in his home only once. The night they both realized what was between them was so much more than friendship.

It was the same night Liza packed her bags, thinking they would both be able to leave Ed Cross, and this place, behind.

They were wrong.

Ben opened his door just as tires crunched down the lane behind them. Liza looked his way. "You expecting company?"

"No." He climbed out just as Troy's truck pulled into view. The ranch hand parked right behind Ben's truck in the narrow drive, looking a little surprised when it was Liza who got out of the driver's seat.

He tipped his head her way. "Ms. Cross."

Her brows went together as she closed the door and headed Troy's direction. "Is everything okay?"

Troy's eyes slid to Ben before going back to Liza. "Not sure."

Liza's head tipped to one side. "What does that mean?"

Troy pulled off his hat, raking one hand through his hair before reseating it. "Means I'm a little concerned."

Ben didn't know Troy well, but he was familiar enough with the younger man to know he was usually a pretty easy-going guy. It didn't bode well if something had Troy concerned. "What about?"

He was fairly sure he knew what, or better who, Troy was worried about. He'd noticed Darrell doing his best to skip out on any and all work possible.

No doubt everyone else was noticing too, which was probably causing unrest among the rest of the ranch hands.

When one man wasn't pulling his weight everyone suffered. It was drilled into his head from the minute he was big enough to help on his family's ranch.

But not everyone was raised with the same work ethic.

Not that his family's singular focus was healthy. It wasn't.

But it instilled a sense of responsibility that served him, and Cross Creek, well.

"I wasn't happy about what happened yesterday." Troy went to the open bed of his truck and reached in. "I went back up on the roof of the bunkhouse today, hopin' I could figure something out."

Ben turned toward Liza, tipping his head toward his cabin. "Why don't you go inside?"

Her jaw dropped open. "No." She moved in at his side, crowding toward the bed of Troy's truck. "This is my ranch too, and if something is going on then I want to know about it."

Troy pulled out four shingles and slapped them down on the ground between them, side by side. "All four of these shingles pulled right out."

Ben stared down at what amounted to asphalt death traps. "You shouldn't have gone up on that roof alone." He'd been lucky as hell when one of the shingles broke free under his boot and Troy was there to slow his appointment with the ground.

"I was tied up." Troy tried to brush it off.

"So was I." He'd been sure his knot was secure. Positive the rope would hold him if he needed it to.

Not that he expected it would come to that.

"Why did you bring these?" Liza crouched down, her eyes narrowing at the shingles lined on the ground. "Are they ruined?"

"No. They're in perfect condition." Troy crouched down, pointing to the neat line of holes just above the tabs. "But they were sure missing some nails."

"Missing nails?" Ben started to bend, but an instant jolt of pain had him settling for looking down. "Where in the hell did they go?"

"That's a good question." Troy picked up the next shingle in line and held it up, offering it to Ben for a closer look. "You can see where they were originally there." He shook his head. "But there was nothin' in them when I went up there."

"That doesn't make any sense." The only way that many nails would be missing was if—

"Someone pulled all the nails out." Liza slowly stood, her eyes moving from the shingles to Ben.

Troy propped his hands on his hips. "That's the only thing I could come up with too. No way could the wind do that."

"Why would someone pull a bunch of nails out of the roof?" The bunkhouse wasn't anything fancy, but it was clean and offered anything a single man could need.

Liza looked Troy over. "What do you think happened?"

Troy shook his head as he reached into his pocket to dig out a toothpick. "I'm not one hundred percent sure."

"But you have suspicions." Liza slowly straightened. "What have you heard?"

Troy pinched the toothpick between his teeth. "There's some hands upset that they aren't gettin' where they want to go."

"There's always hands upset that they're not getting where they want to go." Liza stood tall. "Because they all want to get somewhere that doesn't require hard work."

"I would say that's true in most cases." Troy paused. "But I think you've got a few right now who are carrying more than their fair share of the weight around here, and a few who are doing everything they can to sit on their lazy asses as much as possible."

Liza glanced at Ben before focusing back on Troy. "Like who?"

"Darrell for starters." Ben could start that list for her.

"He's got a couple buddies too." Troy leaned against his truck. "They're the ones doin' ninety-nine percent of the bitching."

"Not surprising." He'd been considering cleaning house but Liza's injury derailed those plans, pulling his attention away from the ranch and onto the woman in charge of it. "I should have cut him loose a month ago."

"Probably. He's causing all sorts of problems." Troy's upper lip lifted. "Outside of his bedtime habits."

"Wh—"

Ben shook his head, cutting Liza off. "You don't want to know."

Liza cringed. "Fine." She huffed out a breath. "We talked about Dustin earlier, but who else do you think is doing well?"

Troy shifted on his feet, eyes going to Ben like he was worried he might be overstepping.

"I'm always interested in hearing second opinions." Normally he wasn't. Not where Cross Creek was concerned.

He was protective as hell of the ranch, and for a long time he pretended it was because he had invested a little of the money he inherited when his siblings bought him out of the ranch.

Money that he eventually learned went to pay off at least a few of Ed Cross's gambling debts.

"As is Ms. Cross." Ben wrapped one arm around Liza's shoulders, pulling her into his side.

To his credit, Troy didn't bat an eye. "Colt. Zach. Dustin." He offered Liza a grin. "And me of course."

She almost managed not to smile back, but her lips eventually lifted. "Of course." Liza took a deep breath, her smile slipping as her eyes fell back to the shingles. "So someone is pissed that we didn't give them a raise."

"Someone is pissed that *I* didn't give them a raise." Ben pulled her a little closer. "They probably assumed that while you were recovering I was the one making all the decisions."

"But I'm not recovering anymore." Liza leaned into him.

She had to be tired.

Tired of constantly having to do everything just right to avoid judgment.

Tired of convincing everyone she was strong enough to run the ranch.

Tired of having to wake up and prove herself day after day.

"We'll handle it." Ben tipped his head toward the shingles. "Anyone else know what you found up there?"

Troy shook his head. "Not a soul."

"Good." Men didn't react well to being called out on their bullshit, so the best way to handle this was to do a clean sweep, removing any problems before they caught wind that they might have been found out. "Keep it that way." Ben backed toward his house, taking Liza with him. "Keep your ears open. Let me know if you hear anything else."

Troy tipped his head. "Will do."

Ben watched as Troy loaded the shingles into his truck and pulled away.

"That's not good." Liza's frown was deep and strong.

And he could almost see her trying to figure out how to string whoever loosened those shingles up by their toenails.

"I'll handle it." He opened the back door of his truck and pulled out the bag from Dianne's.

She scoffed, looking like he'd just taken away any bit of fun left in the world. "Why do you get to handle it?"

Ben closed the door and took her hand in his. "Because I'm less likely to end up killing them."

TWENTY-SIX

LIZA

IT WAS A simple answer. One she could deny if she really wanted to.

But chances were good that Ben was right.

She might just kill whoever was responsible for Ben's slide off the roof, and they'd already sacrificed so much to keep her out of jail the last time that happened.

But the thought of whoever loosened those shingles getting off with only losing their job on the ranch didn't sit well. "Maybe we should call Grady."

"And tell him what?" Ben led her up the stairs to the narrow porch that ran across the whole front of the small cabin he'd pieced together from a few disintegrating buildings that used to be spaced around the property Ed Cross bought sight unseen, thinking he was too smart to ever get taken to the cleaners. "That one of our ranch hands was pissed and set one of our buildings up to leak, thinking they could argue for better wages?"

"Is that what you think happened?" It was a depressing thought to consider that someone who worked at their sides would be willing to risk someone's life to get what they wanted.

Depressing, but not unbelievable.

"It makes more sense than anything." Ben unlocked the door to his home and pushed it wide.

She wasn't sure that particular scenario made more sense than *anything*, but it was something she could see happening.

Unfortunately.

"So we just fire th—" Liza made it two steps into Ben's house before her brain lost track of the conversation. "Oh wow."

This is not what she remembered this place looking like.

"Gotta say," Ben came in behind her, his voice low in her ear, "I don't hate that reaction."

Liza couldn't make her feet budge from where they stalled out.

She expected to walk back in time when she came in here. Had been preparing herself for what revisiting the past might dredge up.

But there was nothing familiar about the space around her.

What used to be as rustic as rustic got, was now sleek and shiny. A sort of modern-meets-cowboy esthetic that centered around leather and wood and steel. "You've been busy."

"Didn't have much else to do." Ben sat the bag from The Baking Rack onto the dining table set longways up the right side of the house, taking up the space just in front of the open kitchen.

"It seemed like you had plenty to do." Ben worked harder than anyone she'd ever met, spending nearly every waking minute of his day on tasks around the ranch.

But from the looks of his house, maybe Ben was awake more than she realized.

"It didn't do me any good to just sit here, Elizabeth." He watched as she wandered into the living room portion of the main part of the house. "I had to do something so I didn't go crazy."

She understood completely. "And here I was eating up my free time watching terrible television."

"I'm not much for the TV."

Liza turned to the back wall. Where most people would have a television stand, Ben had cabinets topped with bookcases. The shelves weren't empty, but they definitely didn't hold enough books to entertain someone for five years.

The actual piece of furniture however, appeared like it took up more than a little bit of time.

CROSSING THE LINE

She ran her hand over the smooth finish of the wood. "You made these."

She didn't have to ask. The odds were pretty good that Ben made just about everything inside this cabin. The man was about as skilled of a carpenter as you could find.

"I did." He continued to silently watch as she moved around his space, looking at the world he'd created.

"They're beautiful." The craftsmanship was impeccable. Each piece fit together perfectly.

"Thank you."

Liza continued her path around the space, over the cow hide covering the smooth polish of the floor. Past the coffee table stacked with hardback books and a pair of reading glasses. A line of framed photographs on the wall above the couch caught her eyes. She leaned closer, trying to get a better look at the large groups of people that seemed to fill each image. "This is your family." Another thing she didn't have to question.

In the many long nights they spent together in the barn, waiting out Ed Cross's frequent alcohol-fueled rages, she and Ben talked about the lives they had before coming to Moss Creek.

And while Ben's childhood wasn't bad or abusive, it also wasn't filled with love and understanding and acceptance, the way hers was.

Liza stopped in front of the center photograph. A man and a woman stood side-by-side, expressions hard and unyielding as they stared out at the camera. "They didn't even smile for pictures?"

She knew Ben's parents weren't particularly kind people, but the faces in front of her didn't even look tolerant, let alone like the type of people who should be rearing ten children.

"I don't know that I ever saw either of them smile." Ben came in at her side, his expression impossible to read as he stared at his parents.

"Do you talk to any of them?"

Ben shrugged. "I call on Christmas. Check and see how they're doing."

"And how are they doing?" Liza understood that sometimes

moving was inevitable, but she couldn't imagine completely losing contact with her parents and sister.

But that was because she loved her parents and sister and they loved her back.

"Fine, I guess." There was a certain amount of sadness in the way he looked at the photographs of his family. "All they want to talk about is the ranch."

"Ours or theirs?"

"Theirs." Ben's eyes dropped. "It's all that's ever mattered to them."

Liza leaned into his side, wrapping her arm around his waist.

There was no point in telling him she was sorry, she'd said it a million times before.

There was no point in telling him he deserved better, hopefully he already knew that.

All she could do was be there for him.

Offer support he wouldn't get from the people who should be providing it.

"They all get together every year for Christmas." Ben sucked in a deep breath. "I didn't find out about it until this past year."

Liza tipped her head back, looking up at his face. "They didn't invite you?"

He shook his head.

Maybe he was right not letting her be the one to deal with the problematic ranch hands, because she did seem to jump right to violence when someone upset her.

The way she was doing right now.

"Why not?" How far was it from Montana to Texas?

She could probably fly down, dish out a couple of well-deserved one-armed ass kickings, and fly right back. Troy was making breakfast anyway, so it's not like there was anything stopping her.

"I turned my back on the ranch, Sweetheart. That's all that matters to them."

"But you're their son." And he was Ben. He was kind and smart and thoughtful and patient. Everything a parent could want in a child.

"In my family everyone has a purpose. I no longer serve my purpose."

Now she definitely wanted to fly to Texas.

She might even take Maryann Pace with her. Something told Liza that woman would be one hell of a wingwoman on a trip like that.

"What was the name of your family's ranch again?" She tried to sound casual, like she wasn't already forming a plot. "I forget."

Ben's somber mood seemed to slip away. He huffed out a little chuckle, shaking his head as his eyes came to hers. "I'm not sure how I survived as long as I did without you."

She'd never been angrier with Ed Cross than she was in this moment.

Not when he smacked her around, giving her so many bruises that she lost count. Not when he said horrible things to her, doing everything he could to wear her down until she broke.

Not even when he came at her, wild eyed and smiling, slashing across her belly with the same knife he'd held to her throat countless times.

"I don't like that look in your eyes, Sweetheart." Ben's gaze turned wary where it fixed on hers.

Like he was a little concerned about what she might do next.

Liza turned to face him. "What look?"

She was caught in an odd situation right now, torn between the urge to rage about the unfairness of all that Ben had been through—

And the desire to make up for her part in it.

"The one that might be homicidal." He took a little step back.

Liza shook her head. "I don't think that's what it is."

The need to punish the people who didn't love Ben the way they should have was fleeing fast, leaving more room for the more interesting of the emotions she was juggling.

Ben lifted one brow as he took a full step back, moving toward the front of the house. "Then I'm not sure I can handle whatever else you're thinkin'."

Liza slowly smiled as she moved in close to him, pressing the tips of her fingers into the firm plane of his chest. "Then you don't know what I'm thinking."

He'd taken care of her. Even when she fought him.

Even when she swore she didn't need his help in spite of everything proving she did.

She added a little pressure to his chest, not so much it would hurt his irritated ribs, but enough to get Ben's boots moving in a direction he probably considered safe. "I don't like thinking of you being back here all alone."

"You were alone too." His argument wasn't as solid as he thought.

"Not like you were." She had Mae and Nora and Clara and Camille. Her parents and Dawn.

Plenty of people to talk to and rely on.

Ben didn't.

"It was fine." He slowly moved across the floor, dark eyes staying on hers.

"That sounds like something I would say." She smiled a little at the opportunity to finally give him back some of what he'd been dishing out for the past few days. "And you get awful bossy when I do it."

"That your way of warning me that you're about to get bossy?" His legs hit the back of one of the armchairs flanking the front window of the living room portion of the house.

Liza dragged her fingers down his middle, over the firm line of his stomach. "Sit down."

Ben watched her for a second. Long enough to make her worry he might try to be difficult.

But then he slowly worked his way into the wide seat, carefully leaning back into the buttery brown leather.

"Undo your pants."

Again he lifted a brow.

But did what she requested, his long fingers working open the buckle of his belt before flipping the button free and lowering the zipper.

She didn't have to prompt him for the next part.

Ben shoved down the fabric, working the tines of the zipper far enough away to remove any risk they might pose, before freeing the hard line of his cock. He gripped it tight, working his fist down the length a few times before moving both hands out to the side, palms up. "Come here."

His voice was rough and raw, tempting her to abandon her original plan.

Ben wouldn't mind.

But that was part of the problem.

Liza shook her head. "No."

She slowly dropped down, going to her knees in front of him, watching as his eyes followed.

He'd done so much for her. All of it without expecting anything in return.

And part of her wanted to give that back to him, provide without taking.

But another part of her wanted to watch him come undone because of something she did.

It was a dangerously heady thought. One that kept her eyes on his as she slid her lips over him.

Around him.

Ran her tongue along the tight skin and velvety head of his straining dick.

Swallowed him down as far as he would go.

Over and over.

Ben's hands came to her hair, holding it back as she sank onto him, cheeks pulling tight as she eased away, dragging out a groan that was like a drug, making her head spin and her heart race.

This man was so strong. Powerful and capable.

And right now he was at her mercy. Driven completely by her and what she offered.

It was intoxicating.

Addicting.

Giving it up wasn't an option.

Giving him up wasn't one either.

He was hers.

And she was happy to prove it.

Liza wrapped one hand around his shaft, adding the squeeze of her fingers under the pull of her lips, setting a pace that pulled his hips off the cushions and had his fingers winding tighter in her hair.

"Elizabeth." Her name rushed from his mouth and his lungs, riding a breath as it ran free.

She lifted her eyes, meeting his as she worked her way back down, pressing until she was filled with him before stopping, keeping him there until he swore, grinding out a curse as she pulled away and immediately sank back down, fist chasing lips along his slick shaft in swift strokes as he went unbelievably hard.

"Fuck." Ben fought her downward momentum. "I can't stop it."

She pressed down over him one last time, pulling in her cheeks as the first heat of his release broke free, watching as his head dropped back and his jaw clenched tight.

Ben's face stayed tipped up toward the ceiling, chest heaving as he tried to catch his breath.

One of his hands slipped from her hair, moving to grab the front of her dress as he attempted to drag her to him. "Come here."

"I don't think so." Liza backed out of his hold. There was no way she was letting him take this tiny victory from her.

Ben was already too far ahead. She needed every opportunity possible to even out things between them.

Because there was no way she was letting this be a one-sided relationship.

Which was going to be an uphill battle considering Ben wasn't used to anyone taking care of him. Looking out for him.

Being there for him.

It went all the way back to his own parents.

No one was ever only on his side.

And she was going to be that. Come hell or high water she would give Ben just as much as he gave her.

His head lifted. "Did you just tell me no?"

"Seems like I did." Liza backed away a little more, just in case he decided to try to make a grab for her.

"Then you must not know what I'm thinkin'." His eyes slowly dragged down the deep blue sundress covering her body.

"I know exactly what you're thinking." She turned toward the table, hoping that refocusing her attention would reduce the temptation to give into him.

Because it was strong.

"I don't think so." Ben shifted around, adjusting his jeans. "Otherwise you'd be over here letting me return the favor."

"I don't want you to return the favor." Liza pulled out a container of Dianna's mousse from the bag and popped the lid off, dragging her tongue across the top of the smooth, rich chocolate.

Ben's nostrils flared as he watched her savor the dessert. "I don't think I like that plan."

She smirked at him, licking her lips. "I don't think I care what you like."

TWENTY-SEVEN

BEN

"I'M NOT SURE I can handle you getting up this early all the time." Liza came in from his bedroom wearing one of his t-shirts, yawning wide as she smashed at her messy hair.

"This is what time I always get up." Ben poured out the first cup of coffee and passed it her way before turning to flip the set of pancakes lined down the electric griddle on his counter.

"But do you really *need* to get up this early?" She yawned again before swallowing down a long drag of coffee.

"I guess I'm just used to it." Ben set down the spatula in his hand and reached out to grab the front of Liza's shirt, using the hold to drag her close. He pressed a kiss to her lips. "Good morning."

She leaned to peek at the food cooking. "I guess it can be good." Her eyes dragged down his bare chest, moving over the bruises still blooming from his fall. "How are you feeling?"

"Not too bad all things considered." He went back to their breakfast, sliding the first set of cakes off onto a plate before pouring the second batch onto the hot surface. "But I'll be a lot better once I do some house cleaning."

"When's that happening?" Liza stayed close at his side, sipping on her coffee as she watched him work.

"The sooner the better." Things might be a little rough at first, but he couldn't help but think they might also be easier without the dead weight holding them back and tearing up their property thinking it will earn them the raise they don't want to gain through hard work or reliability.

Liza grabbed the coffee pot and topped off his cup. "So, today?"

"That's what I'm thinkin'." Ben turned over the last of the pancakes and went to work plating up the sausage he'd already cooked.

"I'll go with you." Liza sounded a little too set on the plan.

"I don't think that's a good idea." He didn't want her to be involved in this in any way, that way her hands were clean.

Just in case one of these assholes decided to be a dick, and considering they weren't even smart enough to think through the ramifications of taking all the nails out of a set of shingles, there was a good chance they'd do something stupid again.

"Why?" Liza crossed her arms, leaning back against the stainless-steel counter. "Because it's what's best for me?"

"That's exactly why." Ben added a stack of pancakes to the first plate and took it to the long table he'd built a few years ago, thinking maybe he'd eventually be able to host the kind of card nights the Pace brothers enjoyed with their ranch hands.

"I don't need you to always protect me, Ben." Liza's voice was surprisingly soft and it lifted his eyes to meet hers.

"I know that." He couldn't stop the sweep of his gaze as it slipped down her long frame.

No one would accuse her of being a damsel in distress. Not ever.

"But a tiger doesn't change his stripes, Sweetheart." He tipped his head toward her breakfast. "Now sit your ass down and eat."

"Have you always been this bossy?"

"No." He gave her a wink as he passed on his way to collect his own food. "You just bring out the best in me."

She always had. Liza opened him up after spending his whole life closed off, thinking that's just how people lived.

But when you're facing a woman spilling all her secrets through tears and fear, it's pretty hard to keep your mouth shut.

"So you're saying that you plan to continue being bossy." Liza lowered into one of the chairs. "And it's all my fault."

"That sounds about right." Ben sat in the chair right beside her. "What's on your schedule for the day?"

"Changing the subject." She took a bite of sausage. "Smart."

"I have my moments."

Liza pursed her lips. "I was thinking I might go into town and run a few errands." She leaned his way. "If you don't mind me using your truck."

"I don't mind at all." Ben was happy to offer Liza a little bit of the freedom she'd been missing. "It's got a full tank."

"So I can go all sorts of places." She grinned, looking light and happy for the first time in a long time.

"You can go wherever you want, Sweetheart." He reached out to smooth down a bit of her hair. "As long as you promise to come back."

Her smile softened. "I can come back here?"

"Of course." He was a little surprised by the question. "You can come here whenever you want."

Liza was quiet for a minute as she poked at her stack of pancakes. "I was thinking maybe we could stay here again tonight."

"You want to stay here?" He felt a little guilty last night when she didn't have her own bed to sleep in and access to all the things that a nighttime required.

"Um," Liza's eyes wouldn't meet his as she continued to stab her flapjacks, "I don't really like the farmhouse."

It wasn't difficult to connect the dots. "I was hoping that it hadn't been too hard on you to have to keep living there."

"It's fine." She rubbed her lips together. "I mean it doesn't even really look like it did back then."

He'd worked hard over the years not to think too hard on the fallout Liza would have to deal with after Ed's death.

If he had he wouldn't have been able to stay away from her, and he had to stay away from her. Suspicion was already there when the city girl killed her husband and inherited everything he had.

Which most people didn't realize wasn't much.

If they suspected she'd also fallen in love with the ranch hand who owned the rest of said inheritance?

Liza would have had a hell of a time convincing everyone, police included, that she acted in self-defense.

"Pack up your stuff and bring it back here." He might not have been able to save her from everything she'd been through since Ed Cross walked into her life, but he could save her from this.

"You want me to pack up everything I own and bring it back here?" She looked from side to side, her eyes skimming his fully-furnished space. "I'm not sure where you would put it all."

"I'm sure I can come up with something." Ben took a bite of his breakfast, the thought of having Liza here at the home he built from the ground up settling him in a way he couldn't explain. "And if I can't then I'll build it."

She reached out, sliding her fingers down his arm where it rested on the table between them. "You don't have to do that."

It was one of many confessions he'd given her during one of the long nights they spent together, talking about the lives that led them each to Moss Creek. "I don't do it because I feel like I have to."

Somehow there was a line dividing his responsibilities at Cross Creek and the ones he carried when he worked his family's ranch. They were almost the same, in load and expectation.

But it was different here.

"I don't want to exploit your skills, Ben." Liza's touch stilled. "I never did. That's why I tried to do so much on my own."

It was one more thing that wasn't easy to hear. "You didn't have to worry about that." He dropped his fork to his plate and spun in his seat, catching her face in his hands as he turned to face her. "I know you would never take advantage of me."

A lot of things had changed, but he knew that never would. It just wasn't in her nature to take advantage of anyone, let alone him.

"I mean," her lips quirked, "I might take advantage of you under the right circumstances."

He pulled her close, bringing her lips to his in a kiss that started off a few steps ahead and only gained speed. He hauled her up from her chair, easily ignoring the stab of pain the movement brought with it. "It's pretty hard to take advantage of the willing."

Liza laughed, her arm looping around his neck as he walked her toward his room. "Aren't we supposed to be working or something?"

"I think we've both worked more than enough." He had her halfway down the hall when someone knocked on his door, sending Liza scooting closer, her eyes going wide as they filled with an old panic.

"It's okay." Ben kept her close as he leaned to peek out the front window. "It's just Troy." It didn't even matter who it was. They didn't have any reason to keep hiding.

But some things were easier to get past than others.

Troy knocked again

Liza eased out of his hold. "I should probably get ready to start my day since yours came to find you." She tapped one finger in the center of his chest. "Then maybe later I'll come take advantage of you."

"YOU SURE YOU don't need backup?" Troy walked along beside him, sticking close as Ben left the mess hall in search of the trio of ranch hands he intended to send back out into the big, beautiful world of unemployment. "I've seen these guys get pretty out of control when they're not getting their way."

Ben stopped, turning to Troy. "Why hasn't anyone said anything?"

Troy hesitated.

"Just tell me."

"A lot of the hands look at this as a dead-end job, so they're not too worried about helping you improve the environment."

It was a brutal truth. One he should have seen coming. "That's my fault."

He hadn't done much to foster a sense of camaraderie among the ranch hands. He'd focused more on busting his ass and making sure the work got done, expecting everyone else to do the same.

"Hell." Ben scrubbed one hand down his face.

He left Texas, walked away from ownership in a successful ranch, all because he hated the way things were done.

And he'd ended up doing things exactly the same way. Maybe he wasn't having kids and dragging them into a work-driven life that lacked love or empathy, but he'd done it with every ranch hand that came through Cross Creek. All the while expecting them to commit themselves fully and give it their best. "I fucked up."

"Don't be too hard on yourself." Troy slapped him on the back "I don't think there's anything you could have done to make the guys you're dealing with now act any better, but you might have heard about their bullshit from the get-go."

"Maybe that would've made all the difference." Maybe he and Liza wouldn't have gone through so many ranch hands over the years. Maybe he could have been having those card games at the table in his cabin, and the years he spent without her would have passed a little more quickly.

Troy shrugged. "Maybe, but beating yourself up about it now isn't going to change anything."

Ben focused on the younger man. He'd assumed Troy was too green to really have much to offer. How many other times had he misjudged a man with potential, all because he didn't live up to the unattainable standards his family ingrained in him?

"I'm sorry I called you bacon boy."

Troy's brows came together. "You never called me bacon boy."

"Not to your face." Ben turned toward the barn where he was fairly confident Darrell and his cohorts were hanging out, hiding from the day's work. "Come on. Let's go piss some men off."

An hour later Darrell and his friends were cut loose, packed up, and shipped out.

"That went about as smooth as I was expecting." Troy eased down into one of the chairs at Ben's dining room table, looking pretty unaffected by all the insults he'd had lobbed his way.

"I don't think I earned us any fans." He hadn't even accused the men of loosening the shingles. Didn't even get a chance to touch on the subject, because the minute they realized Ben was letting them go they went into attack mode, pointing out everything wrong with Cross Creek.

Everything wrong with him.

Called Troy a traitor, a rat, and accused him of offering any variety of sexual favors in return for his new position at the ranch.

Luckily for them, they stopped short of dragging Liza into it.

"It'll be interesting to see what they try to spread around town." It was one more possibility Troy seemed completely unaffected by.

"And that doesn't bother you?" That was another one of many things Ben avoided at all costs. Cross Creek already had a certain reputation, he never wanted to make it worse.

"Nah." Troy leaned back in his chair. "Somebody's always going to be ready to talk shit. That's just how it goes."

"I wish I could be as laid-back about it." Ben started a fresh pot of coffee, his eyes snagging on the empty sink as he passed. The breakfast dishes he told Liza to leave were all gone, along with any crumb that might have been on the counter. She'd cleaned up all of it.

"You're just taking it personally. You gotta stop doing that."

"It is personal." Ben switched on the coffee maker.

"Maybe for Ms. Cross, but not for you. You just work here."

It was what most people thought, but it wasn't the full truth. "I'm actually part owner."

Troy's brows jumped up. "No shit?" He grinned. "That explains a lot."

"Like why I take shit personally?"

"I was thinking more along the lines of you and Ms. Cross." Troy stood up and paced across to the pictures lined across the living room wall. "Explains why it took y'all so long to get together." He squinted at the first photo. "Didn't want to mix business with pleasure."

"Something like that." Ben might be willing to share his ownership of Cross Creek with Troy, but he wasn't quite trusting of the other man enough to tell him about the past he and Liza shared.

"You got a big family." Troy moved down to the second photo. "Are you all ranchers?"

"Yup." His family was one more topic he wasn't ready to discuss with Troy.

Especially not when he'd made the same mistakes he believed they had.

"Must mean it's in your blood." Troy turned away from the photos as the coffee maker beeped, indicating its cycle was complete.

"What about you?" Ben grabbed the coffee cup and filled it, offering it to Troy. "What's in your blood?"

Troy took the coffee, the easy expression he always wore slipping for just a second. "Nothing good."

TWENTY-EIGHT

LIZA

"HEY THERE." DIANNA stood behind one of the gleaming cases in her bakery, smiling wide as Liza and Ben walked through the door. "I think I know what you're here for." She immediately disappeared into the back room.

Liza perused the glassed-in shelves.

Not that it did her any good.

"I guess if I want to actually get to see any of what she makes I'll have to come down in the morning."

"It'll have to be pretty early in the morning. She's usually sold out of half of everything when I get here at eight." Ben took a sip from the latte he picked up a few doors down at the new coffee shop in town.

They'd met the young woman who owned the place and, like Dianna, she was doing one hell of a job.

Moss Creek was suddenly bringing in more transplants than ever. When Liza moved to town she was the first new arrival since Ben came a handful of years before she did.

Now it seemed like they had someone new rolling in all the time, setting up house and setting up shop.

"Makes sense." Liza leaned down to peek at the labels, since that was all she had to go off of. "What's your favorite?"

"Depends." Ben pointed to one of the many empty cake

stands. "I love the maple walnut stack cake." His finger moved. "And the peaches and cream sheet cake."

"Ohhh." Liza leaned closer, squinting at the few crumbs and swipe of white frosting left. "What's in that one?"

"It's a yellow cake soaked in peach nectar and sweetened condensed milk, topped with a whipped cream frosting and slices of fresh peach." Dianna smiled at her from the other side of the case. "It's good."

"Where do you come up with all these ideas?" Liza was impressed as hell with Mae and all the creativity she brought to her food at The Wooden Spoon, but honestly she kind of just thought her best friend was a fluke.

It looked like Dianna was the same kind of fluke.

"I don't know." Dianna straightened. "My grandma used to make all kinds of things up when she cooked." She slid a cake box onto the counter. "Hopefully I get it from her."

Liza poked one finger at a label that caught her eye. "Does that say maple bacon blondies?"

"It does." Dianna wiggled her brows. "Those are a big hit here."

"I can imagine." Liza pulled out her wallet and passed over payment.

Ben offered a grin as he relaxed against the edge of the counter. "Cowboys have better taste than city boys."

Dianna's smile slipped the tiniest bit. "Let's hope so." She passed Liza her change, sliding the cake closer just as another customer came through the door, stealing any chance Liza might have had to figure out why the mention of city boys bothered the pretty baker.

Liza grabbed one of the cards sitting in a holder just beside the register. "Can I make an order over the phone?" She glanced down at the gold embossed logo and phone number.

"Of course." Dianna's smile was back to normal. "Just hit me up."

Liza lifted the card, showing Dianna she had the means. "I will."

Maybe she'd do more than order a cake.

Maybe she'd invite the new arrival to her weekly lunch with Mae and Nora and Clara and Camille.

And not because she hoped Dianna would bring maple bacon blondies.

Not *only* because she hoped Dianna would bring maple bacon blondies.

Ben picked up the cake as the new customers paced along the case, looking over the bits and pieces they had left to pick from.

"Thank you so much." Liza gave Dianna a smile and a wave as she followed Ben out onto the street.

She watched through the window as Dianna passed out the final items from her case, clearing out her stock yet again. "She's doing really well."

"Seems like." Ben balanced the cake in one hand and reached for hers with the other, holding tight as they walked down the street in front of God and everybody.

It was a little nerve wracking after spending so long worried that someone might find out about what happened between them.

But it was also a little freeing. As long as she got past that initial stab of panic.

Liza took a slow breath, trying to calm the fear doing its best to ruin this perfect moment. "Where did Dianna live before she came to Moss Creek?"

"LA. She tried to start a bakery there." Ben tipped his head at a couple as they walked by. "Afternoon."

The twosome passed without a second glance.

Which was good.

And also a little bad.

How much time had she wasted, staying mad at Ben out of self-preservation and stubbornness?

Liza turned, tipping her head over one shoulder to watch as the couple continued down the sidewalk. "No one finds us interesting."

"I find you interesting." Ben shot her a grin.

"Comments like that make it hard to take advantage of you." She smiled back, the regret gnawing at her insides easing only a tiny bit. "I mean no one cares that we're together."

"People have their own shit to worry about." Ben opened the driver's side door of his truck and stepped back, waiting.

Liza didn't immediately climb in. Instead she stayed in front of him, fused in place by a possibility that might be too much to handle. "Do you think they would have ever cared?"

Ben reached out to smooth down her hair as the wind caught it and sent it trailing across her face. "I don't think it would have been worth figuring out."

It was a good and unfortunate point. "I guess."

Ben jerked his chin toward the truck. "Now get up in there so we can go deliver your cake and get back home."

The last bit of upset wiggled free, shoved out by the easy comfort she always had with him. "Bossy."

"Just workin' hard to get myself taken advantage of." He winked as he closed her door, leaving her smiling while he walked around the truck and got into the passenger's seat, looking a little less bothered by the movement than he was the day before.

"How are your ribs?" She was glad the twats responsible for Ben's fall were gone, but she would be happier if Ben had let her push them off the roof like she wanted to.

It only seemed fair.

"Not bad enough to resist the urge to take advantage of me whenever it strikes." He settled into his seat, cake on his lap. "Maybe not right now though." He gave her another grin that sent her stomach flipping. "Wouldn't want to mess up Maryann's cake."

Liza accidentally let her eyes fall to where the cake was positioned.

Considered what might happen if she occupied that spot instead.

"Don't look at me like that, Sweetheart." His gaze met hers. "Not if you're set on going out to Red Cedar Ranch right now."

"Ugh." Liza put the truck in reverse and backed out of their parking spot. "I should have gotten her flowers."

"Shoulda, woulda, coulda." Ben seemed like he was enjoying the hell out of the situation.

And honestly, she was too.

She hadn't spent her time alone, not like it was clear Ben had.

But the relationship she had with her friends wasn't anything like what she had with him.

Which was why something was weighing on her.

"I had to hate you, you know."

Ben reached out, carefully taking her right hand in his and lifting it to his lips. "I know."

It was a realization that would have been impossible to consider before. Impossible to live with.

Which made her wonder—

"How did you make it?" Ben was alone. Not really any friends to speak of. No one to talk to. Nothing to make the time pass faster.

Ben's gaze rested on her face. "By lookin' at you."

His slow drawl dragged out the words, sending her belly flipping as heat raced through her veins, rushing to collect in one particular place.

Liza glanced at the cake again. Maryann didn't know she had it.

She'd never know if Liza tossed it over the backseat and had her way with Ben before ordering a replacement.

"You look like you're considering murdering this cake."

"I am." She eyed the shoulder of the unlined road leading to the Pace's ranch. There wasn't much space to pull off.

Ben chuckled low in his chest. "As much as I like what you're thinkin', it's probably best if we drop it off real quick." His voice lowered. "Then we can get on our way and you can spend your evening however you want."

He knew damn well how she wanted to spend her evening.

Liza huffed out a breath. "Fine." Her foot pressed closer to the floor, sending the dually moving faster down the asphalt toward Red Cedar Ranch. "Maryann better appreciate the sacrifice I'm making for her."

Ben chuckled again. "I don't know that I'd explain it to her."

"She's got four boys and a husband who worships the ground she walks on. I'm sure nothing I can say would shock her."

"I didn't say it would shock her." Ben smirked. "I'm sayin' you might end up giving her some ideas that would end up shocking one of your friends when they roll up on a fogged-up pickup parked out in a field."

Mae and Camille would kill her.

Nora and Clara would think it was fantastic.

Nora might even plan a front seat fornication of her own.

Liza pulled onto the long drive leading back to the main house at Red Cedar Ranch, ready to drop off Maryann's cake and get back on the road.

Unfortunately, when she rang the bell it wasn't Maryann who answered the door.

Technically no one answered the door.

"*It's Ben and Liza.*" Maryann's voice carried through the small speaker on the fancy doorbell the Paces installed after completing the inn at the back of the property, using it to reroute any guests who ended up at the wrong place.

"*We're at The Inn.*" Mae butted in. "*You guys should come on back.*"

"I don't—"

Ben stepped in between her and the camera. "We'd love to."

Liza scoffed.

"*See you soon.*" Maryann sounded excited and she'd done so much for Liza while she was down and miserable after surgery.

Which meant now Liza felt guilty about trying to put the happiness of her libido over the happiness of one of the kindest and most thoughtful women she knew.

"Okay." Liza dug deep and worked up some enthusiasm. "We'll be there in a minute."

She let Ben drag her back down the stairs before loading her into the truck, once again parking her in the driver's seat. She drove them back to The Inn and parked Ben's truck next to Mae's SUV.

Ben leaned to look up at The Inn. "Looks like it's a full house tonight."

"Yeah it does." Clara's minivan was there, along with Nora's car.

So much for making a quick exit.

Ben tipped his head toward the porch. "I think we've been spotted."

Liza followed his line of sight, expecting to see her friends lined up and waiting.

But it wasn't the Pace women propped against the cedar posts.

Ben was out of the truck immediately, cake in hand as he rounded the back of the bed on his way to her door.

She waited, even though it was awkward to just sit there. Ben opened her door, greeting her with a surprised smile. "I was figuring we might be in a race."

"Not this time, cowboy." She took his hand and slid free. "I didn't want you to catch hell." She gave him a little smile. "Next time you probably won't be as lucky."

"I disagree." He kept her hand in his as they walked toward The Inn. "I think my luck finally came in." Ben gave the men on the porch a nod. "Evenin'."

"Good to see you." Brody, the oldest Pace brother, gave him a slap on the back. "How's it going?"

"Not bad." Ben dropped her hand to start offering up shakes as the brothers monopolized his attention, making it easy for Liza to steal away the cake and slip inside, leaving Ben to partake in something that might do him a world of good.

Socializing.

She carried the box from The Baking Rack into the large, open kitchen of The Inn. The women she was expecting to see on the porch were all lined down the counter in front of all kinds of snacks and appetizers. Her eyes lifted to the Happy Birthday banner draped across the upper cabinets. "Are we interrupting?"

"Not at all." Maryann came her way. "We're celebrating The Inn's birthday." She wrapped one arm around Liza's shoulders and gave her a squeeze. "It's so good to see you out and about."

She loved Maryann. Would fight for the woman in a heartbeat.

But sometimes it was tough to be around her. It reminded her of everything she left behind when she moved to Moss Creek and started adding to the list of bad decisions that brought her here.

"I brought you a cake." Liza shoved the box at Maryann. "As a thank you for everything you did while I was recovering."

"Oh, honey. You don't have to thank me for that." She smiled softly. "I love taking care of my girls."

A lump immediately formed in Liza's throat, stealing the smile she was holding with a death grip. Everything in the room suddenly got very blurry.

"It's lemon." Ben's wide body stepped in front of her, blocking Liza from Maryann's view as he snagged away the cake. "Dianna said it was your favorite."

"It is." Maryann still sounded happy and upbeat as she took the cake and set it on the counter.

Ben wrapped one arm around Liza. "Why don't you show me around?" He easily moved her through the crowd, managing to get her out the back door before a single tear fell.

Then he held her close, one hand pressing her face into his chest as she sniffed, trying to suck up the problematic emotions she tried to keep at bay.

He didn't ask any questions. Didn't press her for an explanation.

He just offered support.

Acceptance.

Understanding.

Love.

"Damn it." Liza swiped at fresh tears as they slipped free, ruining the hold she thought she had on them.

"We can stand out here as long as you need."

She didn't doubt his commitment. She'd seen firsthand how willing Ben was to wait for her.

But they couldn't stand out here for much longer. Not when she was positive everyone inside was watching them.

"I'm fine." She wiped her eyes a little harder, getting more aggressive with the ill-timed overflow, then sucked in a deep breath. "I just miss my parents and Dawn."

TWENTY-NINE

BEN

"Hell." Maybe he shouldn't have suggested this after all.

He thought coming over here would be a nice happy little visit. Give Liza some time to spend with her friends.

But it wasn't turning out like that at all.

"We can go." He couldn't stand the sadness on her face. Couldn't handle knowing how bad she was hurting.

"I'm sure that would go over real well." Liza almost smiled. "Can you imagine explaining to Maryann that we didn't want to stay for her party?" She shook her head. "I don't even want to think about how that would play out." Liza took another deep breath, straightening her spine and lifting her chin as she blinked furiously. "I can do it. It will be fine."

Fine wasn't the word he would use to describe this situation.

Ben didn't know what it was like to have parents who supported you and showed their kids love and appreciation, but he could imagine if he had it wouldn't be something that would be easy to leave behind.

Even if it was done with the best of intentions.

"You sure?" He smoothed back her hair. "I am willing to fake a case of the stomach flu."

That earned him a more genuine smile. "I appreciate that you would claim explosive diarrhea to save me, but I think I'll be okay."

"You just say the word. I'll grab my stomach and double over." He'd done way worse for her. Things that almost broke him.

Faking a case of the shits was nothing.

Liza's smile lifted a little more. "I'll be fine. I just had a little moment." She straightened her shoulders. "Hopefully we get some cake out of the deal."

Ben took her hand in his. "I'll be shocked if that cake isn't already cut."

He led Liza back into The Inn, keeping her close at his side so he could fend off any more potential interactions that might send her spiraling into an emotional moment she wouldn't want anyone else to witness.

It gave him a good reason to stick with her, making it clear there was something between them in front of the people she was closest to in town.

But, after partaking in a couple beers, he had to duck away to use the facilities.

Ben leaned into her ear. "I'll be right back."

Liza paused the conversation she was having with Nora about the house Dianne bought from her and Brooks to catch him as he left. She grabbed his shirt, using it to pull Ben back in close as she pushed up on her toes and kissed him right on the lips. It was a bold move, one that stunned him and earned the attention from everyone in the room.

She held his gaze for a second, smiling wide before turning back to Nora, going on like she hadn't just made a clear statement. One no one could misinterpret.

He avoided eye contact with the Pace brothers as he ducked into the bathroom, taking his time, hoping the room might move on.

Ben opened the door and immediately realized that wasn't going to happen.

Brody, Boone, Brooks, and Brett stood just outside.

Waiting for him.

"You want to get some air?" Brody's tone was impossible to read.

"Sure." Ben glanced Liza's way, making sure she was okay

before following the brothers down the main hall and out onto the front porch.

He'd been hoping that five years was long enough to avoid bringing back any lingering suspicions that surrounded Liza.

But maybe he was wrong. Maybe his presence in her life would always put her in danger.

Ben closed the door behind him, staying quiet as the brothers spaced out across the porch. Brody and Brooks sat in two of the rocking chairs. Brett propped up against one of the cedar posts.

But Boone continued to stand, facing him down.

It was quiet long enough to have him counting all the ways he'd fucked up. Thinking about how selfish he'd been, wanting her back at his side.

But then Boone's face split into a wide grin. "It's about fucking time." He grabbed Ben, pulling him in for a backslapping hug.

Ben was more than surprised. He was stunned. "I'm not sure what you mean."

"You and Liza." Brody shook his head as he rocked. "It's been fucking painful watching the two of you dance around each other all these years."

Ben wasn't quite sure how to respond. So he didn't.

Luckily the brothers continued the conversation without him.

"I'm happy for you, man." Boone shook his head. "I know what it's like when you think you do the right thing and then suffer for it."

Ben looked from brother to brother as the reality of all they knew started to sink in. "You all knew?"

"Wasn't real hard to figure out." Brooks tipped his head toward the house. "Hell, Nora put it all together in under a month."

That wasn't good. None of this was good.

"Shit." Ben took off his hat and raked one hand through his hair.

"There's no reason to be upset. You did what you had to do." Brody's expression sobered. "And you did have to do it."

"Which was bullshit." Brooks' nostrils flared. "Everybody

knew Ed Cross was a piece of shit who put his hands on her. There should have been no question that it was self-defense."

"But she wasn't dealing with people who knew Ed Cross. She would have been fine if the state hadn't come in to investigate." Brody focused on Ben. "I hope you know Grady did everything in his power to keep that from happening."

"No." Ben shook his head. "I didn't know that."

"He went to bat for her. Put his job on the line, that's how sure he was she acted in self-defense." Brody frowned. "Those assholes didn't care. They wanted their fingers in it."

"It doesn't matter now." Boone seemed to carry a little of the same relief Ben felt. "It's time to put all that shit behind you guys." He shot Ben a sly smile. "Which it seems like you're doing."

Ben looked from brother to brother before settling on Boone. "What about Mae? Does she know?"

Boone chuckled. "I believe my wife is a little too close to the situation to be able to see things clearly."

"So no."

Boone shook his head, smile holding. "No." He leaned against the pole at his back. "So I'd be ready to catch hell over that one."

Ben glanced over his shoulder back toward the house where he'd left Liza with Mae.

"Liza's fine. Mae won't be upset with her." Boone pointed at Ben. "She'll be upset with you. It's easier."

"Fair enough." He'd happily take Mae's wrath if it meant Liza didn't have to.

"So what now?" Brody asked like he expected Ben would have an answer.

He didn't.

"Hell if I know." Of course he had plans, but none of them really came with a timeline attached. "Whatever happens from here on out is just gravy."

Liza was with him now and that was all that mattered.

"You say that today," Brett piped up for the first time, "but you'll be changing your tune."

"Patience gets harder the closer they are." Boone said it like a man who'd been there before.

He had.

He'd broken up with Mae over a decade ago, thinking it was the best thing for both of them.

But he never got over her. Never forgot the first woman who had his heart.

"I'm just trying to take it one step at a time. I don't want to get ahead of myself." More importantly, he didn't want to get ahead of Liza. She had a lot going on in her life right now, and healing was what she should be focusing on first.

"Good luck with that." Boone crossed his arms over his chest, looking relaxed. "Anything else interesting going on?" His expression shifted, losing a little of the humor it had been carrying. "Outside of that fall you didn't tell anyone about?"

For the second time Ben was surprised. Boone almost seemed a little hurt that Ben hadn't told him about the incident he had on the roof. "It wasn't a big deal. Just a few loose shingles."

"So you *didn't* fall off a roof?" Brody's question carried the same hint of offense as his brother's.

Ben shifted on his feet. "I did fall off the roof, but it wasn't that big of a deal."

The four brothers stared at him.

"It really wasn't. They looked me over, gave me some pain medication, and sent me home."

The Pace boys continued to stare silently.

And he continued to try to explain. "It was just some bumps and bruises." Ben paused, not wanting to give them the rest. Unfortunately, that would probably come back to bite him. "And a few cracked ribs."

"Let me guess. You're right back to work like nothing happened." Brooks was being awfully judgmental for a man who would probably do the same thing.

"Cattle don't take care of themselves."

"That's what you've got ranch hands for. They should be able to take care of shit if you have to be down for a couple of days." Boone clearly didn't understand what it was like to be pinched so tight you couldn't afford reliable help.

"And if they can't, then you need to let your friends know so they can send over some men who will." Brody leaned back in his chair, holding Ben's gaze. "There's no reason for you to be on a horse with cracked ribs."

Ben looked from Brody to Boone, fighting his way through one more realization about himself.

He definitely hadn't been a good boss. Hadn't really encouraged the things he should have among the ranch hands at Cross Creek.

But maybe he also hadn't been a great friend. Probably because he didn't really want to realize he was one.

"I let go of a few ranch hands this morning." Ben scrubbed at his jaw, fighting his way through the discomfort of the situation. "Pretty sure they were responsible for what happened on the roof."

Brody's brows lifted. "How so?"

"I initially thought the damage was from the wind we got a few days ago, but it turns out someone pulled all the nails from a section of shingles." It pissed him off even thinking about it. "A few guys were angry about the way things worked. Wanted to do some damage and figure out a way to increase their pay without having to do any more work." He tipped his head to one side. "Not that they were doing much work to start with."

"They could've killed somebody." Boone appeared to be reasonably shocked by the information.

"I don't think they thought that far ahead." He wasn't sure Darrell and his buddies had enough brain cells between the three of them to accomplish something as complicated as forethought.

"How did they think tearing up a roof would earn them more money?" Brody shook his head. "It doesn't make sense."

"Room and board is part of their compensation. If the bunkhouse isn't habitable because of a leaky roof then we would have to compensate them some other way."

Boone huffed out a humorless laugh. "People never seem to stop shocking me."

The door to The Inn opened, and Maryann peeked out at them. "Get your butts inside. We're getting ready to cut the cake Liza and Ben brought." She came to Ben's side, looping her arm through his. "And it was such a sweet thing to do." She patted his arm with her free hand. "Nora told me about the chairs you made for Liza to sit in while she listened to the wind chimes." She looked around before leaning his way, her voice dropping. "Maybe add a sunshade." Maryann gave him a wink before setting him free and going to the counter where everyone was lined and ready to enjoy their dessert.

"Where did you go?" Liza snuck in close at his side. "One minute you were there and the next you were gone."

Ben wrapped his arm around her, pulling her close. "Went outside and had a chat with Brody and his brothers."

Liza's brows lifted. "Is everything okay?"

Telling her the secret they thought they shared was more public than they realized wasn't anything he wanted to do right this minute, so he settled on offering up something else. Something that bothered him more than he expected. "They offered to send a few ranch hands over until I'm back to one-hundred percent."

Liza's lips lifted in the little smile. "That's really nice of them."

It was more than nice, and he was struggling to come to terms with it.

He'd always thought of the Pace brothers as acquaintances. A group of men who sat in the same small circle he did.

But they'd always treated him like he was more, and he'd never returned the favor. Never even considered it.

"It is." Ben watched the family move around them, trading smiles and jabs the way only people who truly love each other do.

Liza tipped her head up, eyes focusing on his face as he continued to take it all in. "Does it make you sad?"

It made him something. He just couldn't quite put his finger on it. "Why would it make me sad?"

"Because you never had anything like this." Her voice was soft as she delivered the blow.

And it was a blow. One he never saw coming.

Ben tipped his head in a nod. "It does make me sad."

But his sadness wasn't limited to staring down all the things his own family lacked.

Right now he was looking back at himself.

At how he pushed everyone away, thinking they were against him. How he expected the worst in them.

And instead only showed the worst in himself.

Ben wrapped his other arm around Liza, bringing her in closer as the rest of the truth fell into place, digging the ache in his chest deeper.

Because he wasn't the only one who pushed people away.

Liza might not have done it for the same reasons he did, but she was just as guilty of blocking people out of the parts of her life she didn't think they could handle. Keeping them a safe distance from the tough parts.

She had friends and family, but both came with conditions and limits.

Which meant they both stood alone. Solitarily suffering. Refusing to let anyone in.

They both fought to prove they were fine.

Both smiled with a lie on their lips.

Both stayed in the center of a storm, refusing shelter.

And maybe it was time they both stopped.

THIRTY

BEN

"DID YOU HAVE an okay time?"

Liza didn't argue as Ben loaded her into the passenger's seat for the drive home.

She looked exhausted. Like the past month had finally caught up with her.

But she also looked relaxed and happy.

"I did." They ended up staying at The Inn much longer than either of them anticipated. The evening never seemed to really wind down, it just kept going, until finally all the food was gone and everyone was too tired to play another hand of cards.

"I didn't realize you were so good at euchre."

"Neither did Brooks." Ben hadn't played cards in years, but managed to get in the swing of things relatively quickly. He and Mae wiped the floor with Brooks and Brody.

Hopefully she'd remember that when she found out what everyone around her already knew.

"You'll have to teach me how." Liza rested her head against the seat and wiggled her brows. "That way I can play next time."

"Next time?"

"Didn't you hear everyone planning?" Liza's eyes closed but her smile held. "Last I heard we were responsible for bringing another cake."

"I think we could make that happen." Ben reached across the

car, finding her hand with his as they drove through the night. It had been an odd evening. One that had him taking a hard look at the man he wanted to be.

Because he clearly wasn't there yet.

Liza started to snore softly, the sound of her breathing almost as loud as the drone of crickets carrying in through his open window.

It was a perfect night. One he never would have imagined having.

Mostly because he *couldn't* have imagined it. Not even if he tried.

But now that he'd gotten a taste of what it was like to really have a family, all Ben wanted to do was figure out a way to have more.

More people he and Liza could count on. More people that could count on them.

People to share their secrets and heartaches.

People to celebrate their joys and accomplishments.

All he had to do was figure out how to make it happen.

Liza was still sleeping as he turned into the driveway of Cross Creek. He drove right past the farmhouse, not even bothering to stop.

It wasn't her home anymore. Probably never was.

He parked in front of the cabin he'd been working on for almost five years straight, making up projects to distract him from a loneliness he never thought he'd escape.

Liza's lids barely lifted when he opened her door. "Ready for bed?"

She sucked in a breath, straightening in her seat. "Are we home already?"

Ben smiled. "Yeah. We're home."

He helped her out of the truck, sticking close as she wove her way toward the front door, a little unbalanced from the catnap she'd taken on the way home. The second the door was open she went in, dropping her purse on the table that might still someday host card games, before going down the hall and straight into his bedroom.

She came out a few minutes later, face scrubbed clean, wearing one of his shirts.

She'd brought back a few things from the farmhouse, so he'd been expecting to see her in another pair of pajama pants like the ones she wore after her run-in with the calf.

But this was so much better.

Liza paused halfway out of the room, eyes squeezing shut on a yawn that seemed to possess her whole body.

She was beyond exhausted. At least this time it was from staying up having fun instead of working herself into the ground trying to prove a point.

One that only drove home just how perfect this woman was for him.

Liza was one of the only people in his life who never took advantage of his hard-working nature. Never exploited his skills.

Even when she couldn't show it, or admit it, she still cared about him.

Still had his back in a way no one else ever had.

"I think it's past your bedtime." Ben snagged her on his way into his room, urging her into the king-sized bed before covering her up and leaning down to press a kiss to her forehead.

Liza's brows came together. "Where are you going?"

"The bathroom." He gave her a grin. "That okay, Ms. Cross?"

She huffed out a dramatic little breath. "I guess." Her teasing expression slipped. "I think I want to change my name."

He smoothed over her hair, loving the way it stretched across the pillow he used to sleep on alone at night. "I think that can be arranged."

"Where are we going?" Liza had been shockingly patient so far, but he could tell she was getting antsy as they got closer to the outskirts of Billings.

"I told you." He took a turn that would probably clue her in on what their first stop was. "It's a surprise."

Ben hadn't been able to forget the look on Liza's face after he rushed her from The Inn a few nights ago, but coming up with a quick way to ease her pain was harder than he expected.

Until he remembered something he'd heard a few women talking about while he was in line one morning waiting for his donut at The Baking Rack.

Liza wiggled in her seat as they pulled into the little neighborhood, sitting up straighter as he came to a stop in front of the run-down house that bothered both of them.

This was a two birds, one stone sort of evening. One he hoped would do just as much for the older of his two dates.

"I'll be right back." He gave Liza a wink as he got out and headed for Muriel's front door.

It opened before he hit the sidewalk. Muriel slid out, immediately pulling it closed and managing to get it locked tight before he reached the porch. She turned to face him, a bright smile on her face.

"Don't you look pretty."

Muriel's eyebrows were filled in and a few shades darker than normal. Her cheeks were bright pink, and so were her lips. Her steely gray hair was puffed out from her head in tight curls.

"Do you like it?" She lifted one hand to fluff at her hair. "I forgot how nice it looked all curled up."

"I love it." Ben reached one hand out, offering it up as Muriel came down the stairs.

Her hand gripped his tight as she navigated the new set of sturdy steps. Her other hand latched onto the rail as she easily made her way down.

Once she reached the bottom she held up both hands for him to see. "I even painted my fingernails."

Sure enough, the tips of Muriel's fingers were coated in a polish the same color as her lips and cheeks.

The woman knew how to coordinate.

"I'm flattered that you got so fancy for me."

"Pshh." Muriel waved him off. "Women don't get dressed up for men." She started down the sidewalk, heading toward the truck. Her eyes and face lit up when she saw Liza standing on the curb. "They get dressed up for other women."

CROSSING THE LINE

Liza's eyes opened wide as Muriel came her way. "You look beautiful."

Muriel smoothed down the front of her drapey top. "I know." As soon as she reached Liza she snagged the front of her dress, moving it from side to side so the skirts swung around. "So do you."

Liza smiled back. "I know."

This was definitely the right choice.

He'd initially planned an evening that would be just the two of them, but Muriel brought something to the table he couldn't.

Not just yet anyway.

"Now that we've established how pretty everyone is, let's hit the road. I don't want to be late." Ben helped Muriel up into his truck while Liza climbed into the back. He didn't miss that she was starting to use her right arm a little more, mostly just for added balance, but a week ago she hadn't been using it at all and progress was progress.

Ben closed both their doors before climbing in and pulling away.

The women chatted as he drove, covering everything from their physical therapy exercises to their favorite colors and the best place around to get a steak dinner.

They were so engrossed in their conversation they didn't even notice when he pulled up at their destination, parking in front of the storefront in a small strip mall.

"We're here."

Liza leaned forward, peeking up at the sign between the front seats. "Cocktails and Canvas."

"Is this one of those drink while you paint places?" Muriel was definitely the more excited of the two. She slapped her hands together. "I've been wanting to do this." Her excitement dimmed just a little. "Just didn't have anyone to go with me."

"Well now you do." Ben helped Muriel out of the truck, getting her to the sidewalk as Liza continued to stare at the building, her expression impossible to read.

Muriel shooed him away. "Go get her."

Ben was happy to do as he was told. "You ready to go inside?"

Liza's eyes came his way. "I don't think I'm going to be very good at this."

"Who cares?" Ben took her hand. "It's not about being good at everything. Sometimes it's just about having fun."

It was something neither of them had enjoyed much of. And that was one more thing that needed to change.

"I'm not familiar with that word." Liza smiled the tiniest bit. "Could you use it in a sentence?"

"It will be *fun* to paint a picture that you can send to your sister Dawn."

When Liza's eyes immediately jumped to his he knew he'd hit the nail on the head.

He'd seen her wearing around bracelets made of chunky plastic beads or rubber bands laced together. He never really knew where they came from, not until their conversation with Dawn.

"She would love that." Liza was a little breathless.

"I thought she might." He opened the door, holding it as Muriel immediately hustled inside.

Liza did not. She lingered, eyes fixed on his face, jaw a little slack as she stared at him.

Then she grabbed the front of his shirt, fisting it in her hand and pulling his lips to hers in a kiss that earned a whistle from Muriel. She pulled back the tiniest bit, just enough so she could speak. "You make it really hard not to love you."

"That's the plan, Sweetheart." He nudged her. "Now get inside. We've got art to make."

Two hours later they each had a beachy sunset scene. Liza skipped the alcohol, using all her focus and attention to make her painting as perfect as possible.

Muriel on the other hand, took full advantage of the cocktail portion of the evening, drinking down four gin and tonics as she went rogue, crafting her painting into something that looked nothing like anything else in the room.

Because this was definitely not Muriel's first rodeo.

The colors of her painting had more depth. They were complicated and rich. The sweeps of her brush were smooth and flowing, bringing a sense of movement to the water and sky.

"Holy shit, Muriel." Liza leaned over the older woman's shoulder. "That's freaking amazing."

Muriel's smile was different now. Like she was there with them but also far away. "Thank you."

Liza continued to stare at the painting. "You weren't planning to tell us you were an artist?"

Muriel shrugged, but her expression made it clear she was loving the surprise. "Didn't seem relevant."

"Oh my." The instructor stopped behind them, her eyes going wide. "That's fantastic."

"We'll have to hang it up in your house." Ben carefully picked the painting off its easel as Liza helped Muriel off her chair.

"There's nowhere to put it." Muriel's lips immediately pressed together as her eyes snapped his way.

Checking to see if he'd caught the slip.

He had.

"It would be a shame for this not to be on a wall so it can be appreciated." Ben tried to push gently.

He didn't want Muriel to think he would ever judge her for the state of her home. Life was hard. Even harder when you were alone and limited physically.

Probably also financially.

"I'm going to send it to my granddaughter." Muriel swiftly shut down his planned path. "She's an artist too."

Liza smiled. "Just like her grandma." She looped her arm through Muriel's as they moved outside. "Where does she live?"

"New York." Muriel leaned into Liza's side. "Moved there to work at some gallery, hoping she might get some eyes on her own work."

Liza's smile faded.

Muriel continued on, oblivious to the nerve she'd struck. "I tried to tell her that New York is a tough place to build a life." She shook her head. "It's cutthroat there." She patted Liza's hand. "Not like it is here where people help each other out."

Liza nodded, managing a weak smile. "I'm sure she's having fun."

Once upon a time Liza had fun in New York too. It was a story he'd heard only once.

A tale of how the woman who never wanted to burden her parents lost everything and ended up back home.

But only for as long as it took her to finally agree to marry the older man who'd been chasing her for months.

"I hope so." Muriel's lips tipped down in a frown. "But I worry about her."

"I can imagine." Liza passed Muriel off to him when they reached the door. Then she silently climbed into the back seat, hands in her lap as they drove back to Muriel's.

And just like that, the night he hoped would bring Liza an evening of happiness was ending right where it began.

In sadness and regret.

It wasn't Muriel's fault. There's no way she could have known she was dragging up the thing Ben wanted to distract Liza from the most.

To be fair, Muriel didn't know much at the moment.

Her buzz hit almost as soon as she was buckled in, dragging her into a doze before they were even out of the parking lot.

And once again he had a snoring woman in his front seat.

Ben thought her condition might finally provide the opportunity to get a peek inside Muriel's house, but the woman proved to be more spry under the influence than he expected, easily making it up the sidewalk and steps, proving she didn't need any assistance from him. She gave his cheek a quick pinch before sliding in and locking the door behind her.

He turned to find Liza waiting for him. He went straight to her, pulling her close.

She sniffed against his shirt. "What if every decision I made was the wrong one?" She held him tight. "Maybe I should have stayed there. Tried harder to—"

"I've got bad news for you, Sweetheart." He cradled her head in his hand. "You can't change it." He leaned back until her eyes met his. "All you can do is use what you know to decide what to do from here on out."

Which was exactly what he was going to do.

THIRTY-ONE

LIZA

LIZA PARKED BEN'S truck in the only available space left in front of the main house at Moss Creek Ranch.

Apparently she picked a popular day to come get advice from the smartest woman she knew.

She grabbed her purse and slid free, managing to balance a little bit of weight on her right arm as she dropped to the ground. The injured appendage had finally started to feel better over the past week or so, making it much easier to start relying on it for small tasks.

She opened the back door and pulled out the bag of treats she picked up on her way over, hoping it would ease the judgment that was probably coming her way.

Judgment she definitely deserved.

Liza climbed up on the porch and rang the doorbell, again using her right hand. It was a small feat, but it seemed huge.

Especially considering she was beginning to think that arm might never get back to normal.

A stampede of feet came down the hall, making her step back just as the door opened.

An entire group of faces smiled out at her, confirming her suspicions about exactly who all was parked in front of Maryann Pace's home.

"I feel like I keep showing up at party time." She lifted the bag in her hand. "But at least I come bearing gifts."

"Honey," Maryann snagged the bag from The Baking Rack, "you could come over at three in the morning and I would still be happy to see you." She gave Liza a wink. "Especially if you bring something from Dianna."

Dianna was one of the many things she wanted to discuss with the rest of the women occupying Maryann's entryway. "I really like her." Liza closed the door. "It doesn't even have anything to do with how good of a baker she is."

Maryann's brows lifted.

"It only has a little bit to do with how good of a baker she is." Liza smiled, already feeling a little bit better. "She's very sweet and thoughtful." Liza turned toward Maryann's four daughter-in-laws. "I was thinking maybe she could come to lunch one day."

"I'm going to have to start closing down a whole section so we have enough space for all of us." Mae tipped her head towards Camille. "This one finally convinced Mariah to come."

"About time." Mariah was the chef who handled most of the meals at The Inn at Red Cedar Ranch. "I was starting to take it a little personally that she didn't want to hang out with us."

"I think she didn't want to impose." Camille was the newest addition to the Pace family, but she'd lived in Moss Creek her whole life. "And I think she was a little uncertain since sometimes women can be —"

Clara lifted her brows. "Catty?"

Nora held up a finger. "Downright evil?"

Nora learned the hard way that even if they didn't possess one, occasionally women could be giant dicks.

"They can be." It was something Liza herself had experienced before coming to Moss Creek. "It's an unfortunate truth."

"That's one of the reasons I love it here." Nora was a transplant from Seattle. She was a city girl who had been completely resistant to the idea of living someplace like Moss Creek.

But now she was one of its biggest fans and loudest cheerleaders.

"It is pretty different here." Liza never offered up much about the life she lived before coming to Montana.

And maybe that was a mistake.

"I was shocked when I first came here and everyone was so nice to me." It had been a huge culture shock. "Genuinely nice. Not fake nice. Actually nice."

Nora pointed at her. "Right? It was crazy. You think it's a trick."

That's exactly what she thought. "I remember trying to figure out what Maryann wanted from me." Liza sat down in one of the chairs at the kitchen table. "Because that was the only thing that made sense."

She'd never met anyone who didn't have an angle. Some underlying motive fueling their fake kindness.

It was how she ended up not even seeing the end of her career until it was right on top of her.

One day she was out helping scout out new talent for the modeling agency she'd worked at for almost five years, and the next she was replaced, quite literally by a younger model.

She'd aged out of the industry twice. Once on the runway, and once behind the scenes.

And after spending a decade blowing through every penny she made trying to keep up with the women around her, she had no option but to move back home with her parents.

Actually, she had one option.

"I remember when you first moved here." Maryann set the bag of cupcakes on the counter and turned to face Liza, one hand going to her hip. "I wanted so much to come over, pack up everything you owned, and ship you back home to get you away from that asshole."

"Part of me wishes you had." That was some of what brought her to Maryann's today.

It was getting more and more difficult to feel like she'd done the right thing when she came to Moss Creek.

Mae scoffed. "Ow."

"I'm not saying I wish I hadn't met you." Liza spun one of the elastic bracelets stretched around her wrist. "I'm just not sure coming here was the right thing."

"I've been there." Maryann was the last person she expected to sympathize with her.

"Really?" It was shocking to think that Maryann would ever question the life she had. "Why?"

"I left behind my whole family. Everything I knew. Everyone I loved." Maryann carried the large tray of cupcakes to the table and set them down. "And it's not like I could go home all the time and visit. My life here was too busy for that." She lifted the lid and set it off to one side, her expression sad as she looked at the variety of frosted cakes. "I missed a lot."

"Did you feel guilty?"

Maryann's eyes came to her and she softly smiled. "Of course."

That wasn't helpful. Especially considering Liza came here hoping Maryann would have some words of wisdom about how she shouldn't feel guilty. That she'd done the right thing.

"Are you and your parents close?" Nora sat down beside her.

Liza nodded. "As close as we can be."

Nora reached out, resting one hand on Liza's back. "That would be hard."

It *was* hard, but unfortunately it was only the tip of the iceberg.

Liza let her head drop to the table in front of her. "*Everything* is hard."

She'd bottled so much up. Packed away secrets and lies and omissions. Withheld information from her friends and family.

And right now there simply wasn't any more room inside.

"Ben and I had an affair." It wasn't the beginning of their story, not even close, but it was the thing that weighed the heaviest on her.

No one in the room said anything, but the way they looked at her had Liza wondering if she'd just had a lapse in judgment. "It wasn't on purpose." She shouldn't have said anything. Things were going fine. She and Ben were together now. There was no reason to—

"Oh, honey." Maryann's expression was soft. "We knew about you and Ben."

"I didn't." Mae crossed her arms over her chest, eyes scanning the room. "Thanks by the way for no one filling me in."

"It was just once." Liza let her face fall to her hands. "I moved out the next day. Told Ed I was filing for divorce."

Everyone stayed quiet, leaving room for her to keep talking.

"I went and stayed in a hotel a few towns over so no one would know." She thought she was at the beginning of a new life. One that would be complicated and scary, but Ben would be there with her, and that was all that mattered. "Ed called constantly. I finally had to turn my phone off."

She'd planned to leave it off too, but not talking to Ben got the best of her and she switched the phone back on.

That was when she realized one more person knew her and Ben's secret. "Somehow Ed figured out about Ben and I." Just thinking about it made her head hurt and her stomach sick. "He left me a message saying that if I didn't come back he was going to kill him."

Mae snorted. "Right. Like he could've accomplished that."

Maryann shushed her. "Let her get it all out."

"I thought maybe I could convince him there was nothing between us, so I went back." That was mistake number one.

Mistake number two was thinking that since she'd taken the only handgun Ed owned with her she would be safe.

"But he was convinced, rightfully so." Liza stared down at the table. "I knew how dangerous he could be. I should have never gone there."

It was difficult not to carry the burden of taking someone else's life, even when it was the only choice you had. You continued to look for ways you could have avoided it.

"I would've done the same thing." Camille was one of the few women who really understood what she'd been through. Her ex-husband was just as big of a piece of shit as Ed Cross was. "If Junior threatened to kill Brett I would have done whatever it took to protect him."

"I would've gone there too." Nora reached over and took her hand, giving it a little squeeze.

Maryann reached across the table, wrapping Liza's other hand in both of hers. "You can second-guess every decision you've ever made, honey. But it's a waste of time."

Liza nodded, blinking at the burning of her eyes. "That's what Ben said."

"Ben's a smart man. You should listen to him."

Liza let her head fall back. "He's a whole problem himself."

Last night after they left Muriel's, Ben confessed his desire to renovate their new friend's home.

It's a desire Liza shared, however there simply wasn't enough money to do it.

At least she didn't think there was.

"He bought part of Cross Creek from Ed years ago." She shook her head, still not really able to believe everything Ben confessed to her last night. "I assumed it was his life savings. That he sunk it into the ranch and had to stick around so he could get it back."

"Ben owns part of Cross Creek?" Maryann seemed surprised. She blew out a breath. "Makes more sense why the two of you didn't get together right away. They would've thought you killed Ed in cold blood."

"Holy shit." Mae pressed one hand to her forehead. "I didn't even think about that."

"Ben did." He found her that night, cut and bleeding, covered in blood that wasn't only her own, hiding upstairs in her room, thinking Ed was going to wake up and come finish what he started. "He told me I couldn't tell anyone about us. That we had to pretend like it never happened."

"You did a good job." Mae pulled out a chair and sat down.

Liza looked at Maryann. "Obviously not as good as we thought we did." She took a deep breath, trying to steady the nervousness that always came through when she thought about that night. "Anyway, I thought Ben stayed in Moss Creek because he had to." She wiped at the corner of one eye as a bit of moisture tried to sneak free. "But he didn't."

Apparently Ben's family's ranch was worth way more than Cross Creek could ever hope to be worth, and when he chose to leave the family they bought him out of his share, sending him on his way with five hundred thousand dollars, making the sixty thousand he gave Ed Cross a tiny drop in a big bucket, especially once you factored in the interest he'd been accruing over the years.

"He stayed here for you." Maryann's lips curved in a knowing smile.

Liza's face crumpled up as she finally gave in to the tears. "I know, and it sucks."

"How does a man staying here to make sure you're taken care of suck?" Nora was trying really hard to follow along, her question was genuine, not snarky.

"Because what have I ever done for him?" Nothing. It was an easy answer. She'd done nothing for him. "He stayed here, helping me get the ranch out of the red, working his ass off every day. And now, he's making me breakfast and taking me to paint pictures for my sister." She paused to blow her nose on a tissue Maryann passed her way. "He even wants to take care of our new friend Muriel because no one else is."

It all ended up boiling down to one thing.

Ben was too good for her.

He did everything she didn't.

She didn't stay in Moss Creek to take care of him. She stayed because she had to. She wasn't taking him painting and ordering mousse and trying to figure out ways to help him deal with his family issues.

She wasn't even making sure her own family was taken care of as well as she should.

"It sounds to me like you have a to-do list." Maryann said it like it wasn't a big deal. Like Liza wasn't a complete asshole who only thought of herself and ended up twisted into her own problems.

The older woman stood from the table and went to snag a small pad of paper off the counter. She grabbed a pen and clicked it open.

"Number one. Plan something fun for Ben." She wrote it across the paper in neat cursive.

"What's number two?" Liza dabbed at her eyes, waiting for Maryann to write down all the things she should have already been doing.

"We don't worry about number two until we've handled number one." She dropped the pen, folded her hands, and leaned against the table. "So, what would Ben Chamberlain enjoy doing?"

"Well," Liza stared at the paper, her brain racing through everything she knew about the man she loved.

And she absolutely loved Ben Chamberlain. Honestly, everyone should.

"He really had fun playing cards here the other night." It was the part of the evening she enjoyed the most, watching Ben in the Pace brothers joke around enjoying each other's company.

"Perfect." Maryann clapped her hands together like Liza didn't just come up with the most generic thing ever. "Sounds to me like Ben is probably long overdue on a boys' night." She smiled at the women around her. "Luckily we know a few boys."

THIRTY-TWO

BEN

BEN TURNED TO look out the window as gravel crunching under tires pulled his attention from the book on his lap. He slid the biography on Leonardo Da Vinci onto the small table as he stood up from the chair to get a better look at the pickup truck parking in his driveway.

The red color of the paint was familiar enough to drag him to the door and out onto the porch.

"Evenin'." Brody Pace carried a six-pack in one hand and gave Ben a wave with the other.

"Evenin'." Ben leaned against one of the porch posts as the rest of the Pace brothers unloaded from the extended-cab pickup truck. Each one of them carried at least a six-pack, along with a few large shopping bags. "What brings you over to my side of town?"

"Thought we might drink some beer." Brooks was the first to reach his porch. He lifted up the bag in his hand. "Maybe eat some food."

"Oh." Ben planned on spending a quiet evening while Liza hung out with her friends. "Okay."

He waited as the men filed in, going straight to the table to stack up everything they brought.

"You like tacos?" Brody pulled out a large container and popped open the lid. It was filled with sliced beef that immediately filled his little house with the savory scent of cumin and chili powder.

"I do like tacos." He watched as they unpacked a full spread that included tortillas, salsa, chopped lettuce and tomato, shredded cheese, rice, and beans.

"We weren't sure how many plates you had." Boone pulled out a stack of paper plates and plastic forks. "So we brought those too."

Brooks went to the kitchen and started opening drawers. "The only thing we didn't bring was a bottle opener."

"Top drawer. Right beside the sink." Ben raked one hand through his hair as he tried to make sense of the scene around him.

Brooks popped the cap off a bottle of beer and passed it Ben's way. "Here you go."

"Thanks." Ben tipped it back, swallowing down a little before looking at the label. "This is my favorite beer."

"Imagine that." Brody grabbed a plate. "I'm not waitin'. I'm hungry."

Brooks kept cracking open beers and passing them out as his brothers started dishing up food.

Once Brody's plate was full, he sat down in one of the chairs, looking Ben up and down. "You going to eat?"

Ben looked from brother to brother. "I'm confused."

He was friendly with the Pace brothers. Always had a nice chat with them any time he came across one of them in town.

And they'd had fun at The Inn the other night.

But they'd never showed up at Cross Creek like this.

"What are you confused about?" Brett was the last brother to get at the food. He picked up a plate and handed it over to Ben. "It's boys' night."

"I guess I just don't understand why it's here." He knew the Pace brothers got together regularly, sometimes even with their ranch hands.

It was one of many things he envied about them.

But he'd never actually been a part of it.

Not that they hadn't tried. The brothers invited Ben more than a few times, but he'd never taken them up on it.

"It's here because that's the only way we can get you to participate." Brooks shoveled in almost half a soft taco at once. "We knew it couldn't be that you didn't enjoy our company, so we just assumed you must want to have it at your house."

It was a decent observation, one he'd been thinking on since the party at The Inn.

Why hadn't he tried to get friendlier with the Pace brothers? Why hadn't he tried to be friendly with anyone for that matter?

"I never wanted to impose." It even sounded like a lie to him. And he was the one claiming it.

"Considering we invited you all the damn time, I'm hard-pressed to believe you thought you were imposing." Brody was all the way through his food and going back for seconds. "I'm more inclined to think it had something to do with a certain secret you believed no one else knew."

That definitely seemed more likely.

Ben took another swallow of beer as he let that reasoning sit for a minute. "I didn't want to accidentally burden anyone with information they'd rather not know."

Brody tipped his head toward Ben, lifting a brow. "You can go ahead and say you didn't trust us to keep Liza safe, we would understand that."

"Fair enough." He shrugged. "I didn't trust you to keep Liza safe. I was afraid I'd get comfortable," he lifted his beer, "or inebriated, and say something I'd regret."

Boone shook his head, chuckling. "And you thought nobody would notice what was going on."

"Yeah, it's pretty clear when a man starts giving up everything to keep a woman safe." Brody grabbed a tortilla and dropped it onto Ben's plate. "There's really no way to miss it."

"It wasn't personal." Ben moved a little closer to the table, scooping up some meat and dropping it into the center of the tortilla Brody passed off. "I wouldn't of trusted anyone."

"It was a fucked-up situation. I don't blame you one bit." Brody leaned his way. "In all honesty, we had a pool going that if things got too harry you'd confess to killing Ed Cross yourself."

The thought had crossed his mind. "I would have. If I thought they were going to try to put Liza in jail for it."

She'd been through so much. Violence. Abuse. Manipulation.

Ed Cross successfully alienated her from her family, and anyone who would support her, when he moved Liza across the country, isolating her in a way that would ensure his abuse went as unnoticed as possible.

It was a textbook move. One Liza never saw coming.

"Glad it didn't come to that then." Brooks tipped back his beer. "Cause I would have hated to have to claim I was the one who killed Ed."

"Right there with ya." Brett smirked a little. "Woulda been fun though to watch everyone come out of the woodwork claiming they killed Ed."

Ben was stunned to silence.

"Don't look so shocked." Brody leaned forward in his seat. "You've got plenty of people around here who've always had your back."

"I'm not sure why." He'd worked hard to keep some space between himself and everyone else.

Actually it wasn't that hard. It was how Ben lived his whole life up until he met Liza.

He wasn't close to his parents and they weren't close to him. Same with his siblings.

He honestly didn't know he could be close to another person until Liza came along, pulling him in more with every clandestine conversation they shared.

"Because you are a good man." Brody almost sounded angry. "You work hard and you take care of the people around you."

"I can't count the number of times you helped us out when we needed it." Brooks polished off his food. "Even after working a full day here you'd still come work more with us."

"That wasn't a big deal." Work was just that. Work. It had to be done and he was capable of doing it.

"It was to me." Brody's voice carried a surprising amount of emotion. "You helped carry the weight I couldn't when Ashley died."

"Anyone would have done that." He'd been happy to step in when Brody lost his first wife just after she delivered their twin girls.

"Not anyone." Brody pointed his way. "Just you."

"Some people showed up once, but you were the only one who kept comin' back. You were there for us. For our family." Brooks held his gaze. "And we won't ever forget that."

"Which means you're stuck with us." Brody grabbed another beer and popped the lid. "Like it or not." He held the fresh bottle out.

Ben dropped his head.

He was a dumbass. Dense and dumb.

And maybe a little blind.

Ben leaned forward, tapping his beer against Brody's. "I've been stuck with worse."

"That's the fucking truth." Brooks snorted. "I can't believe you actually didn't kill Ed Cross."

"Thought about it." More than a few times. "Probably should have."

"Hindsight's twenty-twenty." Brett kicked his feet up on a chair. "I could have taken Junior Shepard down as a minor, served a few years and been done with it by the time I was eighteen."

"But then I wouldn't have had the pleasure of watching Mae rearrange his face with a cast iron pan." Boone grinned. "And she'd be pissed as hell if you took that honor away from her."

Ben struggled not to smile.

Somehow they'd all managed to come across the best kind of women.

Problematic ones.

The ones some people called bossy.

Loud.

Bitchy.

Intimidating.

Because some people couldn't handle a strong, confident woman who knew her worth.

Thank God.

Ben was just polishing off his first beer when there was a knock at his door.

"Didn't realize you were such a social butterfly." Boone teased him from where he was pulling another beer from the fridge.

Ben opened the door to Troy, Dustin, and Colt, one of the other remaining ranch hands.

Troy leaned to peek around Ben. "Everything okay?"

"Everything's fine." Ben frowned out at the men on his porch. "Why?"

He'd really been hoping for some smooth sailing after clearing out Darryl and his buddies. Just a little time where things were easy, so he could focus on what was most important to him right now.

Who was most important.

"We just saw a truck we didn't recognize come down the driveway." Troy's jaw set. "Wanted to make sure it wasn't anyone who might be a problem."

"Does that mean we have to promise not to be a problem?" Boone stepped into the doorway, beer in hand.

Troy noticeably relaxed. "Hell. I didn't even think about you guys."

"That hurts my feelings a little." Boone lifted up his drink. "Want a beer?"

Troy glanced to Ben.

"Come on in." Ben pushed his door wide. "We've got some food too if you're hungry."

He didn't have to tell Troy and the rest of the boys twice. All three were through the door and snagging drinks and food, rounding out their numbers like someone planned it.

And while no one planned Troy's arrival, someone most definitely orchestrated everything else.

And he was willing to bet all the money he had in the bank on who it was.

Which made everything that much better.

Ben spent the next few hours drinking and playing cards around the table, talking about cattle and corn and football. Weather and work and women.

And while he wasn't completely comfortable talking about Liza and their past, he was okay talking about their present.

And their future.

"You think you'll get married?" Boone tossed out a card, waiting as the trick moved around the table.

"Guess we'll see." Ben threw his addition on top of Brody's. "I don't want to rush her."

Brody snorted. "Sure you don't."

"Let me rephrase that." Ben lined his cards up, tapping the edge of the stack against the table. "I won't rush her."

"You say that now." Brooks nudged Dustin, helping the younger man pick his card. "But before you know it you'll be sweet talkin' her into a trip to the courthouse."

"If for no other reason than so she can get rid of that damn name." Boone swept the cards off, taking the trick that belonged to him and stacking it on his side of the table.

"There's other ways to get rid of a name." Ben watched as Boone slid his finger along the top of his hand, pausing once before making a different selection. "It might be harder to get it off the ranch, but she can get rid of it pretty easily."

"You don't want to change the name of the ranch?" Boone seemed surprised.

Ben shrugged. "It makes sense, even if Ed hadn't bought the place. The way the creeks intersect fits." He turned his attention to Brody, looking for any hint of what might be hiding in the cards in his hand. "But she and I can talk it over and if she really wants to change it then we'll change it."

Brody's eyes narrowed and he seemed to be wavering between a couple options. He finally tossed out a card that trumped Boone's. "It's good that you two work so well together, otherwise that could have gotten real messy."

"I would have signed my portion over to her." Ben tossed in his card, making the trick his as long as Dustin didn't take it from him.

But Dustin was too busy staring at him, jaw dropped. "You own half the ranch?"

"Not half." Ben almost smiled as Brooks leaned back in his seat, making it clear Dustin didn't have anything to fend him off with. "Just part."

"Why doesn't anyone know?" Dustin seemed to recover a little from his initial shock and pulled a card to add to the stack.

"No reason for anyone to know." Even though a few people did.

A few people who obviously knew how to keep their mouths shut considering this was clearly news to Dustin.

Ben swiped the trick off the table. "And it might have undermined Liza's authority." He led the next round, starting off with a low trump card to clear as many of them as possible. "Which we had problems with anyway."

"Some men don't like to take orders from a woman." Dustin picked out a card all by himself.

"Because some men are idiots." Boone went next, tossing out the next lowest trump card.

"Which I appreciate." Brody added his card, proving that Boone and Ben were the only two with any decent cards left in their hands. "Less competition for the rest of us."

"It's a shame that the bar is so low that women are grateful for the bare minimum." Boone shook his head. "A damn shame."

"But it makes us look impressive as hell." Brooks grabbed another beer, bringing one to Ben as he passed. "Course we're not taking old ladies to painting classes, so we're not quite at the same level Chamberlain's at."

The comment removed any doubts he might have had about who set up this evening for him. "I'm sure Muriel would love it if one of you would take her to a painting class." His good mood tempered the tiniest bit as he thought about Muriel sitting all alone in her house.

He looked at the men around the table. It didn't take long for him to work through the rest of the idea percolating in his brain, even with the alcohol fogging it. "You should all meet her sometime."

"Bring her over next week." Brody dunked a chip in what remained of the salsa. "From what I've heard she'll fit right in with the lot of them."

She would.

Muriel was sassy. Willing to speak her mind. Strong and brave and bossy.

"She will." Ben grinned at the thought of her with Maryann and the rest of her group. "She's definitely problematic."

THIRTY-THREE

LIZA

LIZA SWITCHED OFF the headlights as she pulled into the driveway, rolling as close as she could get to the front of the house before parking Ben's truck.

She didn't want to interrupt the fun she hoped he was having.

The Pace boys weren't back yet when she left Maryann's, and she was going to take that as a good sign. They'd been more than happy to pack up and head over to hang out with Ben, so hopefully he was more than happy to have them.

She'd been so caught up in her own problems and sadness that she hadn't noticed how alone he'd been. It was one more thing Liza could add to her list to feel guilty about.

But at least now that wasn't the only list she had.

Liza grabbed her purse and the sheet of paper Maryann sent her on her way with. They'd added a couple more items to it since she was going to knock out number two tonight.

She slid free from the truck, closing her door quietly since even a car door slamming would echo across the open pastures.

She let herself into the farmhouse, but didn't turn on any lights. Ben's house was surrounded by trees, but she wasn't taking any chances.

Not when she and her friends had worked so hard to organize his evening.

Liza dropped her purse in the chair but kept the list with her as she went upstairs to pack a bag.

But not just any bag.

She'd already brought a few things to Ben's place. Her toothbrush. Her face wash. A couple pairs of contacts.

Just whatever it would take to get ready at night, and functional in the morning.

But after talking it over with her friends, it became clear that she needed to offer Ben the same obvious level of commitment that he'd given her.

Which was going to be hard considering his level of commitment was staying at Cross Creek Ranch even when he didn't have to.

Even when they couldn't be together.

Even when she couldn't look his direction.

And now that she was really thinking about it, bringing a few items to his house seemed pretty lame, especially when he'd already made it clear he wanted her staying with him.

But right now it was the best she could do, and at least it was something.

Liza grabbed the biggest bag she had from the closet in her bedroom and started dropping in everything she could think of that was vital to her existence. All her bathroom items went in. Moisturizer, eye cream, deodorant, perfume. All of it.

Then she moved on to clothes. There wasn't any way she would be able to fit her entire wardrobe into the bag, so she just had to settle for items she couldn't live without. That meant every pair of panties and every single bra.

Next she crammed in a couple of her favorite outfits, stuffing them down as tight as she could.

Even then she was already out of room.

"Dammit." She pulled everything out and went to work repacking it, using a little more strategy this time.

The re-pack netted her just enough space to add in her robe and a pair of slippers, but not much else.

Hopefully the symbolism counted for something, because she wasn't going to be able to bring as much as she hoped.

Liza opened the front pouch and was on her way to unplug

the chargers for her phone and tablet, when a strange scuffing pulled her attention toward the stairs.

The house was normally very quiet. There weren't any trees close by to cause scratching branches or scrambling squirrels.

Which is sort of what this sounded like.

She slowly stood, leaning toward her door as she strained to hear better.

Which might have been a mistake, because the sudden slamming of a drawer nearly made her crap her pants.

Someone was in the house.

Papers shuffled together before another drawer slammed, the sound sending her heart rate astronomically high.

Closing her bedroom door would call attention to the fact that she was up there. The hinges were old and creaked with any movement.

Just like the floor under her feet.

Fear of making any sound kept her frozen in place as whoever was in her kitchen continued ransacking the space.

Who came all the way out into the middle of nowhere to rob a house?

The only answer she could come up with didn't make her feel any better. Especially since Darryl and his friends probably weren't too thrilled with her right now.

Liza held her breath as heavy steps moved across the kitchen floor.

They were coming to the stairs.

She didn't have time to process or come up with any sort of viable plan.

All she could do was react. And her reaction was to pick up the heaviest thing within reach, which was a glitter-covered rock her sister made her to use as a paperweight, chuck it in the general direction of the stairs, then slam her door closed and flip the tiny button lock on the knob.

It was admittedly a terrible defense.

And yet somehow successful.

The heavy steps raced down the stairs, through the kitchen, and out the back door.

Liza pressed one hand to her head, fighting to catch her breath as the house went quiet.

She should have kept her damn phone with her, but it was zipped in the purse she dropped just inside the front door.

Hopefully her purse was still just inside the front door, and not clutched in the hand of whoever just broke into her house.

But she wasn't quite ready to go investigate the situation yet.

She didn't actually want to investigate at all.

But without her phone she couldn't really call anyone else to do it for her. That meant she only had herself to rely on.

Liza stood tall, gulping in air in the hopes that it would fuel a sort of bravery she didn't possess.

She could be brave in certain circumstances, but those circumstances always involved other people being in danger.

When it was her ass on the line she tended to struggle.

Step in to protect an innocent child or the man you love? No problem.

She would jump in front of a car or pull a gun.

But when it came time to show herself the same love, all she managed was chucking a glitter-bombed hunk of the Earth's crust into the dark.

That made it sound more impressive than it was.

What she actually did was hurl a chunk of gravel before hiding behind her door like a coward.

And she didn't want to be a coward. Not even when she was the only one who could get hurt because of it.

Liza went to the door, standing right beside it as she listened for any sign that whoever broke into her house hadn't really left. The place was small enough that she could hear just about everything that happened under the roof, and she had definitely heard the burglar run to the back door.

But maybe he was waiting there, lurking in the dark until she came down the stairs to make sure he was gone.

She needed a weapon. Unfortunately she didn't necessarily enjoy keeping them in her house. Liza hadn't touched a gun since the night she had to use one.

Wouldn't have messed around with knives either, but those were pretty tough to avoid.

So she was left with very few options. None to be exact.

Liza tiptoed through her room, looking for anything she could use to defend herself. The only thing that held any promise at all was tucked into the corner of her bathroom. She snagged it from its protective base, being careful not to touch it against any part of her as she pulled it back over one shoulder.

The door barely creaked as she eased it open, doing everything possible to stay as silent as she could.

Luckily, the rest of the house stayed silent too.

Liza sucked in and slid, keeping the opening as small as possible to reduce the chance her movement would be noticed.

Then she tiptoed her way to the top of the stairs, weapon in hand, heart in her throat as she reached the top step.

She could do this. It was fine.

She'd defended herself in this very same house once before.

But that's not who she was worried about that night.

The reason she shot Ed Cross was because of who he planned to find when he was done with her.

And there was no way she was going to let that happen.

The memory was enough to burn her belly with an anger that still lingered.

Still festered.

Liza moved down the steps, riding that wave as it carried her toward the first floor.

And maybe toward whoever thought they could come in and fuck up the first bit of happiness she'd had in a long time.

Just as she reached the first floor, the sound of someone breathing registered, freezing her own breath in her lungs. She adjusted her grip on the plastic handle, getting ready to swing with as much accuracy as she could manage, given she was batting as a lefty.

A shadow moved across the floor, stretching taller as whoever was just inside the backdoor came closer.

She took one step, throwing as much weight as she could manage into the swing, hoping what she lacked in precision she could make up for in momentum. The rubber end connected and the man yelped.

Liza pulled back and swung again. "*Get out of my house.*"

"Jesus Christ." Troy managed to block her second hit. "What in the hell are you doing?"

Liza squinted in the dark. "Troy?" She flipped on the lights, regretting it immediately as the brightness assaulted her dilated pupils. She shielded her eyes with one arm "What am *I* doing?" She blinked hard, trying to acclimate. "What are *you* doing?"

"I just came back from gettin' more beer and saw Ben's truck parked out front. I was wanting to make sure you were okay, since there weren't any lights on." He pointed to the item in her hand. "Did you hit me with a plunger?"

"Don't try to change the subject." Liza pointed at the mess across her kitchen floor. "Why were you going through my stuff?"

Troy's eyes went to the scattered papers. Both hands immediately went up. "I didn't touch anything. I barely got through the door before you hit me."

Liza looked him up and down, trying to decide if she should believe him or not.

Troy pointed to the back door. "This was standing wide open when I passed. That's why I wanted to be sure everything was okay."

She leaned to peek at the door. It looked relatively intact, outside of the doorknob Ben just installed. "Did you see anyone else out there?"

Troy shook his head. "Not a soul." He pulled out a chair. "Maybe you should sit down. You look a little pale."

"I'm okay." That wasn't the complete truth, but right now she wasn't sure about what exactly was going on, and sitting down when Troy could have been the one who broke into her house didn't seem like a smart thing to do. "Where's Ben?"

"He's back at his cabin with the Pace boys." Troy's brows lifted. "You haven't called him yet?"

She shook her head as it started to swim. "No."

Troy fished out his phone and swiped across the screen. As he started to talk she went ahead and took his sitting suggestion, her eyes skimming over the mess of items strewn across her kitchen floor.

"I give him thirty seconds." Troy shoved his phone back into his pocket and crouched down in front of her. "You want some water or something?"

Liza shook her head. "What were they looking for?" She wasn't asking Troy.

Hopefully there was no way he would know.

She was just thinking out loud, trying anything to distract her from the fact that she was dangerously close to melting down.

This was nothing like the night Ed Cross attacked her, but there was still the sense of being violated.

The fear.

The adrenaline.

It all swirled together in a cocktail of familiarity that made her skin crawl and her stomach churn.

She heard Ben coming, registered his boots across the floor as he ran toward her.

But it was like she wasn't actually there. Somehow she was far away.

Detached.

"Grady's on his way." Brody Pace stood in the center of her kitchen as Ben scooped her up and hauled her out into the night, taking her away from everything crowding her mind, cluttering it with the past she would never really be able to put behind her.

No matter how much time went by.

Ben took her straight out to his truck, setting her in the passenger's seat while Troy and the rest of the Pace brothers walked around in the dark, flashlights beaming across the night as they hunted for any sign of who ruined this perfect evening.

Ben pushed her hair back from her face, his eyes on hers. "You okay?"

She shook her head. "Someone broke into the house."

"I know." His hands moved over her face and down her arms, like he was double checking to make sure she wasn't hurt. "Did you see them?"

"No." Liza closed her eyes as the fog started to lift. "I was upstairs."

Ben's hands stilled. "What were you doing upstairs?"

It shouldn't be this hard to remember. It wasn't that long ago.

Her brain just didn't seem to be working properly. "I don't remember."

All she remembered was the fear.

The blood.

No. Wait.

There was no blood this time.

This time was different.

"I was packing." Her words came slowly, each one requiring more effort than it should. "So I could stay with you." She started to shake like she was cold, in spite of the warm summer air. "And then—"

"It's okay." Ben pulled her close, the warmth and strength of his body surrounding her. "Just relax for a minute."

Liza pressed her face into his neck, breathing deep the same way she did on the night that might have left more of an imprint than she wanted to consider. "I don't want to think about what happened anymore."

She shouldn't be thinking about it now.

She should be over it.

Thought she was.

"I know." Ben's hand curved against the back of her head.

"How do I make it stop?" She was so tired of Ed Cross. Tired of thinking about what he put her through.

What he did.

What she had to do.

"I don't know." Ben rested his forehead against hers. "But I sure as hell wish I did."

THIRTY-FOUR

BEN

LIZA LET OUT a breath as they pulled up in front of his house, one Ben felt as much as he heard.

"We can get anything else you want out of there tomorrow." He'd carry it all back by hand if that's what it took to make sure she never had to go back there again.

Liza nodded. "Okay."

He hadn't realized how much that night still affected her. How much of the fear still lingered, waiting for the opportunity to grab hold.

Ben went to her side of the truck, keeping his hands on her as she slid free.

Mostly for his own benefit.

Because Liza wasn't the only one still struggling with memories that carried more weight than they should.

She didn't argue as he kept her close, tucking her into his side tight enough his ribs complained.

They could complain. They'd have to get over it.

Right now all that mattered was Liza. He hadn't been able to be there for her when she needed him most, and he was going to do everything possible to make up for it now.

Liza leaned against him as they walked to the door, her arm around his waist, head against his shoulder.

He led her inside, wishing like hell he'd been able to do this the last time.

She'd been hurt and alone and there was nothing he could do to fix it.

Not without putting suspicion where it didn't belong.

Liza turned to face him as he locked the door, her eyes moving over his face. "Are you okay?"

"Of course I'm okay." He reached out to touch her face, reminding himself she was safe. "Don't worry about me."

Her head barely tipped, pressing the smooth skin of her cheek into his palm. "Why shouldn't I worry about you?"

"Because I'm fine." He stepped closer. "Nothing happened to me."

Nothing had ever happened to him. It was always Liza bearing the brunt of the awful things happening around them.

Liza's brows came together. "That doesn't mean you have to be okay." Her hands came to his chest, sliding up the center. "I wonder if maybe it's worse when it's not you."

"It's not." Couldn't be.

Liza's touch skimmed over his ribs as her eyes stayed on his. "I think it is." She moved in as her hands found his shoulders. "Do you know what I remember most about that night?"

He didn't want to know so he didn't ask.

She offered it up anyway. "The relief I felt when you found me." The tips of her fingers moved over his face. "When I knew you were safe."

Ben closed his eyes, swallowing hard as he dropped his forehead to rest on hers.

"When you fell." Her voice barely shook. "I was so scared but I could be with you, holding your hand, seeing that you were okay." Liza shook her head, rocking it against his. "You didn't have that."

He'd watched the ambulance pull away that night, Liza inside it and covered in blood, pretending like he wasn't breaking apart.

And then he had to do it again, standing in a crowd of people, barely breathing as they took Liza from him once more, broken and bleeding and in pain.

Her hands came back to his face, fingers spreading over his

skin. When he opened his eyes she was still watching him. "I threatened to kick Travis's ass if they didn't let me in the ambulance." She pressed her lips together. "And to make sure Cecily never waited on him at Mae's again."

The tightness in his throat eased a little at the thought of poor Travis Moore trying to negotiate a wound-up Elizabeth Cross. "That's downright vicious, Sweetheart."

"Desperate times call for desperate measures." Liza didn't look sorry at all. "I was willing to do anything to make sure I was with you." Her head barely shook. "But it wasn't for you." She took a little breath. "It was for me." Her eyes dropped. "I couldn't —" Her voice broke.

"I'm fine." His breaks and bruises would heal. "I promise."

"I know." She met his gaze. "And I've been here with you every day to see it." Her chin barely quaked. "You didn't get that, and I can't imagine what it was like for you."

He wanted to tell her it was fine, but he couldn't force it out.

Because it wasn't. Not even close.

"It was hell."

He'd done everything he could to take care of Liza, but his options were limited. Everyone was watching her, trying to figure out if the city girl killed her husband to claim his ranch as her own.

He'd spent the whole time she was in the hospital cleaning the house, bleaching and scrubbing away every trace of what happened. He got rid of the table Ed fell across when she brought his reign of abuse and control to an end, replacing it with the one from his own house.

He burned the sheets. The blankets. The bed. Replacing it all.

Anything she shared with a man who never deserved her.

But watching it burn didn't fix anything.

Liza still couldn't be his.

He still couldn't be by her side as she walked through one of the most horrible things that could happen to a person.

Ben smoothed both hands down her back, trying to soothe a pain that went so deep chances were good nothing could reach it. "But it's over."

"I wanted to think it was." Liza gave him a sad smile. "But

after tonight, I'm not sure it will ever be over. I think it might always be there."

The thought of her having to relive what happened for the rest of her life wasn't anything he could stand. "It will go away."

Liza shook her head. "I don't think it will." Her fingers dragged across his jaw. "But maybe that's okay." Her eyes followed the path of her touch as it slid over his lips. "It will remind me how lucky I am." Her gaze lifted to his. "And that eventually I made a good decision."

"I'm not sure I can look at it like that, Sweetheart." There was no way to put a positive spin on everything she'd been through.

All the suffering.

All the pain.

"Then you're proving my point." She smiled a little as she leaned into him, her lips almost touching his. "It would have been easier if it happened to you." Her expression held the tiniest hint of victory. "Which means you've suffered more than I have."

He didn't like the way that sounded. It was the reason he'd resisted her analysis of their situation in the first place.

Because it absolutely would have been easier if he was the one who went through what she did, but he would never admit that to her, not when it was clear as day that she'd think it meant he got the worse end of the deal. "No."

"You have." Liza was undeterred. "And you did it for me."

He was quiet for a second, letting the clarity she had sink in before offering some of his own. "Everything I do is for you, Elizabeth."

She was so close he could feel her smile against his lips. "I know."

It was what he'd been waiting so long for.

For her to see him.

See that he was always there.

Waiting.

He pulled her in, bringing her mouth to his.

Or maybe she was the one pulling him close, sealing their lips together.

It didn't matter who did what. Why it happened or how.

All that mattered was that she was where she belonged. With him.

Finally.

Liza grabbed at him, hands twisting in his clothes as he tried to get her down the hall and into his room.

Their room.

Their bed.

Their home.

She knocked the hat off his head, sending it to the floor as he did his best to keep her from bumping into anything. When her butt hit the bed she went down, both hands fisted so tight in his shirt that he had no choice but to go with her.

Ben smiled at the strength in her hold. "Seems like that arm's getting better." He grabbed her around the waist, dragging Liza up the bed in short bursts, powering through the pinch in his ribs. "I guess rest was more important than you realized."

"Shut up." There was no aggravation in her voice and the smile on her lips held as she worked his shirt up. "Nobody likes a know-it-all."

"I'm definitely not a know-it-all, Sweetheart." He lifted up, making it easier for her to get his shirt free. "If I was then I'd have figured out how to get you here a hell of a lot sooner." The second his upper half was bare, Ben snagged the banded top of her sundress, easily dragging the gathered fabric down her body, stripping her naked in a single move. "I love these fuckin' dresses."

He hadn't seen her wear many dresses over the years. Not until recently.

"Me too." Liza kicked the pool of soft floral away, sending it over the edge of the mattress.

"Why didn't you wear them before?" He skimmed his nose down her neck, lips running over her satiny skin.

"I wanted people to take me seriously." Her fingers tangled in his hair.

"Sweetheart, I'm not sure people could take you more seriously." He'd watched her go from a woman who lived in fear to one who stood tall, running a world she didn't understand like it was where she was always meant to be.

And maybe it was.

Maybe every decision Liza made was the right one.

The one intended to bring her where she would be appreciated. Understood.

Loved.

"That's not how it started, though." Liza's legs tangled with his. "No one thought I could run Cross Creek."

Ben lifted his head, meeting her eyes. "I did."

She pulled him to her, holding tight as her mouth lifted to his.

He would never get enough of this. Enough of her.

Liza hooked one knee around the back of his, pinning it in place as she pushed against him, rolling their bodies across the bed, switching their positions in one smooth move.

She knelt over him, knees pressed to the blankets, hair loose around her face.

She was fucking stunning.

He slid his hands up her belly, over one of many scars she carried, tracing it with his fingers on his way to catch the weight of her breasts in his palms. He lifted them, dragging his thumbs across her nipples, watching as they pulled tight under his touch. Her eyes closed as he rolled them, pinching just a little with each careful twist.

She moved against him, dragging her pussy over the line of his dick where it strained against his jeans.

"Christ." He was already aching, which didn't bode well for either of them. Ben slid his hands down to her hips, gripping them tight as she continued to work against him, each rub of her body threatening his grip on the moment and on himself.

Liza's eyes opened, lids heavy as they focused on his face.

And what he saw there sent the need racing through his veins into overdrive.

It wasn't the lust that hooded her gaze or the desire pulling one lip between her teeth.

It was something else. Something he always knew was there.

Something no amount of time or distance could kill.

Ben reached up, curving his hand around the back of her neck as he pulled her down to him, rolling her body back under his.

Maybe someday he'd be able to take his time with her. Savor every second as he dragged them out.

But this wasn't someday.

He shucked his jeans, knocking them free as his lips moved against hers, one hand on her face as the other slid his dick along the wet heat of her slit. He pressed in the second he was in place, unable to wait any longer to be inside her.

Liza sucked in a breath, letting it out on a groan that moved from her mouth to his.

He breathed it in, drawing it deep, letting it soothe the ache he would always own.

The ache that would remind him of the sacrifice they both made.

Liza moved with him, rocking in perfect time with each push of his body into hers. She held him tight, eyes locked on his like she was afraid to look away.

Worried this moment might slip away if she let it out of her sight.

He understood the feeling completely.

Because while they'd shared many moments before, this one was different.

This one was real and raw and pure.

It was new and old and undeniable.

It was a beginning.

And an end.

Liza's thighs pressed to his hips, her lips parting as her breath came faster, spurring him on.

Her head tipped, rocking back.

But her eyes stayed on his.

She flexed around him, her impending climax pulling his balls tight, forcing him to fight through.

He'd do it happily. Whatever it took to keep her with him.

She gasped as he hooked one hand behind her left knee, pushing it up as he pressed deeper, sinking completely into her. "*Ben*." Her next breath was ragged. "I'm going to—" She let out a little groan as he worked his body against her, grinding out as much friction as he could manage as his pelvis rubbed her mound.

"That's it." He stayed the course, resisting the urge to speed up as she started to tense. "Give it to me, Elizabeth. Give me what I want."

It's all he'd ever wanted. To know she had what she deserved. To be the one to provide it.

Her back bowed and her eyes went wide, fingers digging into his skin as she jerked under him and contracted around him, milking his own release free.

He buried himself deep, his own heat mixing with hers as he fought for air, face dropping into the tangle of her hair, the sweet scent of her filling his lungs with each burning breath.

Ben nosed against the side of her face, pressing his lips to her temple. "You okay?"

"I think so." She was still a little breathless. "But it seems like I might need to do a little more cardio."

He chuckled. "I think you should hold off on that for a while." Ben eased away, hating the second they were no longer joined. "At least until your leg is all healed up."

Liza's eyes moved over his face, her expression serious. "I need to tell you something."

He smoothed back her hair, running his fingers through the soft strands. "Okay."

She opened her mouth, but hesitated a second before blurting it out. "I love you."

Ben propped up on one arm, savoring the moment for just a second before giving her a smile as he pushed up from the bed to get a towel. "Seems like you might."

THIRTY-FIVE
LIZA

"WHAT WILL HAPPEN if someone opens the door?" Liza stood behind Curtis, watching as the older ranch hand from Red Cedar Ranch installed the camera bell beside the front door on the little farmhouse she used to call home.

Curtis continued working. "I mean, first off they're going to be on camera." He turned her way. "But it's also going to call down to the police station."

"That's good I guess." It would take the police forever to get here, but at least they would get whoever it was on camera. "Will there be a camera on the back door too?"

"Yup." Curtis passed her the box that the new security system came in.

She scanned the front before peeking inside and digging out the manual. The thing was huge. Liza flipped through the pages, eyes losing focus at the vast amount of instructions. "I hope you already know how to work this thing." She stopped at a page that explained how to program it. "It looks complicated."

"I'll take care of it." Ben came up the steps, wrapping one arm around her as he pulled her in from the front porch. "The only thing you need to be worried about is what goes into storage, and what goes to the house."

They'd been at the main house all morning. She and Ben had

come in the day after the break-in and taken out anything important, like paperwork, computers, and valuables.

But then she sort of lost interest in packing up the rest of her things, and managed to stall for over a week.

Long enough that Ben went ahead and took matters into his own hands.

"Where are we taking all the furniture?" Brody Pace stood in the center of her living room, looking at the couch, coffee table, and armchairs. "Because I don't think this is all going to fit in Ben's house."

"Storage, I guess?" Liza hadn't really thought this completely through, primarily because she had so many other wonderful things to think about, and letting her brain go back to this house wasn't something she necessarily enjoyed.

Brody gave her a single nod. "Storage it is."

He and his brothers immediately started carrying out all the big items and stacking them on the back of the flatbed trailer they brought.

It was strange to watch the things she collected over the years walk out the front door. Liza never expected any of it would leave this place, and that included her.

Not that she was *leaving*, leaving. Like it or not, Cross Creek was her home. It belonged to her, and she'd paid a lot for it.

Way more than it was worth.

"You okay?" Ben rested his hands on her shoulders.

"It's just weird. I worked so hard to try to make this place feel like home, but it never did." It wasn't the little house's fault. Under the right circumstances she would have loved it.

"Hopefully you'll feel more at home soon." Ben smoothed over her hair with both hands, keeping them at the back of her head as he pressed a kiss to her lips. "But before that can happen we need to clear this place out."

"I know." She huffed out a breath. "But I would've been fine leaving everything where it was and just buying all new stuff."

Ben gave her a little smile. "I'm not so sure the next person to live here would have been kind to all your white furniture."

"Are you trying to say I'm dirty?" Troy came past carrying an end table. He shot Liza a little wink. "Because I am."

"You're turning out to be helpful to have around." Ben lifted his brows at Troy. "I'd really hate to have to kill you."

Troy didn't look threatened. His grin held all the way out the front door.

"I don't think he's scared of you." Liza huffed out another breath, dragging it into a sigh. "Let's get this over with."

How she managed to live here all these years was impossible to explain, because ever since the night someone broke in it was a struggle just driving past. All she could think about was everything she'd been through there. All the violence. The death. The sadness.

"You want me to empty out all these drawers?" Dustin pointed to the line of cabinets that whoever broke in started to ransack. "Maybe pack everything into a box?"

"We already came in and got all that." Liza waved in the direction of the cabinets that held plates and glasses. "Those are still full, though. You could pack all that up."

Dustin nodded. "Sure. I can do that."

He disappeared out the back door, probably to retrieve one of the many boxes the Pace brothers brought with them.

"Let's go upstairs and get everything out of your room." Ben went first, letting her follow him up.

Liza looked around the bedroom. It was exactly the same as it had been for years, but now it seemed different.

Now she could only see it as the room where Ben found her the night their whole world crumbled down around them. The place where he held her one last time while they waited for the ambulance and police.

"I hate this house." She rubbed her arms, trying to smooth down the unease creeping across her skin.

There was too much here. Too many things she thought she'd overcome.

But it turned out she'd only hidden them, managing to block them away out of self-preservation.

"I know." Ben grabbed the first box and passed it her way. "I do too."

Liza opened up the closet and started grabbing clothes, unhooking as many as she could at once before dropping them in.

She didn't care if she had to re-wash and dry every single thing in there, all that mattered was that this was over, once and for all.

It took less than twenty minutes to pack everything into boxes and shove them to the top of the stairs. The Pace boys and Troy and the rest of the ranch hands made quick work of them, hauling them down and out before stacking them in the back of Ben's truck to be taken back to his house.

Which was about to be bursting at the seams.

It was one more thing for her to feel guilty about in a list that never seemed to stop growing.

"I think we've got everything." Brody stood in the center of the empty house, hands on his hips. "You need anything else from us?"

"You've done plenty." Ben shook Brody's hand. "You sure you don't want me to follow you and get all that unloaded?"

"Positive." Brody went out the front door. "I've got plenty of help." He tipped his head toward where Troy was closing the tailgate on Ben's truck. "Looks like you do too."

Ben watched Troy, a small smile curving his lips. "Looks like."

Brody fished out the keys to his bright red truck. "Let me know when you want this stuff brought back."

"I will." Ben waved as the group loaded up and pulled out of the driveway, taking all her furniture with them.

"You sure they have the room to store all that?" Liza was more than willing to rent a unit, but Brody insisted they had space at Red Cedar Ranch.

"Positive." Ben locked up the house before taking her hand as they crossed the yard. He whistled between his teeth, catching Troy's attention.

As soon as he looked up, Ben tossed the house keys his way.

Dustin managed to catch them midair, swinging them around once before passing them off to Troy. "I guess these belong to you."

Troy snagged the keys away, offering Ben a nod.

They'd discussed their options and settled on the fact that leaving the farmhouse vacant didn't make any sense. Not if there was someone who wanted to live in it.

Troy had been busting his ass around the ranch, so he was the obvious choice, and he'd jumped at the opportunity, not even blinking at the fact that she'd unalived Ed Cross in the kitchen.

Troy added the keys to the ring already in his hand. "I'll meet you back at your place."

"Give us a little bit." Ben hooked one arm around her shoulders.

Troy smirked. "Only a little bit?" He stuck a toothpick between his teeth. "Must suck to get old."

Ben turned toward his truck, an easy grin on his face as they loaded inside. "I'm not too old to kick your ass."

His smile was contagious enough that Liza carried one of her own all the way back to his house.

Or maybe she was just happy. Genuinely, completely happy.

Almost completely happy.

"I'm thinking of going to visit my parents and Dawn." Now that Troy was helping Ben, she had a little more flexibility with her time.

Unfortunately, any traveling she did would have to be alone.

"I think that would be a good idea." Ben reached over to take her hand.

"I wish you could go with me." As much as things had changed, there was still plenty that would probably stay the same for a while.

Like one of them needing to be at the ranch.

"I do too." Ben stroked across her skin as he pulled up in front of their house. There was real regret in his voice.

Like he genuinely wished he could go with her.

Liza slid free of the truck and followed him to the tailgate, managing to balance one of the smaller boxes.

Ben frowned at her. "Leave that here. I'll get it."

"I thought you wanted my arm to be better?" She followed him up the stairs. "Remember all the Advil you made me take?"

"I do want your arm to be better." He opened the door, letting her go inside first. "Which is why I want to be sure you don't overdo it."

"I'm pretty sure carrying a five-pound box of all the stuff my sister's made me doesn't count as overdoing." Liza set the box onto the table and flipped open the top. She pulled out her most prized possession, smiling back at the photo of her parents and Dawn surrounded by seashells fixed to the frame with hot glue.

"You can put that anywhere you want." Ben carried the box in his arms back to the bedroom.

Liza took the photo of her family over to the wall where Ben showcased his.

The images couldn't be any more different.

No one smiled in any of the pictures along the wall. Everyone was just lined up, staring at the camera. No one was embracing or even touching at all. Not even the kids who all sat stoically across the grass in front of Ben and his siblings.

Ben came into the room and stopped, his presence turning her to face him.

"If you ever want to go visit your family then you can."

He barely shook his head. "I don't."

She turned back toward the line of photos. "Are you sure? Because you have pictures of them up where you can see them every day."

"It's a reminder." Ben slowly came her way. "Not to settle." His eyes moved to the line of photographs. "Not to take anyone for granted." He continued coming closer. "Not to fall in line just because that's the way things have always been." His eyes fell. "Not that I've done a particularly good job at any of that." He shrugged. "And I don't hate them. I owe them a lot." His eyes came back to hers. "I wouldn't be standing here without them."

"But you don't miss them?"

He was quiet for a minute. Like he had to think about the question. "I miss what I wish they'd been."

The ache she'd been fighting for days fisted tight, squeezing the breath from her lungs.

There was no way she was ever going to be good enough for this man. No way she would ever equal the level of sacrifice he'd made for her.

But maybe there was one thing she could give him that might at least get her on the board.

Liza wrapped her arms around his waist. "I was thinking about your birthday."

Ben's expression relaxed, like he was happy with the change

in subject. "And you decided that the best thing you could give me was you." He tipped his head to nose along her neck. "On the kitchen table." He caught the lobe of her ear between his teeth. "In my truck." His hand curved along her breast, thumb raking across her nipple through the fabric of her dress. "Maybe in the barn."

"That's a lot of presents you're wanting." Liza sucked in a breath as he tugged down the top of her dress, his head dipping to pull one tight tip into his mouth.

Her pussy immediately clenched as heat raced to collect there, forming an immediate ache.

Ben backed her across the room until her back was against the wall just beside the front door. "Not a lot." His lips moved against hers as he worked the hem of her dress up with one hand. "Just one a lot of times."

His fingers found her immediately. He groaned against her mouth. "Have I told you how much I love these damn dresses?"

Liza's knees went a little weak as he brushed across her, forcing her to fight out a breathy 'yes'.

"I love bein' able to have you whenever I want, Elizabeth." He worked her easily. Skillfully. "I waited a long damn time for this."

She held onto him as her legs threatened to buckle, each pass of his fingers sending her closer and closer to the inevitable. When she started to wobble Ben pushed closer, his body bracing hers as she came undone, clinging to him as everything fell away around her.

Almost everything.
Not Ben.
He was always there.
Always had been.
Always would be.

THIRTY-SIX

LIZA

"EVERYTHING IS READY." Maryann sounded cool and calm.

Thank God someone was.

"I just want it to be perfect for him." Liza peeked out the door, making sure Ben wasn't home yet. "I want him to know how important he is to everyone."

She'd been working like crazy to plan a surprise for a man who'd probably never had a birthday party in his life.

Liza shot a glare at the photo of Ben's parents, wishing she could meet them just one time.

But honestly she should probably thank them. They'd set the bar pretty low.

Hopefully low enough that she would finally be able to make him feel a little of the way he made her feel.

"I am positive this will be the perfect night." Maryann had been her partner in crime, helping Liza pick out and prepare all the food and decorations. They'd gone all out. Invited anyone and everyone who loved Ben.

Because he needed to know that while his given family might not have appreciated him, his found one absolutely did.

Liza took a deep breath, blowing it back out. "Okay. We're going to go pick up the cake in town and then we'll be on our way."

Ben was the only wild card in the scenario. If he was later than she expected then it could throw the whole thing off.

Just then his green truck pulled down the driveway.

"He's here." Her heart rate picked up immediately, and it was only partly because of how he looked in his blue jeans.

"Right on time." Maryann's smile carried through the line. "I love a man you can set your clock by."

Liza tried to calm her breathing. "I'll see you soon."

She disconnected the call and slipped her phone into her purse before trying to find a pose that looked relaxed. She settled on leaning against the kitchen table.

Ben came through the door, his dark eyes immediately finding her and skimming down her body. "Well, hello there."

She smiled, but it felt awkwardly tight as her nerves made it almost impossible to act naturally. "Hey."

He pulled off his hat, tossing it to the sofa as he closed the door behind him. "Are you dishing out birthday presents already?"

If anything could distract her from the panicky feeling skittering over her skin, it was the thought of Ben balancing her on the kitchen table.

But right now there was no time for that.

"It's not your birthday for two more days." That was phase one of her plan.

Don't do anything on his actual birthday. He'd see that coming.

"I don't think that rule is hard and fast." He slowly prowled her way, each step he took threatening all her hard work and planning.

"I need to pick up a cake." It came out fast.

Too fast.

Ben's brows lifted. "A cake?"

"Not for you." She was not good at this. "For the Pace boys. For helping with my stuff."

"When do you need to pick it up?"

"Now."

Ben's brows lifted. "Now?"

Liza nodded, having to stop her head after it continued bobbing. "Right now."

Ben grabbed his hat from where he'd dropped it. "I guess we're goin' to get a cake then."

Twenty minutes later they were walking into The Baking Rack. Dianna was waiting at the counter, looking a little fancier than normal.

Her dark hair was down, curled in big waves that perfectly framed her lovely face. Her brows and eyes were a little more defined than normal, and her cheeks were contoured with a shimmery bronze.

Hopefully Ben wasn't as perceptive when it came to other women as he was when she was involved.

"Hi, guys." Dianna's smile was just as bright as normal. "How's it going?"

She knew darn well how it was going, and her act was definitely more convincing than Liza's was.

"Look at you." Ben pointed Dianna's way and Liza's heart skipped a beat. "You've already got it packed up and ready to go."

Liza let out a little breath.

"You're my last pick-up of the day." Dianna didn't miss a beat. "It's easy to be on the ball when you're in the home stretch."

Liza almost laughed. It was definitely not easy to be on the ball when you were in the home stretch. That's where she was now, and every minute she was bouncing between passing out or melting down.

Because this was important.

Ben spent five freaking years isolating himself to protect her, afraid that letting anyone close would make it more likely they'd see what he was working so hard to hide.

He'd gone a lifetime without a family like he deserved, and when one finally came along he'd pushed them away.

For her.

So that meant she would be the one to rope them back in and wrap them in a big bow.

"That mean you can get out of here?" Ben picked up the bag containing a maple walnut stack cake and slid it off the counter without bothering to look inside.

Another suspicion-raising obstacle cleared.

"It does." Dianna rocked on her heels, smile staying on her face.

Ben leaned against the counter, like he was settling in for a long conversation. "You got something exciting planned?"

"Actually, I do." Dianna's gaze stayed right on Ben as she did her best to keep the show moving.

"Then we won't keep you." Ben straightened, wrapping one arm around Liza as he gave Dianna a wink. "Enjoy your evening."

Dianna winked back at him in an exaggerated move. "I will."

Liza was going to owe her big time, because the baker managed to not only avoid raising Ben's suspicions, but she also managed to nudge his loitering butt right along, putting them back on schedule.

"I think Miss Dianna has a date." Ben held her hand in his as he slowly walked them toward where his truck sat in the public lot. "It's about time someone worked up the balls to ask her out."

"It is." Hopefully Ben wasn't too disappointed in the male population of Moss Creek when he found out she was the one who worked up the balls to ask Dianna out.

Actually it was her, Maryann, and Mae who showed up at the bakery with an invitation to lunch.

And an invitation to a party.

"Whoever it is should invest in a belt with extra holes on it, because I would imagine Dianna could add some girth to a man's middle real quick."

"Is that your way of telling me I'm not a great cook?" Liza gently poked at his middle. "Because you haven't gained a pound."

"It's not the cookin' that makes a man fat, Sweetheart." Ben leaned into her ear. "It's being happy, so hopefully you don't just love me for my body."

"I mean," she made a show of looking him up and down, "it definitely doesn't hurt your cause."

"I guess you'll just have to keep workin' the calories off me then." Ben opened the passenger's door and tipped his head toward the interior of the truck. "Get up in there."

Liza tried not to look panicked. "I was thinking I'd drive."

She didn't want him looking around too hard as they made their way back to The Inn, just in case there were signs of all the cars tucked away in one of the fields.

Ben lifted his brows, but he passed over the keys. "I'm starting to think you like playing chauffeur."

Liza took the keys, clenching them tight in her hand. "I just like feeling normal." She rounded the front of the truck, trying to act as normal as she claimed to feel. Once she was in and buckled her heart started to pound, making her movements jerky as she shifted gears and backed out.

She was going to ruin this if she didn't get herself together.

And if that happened she'd be devastated.

This was her chance to show Ben everything he'd shown her. To let him know how much she appreciated everything he did.

Because it was all for her.

And honestly, that was a lot of pressure.

Liza took slow, deep breaths, fighting for calm as they drove out to Red Cedar Ranch.

Her nerves crept up more with each passing second, and by the time they were passing the main house she could barely string a sentence together. "I called Maryann." Her throat involuntarily swallowed, forcing her to cough a little. "She said they were back at The Inn."

Ben was relaxed in his seat, the bag from Dianna's balanced on his lap. "Hopefully we're not crashin' another party."

She almost choked. "Hopefully not."

There were a number of rental cars and trucks lined out in front of The Inn, just enough to make it seem like any other day at Moss Creek's busiest tourist destination.

She had to give Maryann credit. The woman knew how to pull off a surprise. She'd thought of everything. From the timing, to the hidden parking lot.

And it seemed like it was all going to work.

Ben passed over the cake as they walked to the door. "I'll let you be the one to give it to them."

Liza smiled at Ben's empty hands. "Okay."

He was primed and ready for all the hugs and handshakes

coming his way, completely oblivious to what he was walking into.

She'd pulled it off.

Managed to finally give Ben a little bit of what he deserved.

Maryann came out onto the porch, looking completely normal.

Which was still glamorous. Her swingy bob was styled and sleek and her sheath dress was simple and summery.

"I recognize that bag." She smiled wide. "If you're not careful my boys will come help you out every day."

"I can think of worse things." Ben put one hand on the small of Liza's back, pressing her up the stairs in front of him.

Her eyes were on him as they walked into The Inn. She wanted to see his face when he realized this was a party for him. That the family that found him all showed up to celebrate his—

"Elizabeth." Ben's voice was low. He tipped his head toward the crowd she knew was waiting for them. "Look."

"I know." She couldn't control her wide smile as she turned to face everyone.

But her smile slipped immediately.

And then the cake hit the floor.

BEN

WELL SHIT.

That wasn't the reaction he was expecting.

Not by a long shot.

Liza silently stared at the people in front of her, mouth dropped open, eyes wide.

Ben stepped in a little closer. "Sweetheart?"

She didn't seem to hear him, so he reached up to push her hair behind one shoulder, hoping the added contact might help. "Elizabeth?"

Slowly her hands came to cover her mouth as her whole face crumpled.

Then she started to run, kicking the cake he should have told

Dianne to replace with a decoy, sending the bag tipping over as she rushed across the room.

And straight into her mother's arms.

Maryann came to stand at his side, watching as Liza's dad patted her back and Dawn bounced beside them in excitement. "I think you pulled it off."

"Seems like." He'd been working to get her parents here since that day at Muriel's, crossing his fingers that Dawn would get clearance to travel. When it came through he'd gone straight to Maryann and started planning.

Only to have someone else start planning a party of her own.

"You think she's going to be mad?" It was his only fear. That Liza would be pissed that he'd known about her party plan the whole time.

"Probably." Maryann wiped at the corner of one eye as Liza and her sister held each other in a tight hug, rocking from one side to the other. "But I think it's worth it."

"It's definitely worth it." He'd take all the wrath Liza had to dish out for this moment.

"I hope you recorded this." Dianna stepped in at his side, a cake box in her hands.

"Nora's got it." Ben tipped his head to where Liza's friend was holding up her phone, barely managing to keep it steady as tears trickled down her cheeks.

Dianna looked down at the bag from her bakery. "Glad I didn't put a real cake in there." She carried the box to the island where all the food was set up.

"You're a pretty smart woman." Ben went back to watching Liza as she moved on to hugging her father.

"It doesn't happen often, so be grateful I used it on your cake." Dianna let Maryann help her get the maple walnut cake he'd mentioned once out and stacked on the empty cake stand positioned in the center of the desserts.

It may not be what Liza was thinking, but she'd more than managed to prove her point.

All his favorite foods lined the counter, and all his favorite people filled The Inn. There was no denying the woman loved him just as much as he loved her.

Not that he'd doubted it.

"She seems happy." Muriel was dressed up like she was the night they went out to paint.

Ben made a show of looking her over. "You get all gussied up just for me?"

"Not *just* for you." She wiggled her shoulders, pushing them back. "I figured there'd be some eligible cowboys here." She gave him a wink. "And I'm always looking for young, strong men," her smile turned devilish, "to come shovel my sidewalk."

Ben chuckled. "I bet before the end of the night you'll have more than enough cowboys lined up to keep your sidewalk clear."

"I should get on it then." Muriel elbowed him. "And it looks like someone else wants your attention anyway."

Ben glanced up as Muriel hustled away.

Liza was coming toward him, and it was impossible to tell how she was feeling about the surprise party that turned out to be more surprising than she expected.

She stopped in front of him, glancing at Muriel as she sidled up to Dustin, before bringing her eyes back to his. "You knew about my party."

Ben shook his head. "I knew about *our* party."

"Why did you get to know about it but I didn't?" She didn't seem angry.

She seemed...

Defeated.

"Maryann had to decide what to do. We were both tryin' to surprise the other one on the same day."

Liza glanced over her shoulder at where Maryann was talking to her parents and sister. "You brought my family here." When she turned back to face him her eyes were shimmering. "And all I did was throw you a birthday party."

He knew there was a chance she'd be upset, but he expected anger. Not whatever this was. "It's not a competition, Sweetheart."

She huffed out a bitter laugh. "Thank God, or I'd be in last place."

Ben reached out to wipe at her eyes, catching a few tears as they fell free. "I don't think you understand why I do what I do."

"You do it because you're amazing." She sniffed. "And I can't freaking keep up."

Ben shook his head. "That's not why I do it."

He didn't realize Liza wasn't seeing the reasons he did what he did.

Not all of them anyway.

"I do it for you, that's true." He swiped another tear. "But I do it for me more." He moved in closer, cradling her face in his hands without fear or worry of who would see it and what they would think. "I do it for us." Ben smiled a little. He couldn't help it. "And I do it because I finally fucking can."

THIRTY-SEVEN

BEN

"I'VE GOT A surprise for you."

"Ugh." Liza dropped her head back. "You've got to stop. I'm never going to catch up with you at this point."

She still wasn't over the appearance of her parents and sister at his birthday party, and she didn't pretend like she was.

"It's not a competition." He thought she realized why he did what he did.

But maybe he hadn't been clear enough.

"This isn't just for you." Ben went to the shelf in his living room, opening one of the lower cabinets to pull out one of the many projects he'd been working on over the past five years.

There were times he was certain this one wouldn't see the light of day.

And even a few days ago, he was considering sitting on it a while longer.

But now that Liza's parents were extending their visit it seemed like the time was right.

Liza turned from the plate of pork chops in front of her, twisting in the chair as he crossed the small space between them. She eyed the rolled-up paper in his hand, gaze narrowing with suspicion. "What is it?"

Ben sat down beside her, spreading the paper flat across the table. "Blueprints."

Liza looked over the floorplan in front of them, her focus slowly moving across the lines and letters. "It's a house."

"It is." He picked up the saltshaker and used it to pin down one curling corner. "It could be our house if you wanted it to be."

Liza huffed out a slow breath before stabbing a fork into her pile of mashed potatoes and shoving the bite into her mouth. "You're really frustrating, you know that?"

Ben set the pepper down on the opposite corner. "I had a lot of time on my hands."

"So did I, but I didn't spend it doing nice things for you." She leaned forward, looking over the design. "I definitely didn't spend it planning out our future."

"You spent it saving kids and recovering from almost being killed twice." It was still tough to think about how close he came to losing her on more than one occasion.

"Almost only counts in horseshoes and hand grenades." Liza smirked at him, clearly proud at having seized the opportunity to toss his words back at him.

"And cars and knives."

She shook her head. "Can't add those now. It's too late." She was still smiling when she leaned to focus back on the paper in front of them. "Tell me about this dream house you've been planning." Her lips tipped down in a frown. "It looks expensive."

"I would say you'd be right." He tipped back the beer he'd been nursing through dinner. "If you had to pay for someone else to do everything."

Liza's brows lifted. "You want to build this yourself?"

"Not all of it." He hadn't really thought about the actual building of the house until recently. "I think I could talk Brooks and Nora into helping me come up with a crew to get it weathertight."

Liza smiled a little. "How is Brooks?"

"He's fine." Ben didn't plan to ever keep another secret as long as he lived.

But then Brooks told him Nora was pregnant.

He'd spilled it out over a few beers at The Creekery.

"So you two had fun last night?" Liza had practically shoved him out the door when Brooks called looking for someone to meet him in town. Initially he thought Liza was behind the surprise call.

But then he realized Brooks called all on his own, looking for support from someone outside the situation.

He was scared. Worried for his wife. For the baby they both wanted so badly.

Worked so hard to have after a series of losses.

And he couldn't tell anyone. Not his mother. Not his brothers. Brooks was trying to support Nora when deep down he was falling apart himself.

"Did you talk to him about this little project?" Liza turned his way and draped her legs across his lap.

"Not yet." Last night he'd just listened. Done his best to be there for a man who needed someone to lean on. "Maybe soon."

"So where is the house going?" Liza's small smile held, making him think she wasn't opposed to the idea of building a place of their own.

"Initially I thought maybe just on the other side of the trees here." Ben pointed in the direction of the flat plane of ground he first considered. "But now I'm thinkin' maybe we could put it out in the westmost pasture."

It was a little out of the way and would require putting in another drive, but it offered more space to work with.

And he was thinking they were going to need more space than he originally expected.

"In the pasture?" Liza's brows lifted. "Why all the way out there?"

"It's got the best view and the worst of the creeks run through the back of it." That particular bit of the property was the most problematic to keep cattle on anyway. It wasn't easy to move the herd in and out and the rolling nature of the land made a good bit of it dangerous for calves when the beds flooded.

But there was a great spot near the front that sat up on a little hill, making it high enough that the water would never come close, but they'd still be able to see it from their back windows.

Along with the line of mountains behind it.

Ben ran one finger across the back of the two-bedroom layout. "I was thinkin' we could put big windows all across here."

He moved his finger to the larger of the bedrooms. "Maybe one back here."

Liza gave him a grin. "I guess it's not like anyone would see us naked."

"About that." Ben leaned back in his seat.

Liza's brows slowly lifted. "About what?"

"How would you feel if there was another house next to ours?"

Liza's mouth dropped open.

"Nothing's set in stone yet." There were a lot of loose ends that needed tying up.

A house to sell and pack up.

New doctors to find.

"But I mentioned to your dad that we had plenty of space out here—"

Liza lunged at him, wrapping both arms around his neck, managing to hold him almost as tight with her right arm as she could her left. "I want to be mad at you right now for doing one more damn thing." She sniffed, burying her head into his shoulder. "Why didn't they say anything to me?"

"They didn't want to get your hopes up."

Liza leaned back. "But you did?"

"I wanted you to have something to hope for." Ben slid one hand over her face. "So maybe it'll help you understand why I did everything I did." He hadn't done most of it for anyone but himself.

He needed something to cling to.

Something to carry him through when he felt like giving up.

Liza pressed both hands to his face, pulling him in for a kiss, sniffing a little as she let him go and turned back to the drawing. "Which side would they live on?"

"They can go anywhere they want." He pointed to an outlined spot just across from the kitchen window. "Except there."

"What's there?"

"Your sunflower patch." He tried to come up with a spot she'd be able to see from as many windows as possible, just like the one he planted for her every year now. "We can try it there first, and if you don't like it I'll plant it somewhere else the next year."

Liza's eyes slowly came his way. "The next year?"

"I've got to plant it again anyway, so it won't be a big deal to move it."

"You have to plant them every year?" The question was barely a whisper.

He nodded, not really sure where the conversation was headed. "Yes."

There was something off in her expression. "I thought they reseeded."

"They try, but the birds and squirrels eat every bit of it." Over the years he'd come up with a pretty decent system that involved pre-sprouting the seeds before sowing them and gently raking them in place. As long as he put enough down, there were more than enough to fill the garden Liza cut flowers from nearly every day.

"Goddammit, Ben." She pressed both hands to his face, pulling him in for another kiss. "One day I'm going to get you back for all of this and you're going to be so sorry."

He smiled against her lips. "I doubt I'll be sorry."

———

"I THINK I'VE almost got Muriel to where she'll let me in her house." Troy stood at the front of the barn, chewing on the toothpick in his mouth like he was starving. "It's going to piss me off when I finally get in there, I know it will."

"Don't judge her sons too fast." Ben picked up a hay bale and hefted it to the top of the stack behind it. "You don't know the full situation."

Troy grabbed another bale and piled it to the back. "I know she's living in a house that's falling down around her and no one's doing shit to change that."

"We are." Ben launched another bale, sending it as far back as he could.

They needed to make some space for the Labor Day cut, and with everything going on he'd put it off a little too long, leaving him and Troy out moving the last few bales as the sun went down.

Troy stepped back, surveying the floorspace they'd managed to clear. "You think we've got enough room?"

"No." He'd been working up the amount of hay they cut each year, trying to stay in line with the higher number of cattle they were producing, and it seemed like he was pretty spot on. They should have enough to get them through the winter.

Unfortunately, there was only so much storage space to go around.

"We might have to build another barn." Ben hadn't put any of his own money into the ranch, outside of the initial investment he made, because he knew Liza would never allow it.

And for a long time, chances were good that finding out he wasn't as financially tied to the property as she thought, might have pushed her farther from him instead of pulling her closer.

"Can we do that?" Troy sounded skeptical. Warranted considering the shoestring budget they'd been running the ranch on for the past five years.

But it was all finally paying off, and after years of incremental growth, the ranch was set to double its income next year.

As long as they could keep the cattle fed.

"I think we can make it happen." Liza might still fight him on it, but maybe speeding up some other plans he had in the works might help sway her.

"I think if we can then we should." Troy gave the space one last look. "Cause we're out of room in here." He shot Ben a grin. "Unless you want to give up your wood pile."

"Seems like it's *our* wood pile now." Ben jerked his chin toward the open door. "Get out of here. Go enjoy what's left of your evening."

"I'm plannin' to head down to visit Miss Paige at The Creekery. Have a couple beers and see if I can talk her into comin' home with me."

"You've got your work cut out for you." Ben grabbed one of the Cross Creek branding irons from where someone left it on the floor and hung it back on the wall just inside the door. "Considering you're still sleeping on an air mattress."

"I'm going to invite her over for a camp out. Women love camping."

Ben lifted one brow at Troy. "Do you know many women?"

"Kiss my ass." Troy turned, waving one arm out as he headed for the farmhouse he now called home. "I'll see you in the morning."

"Don't use that camp out line. I'm tellin' you it won't work." Ben chuckled as Troy lifted one finger in the air without turning around.

Paige was going to eat him alive and leave him crying in his beer, just like she did with every other cowboy who thought he would be the one who could figure out how to make her his.

Ben turned to look back down the center aisle of the large barn. The place was nearly packed full.

They definitely needed another building.

Which gave him a great excuse to do something he'd been wanting to do for a long damn time.

Ben pulled out his cell phone and fired off a quick text.

Meet me in the barn.

He'd had it planned out for years.

How he would ask Elizabeth to marry him.

It would be right where it all started. The place where they shared secrets and dreams.

Hopes and fears.

He slid his phone back into place before patting the pocket that held the ring he'd been carrying around since the day she told him she hated him.

Then he went to work setting up a spot, covering a few bales of hay with a drop cloth he kept on hand for painting touch-ups.

Right as he finished up, Troy's boots scuffed across the barn floor behind him.

"You come back for advice?" Ben was grinning when he turned to face the younger ranch hand.

Only it wasn't Troy.

Dustin stood in the center of the barn, an odd expression on his face.

Ben dusted his hands off on his pants. "I thought you were Troy."

"I bet you did." Dustin's tone was cool and clipped. "He's your right-hand man, isn't he?"

Ben huffed out a breath. He didn't have time for this right now.

But he was trying to be better. Better than his parents. "Troy's workin' hard to help the ranch get where we want it to go."

He was hoping Dustin would be like Troy, but right now it was looking more like he might be the same as so many were before him.

A man looking for an easy ride.

Dustin smirked, taking a step closer, one hand coming out from behind his back to reveal a three-foot length of two-by-four clenched in his fist. "I don't think it matters where you want the ranch to go."

A chill ran down Ben's spine as the younger man slowly came toward him, fingers flexing on the section of wood.

He was blocked in. No way out unless he could figure out how to either scale the bales of hay or run through walls.

So all he could do was buy time and hope Dustin wasn't thinking what it looked like he was thinking. "And why's that?"

Dustin's smirk twisted into a sick smile as he lifted the front of his shirt, revealing the angry lines of the Cross Creek brand burned into the skin of his stomach. "Because it's going to be mine."

THIRTY-EIGHT

LIZA

LIZA STEPPED OUT of the shower and went to work wrapping her hair up on top of her head. Like everything else in his house, Ben's bathroom was meticulously crafted.

The walk-in shower was tiled in simple white squares and the floor was done in rectangular stone, perfectly coordinating with the rich wood of the handmade vanity.

It was a small space but every bit of it was expertly done, which made her wonder what Ben could accomplish in the larger footprint of the house he showed her a handful of days ago.

Since then she'd looked at the blueprint countless times, building her own plans and expectations around his.

It was strange to have dreams and hopes for the future.

But definitely something she could get used to.

Once her hair was wound up in a towel Liza opened the door and went out into the room they shared, planning to pull on a pair of pajamas before going out to check on the dinner simmering in the crockpot.

She'd finally managed to corner Ben into a system that gave her almost as many responsibilities as it did him.

It was still not easy to do as much for him as he insisted on doing for her, but at least he wasn't doing everything.

She passed her phone where it sat on the bed, snagging it to check the time.

A text message preview slid across the screen, prompting her to fully unlock her cell so she could see what Ben was up to now.

Liza dropped down to the bed as she opened her messages, pulling up the one Ben sent her ten minutes ago while she was washing her hair.

Meet me in the barn.

He was definitely up to something and, knowing him, it was going to be one more thing that would prove just how incomparable of a human he was.

"Dammit, Benjamin." Liza chucked her phone into the center of the mattress and went to the closet, foregoing the pajamas she was so looking forward to in favor of a pair of joggers and a T-shirt.

The man was going to make her crazy. Every time she finally felt like she was getting somewhere in proving her appreciation for all he did, he would go and one-up himself.

Which was particularly infuriating considering she hadn't managed to one-up him a single time.

And now he wanted her to meet him.

At night.

In the same barn they used to meet in so long ago.

It was exactly the way they started.

And Liza was willing to bet she knew exactly what he was up to.

Not this time.

This time she was going to be the one who surprised Ben.

He'd stayed at Cross Creek.

Helped her take care of a ranch he could have easily walked away from.

He made sure the men that worked for them respected her. Listened to her.

He carried her to bed when she tried to drown out her need for him with sloe gin and shredded cheese.

He saved her when she nearly froze herself to death after passing out in the shower.

He brought her parents to Moss Creek. Was going to build them a house.

Right next to the one he was going to build her.

He made her food and brushed her hair and let her sleep in.

But he was *not* proposing to her in the barn where they first met.

Liza shook out her wet hair before pulling on a pair of sneakers. She marched to the door, digging into her purse to pull out the ring box she knew darn well she'd be needing

It might not be traditional, but for once she was going to be the one doing the surprising.

Liza rushed out the door and down the steps, heading toward the barn on foot.

If he heard her coming Ben would probably be down on one knee as soon as she pulled up, beating her to the punch.

And if anyone was going to be punching tonight, it would be her.

Figuratively.

The barn wasn't super far away, but it also wasn't particularly close, so by the time it came into view she was already huffing and puffing, forcing Liza to slow down and take a few deep breaths so she would be sure she could talk fast if she ended up having to race him to the finish line.

She went back to walking, making her way up the side of the barn, pumping her arms like a woman on a mission.

But the speed of her steps started to slow as a conversation carried through the quiet night air.

Liza stopped, listening to the two male voices. It was hard to make out what they were saying, but she'd recognize one of them anywhere.

Ben wasn't alone in the barn.

She deflated a little.

She thought for sure he was planning something.

And honestly, the thought of springing in with a plan of her own was pretty exciting.

Maybe she'd do it anyway.

Wait until whoever was in there with him left and then she'd strike.

Nailing him with all the love and commitment he could stand.

Liza started up again, but this time she moved a little more slowly, doing her best to make sure Ben wouldn't see or hear her coming.

She edged around the front corner of the barn, sticking to the shadows as she crept closer, intending to get a peek at whoever was inside so she would have an idea of how long she might have to wait.

The conversation happening was louder than she originally realized, carrying out into the night through the open door of the barn.

It almost sounded...

Angry.

"You almost fucked me over." The other man's voice was vaguely familiar. "Thank God you opened your mouth about owning part of the ranch. Otherwise I'd have killed Liza and still had to deal with you." An unhinged laugh crawled down her spine. "And I'm not so sure I could pull off two accidental deaths."

"I'm not so sure you can pull off one." Ben's voice wasn't as strong as she expected it to be based on what the asshole with him was saying.

And that pulled her eyes around the edge of the opening. The building was longer than it was wide, with hay bales stacked along one wall and their tack rooms and storage along the other side, leaving a relatively narrow path to the back.

Which was exactly where Ben and the familiar man were.

She could only see half of Ben, but he was sitting on the floor, eyes a little glazed, something dark stuck to the side of his head.

The other man turned to the side, sending her ducking back behind the edge of the barn.

But not before she recognized who it was.

Fucking Dustin.

"I'd shut the fuck up if I were you." The tone of Dustin's voice turned her stomach.

Almost like—

Liza froze as he kept talking, each word reminding her more and more of someone she used to know.

"The quieter you are, the easier I can make this on you." Dustin didn't sound bothered at all by the fact that he was discussing murder. "Because if you're loud enough that Miss Liza hears then she might just end up in here with you, and we wouldn't want that, would we?"

"You've got to get rid of her either way, so I'm not sure why it would matter to you."

She was going to give Ben a stern talking to when this was all over.

You don't antagonize someone who's trying to kill you. They don't like it.

"See, I thought the same thing." The unwarranted pride in Dustin's voice made the connection she was considering impossible to deny. "But I'm pretty sure Miss Liza's going to need a shoulder to cry on when she finds out you died in an accidental barn fire." Dustin paused, the silence pulling her back to the edge of the door. "And apparently she has a thing for ranch hands, so I should be golden."

She stared at Dustin's back, unable to look away from the way he stood. The way he moved.

There was always something familiar about him, but she chalked it up to running through enough ranch hands that they all blurred together.

But that wasn't why.

"Plus, she clearly likes Cross men." Dustin was moving now, going to a stack of hay bales and cutting through them with the knife in his hand, knocking the dried grass and roughage loose, scattering and kicking it across the floor. "So I figure I'm a shoo-in."

"I hate to burst your bubble, but that woman would never have you." Ben smirked, barely wincing at the movement. "She likes men."

Dustin immediately stepped toward him, packing the momentum behind his foot as he planted it right in the center of Ben's stomach, sending him curling into a fetal position on the hay-covered floor, coughing and retching as Dustin leaned over him. "I really didn't want to leave you to burn to death, but now I think I might."

Or maybe not.

Liza took advantage of Dustin's distraction, leaning as far as she dared to look inside the door for anything that might serve as a weapon. She didn't have time to run and find one, so she was stuck working with what was available.

Her eyes caught on the rack just inside the door.

A line of heavy tools hung from sturdy hooks. Unfortunately none of them would be particularly useful.

It's not like she could sneakily start a chainsaw.

Although it would be fun to slice Dustin up into tiny pieces.

Too bad she couldn't shoot him like she did his daddy.

Liza ducked back just as Dustin started to stand, his arms sticking out too far from his sides, just like Ed's used to.

She risked moving in a little more, reaching for the single item on the rack that might offer her a little added oomph when she went after Dustin.

Because she was most certainly going after him.

And she was going to do whatever it took to take him down, even if she had to claw out his eyeballs and gnaw off his limbs.

Liza swung out of sight just as Dustin turned her way.

She held her breath, waiting for any sign that he'd seen her.

"How long do you think it'll take this whole building to go up?" Dustin sounded casual and calm, one more thing that he got from Ed Cross.

Ed could smack her one second and talk about the weather the next, like nothing ever happened.

It was one of the most disturbing things about him, the ability to be fine one minute and violent the next.

It meant she never knew when it was coming.

And chances were good Dustin worked the same way.

So she couldn't wait for an outburst. If she did then it was too late.

"My money's on two minutes." Dustin laughed. "But I guess soon your money will be my money anyway."

His complete belief that she would ever consider him romantically was enough to make her gag.

But she'd have to throw up about it later.

Right now she had another Cross man to kill.

And that's what she was aiming for.

Fuck assault.

Screw attempted murder.

She was going right for the real deal.

No one was going to take Ben from her.

It was a point she already proved once.

But was happy to reiterate.

"Start counting." The glee in Dustin's voice sent her stomach dropping to her shoes.

Shit.

Liza gripped the handle of the heavy iron, hooking it back over one shoulder. Hopefully she could swing it harder than she could a plunger.

Then she started to run, rounding the corner at full tilt, sneakers moving over the cement floor surprisingly quietly as she raced right at where Dustin stood with a flaming rag in one hand.

But she wasn't fast enough.

The rag dropped just as she closed in, swinging with everything she had, ignoring the protest of her right arm as she forced it to pull as much weight as possible.

Didn't matter if she undid every bit of headway she'd made.

They could amputate the damn thing. As long as Ben was safe.

But her arm held its own, the slice of the branding iron surprisingly smooth as it cut through the air on its way to the side of Dustin's head.

The connection was solid and strong, sending his head jerking to one side a second before he started leaning to the right, stumbling a little as he went down, falling headfirst into one of the bales he split open.

The same bale that was now catching fire at an alarming rate.

There was no time to bask in the moment. Not a second to spare in relief.

Because any celebration would be premature.

Ben was still on the floor.

And they were still both in the back of a barn that was filling with smoke shockingly fast.

Liza rushed deeper into the space, going down to her knees right in front of Ben's crumpled form. "Come on."

"Get out of here." Ben coughed as she grabbed him by the shirt, pulling him up to a sitting position. "I'll be fine."

"Oh no." Liza got her feet under her, squatting down as far as she could before lacing her fingers through the belt around his jeans. "You're not winning like this."

She rocked back, putting her weight into her heels as she pushed against the ground, letting out a ragged sound that got caught between a scream and a grunt as she fought Ben's body up from the floor.

He was mostly on his feet when she realized what she saw on the side of his head earlier was actually blood seeping from one temple.

No wonder he was struggling.

"Put one arm around me." Liza fought his weight, trying to get under it.

"I can't. They're tied." Ben's voice was weak. "Put me down. You need to get out of here."

He was right. She did need to get out of here.

They'd done a great job of keeping their hay dry, and that was working against her. The fire was already making her sweat and the smoke level was creeping dangerously low.

But the only way she was getting out of here was with Ben.

He couldn't walk out of here on his own. Dragging him wasn't a great option either, considering she'd already pushed her right hand about as far as it could go.

That left her one option.

It was the only way she knew was possible for her to carry a full-grown adult.

But she'd never done it with one taller than her.

With his hands tied behind his back.

She'd actually only done it with Dawn, laughing her ass off as her sister squealed and cackled.

Not that she expected that from Ben.

Liza turned, pushing her back into Ben's front as he continued to argue with her.

Luckily he couldn't fight, and his weakened state meant he

immediately slumped against her, putting his weight across her spine.

She reached back, grabbed his thighs, and let out another of the screamy grunts that got him off the ground.

Hopefully it would get him out the door too.

She was almost bent in half, trying to keep him balanced so most of the strain was on her legs, as she moved through the smoke. Halfway there she lost sight of the door, forced to keep moving blindly as her eyes and lungs burned.

Her right hand gave out, losing its grip on the leg it was in charge of, but she kept going, holding tighter with her left hand as she fought through the pain.

It was nothing compared to the pain of losing Ben.

She knew. She'd felt it.

Suddenly it was cooler.

A few steps later she broke through the wall of smoke, making it a few yards from the barn before going down, dropping face first into the grass as she gulped in air.

Ben rolled off her back, coughing between groans.

Liza pushed up just enough to look back at the barn.

There was no saving it.

No saving the man still inside.

Not that she was particularly interested in that.

He tried to take Ben from her, and that never ended well for anyone.

"Elizabeth." Ben's voice was a rough whisper.

She pulled her eyes from the flames, turning to the only thing that mattered.

Ben was battered and bruised, but he was alive.

And there was something important she needed to tell him.

She leaned in, pressing her forehead to his. "I love you."

He tried to laugh but ended up coughing instead, managing a smile anyway. "Seems like."

THIRTY-NINE

BEN

"HE KNOCKED THE shit out of you, didn't he?" Travis Moore inspected the side of Ben's head using the same light he'd shined in his eyes seconds before.

"Really? I hadn't noticed." Ben closed his eyes as his brain continued to throb.

"Stop being a pain in the ass and let him take care of you." Liza was tucked in close at his side, watching every move Travis made as the paramedic tried to do his job. "Does he have a concussion?"

Travis chuckled.

Ben opened his eyes at the sudden silence that followed it, catching the glare Liza shot the medic's way.

"I mean, yeah. He's definitely got a concussion." Travis went back to checking Ben's vitals. "But hopefully that's all."

He felt Liza go stiff beside him.

"I'm fine." Ben closed his eyes again, partly because of the ache and partly because they were still burning from the smoke and soot.

"You're right." Liza scooted closer. "That is frustrating as hell when someone keeps claiming they're fine." She rested her head against his shoulder.

"Told you." He tipped his face toward her, managing to get his lips against the top of her smoke-scented head. "But I really am fine."

She scoffed, the sound quickly moving into a cough.

"You just earned yourself a mask." Travis snapped the clear plastic dome over Liza's face, looking undeterred by her frown.

"Don't even bother telling me you're fine. I know both of you are damn liars." The medic went back to checking Ben over, cataloging each of the injuries Dustin inflicted in his quest to take over the ranch he thought should be his, based on the fact that Ed Cross's blood ran through his veins.

Grady made his way to the open back of the ambulance, leaving the cluster of his fellow officers to come speak to them alone.

"How are you two feeling?"

"They're fine." Travis answered for them. He shot Liza a wink before backing up. "Right?"

Liza made a face behind the mask covering her nose and mouth.

Grady pulled out a notepad from his front pocket. "I heard a little of what happened from the first guys that got here, but can you run back through it so I know I didn't miss anything?"

Ben glanced at where the firefighters were working to put out the last of the flames that tore through the barn that was so much more than simply storage. "One of our ranch hands ended up bein' Ed Cross's illegitimate son." He glanced at Liza, expecting her to be shocked at the revelation.

She didn't appear surprised, which made him wonder just how much she heard before coming in hot, swinging a branding iron like a home run champ.

"Holy shit." Grady looked at him over the pad of paper. "When did you figure that out?"

"About the time he hit me in the head with a two-by-four." The asshole had a surprisingly decent arm on him and managed to knock Ben out for a few seconds.

Long enough to cinch a pair of zip ties around his wrists.

"He knocked the shit out of me then tied me up, planning to burn the barn down with me inside it so he could take what he considered his rightful place as the owner of Cross Creek Ranch."

Grady's eyes moved to Liza before going back to Ben. "Was he going to kill Liza too?"

"He thought she'd take up with him."

Grady's brows lifted high on his head. "You're kidding."

Ben shook his head, wincing a little at the pain the added movement brought on. "No."

"No offense, but if something happened to you I wouldn't touch this woman with a ten-foot pole." Grady had the sense to add the rest of his statement on quickly. "Especially if I was the one responsible for what happened to you." He shook his head. "I've seen what she does when you're on the line."

So had he.

More than once.

It's why no matter what Liza thought, there was never any competition over who did more for the other one.

She took that title home, fair and square. Especially now.

Ben caught Travis's attention and tipped his aching head toward Liza. "You should look her arm over too. She carried my ass out of that place."

Grady shook his head, chuckling low as he continued writing across his notepad. "Doesn't surprise me one bit."

"*Liza.*" A woman's voice carried across the dark yard. "Where in the hell is she?"

"You should probably let her know Liza's over here." Ben leaned to one side, looking for the source of the hollering. "It's her mother."

Grady's arm immediately went up, his unwillingness to end up on the wrong side of the woman who created Liza clear. "She's over here."

Carol Galloway rushed right toward them, with Maryann Pace hot on her heels.

The two women were fast friends, which meant no one was safe from their combined mothering powers.

"Oh." The relief on Carol's face was evident as her eyes landed on where Liza sat at his side. She grabbed her daughter, pulling her close. "I was so worried."

Liza's lips were pressed in a tight frown. "Who called you?"

Carol leaned back, keeping her hands on Liza as she stared

her down with the kind of stern expression only a mother planning to dish out a decently sized guilt trip could manage. "Benjamin had his friend Troy call us." She gave Ben a sweet smile before turning back to her daughter, seriousness returning instantly. "Since you didn't."

"I don't have my phone." It was a conveniently true excuse.

But it was still an excuse.

Liza wouldn't have called her mother if she'd been sitting on a mountain of cell phones.

Because she was still stuck in the mentality that she had to protect her.

"What about you, handsome?" Maryann leaned to one side as she squinted at his temple. "That's a nasty looking bump you've got there."

"Don't worry. I should still be just as good looking." Hopefully it healed fast, because he had shit to do.

Shit Liza probably wouldn't want him sporting a baseball-sized knot for.

"Of course you will." Maryann reached out to pat his cheek before turning to Travis. "Are you taking both of them in?"

"I am." The paramedic looked from him to Liza. "They both inhaled a pretty decent amount of smoke." He nodded to Ben's head. "Plus this one's concussion."

"Good." Carol smoothed down Liza's hair. "We'll follow behind you." She slowly turned toward what remained of the barn. "Anyone else make it out?"

Clearly Troy did a good job of filling them in on what happened.

"No." Ben ran his hand down Liza's back. "Just us."

And it was all because of her.

Liza carried a fearlessness and determination he'd never seen in anyone.

She protected the people she cared about with a fierceness that no man could compete with.

Definitely not Dustin Cross.

Not his father either.

"Good." Carol turned back to them, a familiar look in her eyes.

"Because I'd hate to have to hunt that young man down and handle him myself."

LIZA

"MORNING."

Liza squinted one eye open to find Ben standing beside the bed, a cup of coffee in one hand and a tray of food in the other.

"Are you kidding me right now?" He had to be doing this on purpose.

"Sit up." He set the mug on the nightstand right next to her. "This thing is getting heavy."

Of course it was. The tray probably had half the refrigerator on it.

Liza wrestled her way up, kicking blankets around as she moved. "I thought this wasn't a competition."

"It's not." Ben carefully set the tray across her lap. "Which is good, because if it was I would be in last place."

Liza dropped her head to one side.

"I would." Ben added her coffee to the tray, setting it beside a plate filled with thick waffles and cinnamon syrup, sliced strawberries and bananas, and her favorite sausage links. "And I can promise you that breakfast in bed won't put a dent in it."

This had been going on for nearly a month.

As soon as he was back on his feet, Ben went back to surprising her at almost every turn.

He'd planned a night of pottery painting with Muriel and Dawn. Put together a whole board of ideas for the house he was already knee deep in planning with Brooks and Nora. Handled the insurance claim for the barn. Driven her to the extra physical therapy appointments she earned giving him a piggyback.

The list of all he'd done for her was endless and varied.

Liza lifted her brows at him as he sat down beside her. "Then maybe you should take a little breather."

"You saved my life, Elizabeth." Ben shook his head. "I don't plan to ever let you forget it."

She huffed out a breath. "You don't owe me for saving your life." Liza stabbed at one of the sausages. "I didn't only do it for you."

Ben's lips curved in a slow smile.

One that sent her brain back over what she'd just said.

"Don't you dare try to turn that back around on me." She fought to press down her own smile at his obvious glee over her finally ending up on his side of things. "What you did and what I did are not the same thing."

"You're right." He stole a strawberry, popping it into his mouth. "They're not even close."

"You know what I mean." She didn't like the way he was looking at her.

Like she was finally being forced to admit that maybe she might have been looking at all the things he did in the wrong way.

"I do know what you mean." Ben leaned in close to press a kiss to her lips. "Seems like you might also know what I mean."

He was infuriating in the best possible way.

Always had been.

He made her want to be the best person she could. The best partner she could be.

He didn't judge her even when he thought she was doing something wrong. Just gave her the support and space to figure it out herself, then stood by her side helping her fix it.

Like he'd done with her parents.

She thought they would be filled with questions when they got to Moss Creek and realized maybe it wasn't all she'd been claiming.

But they weren't. Her mother never asked about her arm.

Never questioned how exactly Ed Cross met his untimely demise.

Never asked how it was possible that she and Ben fell in love so easily and completely in such a short period of time.

Because she already knew.

He told them everything, taking that burden and guilt from her, allowing Liza to go back to being just their daughter, no more secrets, no more lies.

"I have something for you." Ben lifted his hand, revealing a white gold band set with three diamonds sitting halfway down his pointer finger.

"It does look like it might fit me better." She pressed her lips together but it was impossible not to smile. "How long have you had that?"

She was willing to bet he'd had it since the night of the fire. That Dustin ruined more plans than the ones he had for their hay.

"Since you told me you hated me."

That answer set her back a little. "But that was—"

"A long time ago." Ben worked the ring loose and held it between them. "But I knew then that we would get here eventually."

Liza reached out to take the ring. "It's beautiful."

It sparkled like crazy, each of the three stones catching the light and bouncing it off each other.

"I'm going to take it as a good sign that you liked it even before I explained it to you."

"I don't need you to explain it to me." She might not be as good as he was at thoughtful gestures, but she definitely knew the man across from her better than anyone else in the world.

Which meant she knew exactly what the meaning behind the ring was.

Liza pointed to one of the smaller diamonds. "Our past." She moved her finger to the other side of the center stone, pointing out the second of the smaller diamonds. "Our present." Liza touched the tip of her finger to the largest of the three. "Our future."

Ben slowly smiled, tipping his head in a nod. "That's right."

"So I guess I should give you this then." Liza reached into the drawer of her nightstand and pulled out the ring box she'd carried through a burning barn and held it out.

Ben looked at it a minute before lifting his eyes to hers.

She wiggled it around. "Take it."

For the first time she really understood what he meant when he said it wasn't a competition.

It wasn't.

Not against each other.

Because they were both *for* each other.

That's what it was really about.

Ben took the box and lifted the hinged lid.

Her smile widened as his eyes moved over the ring inside. "Do you want me to explain it to you?"

Ben barely shook his head as he pulled out the white gold band. "I think I got it." He stared down at the three diamonds set deep in the band.

She'd gone through everything at the jewelry store, passing over all kinds of options until she found this one.

"Now we just have to decide what to do with them." Liza smiled as Ben continued to stare at the ring.

Finally his eyes came to hers. "I don't have any plans today, do you?"

EPILOGUE

BEN

"IS THE WATER warm?" Liza dipped her toe into the creek running behind their new home. "It's not bad, is it?" She stepped the rest of the way in, going to where her sister was squatted down, digging through the rocks as the water moved around them.

"I found a good one." Dawn pulled out a smooth stone the size of her palm and held it up in the air. "Look, Ben. I found one."

He moved toward her, holding out the bucket containing her collection. "I like that one. It would make a good ladybug."

Dawn tossed the rock into the bucket before crouching back down and continuing her search.

He stepped back to take a seat in the line of chairs that stayed set up along the bank, far enough away that even the worst flooding wouldn't reach them.

You're going to have nothing but rocks in your flower beds, son." Liza's dad sat in the sun, his legs stretched out in front of him.

"Less to weed." Ben eased into the chair next to him just as Carol came out with a tray of snacks and iced tea. "And once mine are full I'll send them to your house."

Dennis grinned, knowing full-well Ben would never do that to him.

The man took an inordinate amount of pride in the flowers filling his beds.

Which explained why Liza loved her sunflowers so much.

"Have they found many?" Carol set the tray down on the small table between them.

Ben leaned to peek into the bucket. "They've probably got a few weeks' worth."

Liza and Dawn had a standing date with Muriel. Once a week he went and picked Muriel up from her new home, bringing her back to theirs for an afternoon of painting and food and whatever else they could manage to get themselves into.

They also had a standing weekly lunch date in town with the rest of the problematic women of Moss Creek, which now included Carol, Dianna, and anyone else they could suck into their clutches.

Liza and Dawn dug around the water for another thirty minutes, adding a handful more rocks to their to-paint collection, before finally making their way up into the grass, with pruney toes and smiling faces.

"I need to go start dinner." Carol stood up from her seat while Dennis carried the tray back to their house. She turned to where Dawn was standing at Liza's side. "Are you coming with me, or staying with your sister and Ben?"

"I'm staying with Liza and Ben."

It was the way it usually went, which was more than fine with him.

Ben grabbed the bucket. "I've got the rocks."

"I've got Dawn." Liza dropped down, laughing as her smaller sister grabbed on tight, head back, cackling like crazy as Liza hauled her up the hill the same way she once carried him.

Dawn definitely enjoyed the experience more.

Ben stayed with Carol as everyone else moved ahead of them, hiking up the sloping hill leading to where their homes sat side-by-side.

Carol rested one hand on his shoulder as they walked. "I've been thinking..."

He smiled.

That phrase was usually followed by a wild idea that Carol wanted him to help her bring to fruition.

So far he'd helped her try to dry manure into a lightweight and easy-to-apply fertilizer.

They'd built fabric sail shades to cover her back patio and the furniture that sat under it, along with an array of other items and concoctions.

"Dawn loves the creek so much but it's not always wet." Carol's right eye squinted the way it did when she was envisioning something. "Could we make one?"

"You mean a water feature that runs like a creek?" He'd seen plenty of koi ponds and fountains.

It had to be possible to combine the two.

"It wouldn't have to be big." Carol motioned to the spot just between their houses. "Just something she could have to dip her toes in when the one out back is dry."

Ben gave her a smile as the wheels in his mind started to turn. "I think we could make that happen."

LIZA

"WHAT ARE YOU doing?" Liza went to where Ben was sitting at the table, a line of papers and his laptop out in front of him.

She'd been in the craft room with Dawn for almost two hours, lacing rubber bands into bracelets until her mother came to get her sister for dinner. Ben had been at the table the whole time, quietly working on whatever his next scheme was.

Because he was always scheming. And now he had a scheming buddy.

"Your mom wants to build a water feature for Dawn." He pointed to the screen of his computer. "Something like that."

Liza leaned in, looking over his shoulder at the image. "That seems like a lot of work."

It was two separate levels, one spilling down into the other with a narrow section between them filled with rocks for the water to pass over.

"If you think that's a lot of work then you probably aren't gonna like the plan I came up with."

She snagged one of the papers, pulling it close to look at what appeared to be a building. "Might as well tell me so I can brag about it at lunch tomorrow."

Luckily she had friends who loved hearing her stories about Ben's never-ending fantasticness.

"Right now Dawn has to get out in the snow to come over here in the winter." He turned toward her. "What if she had a nice, warm, dry path to get here?"

"You want to connect our houses with a tunnel?" Honestly, she was surprised it took him this long to come up with it.

"I want to connect our houses with a conservatory." He pulled up a screen showing an indoor room filled with plants and light. "With a water feature she can enjoy year-round." He pointed to the plants hanging from hooks and lining the floor. "I thought your dad might like it too."

Of course he did.

Because Ben never did things halfway when it came to taking care of the people he loved.

And he loved Dawn and her parents.

"They would love it." Liza went to drop down onto the sofa. "A lot."

"What about you?" Ben stood from his chair and slowly crossed the room. "Would you mind our house being connected to theirs?"

"It will cut way down on the snow we drag around in the winter." She lifted her brows. "The real question is, would you mind our house being connected to my parents' house?"

Ben eased down onto the couch beside her, sitting under the pictures lining the wall above it.

There were photos of Maryann and Bill. A shot of her with Mae and Clara and Nora and Camille. One of all their husbands lined along the porch at The Inn. Muriel was there too, grinning as she sat at the large easel in the craft room.

There were plenty more. Her parents and Dawn. The twins and Wyatt and Calvin.

And at the center was the single picture they took at the courthouse the day her name changed from Cross to Chamberlain.

"Sweetheart," Ben pulled her close, tucking her against him, "I think you already know the answer to that."

———

Made in the USA
Columbia, SC
09 July 2025